THE LITTLE ANIMALS

THE LITTLE ANIMALS

by

Sarah Tolmie

SEATTLE

Aqueduct Press, PO Box 95787
Seattle, WA 98145-2787
www.aqueductpress.com

ISBN: 978-1-61976-161-2
Library of Congress Control Number: 2019931450

Cover and Book Design by Kathryn Wilham

Front Cover illustration:
Leeuwenhoek, A_PT_Vol21_1699_p269_figs2-4 ©The Royal Society

Printed in the USA by the employee-owners of Thomson-Shore, Inc.

magnae animae
Ursula K. Le Guin

THE GOOSE GIRL

It is Pentecost. *Pinksteren.* Tomorrow a girl crowned with flowers will parade across the square in front of the Nieuwe Kerk, the bride of spring, followed by a heckling crowd of off-work apprentices. Couples will start courting. Pastors will give thanks for the gift of tongues.

Today geese and their babble occupy the square. Antoni Van Leeuwenhoek is at the market, bargaining. He is a man of middle height, middling complexion, and sober gray eyes, just beginning to get stout, with an itchy dark wig slightly askew. An ordinary man, though this is not his ordinary occupation. He ought to be opening his draper's shop this minute. The housemaid ought to be doing the shopping. But Leeuwenhoek is a most particular man. He prefers to do things himself. So here he is, choosing geese for quills. It is a hateful task, but he is desperate. He has arrived early to beat the tide of arrow-fledgers, down-pullers, scribes, and gluttons. His task outranks all these, did they but know it. Natural philosophy!

The smell of the tarred feet of the huge flock on the air is overpowering. Drovers' dogs guard the laneways. The sounds of hissing and honking are deafening. Some of the green geese are strung on lines, string protruding from the asshole of one into the throat of the next. Herders have fed them fat pork that they will eat and re-eat. Geese are revolting. The drovers are not much better. This is idiots' work. Many are drunk, or slack-faced, or crazy. Getting enough sense out of them to make a deal is a chore. It is the same thing every year.

Suddenly through the gaggle of halfwits and yelling birds the blonde head of a child appears, a girl leading a troop of a dozen geese in a perfect line, like soldiers on parade. She is not much bigger than they are and has no dog, nor even a staff. Her geese are celestially white and twice as big as the others, like harvest birds. They are silent. Their flat feet are bare, except for the first one, which appears to be wearing little red leather boots. They pace past like visiting noblemen. Leeuwenhoek is stunned. Children rarely take animals on the roads, and certainly not girls. It is not like herding them at home. A pasture is one thing, the open road quite another. What can her parents, or her employers, possibly be thinking? A wash of quietness spreads out from the girl and her geese as they cut diagonally through the square, the raucous birds calming, the drovers and householders turning to watch in amazement. He thinks feverishly, Look at the size of them! Think of the feathers! A dozen birds that size, at this season—seventy-two premium quills. Enough for a year, even with all the writing he does. He begins jostling through the crowd in her wake, as the others are still gaping, determined to reach her before some housewife or arbalester's apprentice gets there first. He will buy the lot.

Toiling across the square, trying to avoid bites from enraged geese, he meets precisely the person he had hoped would not be here. Johannes. Now, struggling through the throng, he must struggle with his conscience as well. The man is improvident, infuriating, and disorderly, but he is a great painter. He is a friend. He is even a client, though this is not the moment at which to wonder whether the camera will ever be paid for. He swats away the head of an importuning goose.

"Vermeer!" he shouts over the head of a cross-eyed drover, "go home! You cannot afford those prize geese! I am buying them!" One of the painter's many off-putting habits is haggling for things he cannot buy.

"Antoni!" returns the painter, a smallish dark man, likewise making his way across the square, although much more slowly, ceremoniously standing aside for passing drovers, stopping to let the more determined geese go by. He is not making much headway, and Leeuwenhoek passes him by like a meteor, cutting a swathe through the milling necks. He looks back to see Vermeer standing, doffing his cap, whether to a goose or a person he cannot see, a dark blot in the midst of a rippling, cacophonous, white canvas.

By the time the harried artist has made his way across the square, Leeuwenhoek has bought the geese. At least, he thinks he has. He accomplished this by glaring down several affronted women already waiting there, then trying vainly to speak to the goose girl over the din—could she be deaf? —before spinning her around by the shoulder and thrusting all the money he has into her hands. She is still staring at him, grimy and confused, seemingly unable to speak, as Vermeer straggles out of the crowd.

"Johannes, I have bought them," he says warningly, before the painter can speak. He looks at the girl for some sign of assent. She appears uncomprehending. Leeuwenhoek makes a gesture toward the geese, gathering them to himself, and then pats her tiny, dirty hands holding the money. It is a reasonable sum for twelve geese in prime condition, though perhaps not enough for her extraordinary birds. She finally appears to understand what has happened, looking at the coins for the first time. She is suddenly delighted and does a little, wriggling dance.

Leeuwenhoek nods firmly, as though they have just shaken hands on the deal. The wonderful geese are his.

Vermeer sighs. "Will you at least sell me a few quills?" he asks. "I need new pencils in the worst way."

Leeuwenhoek looks at him severely, trying to muster up his better judgment. It eludes him. "Fine, fine! Of course!" he replies.

Vermeer, looking hopeful, continues, "And some of those fine metal clamps you made for the ends? To hold the brush hairs?"

"Yes," he says, shortly.

He turns back to the goose girl. He has no idea how to part her from her geese, still strangely silent and attentive, like a group of nuns. He has no idea how to herd geese. He asks the girl, carefully looking into her face, speaking slowly, Can you bring them to my house? She nods solemnly. Leeuwenhoek turns abruptly, relieved, and begins to walk away, toward home. The girl follows him, silently. The geese follow her, silently, in a perfect line. He feels like a bishop. Vermeer wanders along beside them, looking at the goose girl.

What marvelous hair you have, he says to her after a while, conversationally. The girl's hair is filthy and partially covered with a kerchief, but it is indeed splendid and copious. She looks over at him and smiles brightly.

"Have you ever cut it?" he continues.

She shakes her head.

"Never?"

She shakes her head once more.

"Good God," Vermeer mutters to himself, squinting at her. Leeuwenhoek glances back at him speculatively. "Virgin hair, Antoni! Look at it! Perfect! Better than sable!"

"Johannes, you have a house full of children with hair for paintbrushes," says Leeuwenhoek.

"They are all born bald and their mother has coarse hair! It's not my fault!" replies the painter in piteous tones. Leeuwenhoek laughs. The girl ignores their conversation, marching straight ahead.

Leeuwenhoek's house is close by, near the fish market. The geese follow the girl obediently into the rear courtyard. There is no gate, as he keeps no other fowl or domestic animals, except cats. He is a townsman. He has no use for country nuisances. The addition of twelve live geese is going to be a bit of a surprise for his wife. Soon enough, though, they will all be hanging somewhere and he will be preparing quills. The larder is Barbara's domain. Meanwhile, he will just have to block the entrance with something so they do not escape. He looks around for some suitable object. The girl stands still in the middle of his courtyard, surrounded by flowerpots, the geese standing around her in a precise semi-circle, like a choir waiting for its cue.

"You appear to have bought her, too," says Vermeer bemusedly, pausing briefly at the entrance. "Mind you keep her well. That hair is priceless." He continues on his way.

Leeuwenhoek stands uncertainly. He shuffles his feet. The goose girl stands among her adoring subjects with her back to him. He walks around to face her, behind the ring of geese. The light is behind her, so her small face is shadowed, while the golden ends of her heavy hair under the kerchief appear molten. A light, clear, toneless voice says: "Do not worry. They will not leave. I am here."

Leeuwenhoek is shocked, as if he had never heard anyone speak before. It is as if one of the geese had spoken. The goose with the red boots looks at him inquiringly. The girl is still.

"Aha, you do, ah, speak," he says, stumbling over his words, which suddenly seem remarkable coming out of his mouth.

"Yes," she says.

"Where did you come from?" he asks. "It can't have been far. Their feet are bare, and none are lame."

"It was far. We came slowly. And the tar does no good. It makes their feet rot."

"Why is this one wearing boots? Who made them?"

"I made them," she says. "He has tender feet."

"Where did you get the leather?"

"I traded a goose for it, in Kampen. She did not like me."

"But these ones do?"

"Yes."

"They will stay in the yard and not run away?"

"Yes, if I tell them."

"Tell them, then," Leeuwenhoek says and watches her curiously. The girl says nothing, to him or the geese, but makes a brief shrugging gesture, a dismissal, a bit like casting seed. The geese, receiving their *congé*, disperse and begin to wander, nibbling at the flowers in the pots. The girl stands unmoving like a wound-down clockwork.

"Can you go home now? Will they stay?"

"Home?" asks the girl, as if repeating a foreign word. She is silent a moment. "Yes, they will stay. Why do you want so many geese?"

"I need pens," says Leeuwenhoek. The girl looks blank.

"Quills. For writing. The long wing feathers."

"Oh!" she replies, seeming relieved, "Then you won't need to kill them."

"I won't?" he says, confused.

"Oh no," says the girl, confidently. "I can pluck them. Two times a year, sometimes three, if you feed them well."

"Truly?" he asks, doubtfully. "Do the feathers grow back so fast? At the same quality?"

"They will," the girl assures him. "The birds will scream and bleed, but I will sing to them and they will forget."

Leeuwenhoek is not keen to become a goose farmer. He has quite enough jobs already, and not all of them make money, as his wife is constantly reminding him. He looks at the enormous, eerily white birds now busy destroying his flowers. One beats the air with perfect, powerful wings, the flight feathers spread out like fingers. He looks at the goose girl.

"What is your name?" he asks finally, as if conceding defeat.

"I do not know," says the girl. "Why do I need one? I can tell you their names, if you like. That is Redboots, and that one is Pansy, that one is Scratch…"

Having been introduced to all the geese in turn, and still uncertain what to do about the girl, Leeuwenhoek goes inside. He sits down at the table in the great room of his house and stares anxiously at the small vase of cuckoo flowers that sits in its own reflection on the highly polished surface. He blew the glass himself and is proud of it, although he has no intention of telling anyone he is a glassblower. It is a professional secret. The vase sits here in plain view all the time, a private joke. Most townspeople of Delft think he is a solid citizen, a draper, a good man of business; a very few interested in such things know him as a lens-grinder, a maker of fine optical instruments. Nothing so frivolous as a glassblower. Guests coming in to his fine paneled room assume it is a Venetian trinket, one that goes with the paintings on the walls, the display of silver and ceramics on the mantel.

And that is the least of the secrets, he reflects, that this vase holds.

Sarah Tolmie

Leeuwenhoek knows that it contains a whole new world, stranger and more populous than the Americas: the world of the *animalcule*. Inside everything we see, everything we touch, this world opens, vaster than the abyss: there is no need to sail off perilously in ships to find it. He may be the greatest explorer in the Republic, and he has never been further than Maastricht. Not that most of his neighbors in the prosperous merchants' town of Delft will believe it, until this precious world that he has discovered through his microscopes yields up items as valuable as tobacco or potatoes or tulips. He has about as much chance of convincing them about the importance of *animalcules* as he would have of convincing that poor simple girl outside.

And what is he to do with her? He just set out to buy geese. Geese! Messy, aimless, honking waddlers, yet, perversely, he needs them, or at least their feathers, in order to record the astonishing new world that he is beginning to find, full of lives as strange to us as those of angels.

❧

Three weeks later Leeuwenhoek knows the names of all of the geese, but not the girl. She is indifferent. He has changed the name of Redboots to Caligula. He is indifferent. The girl is cleaner but still strange and silent.

"She's an odd one," says Barbara. "It's not that I mind keeping her. Now that she's washed, at least. I can't imagine how she's lived so far, poor creature. It's like she's a goose herself. She can tell me nothing about where she came from."

The girl sleeps in the pantry, cares for the geese in the yard, and herds them back and forth at intervals from a pasture he has rented outside of town. He has ordered her, and even pleaded with her, not to keep them overnight in the fields, but she pays no attention. She does not understand his fears. She looks at him stolidly, silently, and then does exactly as she pleases. Mostly she brings them back at night, but not always. She claims that they like to graze at dawn, and that the morning dew is good for them.

Barbara has tried a few names for her—Hannah, Bieke, Anna, Grietje—but none of them have stuck. She responds if addressed directly, but that is all.

"The names just slide off her, somehow," says his wife, mystified. "I can't keep track of the one I've just called her. She doesn't care at all. She's just the girl, the goose girl."

"Think of it like a title," Leeuwenhoek suggests.

"She does have a certain majesty," Barbara replies. "But I'll call her Grietje if the neighbors ask."

"Why would they?"

"People are naturally curious, Antoni," says Barbara, tartly, "about other people. It's only you who are exclusively concerned with bugs."

"Bugs! What? No! They're not bugs, these little animals I see through the microscopes, as I'm always telling you, Barbara—"

"Bugs. Plants. Bits of wood. Scraps of cloth. Dirt. Water droplets."

"Natural philosophy!"

"The *crebbemeester* has already been to see me about the goose droppings. He knows we've taken in the girl. If she leaves our service he'll alert the orphanage. She's our responsibility now."

"It's very good of you to do this, Barbara," says Leeuwenhoek, humbly. "Geese. Strange children. It's a lot to take on. And all for a few quills. It's just—"

"I know, Antoni. I know. Natural philosophy! If this passion spreads there will be a shortage of quills across

the Seven Provinces! You might as well be a scrivener!"
She wags her finger at him in mock severity and then continues more seriously, "We seem to have gotten beyond
quills, though, haven't we? Now it's about that girl, the
poor child."

"We could just slaughter the geese and keep her anyway, as a kitchen maid, I suppose."

"Could we? What would she do? She has no skills in
the house. I don't think she's lived in one for years. She
can barely talk. If we killed those geese I think she would
go mad. Or madder than she is already. They are her family. Her flock."

"She might be a companion for Marieke."

"She shuns Marieke. I think she is afraid of her, afraid
of other children."

"So we leave it as it is?"

"Yes," says Barbara. "Of course, it is all quite crazy."
She has a good heart.

Leeuwenhoek is in possession of twelve new quills,
the longest wing feathers of Redboots-now-Caligula and
the goose called Scratch. They are drying on a reed rack
in his study. In his eagerness, he has even dried one over
the fire—a fussy business, holding the shaft with clamps
and rotating it over the flames like a tiny roast. When he
sharpened it, the shaft was so hard it felt like porcelain.
He had to whet his knives to trim it properly.

The rest he will point as he goes: it is better that they
dry naturally. The birds had screamed horribly, the way
women yell in labor, in deep, vibrating, gasping grunts,
as the girl pulled out the feathers. He had been watching from the kitchen window. She had laid them across
her lap and doubled up their necks under her arm, and,

flexing one wing at a time, yanked out the three main feathers on each side. All the time her mouth had been moving in some soundless song. Afterward, they had tumbled off her lap, trembling and tottering, and rejoined the rest of the flock, which had been standing in a frozen silence, clustered against the furthest wall. Soon enough they had all been drifting and browsing together. The girl had brought him the handful of feathers matter-of-factly. Their tips were bloody.

"It would be best to feed them grain for a few days now," she had said.

"Yes," he had replied, hurriedly, "I will order some."

"If that is all you need," she had continued, "I will pasture them now."

"Yes, go ahead. Do." Casting around for something to say, he had asked, "Are they flightless now, those two?"

"Yes."

"So the others could fly and leave them behind?"

"They would never."

"No?"

"No. A flock sticks together. They almost never fly, anyway."

"Why?"

"Because I walk."

She had led them all off to pasture then in their customary perfect line, the recovered Caligula strutting in front in his red boots, unperturbed.

THE HANDKERCHIEF

Although the goose girl rarely speaks aloud, she can often be heard muttering to herself. The housemaid has spoken of this to Barbara, and even to him. Finally she prevails upon both of them to go and overhear her, very early in the morning, as she lies on her pallet on the pantry floor. So there they are: the anxious maid, Anneliese, dressed and aproned, husband and wife still in their night clothes, Barbara holding up a candle in the darkened kitchen, all of them crouched before the closed pantry door. Leeuwenhoek feels a fool, but he senses that Barbara is rather enjoying herself. She glances at him conspiratorially over the lowered candle flame.

Through the door they hear a steady stream of chatter, then a pause, perhaps a question, followed by another brief spate, as if she were talking to someone.

"You see?" whispers the maid fearfully, "She is mad."

"Perhaps she is talking to the angels, Anneliese," Barbara replies.

"Or praying," says Leeuwenhoek. He straightens up. "I can't see that it is hurting anyone. She talks to the geese all the time. Who else has she had to talk to? Just let her alone."

Anneliese looks unconvinced. "I don't like that girl," she says. "She's unnatural. She never looks at me. She won't speak to me. She only talks to the geese. Like the rest of us weren't there at all. She's not right in the head."

"That may be, Anneliese," says Barbara. "But I don't think she's dangerous, and we've taken her in. She was desperate. It's only charitable."

"She's filthy and covered in fleas, all over scabs…" The maid wipes her hands on her apron.

"Not any more. Not for weeks. I've practically scrubbed her skin off."

"I'm afraid of her."

"Anneliese," says Barbara firmly, "look at her. She's tiny. She's a small girl. She cannot possibly harm you. She looks after the geese and leaves you alone. Let her be. She's hardly ever in the house. Only for mealtimes, and often not even then."

"Why are we keeping geese, anyway?" counters the maid, "We've never even eaten one. What do we need them all for? What do we need her for?"

Barbara and Leeuwenhoek look at each other helplessly.

"Natural philosophy," says Barbara.

"Human decency," says Leeuwenhoek.

The door opens. "Why are you all standing in the kitchen in the dark?" asks the goose girl. She shows no surprise. The maid looks as though she is about to say something, but Barbara glares at her, so she crosses the room to tend the fire.

"We woke early," Leeuwenhoek replies.

"I will go to the geese now," says the girl. She is about to go, and then stops, looking at Barbara. "Can I have some food to take with me?"

Anneliese snorts disapprovingly in the background.

"Of course," says Barbara. "Bread and cheese?"

The girl nods soundlessly. Barbara cuts the bread and cheese herself, generous slices, and ties them into a yellow linen cloth. She hands them to the girl. The child

Sarah Tolmie

does not thank her, but takes the food reverently, holding the bundle close to her body with both hands. She slips out the door.

Barbara turns sharply toward Anneliese and says, with finality, "I will hear no more foolishness about that girl. She is a member of our household, and she eats at our table. With us, with you. No more need be said."

"Mevrouw," replies Anneliese.

❧

Later that morning Leeuwenhoek sees the girl in the courtyard talking to her handkerchief. He is surprised to find that she carries one. Cleanliness is not one of her objects. Usually she stinks of geese. She still has to be occasionally, more or less forcibly, bathed, with his wife standing over the tub. She is a tolerant woman, Barbara, but she would never allow an object as greasy and reeking as the goose girl had been to share a house with her only daughter.

The girl's fine linen handkerchief is filthy, no good for cleaning anything. Leeuwenhoek, looking from the window, sees her small form sitting on an upturned bucket, smoothing a wide square of cloth across her knees, plucking it and straightening it, addressing it earnestly, her head bent down, shoulders hunched. Leeuwenhoek sees that the white fabric is covered with what look like bloodstains: three great darkened splotches. The girl is staring at them raptly. The geese bustle around her and she ignores them. Her lips are moving.

Unable to contain his curiosity, Leeuwenhoek steps toward her quietly across the courtyard. "Are you talking to the geese?" he asks.

"No," says the girl, "to the little animals."

"The what?" asks Leeuwenhoek, sharply.

She continues dreamily, still looking down. "I thought it was my mother talking for the longest time. She died long ago. This was her hankie. It started speaking to me in the forest, during the winter."

"In the forest? What forest? This winter?" He is momentarily distracted from her impossible reply about the little animals, which he must have misheard.

"I don't know," she says, "just the forest. In winter. I saw many strange things there. The blood spots began to speak to me there. But not with just one voice, and nothing like my mother's. I think there are little animals in the blood."

"Little animals?" says Leeuwenhoek, with a feeling of unreality. "They speak? To you? How?"

"It is not exactly speaking. Sometimes it is like singing, heard very far away."

"What, in words?"

"No, not words. Feelings just unfold, sort of, inside me."

"The animalcules—the little animals—can you see them? What do they look like? What do they say?"

"I cannot see them. They are too small. Sometimes they are hungry, or angry. They want to grow. There seem to be fewer now than there were before."

"Is it only from the blood that they speak?"

"I hear them best from there. That is where I am used to listening. But I think they are everywhere."

"My God," says Leeuwenhoek, in amazement. "Have you told anybody else?"

"No. Why? Can you hear them, too?"

"No," he replies, with a rush of pride, "But I can see them."

"Ah," says the goose girl with innocent satisfaction. "Can you see them now? Do you have your own blood?"

"No," says Leeuwenhoek, "I need a machine, called a microscope. It makes tiny things appear big. You have to look through a lens, a special kind of eye. I have not yet looked at blood. Only water. And wood. And cloth. And grass. Some other things."

"You should look at blood. There are many animals in it," says the girl.

"Thank you," he replies, "I will." He stands there, nonplussed.

The goose girl folds up her handkerchief carefully and tucks it into her bosom. As she rises from the bucket, the geese look up at her attentively. She nods approvingly at them, at him. Leeuwenhoek's audience is over. She leads the geese away to pasture. He watches them waddle out of the new gate, hearing the tiny slaps of their flat feet on the cobbles as they depart. The interlocking pattern of the now-empty stones assaults his eyes, and he stares down at it fixedly until the lines begin to swim. He feels nauseous. Swaying slightly, he goes in.

⤚⤙

Grinding lenses is tedious, painstaking business. It is also, he has learned, largely unnecessary. Nonetheless, he spends a certain amount of time doing it, for the microscopes he sells or displays. They are his bait. People admire them and even buy them, but they are misdirection, such as conjurors perform at fairs with walnut shells. Grinding is fiddly, repetitive work, but it affords him time to think.

He sits at the lathe in his study, buffing a nearly finished lentil of glass held in a form with soft leather. He cannot trust himself to do anything else, as his hands are trembling. He simply cannot believe the foregoing conversation. That a child who has grown up half-wild and half-starved on fields and roads might hear voices, that he can accept. Half her compatriots, herders and drovers, are insane. Anneliese's assessment of the girl is probably quite right. What he cannot account for is his own opinion. More conscientiously, his own desire. He *wants* the girl to be hearing *animalcules.*

Surely that is what they must be, these little animals that the girl hears? Animalcules? The minuscule creatures that he sees, so many times magnified? What else could they be? They must be! The girl may be mad, but that need not prevent her from speaking the truth. Churchmen impute a certain kind of truth to the mad, a holy innocence. That must be what it is. After all, he has worried from time to time about his own sanity. He sees monsters: creatures more bizarre than those painted by Bosch, with many legs and no heads and bodies that make no sense. And it seems they are omnipresent. They infect the world like lice. The goose girl claims that they feel angry, hungry. He has never thought about their feelings. What do they want of us, the *animalcules?* Do they know we are here? Are they our enemies?

We are greatly outnumbered.

But people are made in God's image. Compared to animalcules we are huge, gods ourselves. They inhabit us as we inhabit the world.

We are worlds.

Such thoughts give him vertigo. They make him fear that he is living through a monstrous time, in which infinity is creeping into everything. Occasionally he has looked through the artificial eye of the microscope and has had to clutch the table for fear of falling in. Into the inexplicable, teeming world of the animalcule, in which he would not last a minute but would be torn apart by millions of chomping jaws. Likewise he has looked at the sky, that space above the terrestrial sphere that has suddenly, horribly expanded into unguessable distances filled with huge masses, and felt himself shooting unfathomably upward. Such are the perils of the lens-maker.

Does the goose girl hear the stars singing, as well?

He should just send her away.

PLAGUE

Vermeer comes by, as if casually. He is angling for quills. Leeuwenhoek finds, to his own irritation, that he has already mentally set aside three of them for him, those with the heaviest shafts that will open up widest to receive the brush hairs. The problem with being a true artisan is that it is so easy to be exploited by your friends. Most people are not interested in making things. Vermeer, who is exclusively interested in making paintings, knows this quite well. He has already talked Leeuwenhoek into making a *camera obscura*, an elegant little device in a mahogany box, with a wonderful crisp mirror that he silvered himself. And a ground lens, as high magnification is not its object, merely accurate reflection. The painter is full of enthusiasm for it, talks of it as if he had invented it himself, and has not paid a single florin for it. Leeuwenhoek wants to strangle him, but at the same time knows that by tomorrow afternoon he will be puttering around with tiny brass fittings for Vermeer's pencils, provided, gratis, from his own geese.

He has a passion for constructing things. He had perversely enjoyed fitting together the pieces of the new gate, even as he grew ever more convinced that raising geese in town was a ridiculous enterprise, one sure to attract the ire of the Council of Forty. Indeed, the *buurtmeester* has just been to see him about the geese. "Any complaints about noise, stink, or nuisance, Antoni, and you'll be up for a reprimand. You know that's embarrassing. Bad for business, too. More than once, and they'll have to go. What in hell are you keeping geese for, anyway?"

Leeuwenhoek had tactfully not replied with the speech about the damnable nosiness of neighbors in the free Dutch Republic that sprang to mind. He had given the man a glass of genever and sent him on his way. Barbara had spoken to their nearest neighbors months ago and promised them unlimited free goose shit for their garden if they would kindly permit the sweepings from the courtyard to be collected by the *crebbemeester* at the collection point opposite their door. They had had no objection, as they kept a fair-sized orchard in back.

Moreover, their neighbor is Cornelis s'Gravesend, the town anatomist. Leeuwenhoek had convinced the man without much trouble, though perhaps without much truth, that he is raising geese for the purposes of experiment. After all, he too is a natural philosopher. So there is really no need to worry about the *buurtmeester*. He can go and enforce the endless bylaws somewhere else.

"How is your goose girl?" asks Vermeer.

"What makes you think she is still here?" counters Leeuwenhoek.

"You have a spanking new gate—very fine, I must say—and the yard is covered with goose shit," replies Vermeer. "Unless you have added goose herding to your list of professions?"

Leeuwenhoek sighs. "The girl is fine. Strange. I think she may be a seer, or a saint. She hears voices—"

"I want some of her hair," says Vermeer.

"Johannes!"

"People are always collecting the hair of saints."

"Catholics," retorts Leeuwenhoek.

Vermeer crosses himself and looks expectant. Leeuwenhoek laughs reluctantly. He always forgives Johannes. He can't help it.

"She has the geese at pasture."

"I will wait."

"All day? She may keep them overnight."

"Well, will you collect it, then? When she returns?"

"Johannes, it is an odd request—"

"Antoni, she is an odd child, and not even your child! Who cares? Just ask her for a few hairs. Who has ever seen hair like hers? Make sure you get close to the scalp. It is softest there."

Vermeer can already tell that Leeuwenhoek will do it. He rises to leave, and wrings Leeuwenhoek's hand, saying "You must come and see the camera. It is superb." He departs.

Leeuwenhoek, rattled, calms himself by contemplating the design of the brush clasps. He begins to trim the feathers for the artist's pencils. He slices the quills open with his finest blade and puts them in a tray to soak. He makes several rough sketches.

Then, suddenly, the girl is home. It is raining, so she has brought the geese back early. They will shelter, honking querulously, under the eaves until the weather lets up. Their outrage is comical for water birds. He calls to her through the kitchen window, "Come in and dry by the fire!"

She comes in. She looks out of place indoors. She stands extraordinarily still. Leeuwenhoek is made aware of the hardness and regularity of all the surfaces, the cold flagstones of the floor, the terse uprightness of the walls. His house is a trap. She stands there like a goose, with the same effortless watchfulness and precision.

"You remember my friend Johannes, the one we met at the market, the first day you came here?" he begins uneasily.

She nods, and draws closer to the fire, spreading out chilled, blue hands.

"He is an artist. He paints wonderful, small paint-ings. Precious. Filled with light. He praised your hair, remember?"

"Yes," she replies, "he wanted some. Why? Is he look-ing for the little animals, too? On hairs, and in blood, and things, like you?"

"Ah, no," he replies, surprised, "no, for paintbrushes. Human hair, especially the hair of children, makes the finest brushes. Pencils with the finest points."

"He wants my hairs for this?"

"Yes," he says, sheepishly.

She says nothing, but starts to unwrap the damp ker-chief from around her hair. She unties two small pieces of dirty ribbon that she carefully tucks down her front, and her heavy braids begin to unravel. Leeuwenhoek is struck with a sense of looming inappropriateness. Watch-ing a woman bare her hair is an intimate thing, even one as young as this. He is not normally aroused by children. Yet this does not quite capture the problem. It is more like seeing an angel, or an animal, undress. As if she were about to take off her skin.

He departs back to his study to fetch scissors, almost trotting.

When he comes back the goose girl is standing in front of the fire, wholly obscured by her hair, a rippled, glinting curtain that falls clear to the floor. He fears she may be naked behind it, seeing a small sodden mass near the hearth. As he approaches, clearing his throat, he sees it is only her apron. His relief is unspeakable.

The girl turns toward him without speaking, takes hold of a handful of her magnificent hair, and yanks it casually out of her scalp. Leeuwenhoek starts and yelps, nearly jumping backwards. The girl shows no sign of emotion. She hands over the hank of hair and begins the long task of braiding it back up, combing it with her fingers. He looks to see if the tips are bloody, like the goose feathers. They are not. He accepts it like one of the gifts of the magi, or as if it might turn into vipers.

He carries the hair into the study and lays it on the desk next to the soaking quills, which are unfurling beautifully. His fingers feel hot. He is tempted simply to lock himself in the study. But he has invited the girl in. She is a guest in his house who needs food and fire. A fellow pilgrim. Otherwise she might as well be sitting outside, under the eaves with the geese, in the rain.

When he returns to the kitchen, the girl is winding the finished braids around her head, tucking in the ends, and tying it all up again with the kerchief. He leaves her to it. When she is done, he opens his mouth and says the first thing that presents itself, popping into his head like a jack-in-the-box. He asks her: "what did you see in the forest, when you were traveling? You said that you saw strange things." He realizes, as soon as he utters it, that he is prompting her to say more about animalcules.

The girl looks him full in the face for a moment. Then, as if she has received the answer to a question she did not pose in words, she sits abruptly down on the floor near the fire. Leeuwenhoek suppresses the urge to do the same; the idea of sitting in a chair seems suddenly pretentious. Nonetheless, he draws one out from the table and sits down. The goose girl gazes into the flames and speaks in her light monotone.

"We were in the woods a long time," she says. "It was always raining or snowing. The geese did not like it. They smelled foxes and things and were afraid. They never left me alone for a minute. I had been sick, in Kampen. A woman looked after me. But once I had left, I got sick again, shivering. The hankie, my mother's one, I began to hear it buzzing, or whispering, like bees in the distance, as it lay inside my dress. Maybe it got warm and woke up because I was hot. I thought it was my mother talking to me."

"What did it say?" interrupts Leeuwenhoek.

"Warnings, it seemed like. Excitements. Fears. Not in words. A kind of reaching out. I thought it was my mother, comforting me. Maybe singing, like at night time."

"But you think that no longer?"

"No. The little animals, they are talking amongst themselves. Not to me. I just—"

"Overhear them?" he suggests.

She looks at him meditatively. "Overhear? Yes. I overhear them."

Leeuwenhoek, needing time to think about this, returns to his original question: "What did you see in the forest?"

"Many things. Some were just the dreams of fever. But one morning, just past dawn, we were sheltering under a big tree on the edge of a clearing, the geese were still sleeping, and I saw a huge figure, as tall as a tree, but made of a dark mist, like smoke or twilight. Striding. It was a woman, a huge, huge woman, heading back toward the town we had left. Kampen. There was a sound like wind in the trees. She made no marks in the grass, not even in the dew. She had enormous dark eyes like bruises in a white face. I could see the sun rising right through her. She walked right past without seeing me. The geese all woke up at once, hissing and honking. And the hankie inside my dress, it was buzzing and muttering crazily. It pulled and pulled: it wanted me to follow. I was afraid. I did not want to follow. So I pulled out the hankie and threw it on the ground."

"My God," says Leeuwenhoek, "what was it?"

The goose girl replies, with her implacable authority, "Plague."

"Plague?"

"Yes. Soon after, plague came to Kampen. Many people died. I heard about it on the road. We saw it coming. The geese, and me. That is what I think."

Leeuwenhoek has no idea what to think, other than to be glad she is not his daughter. They seem to have strayed from the topic of animalcules, or from any interpretation of them that he can understand.

"My mother died of plague, in our village, before. Almost everyone died, so I took the geese and left."

"When?"

"Long ago. I think that the little animals in the hankie knew Plague when she passed by. They were calling to her."

"They were calling? Why?" He finds that he is asking in all seriousness, as if the girl were an oracle. The interpreter of the animalcules.

"Maybe they are her children."

Leeuwenhoek pictures tiny, crawling creatures in the blood on the handkerchief waving and crying out to Plague, their mother. His head spins. He imagines temples, congregations, avenues, at a scale far too small to see, inhabited by minuscule, orderly monsters. Monsters with mothers. Hierarchies and conclaves and councils. A town of animalcules. He will never be able to move again, lest he crush whole civilizations.

But then, what civilization would cheer for Plague?

The girl looks up. "The rain is stopping," she says. "I will return to the geese now. If I can hear the little animals in the blood on the hankie, maybe you can see them. Do you want to look?"

"Yes," says Leeuwenhoek, seizing this idea. If he can see animalcules there, he will be somewhat further ahead. She will become a more credible witness. He will have evidence. He pauses for a moment, then adds, "have you told anyone else about this vision?"

"What is a vision?" says the girl. "It was just something I saw. No, I have not told anyone. I don't like talking to people."

"Good," says Leeuwenhoek, "and my advice is: Don't tell anyone, at least for now. A vision is a moment of seeing something that nobody else can see."

"Ah," she replies, "like you seeing the little animals?" Not waiting for his reply, she nods serenely and passes out the door, back to her waiting flock.

❧

On rainy evenings, the goose girl is more likely to eat with them. She prefers to eat her food outdoors. Where she can run away with it, Barbara thinks, if anything threatens.

It is pouring heavily. So the girl is in the kitchen, by the hearth. Barbara has instructed her to wash her hands and face; she has to do this every time. The girl does not learn. Now the child is sitting quietly on the hearthstones, off to one side, waiting. She does not offer to help. She never has. She sits silently, warily, like a strange cat.

Barbara reaches a hand across her to a kettle hanging over the hearth.

"You are burned," the girl observes, in her emotionless voice. She does not say "you were burned."

"Yes," says Barbara.

"So is Scratch," says the girl. "That is why she is lame. She scratched and scratched at that foot when she first came, until it bled. She burned it in a fire."

"When?"

"I did not see the fire. Only in her mind. She ran to us, one day, when we passed, all alone, black with smoke. She stayed with us."

"In her mind?"

"Yes. A goose's mind is different. But it was fire: the roar and smell."

Barbara takes her hand away from the kettle.

"Why did you not call her Blackie, or Blackfeather, then?"

"Because she scratched. All the time. At that foot. Even after it healed. She would not stop. Sometimes she still does it. If she is tired, or cold."

"The poor thing," says Barbara, hoarsely.

"A burn never goes away," says the girl, "does it?"

"No," says Barbara, "it scars." She wraps both her hands in heavy cloth, and lifts off the soup. "Here we are. Time for supper."

⌁

Spring has advanced. Vermeer has come, disingenuously, to collect the brushes, with another invitation to come and see the camera. Sooner or later, Leeuwenhoek knows, he will indeed go to see it *in situ*. He is reluctant, though. For one thing, if he goes to the studio, there is no telling what he might end up buying.

The brushes, however, proved almost miraculously straight and strong, as if made of ivory. The perfect, fine golden hairs stood up at the ends like candle flames, making the brazen fittings look dark. He had seriously thought about gilding them, which was sheer folly. Who would waste gold on goose feathers and a tuft of hair? He is not a papist, making reliquaries. It was only that the little pencils were such beautiful objects of human art. Crafting them, all the while, he had felt like a doll maker.

He has, in fact, furtively, made some miniature furnishings for the superb dollhouse that Barbara had brought into the marriage as part of her dowry. It is a magnificent piece, made in Amsterdam by guildsmen, with twelve rooms. His carpentry is not really fine enough for it, though Barbara has never complained. Certainly he has never begrudged her the best cloth from the shop for it. The dolls dine on silk; the family, linen. He has put together a few tiny framed mirrors and a brass coal scuttle. Small, made things create tenderness.

Animalcules do not do so. At least, not for him. Perhaps for the goose girl. For him, the attraction of their tininess is different. They are unmade. It is interesting to speculate about the circumstances of their lives. For lives they definitely are. He has seen them eat and excrete, move, merge, grow, burst, and, most strangely, split. They are not parts of the things they inhabit, the enormities and rifts and fibrous roughnesses of fabric or skin or hair; they are themselves. Motile. Alive. Separate. What, if anything, do they think? And if they don't think—he has seen no evidence of brains or nerves or organs of cognition that he can recognize—how can they be so active? Plants have no organs for thinking and they can move, but not with the restless determination he has seen in *animalcules*. Yet animalcules share almost nothing in bodily form with animals of larger scale: they are not really animals.

Animalcules. Little animals. Words fool us. We get so used to them, we use the same ones for everything. Then we think we understand.

HONEYDEW

The girl says that the honeydew has appeared in the pond where she pastures the geese. He is coming to collect some. It is dense this year; the whole pond is engulfed in a bright green glow. The geese do not like it. They avoid deep dives, she says, and graze only out of the water. What do they fear?

The Romans used geese as sentinels, trusting their animal vigilance. Local farmers say the shocking bright color that appears so suddenly in the waters at this time of year is caused by the heavy spring dews leaking into the ponds. Blue-green fibrous filaments appear in cattle wades and duck ponds, anywhere there is a high traffic of animals, suddenly, in spring, due to the meeting of two waters. At all other times of the year, dew is harmless. In spring, it carries poison.

Dew. All the year round the fowl sip it happily and eat grass stems laden with it. But when it comes, they mistrust the honeydew. They eat the dew-wet grass and avoid the matted ponds. Leeuwenhoek is more inclined to trust geese than farmers. Honeydew has nothing to do with dew, he thinks. He no longer shares the widespread belief that things can instantly change their state, or be born of nothing. All things are themselves. And the world is full of dormancies, latencies, seeds of things waiting to happen. When certain conditions are met, things grow, things die. Perhaps if he learns what the honeydew is, he will figure out how it comes into being.

He is up to his knees in mucky pond water. The geese are looking at him curiously. They are not accustomed to seeing people in their pond. People do not go into ponds. Not adults, anyway. Perhaps the geese find it comical. He is embarrassed. Not because he fears the judgment of geese, but because their attention has made him realize how childlike he must seem. As a boy, like all boys, he was happiest when wet. Now he thinks, as he waits for the disturbed bottom to settle around his freezing feet, good God, how many times this year have I been in this pond? A dozen, at least. He has taken phials and phials of water, at various seasons, for various purposes. It is a veritable city of animalcules. It was, indeed, his constant pilgrimages to this pond that allowed him to find and rent the surrounding pasture. So the geese have reason to be glad of his philosophical inquiries. He glares at them. They are unrepentant. He dips his glass jar down in a wide arc, scoops up some honeydew, and trudges out.

As he is wrestling his stockings and shoes back on, the girl appears from the field's one small copse, where she has been relieving herself. He had noticed her squatting there as he came up the lane. She approaches him, blunt and clear as a goose, etched against the early morning sky like an ink drawing. He is sitting on the ground. It is rare that a grown man looks up at a child. He feels caught out. His buttocks are wet and cold on the dewy grass. His shoe buckles suddenly appear an impenetrable mystery, as they did when he was seven.

"Why are you here?" asks the girl. He is trespassing. This is her domain.

He resists the urge to explain that he is, in fact, sitting on property that he has legally rented upon which geese that he purchased at market reside, and says, "Collecting honeydew."

She accepts this as perfectly natural. "The geese hate it," she says.

"Do they?" he asks. "They eat water plants, though, do they not?"

"Yes. Maybe it is not a plant."

"It is green. It needs water. It takes energy from the sun. Plants do those things."

"Does anything else do those things?"

"Well, animals need water to live, and some kinds take strength from the warmth of the sun. Toads and such. Only plants, though, are green."

The goose girl is unconvinced. "Frogs are green. Some plants have leaves that are red and yellow. Or flowers."

"True. But most plants are green. It is part of their plantness, the condition of being a plant."

"Most frogs are still green. They are not plants. Are they?"

"No. Animals, that can move around on their own. Plants cannot do that."

"You call honeydew a plant, and it moves around. Or maybe it is just the water."

Leeuwenhoek has made no progress with his shoe buckles. He puts his hands on his knees. "You're right," he says. "It's very hard to make these distinctions—what is a plant? what is an animal? —if all you have is words. Words make everything the same. It drives me mad. Through a microscope, everything looks different. Absolutely clear. The substances of a plant and an animal are distinct; they have different parts; the bits are arranged in different ways. It's very confusing that we have to use the same words to describe them—words like green, say. A frog is green, and so is a leaf. So we think there's something the same about them. But if I look at the muscle of a frog and a fragment of leaf through a microscope, they have completely different structures—they are built in a different way, out of different materials. A plant doesn't even look green through a microscope, did you know that?"

"No," replies the girl.

He smiles at this phlegmatic answer. He spends a moment concentrating on the shoe buckles. He goes on in a calmer fashion, "well, neither did Aristotle. He was an ancient philosopher; according to him, things are either animal, vegetable, or mineral."

"Is that all?" says the girl. "What is mineral?"

"Like a rock. A rock is mineral. Or metal, ores smelted from rock. Not alive."

"Rocks are not alive?"

"No."

"But what if little animals live on them? How can you tell where the little animal stops and the rock begins?"

Leeuwenhoek has thought along these lines and exhausted himself. He is determined to defend the rights of animalcules to a separate existence. He is wounded that she, their champion and interlocutor, should say such a thing.

"With a good enough lens, you could see them," he replies shortly. "Animalcules can move and the rock does not. They change, and the rock does not."

She looks as though she is about to argue.

"Why do you think honeydew is not a plant?" he asks quickly.

"I just wondered if it had some other way of being alive."

"You mean, not as animal or vegetable?"

"Yes," she says.

"I don't know, but I think it possible," he admits.

Shoe buckles mastered, he rises, picking up his jar of glowing green filaments. He nods to the girl, resisting the impulse to bow, and lumbers off through the mud in his wet breeches.

⟶

Honeydew is not a plant.

Two days have passed since his trip to the field. He is still in a daze.

The geese are right. The girl is right. Honeydew is green and it needs the sun, but it lacks the interior structures that he has seen in wood and flower stems and leaves, those vessels and fibers that make a plant a plant, that allow it to feed itself and to cohere as a single life. Each minuscule speck of honeydew is its own being, somehow, even lacking those things; it gathers up vital force inside itself and drifts about, as plants do not. Yet he cannot escape the opposite conviction, either: that the whole blanket, or carpet, or cloud of them all act together, that they are many units that make up a single being. Like trees in a forest, but also unlike. When we speak of a forest, what do we mean? We mean a group of trees, all growing together in a single place, one that we may walk through or place on a map. It is a term of geography. We do not think of a forest as a being capable of acting, though we may say "the forest grows" or "it spreads." Except in children's tales, we do not think of trees as actively doing anything, individually or collectively. This is indeed the meaning of vegetable life.

Is honeydew animal or vegetable? One or many?

Should we speak of a forest of honeydew? A herd? A garden? A colony?

An army?

The honeydew, he can describe it in detail; he can draw it; but he has no idea what it is. A fish? A leaf? A mushroom? Small wonder the geese distrust it. It has another way of being alive, just as the girl said.

Categorical problems such as this make him giddy. They do not suit the shape of his mind. He is much happier just looking at the honeydew particles, enumerating their parts, drawing and measuring and recording them. He feels like their caretaker, somewhere between an advocate and a valet. He is not a scholar or a theologian. Metaphysical speculation makes him uneasy. It is best left to those who know Latin.

He is also affected by the sheer beauty of the honeydew: the traces of jewel greens and blues he can sometimes see in them, their minuscule translucencies and fine, crisp edges. The uniformity and elegance of their patterns in the water. Their spirals, like stairs in a tower. The draper in him thinks, Imagine the tapestries they would make! Gobelin! Printed cloth! Finer and more intricate than the flowers and sinuous oriental plants turned out by the French factories. Ah, now—honeydew tapestries. Could he find buyers? Who would make the cartoons? He would not trust that to his own hand. He has only ever been a cloth seller, not a cloth maker…

The need to see the quality of fabric clearly, to count the threads and see their individual densities, is what had made him into a lens-maker in the first place. He recalls, fondly, shocking a room full of weavers into silence the first time he had pulled out a magnifying glass of his own making and showed them their own work at higher magnification than they had ever seen before. He had lost a lot of business that day, but he was never cheated again.

Could he go back to those weavers now and say, Look what else I have seen through my lenses? Look, how beautiful! What patterns! Think of the money we could make!

~

"Antoni," says Vermeer, three days later, in long-suffering tones, "No one is going to buy a tapestry covered in green bugs."

"But they're not bugs, they're—"

"What, then, Antoni?"

"Well, plants, sort of, but free-floating and yet interlocking—"

"I see. That will make all the difference. They will line up for tablecloths and carpets woven with special, invisible, movable, green plants that only you have ever seen. Particularly when you tell them it is honeydew, that makes all their animals sick in the springtime and smells like shit."

The idea of Vermeer giving him sensible advice is galling.

"Well, I won't tell them, then! I will just say it's a formal pattern."

"Most patterns are simple. These are far from simple." Vermeer gestures to the litter of drawings on the study table.

"They could be simplified."

"And would you like them then? Would you be happy with them? You know you'd go mad if I changed a single line." Vermeer picks up a pen and approaches the top sketch threateningly. Leeuwenhoek clenches his jaw. He stares firmly at the painter. Vermeer glances at him humorously and becomes absorbed in the drawings. "These, now. What are these? Hairs? Tongues? Penises?"

"For want of a better word I call them branches. Or legs. Or whips. For locomotion."

"Antoni, you need to talk to learned men about these things. Whips, good God, man! You need fancy Latin words for this."

"I know. You're right. But who? I know a few people who are doing this in the Republic but they're more important than me. Huygens is a snob; Hudde, for God's sake, he's the mayor of Amsterdam. Who else could I talk to, in Dutch?"

"If you send mostly pictures, you wouldn't have to talk at all. You could correspond with anybody in Europe."

"No, I would. I do. The creatures move and shift. I need to label the parts. There are processes I need to describe. Also, my drawings are terrible."

"You need an amanuensis," says Vermeer casually, delicately moving pages. Leeuwenhoek freezes. Vermeer looks at him. "Not me. Absolutely not me. I am not reliable. And I hate drawing. I am a painter, Antoni. What you need is a limner, a cartoonist." He looks thoughtful a moment. "Like one who has worked for the weavers, Antoni. A man who can draw fine, simple forms."

Leeuwenhoek is thunderstruck at this practical idea. His friend gives him a knowing look. "But first, Antoni, you have to decide what you're doing. Studying bugs for natural philosophy is one thing; making them into weaver's cartoons is quite another. One is—what? art?—and the other is industry. You need to think about what you want out of these enterprises. They are not the same."

"But if I find the right man? Surely he could do both jobs?"

"Who would that be, Antoni? A weaver's apprentice, trained limner, and bug anatomist? With a head for business and a flair for natural philosophy?"

Leeuwenhoek laughs. "Yes, him."

"Well, there might be one such man in Delft. If you find him, hire him," says Vermeer.

The English Chapel

Several days later Leeuwenhoek is sitting in the English chapel, between services. He does this occasionally, though not without guilt. At least the English have the right ideas about God. Some of them, anyway. His old master in Amsterdam, years ago, had been a Scot, William Davidson. Nobody could say he wasn't a good Calvinist. Almost too good. Of course, a Scot is not an Englishman. Though the island now has a Scottish king. Charles, is it? But then, doesn't everyone say he's secretly a Catholic? Raised in France? Really, it is a pity that their godly republic foundered. Princes are unreliable.

He likes the architecture of this chapel. It is much smaller than the impressive dimensions of the Nieuwe Kerk, of course. The English congregation used to hold services there, in between the Dutch ones, but it became too inconvenient. They had to hold them at outlandish times and sometimes couldn't get in at all on holy days. They built their own chapel. He has seen village churches like it: a plain rectangular room, seating perhaps forty people, with a small vestry behind. This room is ever so slightly more ornate, though, to his eye. Spare, dark pews, no images, just like a Dutch church, but the proportions are a tiny bit different. Also, behind the chapel itself, and presumably not on consecrated ground, is a small flat for the English rector. This has always struck him as profane, even though it has a separate entrance. The English must have thought it unseemly for their pastor to live in rented rooms. And no doubt the lodgings are part of his preferment. Leeuwenhoek has heard people say—usually when trade tensions with England are high—that the English priest has to live alone because he's a spy. Leeuwenhoek knows the Reverend Forsythe. The man is so unworldly that this possibility strikes him as unlikely.

English is spoken in this chapel. He has spoken, haltingly, to the rector in that language. They communicate better in Dutch, though Forsythe's accent is noticeable. He feels a kind of kinship with him, as he does with the chapel itself. Barbara's father, a brewer, had lived and traded in Norwich for many years. She had spoken English fluently until the age of nine, and still has friends in the congregation. People, usually traders' exhausted wives with young children and little Dutch, still come to her for help. It is not unusual for Leeuwenhoek to come into the great room from the shop, or from an errand outside, to find Barbara holding the hands of a weeping woman in foreign clothes, seated in front of the dollhouse. Months later, better settled and with more command of the language, these same women come by with gifts of food and brandy and London gin, with tidy children and gossip from two nations. Some are among his best customers at the drapers' shop. He has reason to be grateful to the English chapel.

What Leeuwenhoek likes about the building, with its whitewash a shade off, its moldings a thumb's breadth too wide, he likes about English, too. When he overhears an English conversation, or catches the tail end of a sermon, something tugs on his imagination; it is as if the speakers are standing just on the other side of a heavy linen veil. Close, yet muffled. Language is going on, and he is not obliged to understand it fully. The effect is soothing. He comes here from time to time to rest his mind. An English silence stuffs itself into his ears, briefly stems the endless tide of words in his head, the brimming minutiae of his investigations into the lives of the animalcules.

He is sitting in a trancelike state, perhaps that peace that passes all understanding, in an empty pew, when his friend Dr Reinier De Graaf walks by, the heels of his boots ringing in the narrow aisle. He cannot possibly have any spiritual reason to be there, as he is a Catholic. Therefore, he must have some business with the rector or his staff. Leeuwenhoek hails him. De Graaf stops immediately and drops onto the bench beside him. Leeuwenhoek cannot help but wonder if this is sacrilege. De Graaf looks at him wryly and says, "We are neither of us a good fit in this pew, Antoni. What are you doing here?"

Leeuwenhoek replies, a trifle defensively, "Praying." Yes, praying. To the God of the animalcules. In the English chapel. Divinity is everywhere.

"And I am here bringing a remedy for the sexton's wife, who has a female complaint," says De Graaf. He is the only doctor Leeuwenhoek knows of who specializes in the diseases of women. No doubt it is because he trained in France. Of course, it is mostly their husbands he deals with, as the women suspect him and carry on dealing with midwives and priests and charlatans just as they have always done. He had tried in vain to persuade Barbara to be examined by him when she had puerperal fever after their third child was born. Again after the fourth. Scandalized, she had refused both times. The third baby had died three weeks after birth, two years ago. They are still in mourning for the loss of their fourth infant, a son, Philips. He had died at five weeks, six months ago. All this time Barbara has carried on trusting only in her circle of women: healers and herbalists and old wives. Next time he ought to insist.

"Are you here working on your English?" inquires De Graaf. "Because it is better to do that when people are actually speaking."

"I am sitting here thinking about animalcules," admits Leeuwenhoek.

"Ah. How go your inquiries with those beautiful little microscopes? I have never seen anything like them, as I've said a hundred times."

"I have seen so many new things that it fills me with wonder. I have pages of notes. But what should I do with them?"

"Write a book."

"What, like the *Micrographia*? That fellow, Hooke, he is a philosopher. He writes in Latin as well as English. No one would listen to me, a linen-draper. Half the time I am not sure my notes make sense at all. It's just that these creatures are so irresistibly fascinating—"

"Send your observations to the Royal Society, then. Hooke is a member. You know he, at least, would be interested."

"Reinier, that's ridiculous. They would never read letters from a Dutch haberdasher."

"I bet they would, once they saw your results. Once they understood the quality of your microscopes. I will write to them as your advocate, perform the introduction, as a *bona fide* medical doctor, graduate of Angers and Leiden, etcetera etcetera. That is all it will take. These philosophers are not dukes, Antoni. Most of them are just middling men. Though in England, they say, even the king takes an interest."

"Reinier, we are at war with England. They will dismiss me as a cheesemonger."

"Antoni, here we are, two seekers after knowledge in the English church in Delft. A Catholic and a Calvinist.

Neither of us English. Neither God nor reason pays any attention to these wars."

Leeuwenhoek steels himself. "You are right, Reinier. I agree. Go ahead. Write an introduction. We will see what they say. Perhaps the passion for philosophy will trump all other things. Sometimes I feel that if I don't share all these observations I will go mad."

"As a fellow natural philosopher, it is my duty, then, to save you for posterity," says De Graaf, earnestly. "Now I must deliver this package." He rises, nods briskly in farewell, and strides quickly up the aisle.

Leeuwenhoek continues to sit in the pew, trying to recapture his trancelike state. But it has fled. The inside of his skull is now as full of wrigglings and tiny gesticulations as a specimen jar. Could he possibly interest the Royal Society in his discoveries? In his inchoate notes? He hears footsteps ringing once more off the bare walls. Perhaps De Graaf has forgotten something. He looks up to find the English priest, the Reverend David Forsythe, coming down the aisle. Leeuwenhoek rises to greet him, a pastor in his own church.

"Antoni!" exclaims the Englishman, shaking his hand cordially—he has a firm handshake for a man who otherwise appears timid— "what are you doing here? Is it Barbara? Is she consoling another new member of my congregation? Do you need anything?"

"No, no, I am fine! As is Barbara!" replies Leeuwenhoek quickly. This is typical of the reverend, who is a very different kind of clergyman from their own pastor, a stern unsmiling man of sixty who has scarcely left the precincts of the Nieuwe Kerk for thirty years. Forsythe, though personally unassuming, is a man who has left his homeland to do God's work in a foreign country. This bespeaks an adventurous spirit. He has worked like the very devil to improve his Dutch, knows everyone in town, and is ever eager to be helpful. He is in many respects a kind of unofficial diplomat. Barbara admires him tremendously.

"You are here seeking a peaceful moment, then?" says Forsythe. "A bit out of the way? I cannot blame you. Everyone in this town is so industrious. Business dogs us everywhere. It seems impossible just to sit still, even in the house of God. And yet sometimes we'd very much like to."

"Exactly, reverend, exactly!" Leeuwenhoek says gratefully.

Forsythe makes the briefest of bows. "Then I will leave you to it, provided that there is nothing else I can do for you," he says, smiling. "And give my regards to your lovely wife." Leeuwenhoek nods politely in reply. The rector turns back up the aisle and disappears into the vestry.

Leeuwenhoek sits for a further moment wondering guiltily whether his conversation with De Graaf counts as business or not. Then he departs.

~

When Leeuwenhoek gets home, the goose girl is waiting. She has brought a gift: five stems of fresh timothy. She unwraps them, slightly wilted, from her apron, and hands them over ceremoniously. He receives them in due form but has no idea what to do with them. He stands there in puzzlement.

"You eat them," she says, as if it were obvious. It is obvious, to her; she lives with geese.

"But—it is grass. We don't eat grass."

"You just eat the lightest green part. You have to pull it out," she says, and shows him how to pull the inner stem out of its sheath. He nibbles on the exposed end of the stalk, politely. It is surprisingly sweet. He quickly consumes the ends of the other four stems.

"Thank you," he says to her. She nods. Not knowing what else to do with them, he lets the uneaten parts fall to the ground. A goose rushes toward them, and they are quickly gone. "You were right, you know," he continues. "About the honeydew. I don't think it is a plant."

"What is it, then?" she asks.

"Something else, another kind of life that probably deserves a new name."

"Name it, then."

Coming from a girl who has not seen fit even to name herself, he considers this a rather peremptory demand. "I think I will leave that to other people."

"What people?"

"I thought, some natural philosophers in England. Famous men, who write books. I have decided to write to them about my discoveries."

"England?" she says, blankly. Leeuwenhoek blinks.

"An island across the water from us, across the North Sea."

"And men there know about the little animals?"

"Yes. I imagine so. Some of them."

"I wonder what names they will choose," she says musingly, watching the geese mill around her feet in the hope of more grass.

"I have no idea. We might not even understand the words. They are likely to be in Latin."

She gives him another blank stare.

"Latin? Like the name of Caligula? The Roman emperor?"

She gives no sign of understanding.

"Latin," he repeats, as neutrally as possible. "The ancient language that priests used to speak in churches, before the great reform. They still speak it, in some places. Italy, France. Spain. Not here."

"Sometimes people have spoken to me, and the words have made no sense. Was that Latin?"

"Unlikely," he replies. "French, perhaps. Or Spanish." It is possible that she has never thought of other languages, that she assumes there is just the one. He ought to pity her in her animal ignorance, but it would be like pitying a cloud. Or a goose. What would be the point?

"So the priests from England will name the little animals in the honeydew?"

"Ah," says Leeuwenhoek, thinking it over. Finally he shrugs and says, "Yes."

LITTLE BOOTS

In the morning, Caligula is dead. The goose girl is stricken. She has been crying, Leeuwenhoek sees, when she comes to wake him, flinging open his bedroom door just after daybreak. She has never even been in this part of the house before. Her normally light voice is hoarse.

"You killed him!" she says accusingly. She leads Leeuwenhoek outside.

Caligula is lying on the cobbles. The other birds are shunning the body and keep away. The goose's body is uninjured, so it was not animals. His neck is stretched out in distress, his beak flecked with foam. The stones around him are green with excrement. The exposed bottoms of his little red boots are sadly worn.

"What? How could I have killed him?" asks Leeuwenhoek in surprise.

"It was the grass. The little animals on the grass. Your spit was on it."

"What? How could that kill a healthy goose? How do you know, anyway? Perhaps he had some disease."

"No. Not before. Now he does. That is why the others are staying away."

"How do you know?"

"They told me," she says impatiently. "And I hear the little animals in him, everywhere. Muttering. Buzzing like bees."

Leeuwenhoek stares at her, dumbfounded. He ought to be afraid. Priests perform exorcisms for less. Popish nonsense, of course. In France or any of the German principalities they would try her for witchcraft. Having more sense, people here had given that up decades ago. Perhaps he should take her to the madhouse? Or the orphanage, after all? There's no end to the ways an unpredictable, crazy child, even a servant, can embarrass a family. Solid respectability is very necessary for a retailer.

But then he would lose his best witness to the animalcules. His strange ally. It is more than possible that she is right. In principle, her statement makes sense. The little animals are everywhere. And they travel. Some might pass from a man to an animal, or vice versa. In spit, in sweat, through the air or water. Some might be tolerated by one organism but not another.

At present, of course, he can prove none of this. Nor could she. If he talks in these terms to anybody else he will just end up in the madhouse himself.

"Do not eat him," the girl warns.

Certainly not. The goose's body is polluted. He will burn it.

"I am very sorry," he says to her. "I did not know such a thing could happen. Poor Caligula."

"Nor did I. I did not know geese could die of plague," she replies.

"Plague, like the kind you saw in the woods, going to Kampen?" he asks quickly.

"Not exactly that kind. But some kind. I hear them, the little animals. They are wicked. Kill them. I felt him die. It hurt a lot."

"I will burn his body, then. Fire is cleansing."

"Good. They are eating him. Eating his blood. I hear them singing. They are filled with joy. Soon they will be dead," she says bleakly.

"I don't understand what could have happened," he says, perplexed. "What little animals could live inside me that could kill him so quickly? Why am I not dead? Could it spread to the rest of the flock?" He looks over at the rest of the geese huddled against the far wall. They are silent, like mourners.

"I don't know," replies the goose girl. "But they are afraid. Their fear protects them."

"I suppose that is what fear is for."

"Yes," she says, staring down at the dead bird.

"Say nothing about this to anybody," says Leeuwenhoek suddenly. "Promise me."

"Why not?" says the girl.

"People fear disease. No-one understands the little animals and what they do. If anyone found out that you know about this sickness in Caligula, they might think you caused it. Or me. With our inquiries, or our knowledge. Or they might insist all the birds be destroyed. Best to say nothing and just try to find out what happened. If we can."

The girl nods.

Leeuwenhoek moves to collect the body, though with no clear idea what to do with it. The midden? The kitchen fire? He doesn't want to burn down the house.

"Leave it," says the girl. "Burn him where he lies. Burn the ground. Burn it all."

In some respects this is easier. He will not have to touch Caligula, which he is now very reluctant to do. He is learning goose wisdom. But it will make a spectacle and a smell. What will he do if the neighbors complain? He will just have to say it is some kind of bird pest and that he is being careful of his flock. It is a matter of public safety. The courtyard and the goose are both his property. He leaves the girl standing guard and goes to the kitchen to find oil. He wants an immediate, hot flame.

Looking around the kitchen, he finds a crock of fat. It is probably goose fat, he thinks, with a shudder. He knows Barbara will be furious if he uses the butter. He melts the fat over the fire until it is liquid and smoking, and carries the hot pan out to the courtyard. He pours it over the body and the ground. Fortunately Caligula is a good distance from the walls. He carries the pan back in, and brings out a brand from the fire with tongs. He drops it in a pool of fat. With a whoomph and a rising roar, fire spreads instantly, accompanied by the horrid smell of burning feathers. Then burning leather. Then scorching goose. Caligula lies in state, engulfed in pagan flame. Leeuwenhoek wonders if the Roman emperors smelt this tasty as they were burning.

"It is a shame about the boots," says the girl.

THUNDERCLAP

Caligula's pyre cracks a single cobblestone in the front courtyard. As it splits, it makes a quick, sharp, carrying retort. Barbara comes rushing downstairs, wrapped in shawls, to find her husband and the girl presiding over the goose funeral. "What is happening, Antoni?" she demands.

"Nothing, nothing," he replies soothingly. "It is a cleanliness measure. The bird may have a pest that could spread to the rest of the flock. The fire cracked a stone. That's all."

Barbara blocks the kitchen doorway, preventing a curious Marieke from coming out. "Go back upstairs," she says to her daughter, tightly. Marieke protests violently, but Barbara is adamant. The little girl has to content herself with watching the thrilling blaze from an upper window. Leeuwenhoek sees her tearful face through the glass. Eventually, determined at least to have the last word, she laboriously opens the window and calls down hoarsely to her father, "It smells so good!"

"Yes, roast goose!" he calls back up. Marieke seems satisfied. When he next looks up, her face is gone from the window. When only bone and ashes are left—surely they are safe by now—he sweeps them up, ready to deposit them at the midden near the s'Gravesends', then realizes that he has no basket. He does not want to sweep them all the way across the yard, scattering them in the air.

"Can you go to the kitchen and ask Barbara for a basket?" he asks. "I don't want these ashes to get everywhere."

The goose girl turns and heads for the kitchen door. Five minutes later, she is back, though without a basket. Her hands are empty.

"Barbara is sleeping," says the girl.

"What?" says Leeuwenhoek. "Now, in the kitchen?" He is immediately worried. "Look, do you mean she's lying down—fallen?"

"No, she is sitting. She is asleep but her eyes are open."

"Almighty God! What—"

"She is not dead," says the goose girl, "only sleeping. Like a goose does, watching. She did not see me. I did not move. A goose notices only if you move quickly, if it is sleeping that way. Though usually they close one eye. Hers are both open."

Leeuwenhoek drops the ashes and runs for the kitchen. Dashing through the door, he finds Barbara, whey-faced, silent, not working, sitting at the kitchen table, her eyes averted from the fire. He takes one look at her tense, crouching body, her fixed, inward-turned gaze, and goes to sit beside her, dragging a chair close. He unclenches and smoothes and strokes her hands, which are clutched tight in her lap, obscuring the raised red welt of the old burn scarring her right palm.

It has been years since he saw her like this. After the disaster, she had been like this often; sometimes it had taken an hour or more before she could speak. The goose girl was not wholly wrong to say she was sleeping. It is something like sleep.

Leeuwenhoek strokes his wife's hands methodically, ten, twenty, thirty times, thinking: it was the open fire. It was the loud sound. I should have warned her to stay in, not to come down. Such a fool.

Barbara had been at home the day of the Thunderclap. They had only just been married. He himself was traveling back from Amsterdam, slowly, in a barge, supervising the shipment of the expensive dollhouse. They were not yet living in the house on Hippolytusbuurt, but around the corner, in a house owned by relatives. From miles outside the city, he had heard a dreadful, tearing boom. He thought the French were attacking. All shipping stopped moving. Barge-masters conferred anxiously; crew and passengers waited; eventually they moved on cautiously. They arrived, hours later, to find no men in uniform, no rebels, but a city decimated, the heart blown right out of it. Practically the whole east end was gone. Some idiot had taken a lantern into the powder magazine, he heard, as he gazed over an awful wilderness of broken glass, twisted beams, and fire.

People rushed off the boat in disorder, desperate to check on their families and property. So did he. Days later, he remembered the dollhouse. When he went back to look for it, he found that someone had providently moved it into a warehouse in the midst of all the chaos. He described it in detail, signed an affidavit, and got it back. Of course, he had no house to put it in. For a while, the dollhouse was the only house they owned.

He had picked his way through the east end, past heaps of scorched masonry that had once been his neighbors' houses and shops. His own house, when he got there, was an abstract pile of rubble. Domestic items, including one eerily intact large ceramic vase, littered the streets, blown out through windows as houses collapsed.

In the middle of the fish market he found a forlorn group of people. Some were wounded, some burned, all coughing from smoke and deaf from the blast. Barbara was among them. He wept with relief when he found her. She did not recognize him. After a while, he led her stumbling away, and they took refuge with her relatives on the other side of the city. There things were shaken up and windows were blown out, but the buildings were still standing. After several days, Barbara was able to talk; she thanked him for rescuing her. Her aunt looked after the terrible burn right across her right hand. She heard ringing in her ears for weeks, and eventually went deaf in the left ear. She was never able to say what had happened, how she had escaped the collapsing house. Only a few broken phrases. There was a gap in her memory, like pages torn out of a book.

The competent, confident young woman he had married vanished for a time. She trembled and vomited at the sight of the kitchen fire. Months passed before she could sit by a hearth or help in the kitchen. Her hand was a long time healing and caused her great pain. She could not bear loud noises. She was very reluctant to touch walls or doorways, fearing that they might collapse at her touch. Leeuwenhoek was terrified that she might be permanently afflicted. All the business of getting their lives back to rights he had done himself. Barbara's aunt, though, had been patient and ingenious. She had somehow nursed her through a long period in which Barbara could do little but sit and stare, occasionally read, and walk slowly back and forth from her aunt's house to church. At any other time, this behavior would have been shameful, even scandalous—mad. But families all through the city were dealing with people in similar conditions. Pastors prayed for them in the churches and urged compassion. All the wards in the hospital and the orphanage and the old people's homes were full, every bed in the city, with people wounded not just in body but in mind.

Leeuwenhoek busied himself with finagling and persuading creditors and family members and so on, and purchased the house on Hippolytusbuurt. It needed fixing, having partly collapsed. A little under a year after the explosion, he had brought the dollhouse out of storage, given it pride of place in the great room of the house, and ceremonially walked Barbara over to their new home. That had been ten years ago. She had gone from strength to strength ever since, regaining her authority, becoming a responsible householder, a respected citizen, an attentive mother. The only lingering sign of this past horror is a dread of thunder. She is always nervous in storms.

Leeuwenhoek sits at the table, stroking his wife's hands, calling her back to herself. Eventually, after many minutes, Barbara stirs and mutters. She looks down at her hands, seeing her husband holding them, smoothing them with his thumbs. "Antoni," she says, dazed, and begins to cry quietly. "I am so sorry. It was just—"

"I know," says Leeuwenhoek. "But everything is cleared away now. Marieke can come down, go out. It will be fine, my dear love."

"Maybe later," says Barbara, wiping her eyes on her apron. She looks up at her husband. "I had better go to her. I yelled at her. She was confused." Tears well from her eyes again. "But I was afraid to let her go out."

"Because of the fire?" asks Leeuwenhoek softly.

"And the sickness. You said the bird had a pest. What kind of pest? I couldn't let her go near."

Leeuwenhoek recognizes a deep fear that he knows well in Barbara. One fear brings out another.

They have lost three infants to fever. A girl, before Marieke, two boys since. Marieke, now seven, is their only child. It is not uncommon for young children to die, but this does not make it any easier. Each baby had been gorgeously swaddled in silk and linen grave clothes as it went into the ground at the Oude Kerk, members of a respectable haberdasher's family. Barbara has a helpless fear of contagion. All sicknesses, pests, fevers, they terrify her. If a neighbor is ill, or there is rumor of any kind of plague in town, she keeps her daughter inside for weeks at a time.

He should never have mentioned that the goose was ill. Even animal sickness is a threat. She had drowned the family cat for its constant coughing when Marieke was five. She had blamed it for the death of their infant son, Philips. The cat was coughing; the baby was coughing: that was enough for her. He had thought this action senseless at the time but in light of what has just happened with the goose he is now not so sure. If it is possible for his saliva to have somehow killed Caligula, it is surely equally possible for an animal to pass contagion to a human being. This is, however, not something he will discuss with Barbara, and certainly not on the strength of something so tenuous as the word of the goose girl. If his wife had even the remotest suspicion that the geese—or the girl—posed any danger to the health of their one surviving child, she would slaughter every goose and the girl would be at the orphanage with her next breath. Barbara has been the goose girl's champion up to now, but on this point her terror knows no bounds.

"You know I can't bear the thought of Marieke in danger, Antoni," she says, and draws a long, shaky breath. "Sickness…and fire… I can't have her ending up like me."

"What? Barbara, you are fine—indeed, wonderful. A lovely, wise, respectable woman, my beloved wife, dear to my heart, and healthy as a horse. How could it be bad if she ended up like you?"

"Barren, Antoni," whispers Barbara, staring down at her burned hand. "Womb-sick. Surely you have realized that is why our babies die? Why they burn up in fevers, cough themselves away in the cool air? They are born too hot."

"Barbara—"

"Antoni, it was the fire! Of course it was! That terrible day, the scorching heat, half my clothes burned away—it changed me. It dried me up like a stick. So my babies are born too hot, too dry. We must keep Marieke away from fire! She is already tainted…"

"Barbara!"

"Oh God, oh God, like that poor child, the fire-baby, Klaartje, that poor child, born too soon, scorched all down the right side—it was less than two years after—" Barbara is trembling all over. Leeuwenhoek kneels on the floor before her and wraps her body in his arms. Her hands close over his shoulders like a vice.

"It was a birthmark, Barbara. A strawberry mark, just colored skin. Nothing to do with fire. She was born too early, too small. Bad luck, terrible luck, accident, Barbara. You know it happens to many women. It happens all the time. You are fine. You have always been fine. The Thunderclap did nothing to you. It couldn't have. That is not how the world works. Think of it—what? A baby born differently because it is raining, or the sun shining, or a fire burning? On a Tuesday different from a Wednesday? No. Every one of us would be different then! We are born as God made us, Barbara. The rest is silliness. Hush, now."

"But the midwife said—"

He suppresses a surge of resentment. The midwife is a superstitious old fool. Barbara's head is full of her cant. "It doesn't matter what she said! A mark on a baby's skin inside the womb can have nothing to do with a fire outside it! Nothing! Ask Reinier, my love, if you don't believe me. People have their young just like animals do, and by the same processes. He can tell you all about them. If what that fool woman said were true, then, logically, if we wanted hot-blooded horses, all we'd need to do is set the barns on fire while the mares were in foal!"

Barbara snorts with horrified laughter. Color begins to creep back into her cheeks. Loosing her grip on his shoulders, she wipes her damp face and nose with her apron. "I can't believe you just compared me to a pregnant mare," she says, in an attempt at her usual, teasing tone.

"I didn't!"

"By implication. It is highly undignified to compare your wife to a horse."

"Yet I have the feeling I have heard the comparison before—probably in some bawdy song?"

"Worse and worse. I shall take insult."

"Yet you were acting just like one, weren't you? One of those fancy, high-strung Arab horses that they use for racing, that spook at nothing?"

"Outrageous!"

"With long, slim legs, and narrow hooves, and ribbons braided into their manes? Tremendously expensive of upkeep? The best food, and heavy blankets all night to keep off drafts?"

"What? Never! Unseemly decadence!" Barbara says, giggling now in relief. Leeuwenhoek rises from the floor, knees protesting. His wife stands up, too. "Thank you, Antoni," she says softly. He picks up her hand and kisses the burnt palm, then carefully folds it shut.

"There," he says, "you can take this up to Marieke, to placate her."

Barbara holds up her closed fist and shakes it lightly, as if checking to see that the kiss is still rattling around inside. She gives him a faint smile and heads for the stairs, still looking pale.

Leeuwenhoek walks through the house to open the draper's shop. He is late. As he turns the key in the door, he thinks of Barbara opening her hand upstairs in Marieke's little room, just through the wall, and the kiss fluttering out like a butterfly.

SOOT AND SPIT

The variety of smells generated by the burning of Caligula ("It smells so good, Papa!") sets Leeuwenhoek to thinking about the sense of smell. How, exactly, is the act of smelling effected? By what tissues, or vessels, or porosities in the nose? In the throat? In the brain, or the diaphragm? Reinier might know. Is it a matter of tiny particles? Do we sniff these up our noses? By what manner are they distinguished, if that is so? By shape? By density? How do they work upon us so that we perceive distinct smells? Might we have different-shaped receptacles to take in different particles? Or do things give off gases?

Matter exists as solid, liquid, or gas. Most solids, he has found, are full of tiny things, particles and living animalcules. Most liquids, too. Gases, ethereal matter, must surely be the same. Air is not nothing, except in a vacuum. He has read of experiments in vacuums, made with pumps. These are fashionable and ingenious. The pumps are cunning, and he would love to build one. Gases are doubtless full of animalcules, also, like solids and liquids. All matter harbors them. Is it these we smell, when we inhale? Tiny things riding on the wind?

But what are they riding *on*? Of what is the wind itself composed?

This is the problem with the world of animalcules. Once you have begun to think at their scale, everything is in danger of becoming philosophical. As far as he can see, there is no reason not to assume that all solids, all liquids, all gases are not made of yet tinier things, and those of yet tinier ones, and tinier, and tinier, down to some final, minuscule unit long out of the range of perceptibility. Or perhaps it never stops.

He is holding a jar over the kitchen fire. Smoke flows into it in liquid, curling patterns. Soot forms in the jar, solids falling right out of the air and clinging together on the glass. He carries the jar into his study and examines the particles through his microscope. They fall into a pleasing, overlapping pattern, finer than the finest ink drawing, as if they are trying to return to the wood grain that gave them birth. He is both pleased and annoyed at his own fancy. It is perfectly clear that unseeable forces—chemical, physical, divine—act upon us every second. Their cumulative powers far outweigh our will. It is as if, by sheer accident, looking through his lenses, he has discovered fate. And yet now, this minute, looking at soot, he sees trees; his mind is determined to exert itself, to determine the shape of things. This is a battle he can never win. To allow himself, the discoverer, to be dwarfed by the simple properties of God's creation, or to insist upon his rights, those that his mind, made in the image of God's own reason, inevitably imposes by way of understanding. Indeed, such is the battle of Calvinism itself.

He is not comfortable on these theological heights. He turns to the next treasure he has been keeping in his study: a jar of saliva. Not his own. This also, in a way, he owes to the death of the goose. Just one other person (thankfully not the *buurtmeester*) had reacted to the burning of Caligula in the courtyard: Old Willem, a great uncle and hanger-on of the s'Gravesends. He had been out sweeping.

The old fellow had got, as they say, spitting mad. In the midst of a wide-ranging harangue about fire wardens, town bylaws, public foulness, flyblown carcasses, idiot

children, vagabondage, unregulated household econo-
mies, loose women, business malpractice, idolatry, incest,
and papism, he had horked an enormous glob of phlegm
over the gate. It lay there, glistening wetly, the size of an
oyster. Leeuwenhoek had noticed his impressively blackened teeth.

As he leaned over the gate and talked to the horrible
old gossip for the next half hour, the man's breath had
nearly knocked him down. "Stupid, is she, that little girl
you got to herd over there? Never heard her say a word
yet. And now she's gone and let one die on you, dumb
little cow," had been the old man's first remark.

After twenty minutes of this Leeuwenhoek had soft-
ened him up enough to say: "Now, Willem, you know that I
occasionally conduct experiments? With optical devices?"

"Why would you want to do that, seeing as you're a
successful businessman already?" the old fellow had replied truculently.

"There is good money in selling lenses."

Willem had nodded, judiciously.

"I am hoping that you might be willing to help me
with one of these experiments," Leeuwenhoek went on.

"Me? How?"

"By allowing me to use a sample of your spit."

"Good God, man, what for?" said Willem, and then:
"Why don't you just use your own?"

"I certainly intend to use my own. But it is best to have
several examples."

"What good could it do?"

"It would be an important contribution to knowledge.
Perhaps by looking at it through the microscope, I can
tell what is in it, or what it is made of."

"I can tell you that right now, you fool. It is spit," the
old man had retorted, shaking his head.

"Perhaps it will become a celebrated experiment, recorded in books."

"In books, you say? What, like Holy Writ?"

After a bit more pompous delay, Willem had finally nodded. Leeuwenhoek got him to spit into a clean jar, and he allowed one of his blackened front teeth to be scraped. He had wandered off then to finish sweeping, wondering aloud if his spit would ever become famous, and still eyeing the goose girl as she cleaned up Caligula's ashes.

Here, in Leeuwenhoek's hands, is the jar of Willem's saliva. He is a grownup contemplating a jar of spit. If he mixed in some mud and a couple of garden snails, it would be enough to delight any seven-year-old boy. Likely he could sell it to an old woman in the market to use in some foolish witch brew. But his is a nobler purpose, surely.

Some people are spoken of as poisonous. A figure of speech. The death of Caligula had shown him, all too clearly, that people can *be* poisonous. That he himself is poisonous, at least to geese. Perhaps by examining the properties of saliva he can begin to figure out why. Of course, he is not a doctor, like Reinier. Maybe he really does have more in common with little boys and their games of spit and mud.

Surely if any man's mouth is poisonous, it is Old Willem's.

He prepares his specimen and turns it to the light. Incredibly, there is nothing. There are no little animals in Willem's spit, even though his mouth had smelled like a privy in springtime.

He tries his own. It is likewise clean. Infuriating. How can this be? He knows they are there, the *animalcules* that killed the goose. The goose girl has said so. He believes her. Perhaps he ought not to, but he does. Her explanation of the goose's death was satisfying. And now he cannot prove it.

This is his best microscope, incredibly powerful, able to magnify things nearly 300 times with excellent focus, and still there is nothing. Nothing except some clusters of clear round globules that are almost certainly flaws in the glass. Bubbles in the lens. Though he knows his own lenses well and can't recall seeing these bubbles before. Perhaps—

No. He cannot begin to doubt his own eyes. That would defeat the whole purpose of microscopy. Damn it all! He cannot see far enough, well enough. The goose girl has beaten him with her inscrutable powers. It is mortifying. He imagines the triumphant, invisible animalcules in the saliva having a parade, singing, waving tiny banners. Still hidden. Saved.

He sits disconsolately on his bench. It is unlikely enough, he reflects, that anyone would believe that any kind of animalcule could kill a goose. Most people do not know that animalcules exist. He is not even sure that Barbara believes in them, though he has shown her numerous times. Her eyesight is not nearly as good as his. Nor is it likely that he could manage to kill the little animals who had passed from him to Caligula along the grass stem, assuming he could even distinguish them from others. What, he should destroy all his own saliva? All the spit in the world?

Probably he should just not kiss any geese.

He wipes off the pin of the microscope and installs a fragment of the black matter from Willem's tooth. After the aridity of the saliva, it is a festival. Several different kinds of tiny creatures dance in front of his eye: drifting spirals, long rods, and one especially lively type, moving so fast he cannot ascertain its shape. These ones dash about, looking fleetingly oblong, fleeting roundish, speeding by on their own minuscule business. It is a miracle and a relief. The tiny world continues. He is not its master. Thank God. Who could command such a host?

Perhaps this is why animals lick their wounds. Even people do. He had absently sucked his own thumb after stabbing it with one of the tiny brass fittings of Vermeer's pencils. Saliva is clean. Not entirely free of animalcules, if the goose girl is right, but evidently containing fewer than the rest of the mouth. Perhaps fewer than the exterior surfaces of the skin.

Cheered, he begins to take notes.

BLOOD

Leeuwenhoek feels he has failed Caligula, but the goose girl shows no sign of caring. After her brief outburst of passion, she has reverted to her animal calm. Now she looks after a flock of eleven. It is high summer, and, with the good grazing, the geese have grown to astonishing size. They remain impeccably white, not so much as a stained feather. When he sees the girl leading them back along the street at dusk, they almost seem to glow, luminous like the honeydew. Dogs are afraid of them. They have quite a following among the local children. Leeuwenhoek himself does not want to touch them.

"Just don't share food with them," says the girl.

"There is little chance of that," he replies.

"I do it all the time," she says, shrugging.

Her life is incomprehensible. It is not important that he cannot dine with geese. Still, he feels like a leper.

"Have you heard them, the little animals that were in Caligula, again? Anywhere? Can you hear them in me?"

The goose girl considers. "No," she says. "Then there were many of them. If there are any left inside you, they are quiet. Or perhaps they are too few."

"I could not find them with my microscope, either," he admits. "I think they are too small."

"Perhaps they could be grown bigger," she replies.

This is an entirely new idea. "What?" says Leeuwenhoek, "like in a garden?"

"Or a farm. My geese are much bigger than wild geese. I wonder what the little animals eat."

"Didn't you say they were eating the blood of Caligula?"

"Yes. Stealing it, or part of it. The red part."

"You mean, the part that makes it red? Isn't it all red?"

"No."

He is about to protest, but then he thinks of Willem. *It is spit, you fool.*

Leeuwenhoek already knows that colors are completely different in the world of the animalcule. Colored fluids are clear. Clear fluid contains tiny colorful creatures. Ordinary beach sand from Scheveningen is a revelation, more tiny jewels in a single pinch than the hoard of the Grand Turk. There is no reason to dismiss the idea that blood has many parts and only some are red. He knows as a cloth merchant and an optician that the colors we see are the result of the way light falls on things. Lighting is the greatest challenge in microscopy. If he could only get more focused light on his subjects, the largely colorless sphere his eye sees through the lens would be vividly transformed. He has many times wished for a transparent head. He spends hours each week making precise adjustments to his shutters in the study, striving to get an optimal slice of clear, bright light to fall on his tiny specimens.

"Obviously," he says, pushing down his doubts, "they must eat something. And when they find foods they like, they must expand—in number, or in size, or both."

"So if we fed them more goose blood, they would grow, these ones?"

"They would multiply, yes. It seems they did before. But I don't know that they would grow bigger."

"Do you want some blood?" asks the girl. "I can get it."

Leeuwenhoek hesitates. The girl is moving too fast for him. She has already made him into a goose farmer. Does he want to be an *animalcule* farmer? Especially if the livestock is dangerous? The world is dangerous enough already. Nor can he explain, to her or to anyone, his attitude, neutral yet protective, toward these littlest of animals. He has no desire to control them. He is rarely sure what they do. It is simply delightful that they are there, that their world exists. He has heard that angels take this attitude toward men. So, perhaps his is an angelic regard for the animalcules.

"No," he replies. "Remember, you said those little animals were wicked? I don't want to make more of them. There are many others that I can see easily, everywhere."

The goose girl nods.

"Do you want to look at the blood on my handkerchief?" she asks.

"That, yes," he says, "if you don't mind."

"I don't mind," she says.

"Are they still speaking, or singing, the animalcules you heard on it?"

"Less. I can't hear them all the time. It happens mostly when I am just falling asleep, or just waking. Or sick. Or very sad. Then the faraway feeling comes."

There is little he can say to this. Who could? Priests, perhaps, or the doctors who work at the madhouse. But they would dismiss her observations as ravings. He wants them to be true. He cannot bear to have doubt cast on the world of the animalcules.

"Do you have the hankie with you?" he inquires.

She pulls it, carefully folded, out of her bodice, and hands it to him. It is warm. He pinches it between his fingers lightly and wishes for forceps. It is a valuable specimen. He moves to carry it to his study, and the girl moves with him. Clearly she is willing to lend it but cannot be parted from it. She owns almost nothing, but those few things she owns are part of her. Leeuwenhoek pictures her in the whitewashed stone chambers of the madhouse, hemmed in by other people, without her geese, the hankie stolen or washed clean. His heart constricts.

She walks along beside him through the courtyard, through the house, all the way to the study. Marieke, playing with the dollhouse, looks up in surprise. The goose girl is not companionable, he thinks: she simply must remain within a few feet of this scrap of cloth.

He lays it carefully on the table, fetches some silver tweezers, and unfolds it. The girl stands silently watching. There are the three dark, irregular blotches staining the linen.

"Where exactly did you get it? It was your mother's?" asks Leeuwenhoek, looking for vials.

"It was in her hand. She had been coughing up blood. Then she stopped. I waited for a long time. Then I took it," she replies.

"No one else came?" he asks, searching for his finest scraping tool. He is determined not to damage the fibers.

"They were all dead."

Marieke has never seen even a goose die. She had been shocked to see the body of Caligula and had first thought they were burning him alive. She has never connected the meat on her table with living creatures. She asks occasionally about the goose with the red boots: why is he not with the other geese any more? Where did he go? She used to ask the same thing about her infant brothers, until she forgot them.

Leeuwenhoek locates the tool. He finds himself narrating what he is about to do, feeling uncomfortable and foolish even as he does so. Usually he works in silence. "You see," he says, "first I scrape off the tiniest amount from the surface of the cloth, here where it is crusted. Fine. I put it into this jar and seal it. So. Then another fragment, here, into this jar. Yes, and then a third, into this one. Now you may have the kerchief back."

The girl folds it on itself, protecting the blood, and stuffs it into the bosom of her dress.

He rattles on: "the first jar, I think, I will examine dry, as a solid particle. And the second wet, mixed with clean water, or saliva."

"Saliva?"

"Spit."

"No, don't do that. What if the little animals in the spit attack these ones, and kill them?"

"With clean water, then."

"Aren't there little animals in water?"

"In most water, yes. But I always check that first. It helps if you boil it. Or get it in a clean jar right from the well."

"What about the third jar?"

"I don't know yet. I always find it is helpful to have a third sample, so I can change my mind as I go, or repeat things."

"Mix it with blood," says the girl, emphatically.

"Goose blood?"

"No. Mine. These animals come from my mother. They like our blood."

The goose girl is dogged. They have come back full circle to animalcule-farming. Leeuwenhoek is still hesitant. Plague is more terrifying than diseases of geese.

"Let me see what is in the dry blood first," he says, temporizing.

The goose girl inclines her head. "I will return to the geese now. Greet the little animals from me, if you see them."

"How would I do that?" he asks, intrigued.

"I don't know how you would do it. Just say hello."

"In words?"

"No," she replies impatiently, "not in words. Like you do with geese."

"If I have to talk to the geese, I use words."

She looks at him distantly, perhaps pityingly, and marches out.

Leeuwenhoek is left feeling inadequate. Not having access to her peremptory vision—can it justly be called vision if she hears it, or feels it without seeing?—he plods on with philosophical method. Opening the first vial, he shaves off a thin fragment of the crusted blood and deposits it on the pin of the microscope. It is precarious, as it is too small to impale securely. A wind, or a breath, may blow it off. He has found that one remedy for this is to move very slowly. He doesn't puff if he is not exerting himself, and he creates less breeze. So, with the exacting deliberation of a drunk man aiming at a keyhole, he carries the scope to the window. Not too close, for fear of wind, and because he needs a fairly narrow, exact band of illumination to strike the lens. He goes just close enough, placing his feet deliberately on a shiny patch in the middle of the floor, shielding the specimen with his hand, and then, holding his breath, lifts the tiny machine, and its tinier passenger, to his eye.

He adjusts the pin for focus. The usual brownish blur resolves slowly into a colorless field populated by puffy discs. They resemble a certain kind of raised biscuit that Barbara makes, with indented middles, as if a thumb had pressed into them.

Are these plump cartwheels the inimical creatures that killed the girl's mother?

Not everything that lives inside us is kind. He has seen the organs of animals destroyed by little flounders that grow inside them. Calves. Hares. Sheep. Tiny inhabitants in insurrection. They are strangely brave, killing their hosts. They are republicans. Kill the king, eat his meat. What then? In the case of the flukes, the interior worms that have brought the creatures to death, he knows: they die. They go down with the state, their animal hosts. He also knows: they spawn. Eggs pass out of the dying beasts onto the grass. New beasts eat them. If the parents die, what matter? The offspring live again in a new host, a new state, moving from kingdom to kingdom. *Le roi est mort, vive le roi.*

These flattened globules, they could be part of the structure of the blood, like the interior divisions or pockets he has seen in wood and leaves. Hooke had called them *cells,* like the chambers of monks or bees, when he saw them in cork. It is interesting to think of a liquid as having a structure. This could even be the part that gives blood its red color, as the goose girl said.

This blood is old, and dead, and dry. All its parts are desiccated. Surely it cannot be alive? Does blood live outside the body? Is it alive at all? Or is it an inert substance? The blood of the dead mother, if it is itself dead, how could it speak to the living child? It couldn't. Not in any way he can explain. The work of a natural philosopher has nothing do with hauntings or religious visitations. Those are the provinces of priests. Yet it seems to him unlikely that the goose girl's acute powers of observation defy empirical explanation. There are few phenomena that do.

The way he looks at the world, it must have been something still alive that made itself known to the child. Something *in* the blood on the handkerchief, not the unliving blood itself. Something dwindling? Something dormant, waiting?

Nothing is moving. Nothing is obviously alive. The animalcules that spoke to the girl, if they still live, are hiding; this blood is their forest. Perhaps the invisible creatures eat these handsome discs. They are surrounded by food. Then again, aren't we all? What do humans do in a forest? They hunt for food.

What he sees through the lens now appears regular and orderly. He is looking for a stranger, something anomalous. The creatures he is looking for, they could have disintegrated. He has seen the covering membranes of animalcules pop and their insides disperse. Or they might be too small to see. In our world, we tend to fear the largest creatures. Perhaps in the microscopic world, we should fear the littlest ones. He may yet produce a lens that can capture them. But for now, they have gotten away, the plague animalcules, if so they be, the ones who had called out to the monstrous figure the goose girl saw in the woods—

He would have to be mad to believe that story. Perhaps it had been a fever dream? The child's bewildered memory of a lost mother? The girl's own wild mind seeking to impose some shape on her experiences, as he himself saw wood grain in the patterns of soot? Or as Barbara sees herself as burnt on the inside from the Thunderclap? Best to leave it alone.

It is entirely plausible that exceptionally tiny foreign animalcules could have inhabited this blood, and that traces of them remain. If only he could flag the little creatures, force them to identify themselves. They could be lurking there, right now, those tiny malign beings, hiding in plain sight as if written in invisible ink. If only he had the lemon juice he has used to fool Marieke—magic words! look, the fire brings them up, up out of plain paper! Alchemy!

Chemistry.

Sarah Tolmie

He is a cloth merchant; of necessity, he knows a little chemistry.

Dying fabric is a matter of chemistry. Fabrics are made of living things: plants, animals. Each of them absorbs pigment differently. False silk can be discovered by the way it takes up the dye. Some dyes will stain skin, some will wash off. Specific dyes cling to one thing and not another.

Logically, these rules should also apply in the microscopic world, in which there is a diversity of material. So if the animalcules that carry plague are one thing, and the blood another? Perhaps they could be dyed, made to show themselves that way. Colors could be used to differentiate things—one animalcule from another, an animalcule from its surroundings, or even to distinguish parts of the same substance. Why not? Like the painters say: figure and ground. Brought up, perhaps, by saffron, or cochineal, or any of the dyes he knows as a haberdasher...

Could chemistry be the secret language of the tiny world? Greet the little animals for me, the girl said. He can never greet them in words. But this way, he might at least coax them to say *hello, here I am*—and so begin a conversation.

GLASS

The dried blood from the handkerchief is unfortunately silent. What if he liquefies it? Would that bring it
back to life? Seeds and tiny creatures, though dormant
for long periods, can be reanimated by water. Insects are
not spontaneously born from the ground every spring;
they emerge from minuscule eggs, activated by warmth
and rain. Specimens on his shelves have dried after long
inspection and looked dead, only to revive if moistened.

He told the goose girl he would examine the blood
wet and dry. He keeps his word. Plus, he is methodical.
Once he has come up with a plan, he suffers from a men-
tal itch if he does not carry it out. The devout are com-
monly compelled to pray or to confess. His compulsion
is similar.

He will have to use the secret tools. This always gives
him a curious feeling: a combination of enormous, eu-
phoric, stifled laughter and of hateful anxiety, the fear
of being found out. A return to childhood, every time.
Though grown men have a passion for secrets and rituals
entirely equal to those silences and bits of arcane knowledge cherished by children. Belonging to any guild in
the world is enough to tell you that.

He closes the shutters. He takes the scope from his
eye and places it carefully on the table. He checks the
door. Then, trying not to tiptoe or otherwise behave himself in a ridiculous manner, he goes to the chest at the
side of the room and removes the false bottom from the
lowest drawer. Nestled neatly in oiled cloth wrappings are

the components of a small lamp. They are quite simple, and he assembles them quickly. He fills the well with oil, ignites the top of the flue, and fans it into heat with small bellows. He unwraps several pairs of tools that look like tweezers. From a small wooden box in the hidden drawer he picks out a small, clear glass bead, about the size of a gooseberry. There is nothing special about this bead. He gets them from a friend at the East India Company headquarters in town. He always claims they are for his daughter, that she uses them to decorate the dollhouse.

To children, and to tribal chieftains from far corners of the world, such beads are wonders. Europeans figured out how to make good clear glass a century ago; it spread out from Murano, despite all the Doges could do. All secret techniques are found out in the end.

The beads, which are cheap and plentiful, churned out from glass factories in Amsterdam and elsewhere, provide him with a wonderful shortcut. Each one is a tiny parison, a tube formed around a central bubble, the foundation of the glassblower's art. If you want to make twenty-five cheap beads, you heat up glass and blow it into thin tubes or capillaries. Then you chop them up and round each piece. There are several methods of rounding, all quite ingenious, and also for layering on colors—glass-working is delightfully complex, as he has learned, even as an amateur—but these do not concern him. What he wants is the tubing. The cheapest beads will give it to him, even rejects that are imperfectly rounded. Each one of these glass bubbles is enough to yield a tiny specimen bottle, a hollow thread of glass, sometimes two. All he has to do is reheat the bead at his hot lamp, draw it out further, and then seal one end. Stoppering the other with a daub of wax or cork gives him a skinny little tube to fill with water or saliva—or blood. These he can affix to his scopes with clamps to examine at his leisure.

His miniature lamp, well aerated, is now hot. In a small dish he prepares a little mud, just a pinch of powdered clay and his own spit and a drop of his lamp oil. He spreads the slippery stuff over his smallest awl, really just a thin metal rod, and threads the bead onto it. Then he holds it over the lamp and rotates it, like cooking meat on a spit. The bead narrows and thins and begins to creep along the rod, molten.

He takes it off the flame. Now comes the awkward part. He has destroyed many at this stage. But no matter. They are cheap. Using two pairs of tweezers, he eases the ductile glass tube from the awl, hoping that the mud is still slippery enough to release it. This time, it is. Before it cools too much, holding each end firmly with tweezers, he draws it out, pulling his two hands apart. Now the lowly bead is an instrument of science, a fine glass capillary. This one is excellent, more than two hands long. He lays it down carefully on a ceramic tile, trying not to bend it.

When it has cooled sufficiently, he picks it up from the tile, holds it between the two tweezers again, and holds the middle of the tube over the lamp. He attempts to rotate it without dropping it, with minimal success, and draws it out slightly more. The tube thins and thins, closing in on itself, and finally burns right through. Now he has two perfect, very fine tubes. He is immensely proud of himself. He burns off the points and tidies up the sealed ends. He lets his flame cool and anneals them. When they are perfectly cool he will buff the opposite ends neatly so he can seal them with cork, or wax.

Leeuwenhoek looks fondly at the small, shiny things lying on the tile. Every time he gets out this equipment, he can barely resist playing with it all day. Glassworkers are lucky. What if he were to heat up a glass thread and curl it round and round on itself, and pull out a tiny handle? A glass mug! For the dollhouse! Or he could make a clay mold, just using a coin, and make little glass plates! Marieke would be delighted. Likely Barbara would be too, if they were good enough. But he cannot afford to be known as a glass blower.

It is sad. The joyless secrets of adulthood must take precedence. He is beginning to make some money selling lenses. Excellent ground and polished lenses, and sometimes scopes or viewers to house them. The best ones, which are not ground, he keeps for himself. He kids himself that this is policy, the thrift of the wise merchant who raises the value of goods by withholding them. But this is not true. He doesn't need to sell lenses at all. He makes a fine living as a draper and from his city offices. Selling instruments just gives him an excuse to make them. The compulsive desire for inquiry, and for making the instruments of inquiry, is difficult to explain, even to himself.

Knowledge, true knowledge, is not based on scarcity. Knowledge is meant to be free, like air or water. He did not make animalcules. They are the creation of divinity. His excellent lenses enable him to see them, that is all. He is determined—desperate, even—to share the knowledge he gains from them.

Yet his best lenses, the special ones, he makes. He makes them in a particular way; they are objects of human art. His art. They are his, and his alone. The very idea of sharing them makes him want to hiss like an angry goose.

He tidies up the ends of his new capillaries with the lathe. They are ready.

Mixtures

Leeuwenhoek puts away the secret tools, as always, with a pang. He opens the shutters, flooding the room with late afternoon light. He fetches a lidded jar of clean water and pours a little into a mixing vessel. Then, before he can lose his nerve, he drops in the second of his three tiny chunks of crusted blood, and stirs it up. Using a threadlike pipette—which he also made himself—he forces a little of the rusty brown mixture into the tiny glass vessel and stoppers it.

In the intense slice of light from the window several paces away, he sees them again, the bulging discs, like wheels. They look juicier now. But nothing else seems to be happening. This does not surprise him. Things often become more lively after a wet specimen has stood for a few days. They age like wine.

As to adding the third chip of dried blood to a vial of fresh blood, his mind veers away from it. He has never used blood to prepare a specimen before. And the idea of providing the invisible animalcules that might cause the plague with nourishment is unnerving. He wishes he had the goose girl's iron will.

❧

As Leeuwenhoek begins work in his study, the girl herself goes back through the big house, past the child playing with the small house. The child looks up as she passes. The goose girl ignores it. She does not like children and often does not understand what they say. Frequently they are cruel.

She is almost out of the room with the tiny house. The child says, "Wait!"

"Why?" says the goose girl.

"Don't you want to play?" says the child.

"No," she replies.

"Why not?"

"I don't know how. What do you do with that tiny house?"

"You do the same things people do in a big house, only smaller."

"Why?"

The child considers. "Mostly they don't let us do them in the big houses yet."

"That's why I hate living in houses. I never know what goes on, and I can't do most of it."

"Yes," agrees the child. "What's your name?"

"I don't have a name."

"But what do people call you?"

"I don't know. They call to me if they have food for me, and yell at me if they want me to go away."

"My name is Marieke." After a minute, she goes on, "this dollhouse belongs to my mother."

"To Barbara?"

"You mustn't call her that! Are you allowed to call her that?" says the child, Marieke.

"Isn't that her name?"

"Only the pastor calls her that. And Papa," says Marieke.

"Antoni?"

"I don't know. I think so. Papa, with the microscopes."

"Antoni."

"Are you really a child?" asks Marieke. "I didn't know children were allowed to use those names. No one else does."

"What do they say?"

"Oh, they say Mijnheer Van Leeuwenhoek and Mevrouw Van Leeuwenhoek and all that."

The goose girl pauses. "I don't know who those people are," she says finally.

"Me neither," says Marieke, "I know Mama and Papa. Mama more."

"Yes," says the goose girl. "It is a beautiful small house," she adds, after a moment. Then she leaves.

Presently, she is out in the courtyard once more. The handkerchief is tucked in her bodice, where it should be. The geese are waiting.

She knows Antoni is right about putting the blood in water. Once she had leaned over a stream to drink and the kerchief had fallen out. It had spread out on the water like a leaf and nearly floated away. As the current bore it almost out of her reach, it had screamed aloud, a high thin wail. Even the geese had heard it. She had thrown herself into the water to recover it, brimming with terror. It was the only thing she had: the last bit of her mother. She could not lose it. It was like her mother screaming: *save me, save me*! But when she got it back into her hands again and laid it out on the grass in the sun, careful not to wring it, she heard not a scream, but a hum, like a crowd in the distance, a buzz of many tiny voices, alarmed and newly woken. The hankie, she had realized, was a little boat. Like the huge barges she had seen floating by on the slow rivers, full of life.

Was that the first time she had heard the voices? Right around that time she had gotten sick, soon after the fall into the water. She had wandered, pale and sweating, into the village. The woman had looked after her. In Kampen. To her, all villages are Kampen. That is the name.

Now she is in a much bigger town with a name: Delft. Water runs through it. Antoni, who owns them all now, has said the name to her many times. He has always lived here. She remembers the name for his sake. When she leaves, she will forget it. For now, she is content. The geese are happy. The food is excellent, though she does not always know what it is. The house is warm; it is worth sleeping under a roof, between walls, to be that warm. It is interesting to use the words that people use. Sometimes she goes a long time without doing so and nearly forgets them. But they come back. That is the way it is with things that she learned when she was too small to remember. Like who her mother was, and the smell of the dark cottage and the goose yard, and the sound of coughing.

The first day, when they had met Antoni at the market, he had given them a lot of money. She still has it. She keeps it under her pallet in a little pile that she can feel under her head. She does not need it now. The geese do not care about it. They do not understand money. You cannot eat it. What she knows about money is this: you have to do something to get it. Like she had done on the road with the old man, also dirty and ragged, and not much bigger than she was—she had pulled and pulled on a small muscly part of him that stuck out from his clothes like the head of a goose. He had given her a coin for it. He looked as poor as she was, so it must have been very important to him. Or, for money, you have to give something away, like she had with Dig in a village, maybe Kampen; she had left that quarrelsome nasty goose with a man there and gotten some money and some leather and thread for Redboots. Dig had been a goose who ruined everything. Looking out of her eyes, everything was ugly. The others were afraid of her unpredictable temper. Geese like that, you have to get rid of them, or kill them.

After that had happened with Dig, she understood that geese had value; they could be traded for money, and as long as she was with them, she could too. It did not matter to her, or the geese, if someone thought that he owned them, as long as they stayed together. What people think does not matter. Only what they do. Redboots and the others had really wanted to go to the market that day, when they met Antoni. They were excited by such a large flock, and there were grain and salt and meat smells. They had walked into the crowded square, and stopped, and then Antoni had come and offered them the money. After a minute, she had understood why, and then they all went with him.

Now she has it for the road. That is when she will need it. When the luck runs out, or the geese get restless, and they go. People along the road will sometimes give you food, or shelter. But never money. That is something people keep to buy safety for themselves. People will help you, if you have it. That is its magic.

She will ask Antoni again if he wants some blood. After all, her body is full of it. This would be the first time she had a use for it. She is sure that the little animals from the hankie would like it. They are dying. Or resting. It makes her uneasy. She does not want them to go away. Yet, when she had seen Plague in the woods, the huge figure had been terrifying. She still sees those enormous bruised eyes in her sleep, hears the rasping, whistling, coughing sound of her passage. She would not want to meet Plague again. Perhaps seeing is worse than hearing. Plague's tiny children on the handkerchief, when she hears their voices—like the thinnest threads in her mind—she can imagine them as like herself. She has never had to see them. If they are ugly and threatening, she does not know.

But she would be lonely without them. They have been with her for a long time. Like the geese, they are part of her. Not all parts of us are nice. Not all are the same. Not all are safe.

Antoni does not understand this. He is the kind of person who thinks he is just himself. Perhaps he is. She has no idea what it is like to be him. But it seems to her that people who live in towns think this way. They live all crowded together, flocks and flocks of them, and yet each one thinks he is alone. To her, most people appear the same, or all joined together; the way they walk, in neat lines, all going one way, then another, along streets, makes her think of ants. A town is a kind of nest or hive. People buzz and mill at churches and markets like insects do at carcasses or flowers. It is hard to tell one from another, except for the very few she knows well: Antoni, Barbara. The painter, Johannes.

These people, the few kind people whom she recognizes, they call her by various names. They see her as a girl, as one person, the way they see each other. She rarely remembers the names, because she is not just one person, not only this girl with two legs and heavy braided hair, who wears clothes and keeps a handkerchief and sweeps the courtyard. She is also Daisy and Scratch and Turntoe. She had been Redboots until he died. She had even been Dig.

When she talks to Antoni, or Barbara, she sees the world that they see, and lives in it: the world in which people own houses and instruments and boats, in which objects are made to fit into people's hands and doors are almost twice her height. When she is on the road with the geese she lives in their world: the grass and trees are taller, the smells much stronger. She knows what to eat and what not to eat. There is less color. She sees things from many places at once and has different feelings about them. She often does not recognize human objects: gates, stiles, a dropped basket. But then she can fly.

The little animals, when she hears them, sometimes she gets flashes of their world. Not like flashes of light, things that you see, like sun bouncing off a windowpane, but bursts of sound or feeling. A liquid feeling, a gurgling sound, the feeling of being in water, or of having edges, or of motion. These are very faint and hard to remember. She has nothing to remember them with. Whatever their world is like, it must be very different. She could never explain it. Such things do not go into words.

She could never explain even the goose-world to Antoni, and it is much closer to his. She does not intend to try. Geese do not feel compelled to explain themselves. Only people do.

THE LETTER

"I have written to the Royal Society, Antoni," says De Graaf. He is sitting in Leeuwenhoek's great room downstairs, staring idly at the blown glass vase, which is today filled with orange tulips. Following his gaze, Leeuwenhoek feels a familiar flash of secret amusement. Fooling our friends is pleasurable, even when they are advancing our cause.

"They are busy men. This will all take months. In the meantime, I suggest that you assemble some of your most interesting notes into a letter, and send it as soon as you can. Then they will have some evidence to back up the extravagant claims I have made on your behalf."

"What extravagant claims, Reinier? I am a haberdasher. They are probably horse-laughing already."

"That you construct the finest simple microscopes in Europe, you fool! And see things through them that no philosopher or medical man I know has ever seen. That is inarguable."

"So I just send them a letter, in Dutch? Greetings, esteemed members of the Royal Society of London, here are some microscopical observations from a cloth merchant in Delft, and yes, that is how I spell microscope in Dutch, and—"

"You are waffling, Antoni. Do it. You will go mad otherwise. Your results will speak for you, in whatever language. Plenty of people in England can read Dutch. How else can we keep the wars going?"

"Fine. Where do you suggest I start?"

"With your most interesting observations. Include drawings. And if you have discovered something that contradicts a famous book, include that. Philosophers love a good argument."

"Hah! I have found many things that are clearly wrong, even in Hooke himself. But I love the *Micrographia,* and often use it to guide experiments. Even though I can barely read it, it helps me think. That is what these learned men are good for; they have the knack of putting the story together."

"Send a series of observations that you have seen nowhere else. Ones that surprised you. Do not worry too much about the story, or the style. They will edit them—and translate them, I imagine—when they publish them."

"They will publish them?"

"Of course they will, Antoni! What do you think the Society is for? Record-keeping! It's the new clerisy! Their entire purpose is to record their own experiments and transactions, and those they deem worthy from elsewhere. Posterity is their aim. They have volumes and volumes hidden away in some library somewhere, of every burp and fart that the least significant member has ever emitted. Yours will be among them."

"That is really a great relief to me, Reinier."

Leeuwenhoek pulls open a drawer in the shining table and removes a sheaf of papers, trying to appear unconcerned. In reality, he has been in a ferment for weeks, ever since De Graaf first mentioned the Royal Society idea to him. The thought that he might be accepted among this group of eminent philosophers had burst upon him like shot from a culverin. It tickles his vanity in a way nothing ever has before. Clutching a wad of papers in his hand, he turns as if casually to his friend: "As it happens, Reinier, I confess, I have already been thinking about this.

Here are some of my earliest observations, done on pond water. Many types of animalcules never before cataloged (to my knowledge) appear here. I was utterly astonished at the time at their variety and activity and beauty—not to mention the fact that they were there at all. There are five types here: these ones, long and narrow, these, rounded, these, with little whiplike legs..." He extends the papers to the doctor, who waves them away.

"Enough, Antoni! Enough. Transcribe it; send it."

"But what if it grows too long? I have such a mass of material—"

"It will not be too long. It cannot be too long. These men are as crazy for detail as you are."

"I suppose so."

"Yes." De Graaf shifts his tall, languid frame in the chair and rises. "I must be going. Give my best to Barbara and *la petite* Marieke. Barbara will remember enough English to help you with the greeting, at least."

"Barbara thinks all this is folly. She is too nearsighted to see anything through the lenses. I am sure that, privately, she thinks I am insane."

"She is not very modern, Barbara."

"No."

"You should let me see her, next time she falls pregnant."

"I know. But she resists. She is full of ridiculous notions from that fool midwife. It breaks my heart that she will not see reason. But her fears are very real. Think what she has suffered."

"Insist. You have lost two sons now."

"I know, Reinier. All too well. Goodbye. Thank you for the encouragement." The path that his friend has set him on—toward the eminence of the Royal Society—is so overwhelming that Leeuwenhoek rises from his chair and gives him a brief bow. This is not in his usual repertoire. Calvinists do not bow. Not like papists with their bendy spines. De Graaf laughs, executes a much more elegant, courtly bow, and departs chuckling.

Leeuwenhoek spends two days feverishly going over his notes, making fair copy. His drawings are awful. Some simple diagrams are passable, but anything more ambitious is a complete failure. His pride will not let him send the letter in this state. He must find that amanuensis that Vermeer talked about. He knows various people, including some relatives, in the Guild of St Luke, the artists' guild. —Why is there no natural philosopher's guild? Well, there is one simple answer: they make no money. —Yet that is what the Royal Society really is, he supposes: a guild. Doubtless they will end up making money sometime. The English always do. Could he really end up a member? That would be something. Quite different from the tedium of the Guild of St Nicholas and its endless cloth statutes and measurements and reviews. Being a member of a merchant's guild is excruciatingly boring. Slightly better, but only slightly, is working for the survey office, where at least he gets to use some interesting instruments and do some calculations; sooner or later he will do the examination and become a *Landmeter*. Everything needs official surveying. A nice salary comes with it, and you can't get by in Delft without taking on some of these city offices, or people think you're a criminal. Still, it would be a joy to belong to a body of men who were untrammeled by these mercantile concerns. Mijnheer Antoni Van Leeuwenhoek, member of the Royal Society. Is there some kind of insignia?

His mother's family are regents, so he has city jobs that already come with insignia. It's just that the honorifics come attached to jobs he would rather not perform.

People who do not have to do these endless government tasks think they are sinecures, but they never are. He's a *Camerabewaarder* at the Stadthuis, which doesn't sound like much: on paper, this means keeping one important room ready for use by the magistrates and their clients. However, no-one is going to pay you a salary of 200 guilders for that—it also means organizing the blasted clients, keeping lists and appointment times, running constant errands, acting as unofficial notary, and generally trying to keep a group of rich, complaining people content with their access to city government three days a week. As Leeuwenhoek is a quiet, methodical person with a head for figures, he is unfortunately very good at it and can look forward to much more of the same for the rest of his life, under various titles. He tries to be public-minded, but there are days on which he wants to throw large numbers of overdressed, overpaid, overzealous people into the canal, along with their cats, canaries, virginals, decorated missals, tuns of sherry, wheels of cheese, donations to the orphanage, and all other miscellaneous materials of legal contest. Preferably weighted with stones. Of course, the time might come at which he would be made responsible for dredging, and then he would be filled with regret at the corpses and wreckage.

The Guild of St Luke is not far away, across the market square and onward through a few narrow streets. He enters the dark guildhall. A fine collection of paintings by members and some investment pieces from elsewhere, the best in town, line every inch of wall, though now they are dark blurs as his eyes adjust to the low light. A dining table is set, quite elegantly, in the middle of the hall, though it is only midday. They must be having a festivity this evening. A rumbling noise issues from one hallway, and a man appears, rolling a wine barrel. This is a stroke of luck, as the man is Fortunatus, a friend of the man he is seeking. Neither he, nor DeWitt, the man Leeuwenhoek is looking for, are really artists: one is a pigment seller and the other a panel-preparer. They can paint enough to keep up appearances, but that is not really their purpose in the guild. They are suppliers. Like all suppliers, they know everybody.

Leeuwenhoek hails the man loudly over the sound of the rattling barrel: "Fortunatus! I am looking for DeWitt! Have you seen him? Is he coming this evening? What time does the ceremony begin?"

Fortunatus looks up, stopping the barrel. "DeWitt? No, he's not here. But he should be coming this evening. All starts at five. Shall I tell him you're looking for him?"

"Yes, please. Tell him I will drop by beforehand. At the front entrance. Can't come in during session; I'm not a member."

Fortunatus gives a grunt of assent and starts the barrel rolling again, diagonally across the room. He disappears down another corridor. Leeuwenhoek goes home to get some profitable work done at the shop.

At half past four, Leeuwenhoek is there again, loitering in front of the arched entrance. After about ten minutes, artists of various stripes start to turn up in ones and twos—not very social, artists, on the whole—and trickle into the building. Vermeer is one of them. Leeuwenhoek is surprised. He must be in funds. His membership in the guild comes and goes according to his credit. When he's solvent he has even been President. Maybe this is the time to press him to pay for the camera. Vermeer wrings his hand warmly and seems ready to launch into a spate of conversation when Leeuwenhoek sees DeWitt approaching. "Another time, Johannes," he says firmly, "but be assured I am taking your advice and trying to find a cartoonist."

He steps forward to intercept DeWitt, a flaxen pale man, with white eyelashes and brows; he is so eerily pale that Leeuwenhoek always expects him to have pink eyes, like a rabbit. As it is, his blue eyes look black in his white face as he turns his unemotional gaze to Leeuwenhoek. "Antoni. Hello. Fortunatus mentioned that you wanted to see me." He has a singularly quiet, colorless manner, as if his trade of whitening and priming panels has bleached out his person.

"Yes, Matthias, I do. Don't let me keep you from the feast. I was wondering if you could recommend a draughtsman, possibly a cartoonist who has worked with the weavers."

"What for?"

"To do small, detailed drawings of microscopical specimens. In pen and ink. Or crayon."

"For you?"

"Yes. I am entering into correspondence with the Royal Society in England." Leeuwenhoek stands a little straighter.

"The Royal Society of what?" asks DeWitt, blandly.

"It is a group of natural philosophers in London who conduct experiments, using microscopes and other instruments."

"At what pay?"

"Well, at guild rates if he is a member. Or we will have to negotiate, if he is not."

"Would you consider my son?" says DeWitt, unexpectedly. "He is a fine draughtsman."

"Is he a member of the guild, then?"

"No."

"How old is he?"

"Eighteen."

"Then surely he should be apprenticed."

"He is, informally, to me. We have not tried to admit him to St Luke's. I don't think it would prove worth the money. He cannot see colors."

"What, not at all? How do you know?"

"He can make no distinction between red and green. From what he says, they appear to him as shades of gray. Nor can he tell purple from blue, orange from red. All the same, he is a superb draughtsman, far better than I am at line drawing. Better than many guild members. And for the moment his work comes cheap."

"Good heavens. The boy himself is a natural wonder. Can you send him to me tomorrow afternoon?"

"Yes. He will be very pleased to have a trial of his skill." DeWitt nods politely, and the matter is concluded. His pale figure is swallowed up by the shadowy entrance of the guildhall. Leeuwenhoek gazes after him for a minute. A painter with a blind son. Or, not exactly blind. Color-blind? Still, at least he has a son.

At precisely two in the afternoon, according to Leeuwenhoek's atrociously expensive pendulum clock—a philosophical wonder that he has owned for one year and so far managed not to take apart and put back together again by rigorously thinking of his investment—DeWitt's son arrives. His name is Pierre. Not only is he crippled, but he has a French name. But then, these painters, half of them are Flemings.

The boy shares his father's ethereal lightness. His hair is white blonde and he has a light, husky voice and pale eyes. They are a family from whom color has been refined away, or perhaps not technically achieved. *Grisaille.*

In the boy's case, the colors have apparently leaked right out of his eyes.

Leeuwenhoek, embarrassed, shows him some of his rough drawings. The boy is determinedly polite about them. No doubt his father has threatened him with dire punishment if he does not get this job. At Leeuwenhoek's request, he sits himself down and begins to copy one in reddish crayon. Then another in ink. Leeuwenhoek is impressed. They are instantly beautiful and legible. The animalcules have found their portraitist. Thank God.

"Pierre, these are lovely! That is, highly acceptable. I am happy to offer you the work if you want it." He keeps himself from effusing so as not to drive up the price.

The boy is pitiably grateful. He tries not to say too much so as not to blow it at the last minute. Seeing this, Leeuwenhoek finds himself morally unable to short him on the wage. They agree on a piecework price for this job—illustrating the letter, which Leeuwenhoek indicates ought to be the first of many—that is not far below the guild rate. As he is not a member, they need no contract, and merely shake hands on it. After this ritual, the lad actually appears to be glowing, lit from within like a lantern. Leeuwenhoek resists the temptation to shove him into a closet just to see if this is truly the case.

As he is leaving, carrying Leeuwenhoek's terrible drawings carefully in a folder, with a promise to have them back in three days' time, Pierre bursts out: "But the creatures! What are they? Are they real?"

"They are tiny creatures, animalcules I call them, that I have seen through my microscope. In plain pond water."

"They live there all the time? Do they move around?"

"Yes, they are quite active. That is one reason they are so hard to draw."

"Can I see?" The boy is agog, but he continues, professionally: "It would improve the drawings, I expect."

Leeuwenhoek has never had anyone, except for Reinier, who is a doctor of medicine, ask to look into the microscope. Even the goose girl has not done so. He is thunderstruck.

"You mean, now? I no longer have exactly those specimens. Though I have others, such that you could get an idea of their scale."

"Now would be excellent, if that is convenient for you," replies the boy.

"Ah. Yes. Yes. It does make sense. It will result in a better product," says Leeuwenhoek, confusedly, rising from his seat. "Come with me to my study." He leads Pierre to the room next door, through a short passage, and opens the heavy shutters for light. The boy follows him so closely he is slightly underfoot, like a cat.

Leeuwenhoek looks through various jars and glass capillaries that line the shelves. A couple have viewing lenses attached, screwed on to the side. These are a bit clunky, but with them he can keep an eye on a specimen for a long time. One of these might do. He looks through labels. Smoke. Pepper water. Oak. Cochineal. "Ah, here is water. Well water. It always has less in it, but it has been sitting for a while. Mind you, these are not my best lenses." He has no intention of showing Pierre his best lenses. They are hidden in an invisible drawer at the base of the lathe. The lathe that he does not use to make them, another of his infantile jokes. He is feeling a bit nervous, as if about to make introductions of relatives he does not know very well. Pierre, too, is gratifyingly excited. He looks around the room with its tools and glittering jars as if he is about to explode.

"These are all your specimens? Things you have collected? And these—animalcules?—live in them? Do they live everywhere?"

"I believe so. We share the whole world with them. Who would have thought it?"

Pierre approaches a shelf. "Smoke?" he asks, "How do you collect smoke?" He goes off on a professional tangent: "Smoke, now, smoke is a horror to draw. It depends on the currents of the air. Have you noticed how little smoke there is in domestic paintings? It drives me mad, all these perfect, smokeless fires and all of us going around with soot in our hair…"

"Come toward the window," says Leeuwenhoek. Pierre is there instantly. He accepts the fragile capillary with its viewer as if it were the relic of a saint. "Hold it to the light. Not too close. Keep your head out of the way. Try to look through the center of the lens."

Pierre stands a few paces from the window, a lightness bathed in light. He holds the little jar up to his eye and moves his head delicately, and his shoulders and feet, finding angles. He looks like he is doing a very small dance. It has a certain comedy to it but also a technical seriousness. It goes on for some time. Leeuwenhoek is reminded of an automaton he once saw in Amsterdam, finest of its kind he had ever encountered: it was of an angel, white and gold, with brilliant cobalt wings. Unlike many such devices, which try too hard, its movements were slight: a slight incline of the head, a modest movement of the wings, not as if it were trying to take off, but just settling its feathers. Supremely tasteful, utterly blasphemous.

"My God," says Pierre suddenly. "Jesus Christ our Lord and Savior, what is that? That, my God, right there?"

Leeuwenhoek recognizes an error he often falls prey to himself. "You forget, I cannot see it," he says. "Only one at a time."

"Right, yes," says the boy, hurriedly. He has dropped his politeness. "My God, my God, my God, that thing, what is it—hup, what, now it's gone—what, there it is again, it's covered with hairs or legs or something—Jesus, it's the size of a carthorse, wait, no, it can't be—" He takes his eye away from the viewer to glare at the tiny vial. Then he looks back into the viewer. "Master Leeuwenhoek," he says, "this is incredible. It is a miracle."

"I find it so, myself," admits Leeuwenhoek. "Could you draw what you saw?"

"Yes. I think so. To get everything I would have to look for more time. But the rough idea, that I could do now. Is there paper handy?"

Leeuwenhoek casts around, finds a sheaf of notes, and turns a page over. He locates a pen, one of Caligula's magnificent quills. He opens the ink pot. "Here," he says. Pierre puts the viewer reverently on a shelf and comes forward. He sits down, takes up the pen, does a few trials on the edge of the page, and then draws, at once, with no false starts or hesitations, the little creature that Leeuwenhoek calls a wheel bug. There it is, rounded and gelatinous, sitting dimensionally on top of the page, like a blob of spit, except covered with a ring of tiny, waving hairs. "Ah, one of those!" he says, delightedly, "They are remarkable! Do you know, I have seen one split right in half? And then there are two, both living? Incredible! I think that is how they reproduce, I mean, the only way... not by sexual reproduction."

"What?" says the boy, distractedly. He is doing another drawing, flattening the creature out in the manner of a diagram. He draws an elegant series of pointed arrows emanating from it. "For labels," he says.

"Sexual reproduction. Mating," repeats Leeuwenhoek.

"Ah," says Pierre, blushing slightly. It is obvious, given his pallor.

"Imagine working for my friend Reinier—Doctor De Graaf. You'd be drawing penises all the time. And lady parts. In cross-section, and straight on, and all the vessels within, and so on. Fortunately, there seem to be options other than sex in the world of the animalcule," says Leeuwenhoek.

Pierre squirms visibly, but he looks fixedly down at his drawing and says, "No matter. I can draw anything."

"Good lad. Now you had better be going. Come to me if there are any details you can't make out. Get it done as soon as you can and I will get the letter onto the next boat. Then we can start working on the next one. Maybe the pepper water…" He stops, so as not to distract the boy. Or himself.

Pierre charges out of the house like a dog making off with a stolen beefsteak, not at all like the reserved boy who had first come in. Leeuwenhoek watches from the window as he dashes across the market, narrowly avoiding collision with a farm cart loaded with squawking chickens. Shouting and cacophony ensue. The boy makes a rude sign at the irate farmer and peels off around the corner, out of sight.

Matthias DeWitt is a lucky man, thinks Leeuwenhoek, striving not to be bitter.

PLAGUE'S DAUGHTER

The letter is away. The eager Pierre had finished the drawings by the next day. They had utterly transformed the professionalism of the whole thing. Leeuwenhoek senses that he, too, is wildly excited and interested, speculating about their reception, though the Royal Society can hardly occupy the same status in his mind as it does in his own. He had run into Matthias DeWitt coming out of the Mechelen, the inn and art dealership once owned by Vermeer's harebrained father, and received a much more expansive greeting than usual. Probably Pierre is talking his ear off. As he himself had been burdened down by a load of taffeta that they wanted for some interior draperies, he could not stop to talk. Always chop-chop for the Mechelen, the fanciest watering hole in town. It remains a haven for artists and a lot of informal trade goes on there, and some paintings are sold off the walls. Still, the food is better and the art is worse since Janzoon's day. Vermeer's father had always been a man with more taste than sense. Not much of an innkeeper.

The blood and water mixture has now been sitting for a week in his study. Somehow he has been reluctant to approach it. This is unlike him, as he is usually filled with zeal for any ongoing project. Today he steels himself to take it down from the shelf. He takes out his best lens from the drawer underneath the lathe. Then he opens the shutters. To the naked eye, the capillary's contents are cloudy and dark.

Seen through the lens, as usual, the color is dispelled. What he sees is light and clear. The bulging discs are there, now fatter, like loaves. They look delicious. After a considerable time, he sees a number of the oval animalcules that he is accustomed to seeing in water. They appear huge, swimming through the inert, rounded cells, whatever they are, little packages of something.

And that is all. Perhaps this is what he has been protecting himself against: disappointment. This will not be an experiment that he shares with the Royal Society. Who will he share it with, then? The goose girl? In many respects it is, properly, her experiment. But she is not at home. It is a beautiful day, and she is out with the geese at pasture. He will have to talk to her, and show her the vial, this evening. He could try to show it to Barbara, but she is unable to see much through his lenses, and what would he say, anyway—here is a specimen in which I hoped to find one thing, but found something quite different? Or possibly nothing at all? If she asked, he could never tell her that the creature he had initially been seeking might be the cause of the plague. Might even *be* plague itself. To Barbara this would make about as much sense as if he explained that Plague was a twenty-foot-high spectral figure stalking through the woods. Either way, he would probably end up sleeping at the Mechelen, and his wife would rampage through his study, destroying all his specimens. He would end up divorced. The consistory would support Barbara (all too justly) in her claim against him—of putting their only child at risk.

It is much safer to talk to the goose girl. For one thing, who but himself would ever believe her?

He tidies up. He puts away the best lens. He checks on his clerk, Joost, who is minding the draper's shop. He considers going through his endless notes to see what to put in the next letter. This might assuage his feelings of failure.

Half an hour later he is walking out of town to see the girl, the vial in his pocket, carefully wrapped in a handkerchief. He is seething. Not only because he is wasting his valuable time on a fool's errand, but because, in a moment of spastic stupidity, he had managed to throw the nice little brass microscope he had had in his other pocket—not his very best quality, which he does not carry about, but still, a good one, and fairly new—over the low parapet of the bridge and into the canal. Being one of those people who prefer a neatly patterned life, he had stopped in the exact middle of the bridge, paces from the house, as he always did, and peered over the low wall into the slow water. Usually when he does this he is filled with a sense of vague peace and civic pride, considering the general order and efficiency of it all, the cleanliness of the water, so carefully inspected and kept flowing by the Water Board, the not inconsiderable engineering feats of daily life in Delft. Today, like a complete ass, he had put his hand thoughtlessly into his right pocket (he always carries specimens in his left) to pull out a handkerchief to mop his brow, and in pulling it out, had dislodged the tiny brass instrument that also reposed there, which had snagged on the cloth and then flown, rather dramatically, over the edge and into the brown water. The whole incident had transpired with a perverse deliberateness; had anyone been watching (and thank God there was no one) it would doubtless have looked like he had thrown it in on purpose, the way boys do with pebbles and whatnot. He could even have been fined. Tossing foreign objects into the canals is illegal.

Then, possessed by rage at the folly of everything, he had gone straight on toward the road that heads out of town without bothering to return home for a new scope. Now, as he approaches the pasture with the glowing blue-green eye of the pond at the center, he thinks that this was stupid. But there is nothing he can do about it. He looks around for the goose girl and sees the flash of her white apron some distance away. He trudges toward her over springy grass littered with goose shit.

"Ah," says the girl, turning soundlessly and movelessly, as if on a potter's wheel, "You have brought the blood."

Leeuwenhoek's anger evaporates instantly, like a water droplet hitting hot glass. Pfft. Gone. From a liquid to a gas, drifting away. Most men are made angry by things they do not understand. Leeuwenhoek is not. His useless self-loathing turns off and is replaced by the bright, equivocal feeling he associates with all forms of inquiry. Today's will not be a useless venture after all. The girl does not even need the scope. She is some kind of magician. He ought to be insulted by her hocus-pocus, but for some reason he is not. He does not know how she arrives at her pronouncements, but he, or someone, might yet discover it. All secret techniques are found out in the end.

He lets out his breath in an explosive "hah" and says, "What? You hear them? The little animals?"

"Yes. They are very active," replies the girl serenely. "I could hear them as you came up the lane. I thought it would be so."

"You did?"

"Yes. The hankie got wet once before and they seemed to come alive. They even screamed."

The girl is not lying. She may not even know how to do so. "How is it, do you think," he asks her, "that you know what you know? Do you have any idea why you can hear animalcules, and I cannot? When did it begin?"

"It is not just the little animals. It is many things. Like the geese. And other things."

"The geese, yes, they listen to you. And you to them. The animalcules are like this in some way, also? What else do you hear?"

"Why do you want to know?"

"I don't know. I am possessed by the urge to learn things."

"How does that help?"

"I am not sure that it does."

"Sit down," says the girl.

"What? Why?"

"You are too tall. Like a tree. I don't like it, and neither do the geese."

Leeuwenhoek sits down on the soft turf. He takes the capillary from his pocket as he sits, so as not to break it. But he does not unwrap it, so it does not overheat in the hot sun. The whole scene feels flattened and unreal, as if he is in a painting. The goose girl looks oddly proportioned from the ground, towering over him, receding into the bright sky. Something in her posture relaxes. Several of the geese, who had raised their heads alertly to watch the goings-on, go back to grazing. Somehow influenced by this atmosphere of intimacy, Leeuwenhoek says, to his own surprise, "I have been having a bad day." He goes on, sheepishly, telling her about his inability to see anything in the blood and the fiasco at the bridge and the loss of the scope. She listens soberly.

She does not say "I am sorry" or any conventional thing. He has never heard her apologize. It now strikes him how unusual this is: children spend much of their time apologizing. He remembers Barbara teaching Marieke—*hello, goodbye, please, thank you, excuse me, I'm sorry.* The goose girl says none of these. Yet he senses in her a general softening of her animal rigor.

"So, you were right," says the girl, "about putting the little animals in water. They have woken up. But you still could not see them?"

"I conclude they are too small. Even my best lens cannot capture them. But you have no such limits, it seems. How can that be?"

"I do not know. I guess they are small, but loud. Or maybe size has nothing to do with it. Something is alive, or not alive, and if it is, I can hear it. Especially if I already know it is there."

"If something is familiar, or has already drawn your attention, then you hear it more clearly? So what draws your attention in the first place? How can you pick that one thing out of many—do you hear many, all the time?"

"Yes, I hear many. I think. All the time. If I am quiet, and not busy, there are waves of sound whispering all around me. Like the ripples on water when you drop a pebble in, but coming toward me, not going away."

"Incredible. If the honeydew comes back to the pond, will you hear that?"

"I guess so. It might be hard to find it, among the voices. There are many there now."

"If I isolated them—took them away from the others—and held them in a vial like this one, would that make it easier?"

"Yes. Even talking to you about the little animals in the blood makes them more clear in my mind. They seem more real. I first noticed them because that blood was all I had left of my mother; it was dear to me."

"I have read that natural philosophy is supposed to be a passionless pursuit. We are the servants of reason. But I have never found that to be true. Why do anything if you have no passion for it? Why do one thing rather than another? I am as driven to examine strange creatures through microscopes as Lancelot was driven to run mad for love in French romances."

"Who is Lancelot?"

"Oh, a famous knight from books. He lived hundreds of years ago, if he lived at all."

"Ah. Then why does it matter what he does? Did?"

"Lancelot? He is famous throughout all Europe, even today."

"How can someone who was never alive be important?"

Leeuwenhoek is stumped. He does not feel that he is the best advocate for Lancelot. He has read few romances. As a rule he finds them boring. Yet he feels duty-bound to say something.

"Stories about Lancelot are adventurous and interesting; people enjoy reading them. They learn things from them, and from him, even if he was never alive. He is an idea. He acted nobly and was an example of the passion of love."

"But you said he was mad? Everyone is afraid of mad people."

"As I recall it, there was one time that he went mad and ran off into the woods because of his love for Queen Guinevere, whom he could not have. She was married to another man, the king, Arthur. But most of the time he did not act crazy. He was very brave."

"I have spent most of my life in the woods. People have chased me and thrown rocks at me, called me crazy. I don't think they were learning anything from me. But I am alive, and Lancelot is not. So I am more important than he is."

There is no way Leeuwenhoek can argue with this. He even agrees. Yet her sympathy has such stern limits. She can feel every living thing for miles around, but there is no way he can convey to her the value of that French scribe who lived all those centuries ago, and all the thousands of people who have admired and copied his work since then, and then others because of them, and so on, and on. This is a spreading and intricate form of life, as complex as the honeydew, as large as any forest, but the goose girl does not hear it. She cannot read. It is so very difficult to be fully human if you cannot read. Should he not try to teach her? Would Barbara consider it? Marieke reads quite well. But then, why would a goose herd need to read? He is quiet for a minute and then goes back to the topic of animalcules.

"What can you tell me about the little animals in the blood now? What are they doing?"

"Being themselves. It is hard to say. They are active, and happy. They like being alive. I think they are eating? Something in the blood, or the water."

"I wonder if they will eat all of it, and run out? Then they would die, or go dormant again. Sleeping, I mean."

"Yes, perhaps. Or maybe they will grow so many, or so big, that they will fill up all the water. Then what would happen?"

"Well, I doubt they can explode the glass, so likely they would reach their maximum and then begin to die off."

"Are you going to put some in blood?" she asks.

Here it is again. Leeuwenhoek has been expecting her to ask this, though he still has no good answer. "I am afraid to," he finally admits. "Plague is terrible."

"I remember," says the goose girl. "May I hold the vial?"

Leeuwenhoek hands her the capillary cautiously. She unwraps it and holds it in her bare, dirty hand. He is afraid that she will break it and drink it or do some unexpected thing, but she just holds it lightly, silently, her expression rapt. "It is like the handkerchief," she says, finally, "like it used to be."

Leeuwenhoek thinks of Marieke, at home playing with her mother's elegant dollhouse. The goose girl stands in the bare field, holding a vial of water and blood, the only gift that plague can give her daughter.

REPLIES

Leeuwenhoek and Pierre have gone on with the letters. Both were too impatient to wait for the Society to reply. They have done pepper water, animalcules from well water, some fine cross-sections of wood and leaves, illustrating their fibers. There is practically nothing that Leeuwenhoek is unwilling to look at through the microscope; everything is miraculously transformed.

Pierre is becoming extremely skilled with the scopes. He is also revealing an unexpectedly cheeky side. So in addition to getting an excellent draughtsman below market rates, Leeuwenhoek has found himself with a true assistant: a keen and funny and insightful fellow observer. He likes the boy a lot. He tries to avoid thinking of Pierre as a son, considering any such thought disloyal to Barbara, and really the lad is too old, unless, as parents, they had started indecently early.

Pierre's inability to see colors makes him a better microscopist. His training as an artist helps as well. His eye is accustomed to seeking out the edges of things; he has an acuity about light and shadow, transparence and opacity, fore- and background, and he is not distracted by the slight spreading blurs of color that sometimes annoy Leeuwenhoek. He is becoming accustomed to asking Pierre for a second opinion on things he finds it hard to make out himself. As he himself has the best natural vision of anyone he has ever met, he finds this perverse, but useful. A draughtsman as good as Pierre should be making a living as a cartographer, or as a marine or military artist, many of whom work almost exclusively in pen and ink. The fact that he is not shows a prime failure of imagination on the part of his father—one for which, however, Leeuwenhoek cannot help but be grateful.

Pierre is now allowed to use the best lenses. He can hardly exclude his amanuensis from seeing his best results. He has used them with Pierre without fanfare, no indications that they are unusual, or even better. He always has them out when Pierre arrives, so no mystery accrues about them being kept in a separate place. As they look the same once installed in a metal housing, and the boy knows little about lens construction—though a fair amount, practically, about optics—he figures he is safe. He has several times allowed Pierre to walk in on him at the lathe, industriously polishing away. This tomfoolery always makes him feel embarrassed. It is not like misleading guests, or even Reinier; Pierre is a practical worker with these tools, and he looks up to his master. He knows he is acting in bad faith. But then, these lenses are his masterwork, and Pierre, if he is anything, is still an apprentice. He is allowed a certain professional license.

Consequently, Pierre is in the house, in the study where Leeuwenhoek is teaching him how to prepare specimens, when the Society's reply finally arrives.

~~~

Mijnheer Antoni Van Leeuwenhoek,
Hippolytusbuurt, Delft in Holland

The Society has received your letter containing microscopical descriptions of *animalcula* in water and read it with interest. While we wish to offer the utmost encouragement to interested amateurs, we regret to say that many of your observations seem to us fantastical, and more to the point, we cannot reproduce them with our own microscopical equipment. Therefore we cannot consider them to be of philosophical value.

I remain yours, sir, in deepest respect,
Henry Oldenburg
Secretary, The Royal Society of London

This is crushing. Even more insulting, the letter is followed by a translation into something resembling Dutch but that is more properly German. Leeuwenhoek is filled with a mixture of shame and rage. If there were a fire in the room he would toss it in. But there is none because it is bad for specimens to be too warm. Reinier is in Paris on some medical business; this is just as well, as it prevents him taking out his frustrations upon him for his obviously useless introduction. As it is, he hands the letter, wordlessly, to Pierre, who is standing at the workbench looking expectant. Leeuwenhoek's hands are shaking.

Pierre puzzles over its odd language for a while. Eventually he looks up. "Why is it signed by a German?" he asks, aggressively. "Lutheran dog. He's probably a spy for some princeling. What does he have to do with the Royal Society of London?" Pierre has a Fleming's contempt for Germans. His family comes from Ghent. Leeuwenhoek suspects that his mother speaks to him in French, and that she, at least, may be a Catholic. Dutch is acceptable; German barbarous.

"And what does it matter to you if their microscopes are too lousy to see what you've seen? What does that matter? I thought they were supposed to be professionals! What? Learned men? Stupid English snobs! That's like saying you've sent them a painting that can't possibly be a painting because no one in England can paint one like it! Have you ever seen an English painting? It's like they do them with pig's trotters! Jesus Christ, Lord and Savior!"

Leeuwenhoek is touched by Pierre's ire. He lets him go on for some time. He is eighteen, and therefore can say a whole lot of things that he, the sober adult, ought not to. Seeing Pierre's hurt and anger expressing itself, he gradually feels calmer. His heart stops thundering in his chest. Finally he gives the boy a significant glance and raises his finger, like a statue of Socrates. Pierre shuts up instantly. His fair hair bristles and stands up on end in continued protest, but he is quiet.

"But should we send the next letter?" Leeuwenhoek asks him seriously.

"Yes!" replies Pierre, immediately. "Yes! Of course! Master Leeuwenhoek, this is an insult! You must show them the truth! And the drawings of the little animals from the pepper water are beautiful, and—"

Leeuwenhoek does his Socrates gesture again. Pierre subsides. "Thank you, Pierre. I think you are right. We will send it. If they are true philosophers, they must admit they are in the wrong. Inquiry must move them. I will give it to Grisse tonight; he is traveling to Amsterdam and can send it from there." The boy looks ready to sob with relief. Leeuwenhoek squeezes his shoulder lightly. It makes both of them feel better.

They finish preparing the specimens. They look at them, in the strong northern light from the window, with a magnification and a focus that the Royal Society of London does not have.

Apprenticeship

The geese are sleepy. Two of them have sore feet from walking on the hard summer roads. They are expecting a thunderstorm. Therefore, they are not inclined to go to pasture. They are loitering around the courtyard, and the girl is with them, sitting on the upturned bucket. She sings to them softly and vaguely. Turntoe is watching, neck upraised. The rest are milling about, or grooming, or sleeping.

Pierre marches into this scene of companionship, through the rear gate. He stops short, surprised to find the yard full of geese. Usually they are long away when he gets there. Before he even notices the goose girl, Turntoe advances on him, hissing, lifting her wings. The others wake up and peer at him, alert and suspicious. Pierre backs away toward the kitchen door.

"No," says the girl, idly. Turntoe immediately loses interest; stretching her neck and fluffing her feathers, she withdraws to a shady corner to rest her sore feet. Scratch takes her place as sentinel.

Pierre looks at the girl. He had thought she was speaking to him, but obviously she had not been. The girl looks back at him. "Her time was up, anyway. And her feet are sore. She has a bad leg."

"Who are you?" asks Pierre, stupidly. It is perfectly obvious who she is; she herds the geese. He has known that Leeuwenhoek keeps geese—for the quills, apparently, though surely he could just buy them—since he began here. Half the time the courtyard is covered in shit.

"I am with them," says the girl.

Pierre tries to pull himself together. "I mean, why are you here? Should they not be at pasture?"

"It is going to rain," replies the girl, "and they are tired today. Did you know you have something on your jacket? A big white mark?"

Pierre looks down at his front. There is nothing. "No, I don't," he says to her.

"No, on the back. Like dust, or flour."

"Look, that's ridiculous. How can you possibly know that?" asks Pierre. He had knocked over a jar of gypsum in his father's workshop on the way out, but had carefully brushed down his jacket—the front of it, for how could any have got on his back?—and scooped up as much of the white powder as he could, replacing the broken jar with another from the shelf. The old jar he had thrown into the midden. Now he is likely looking forward to a beating when he gets home, depending on the price of gypsum.

"I can see it. There are two geese standing behind you."

"Is this a joke?" asks Pierre.

"Crunch and Flathead. Right there," —she gestures, so he turns around to see two geese looking at him attentively, almost self-consciously, as dogs will when you talk about them— "they showed me."

"Are you insane? What do you mean?" asks Pierre, stripping off his jacket. Crazy girl. He turns the jacket round. There is a big white splotch on the back, the devil's handprint marking out his guilt. "Jesus Christ, Lord and Savior," he says. He begins to brush it off, totally at a loss.

The girl goes back to the wordless singing she was doing before. After a while she says, "you are the pale one who works with Antoni. You have that stuff in your hair, too, but nobody can see it. You are already white as a goose."

Pierre begins to ruffle and shake his hair, before he puts his jacket back on. He is shocked. He would never use his master's first name.

"So you look at the little animals, too? What do they look like?" says the goose girl.

Pierre wonders if he might be dreaming. He is actually still at home in his bed. He has not yet departed for Leeuwenhoek's, or knocked over the gypsum, which would at least be a relief. "You know about them?" he asks the girl. "Which ones? Have you looked through the master's microscopes, too?"

"No," she says. "I have not seen them, those little creatures that live in water and spit and blood, and all over. Sometimes I hear them, though. The watery ones, what are they like, when you see them?"

"Ah. Well," says Pierre weakly, "there are several kinds. Some are oval, some round, some are long and thin, like sticks. One round kind is covered with little hairs, or legs. One long kind can kind of flow internally and inch along like a caterpillar. They can all move, somehow, through the water. They are clear, like gelatin, or snot, or spit. You can just see the edges of them. If the master will permit it, I can show you some drawings—" He breaks off and then asks sharply, "Does he know that you know all this?"

"Oh, yes. We have talked about it."

"Then why has he not shown you himself?"

"I don't know. We always get to talking about other things. But I would like to see them. I wonder if I could tell which was which?"

"Which animalcule was which? Well, yes, you would see them. They do look very different from one another."

"No, I mean, which one goes with which voice."

No opinion presents itself to Pierre about this matter. He says nothing.

"So you just see the edges of them, like a black line? Can you see the water through them? Do they have any colors?" the girl goes on.

"Yes, like a black and white drawing. I think you can see the water behind them. Sometimes you can see one animalcule right through another. If they have colors, I cannot see them." He pauses. "I do not see color," he continues, peremptorily, as if this is an important decision he has made.

"Neither do the geese," says the girl.

"Oh my God, really?" says Pierre, in astonishment. He turns to stare at the nearest goose, as if this fact will suddenly become obvious. But of course it is no more evident than when anybody else looks at him. "Lord and Savior," he says, "You mean, all this time, I've been a goose?"

The goose girl does not laugh. With a joker's instinct, he understands that she does not reject his statement, or disapprove of his levity. The words just mean something else to her.

"Yes," she says. "A white goose."

Pierre is still trying to fit all these ideas into his mind when he hears the clock strike. It is two o'clock, and he is due inside. "I must go," he says to the girl, turning to the kitchen door. He is rather proud that he uses this door now, as it marks him as an intimate of the household, a true servant.

The goose girl nods. "Say hello to the little animals for me. And to Antoni," she says. Pierre walks into the cool interior of the rear kitchen, shaking his head.

IN CAMERA

Leeuwenhoek and Pierre are in the study examining cochineal. Leeuwenhoek is reasonably sure he has found an uncrushed, diaphanous insect wing, but he wants Pierre's opinion, chiefly as to whether he can draw it. Therefore, Pierre is a few paces from the strong light of the window, squinting into a tiny lens right next to his eye, muttering to himself: "yes, I think so. Hup, shit, where's it gone? Ah, there. Well, now, that's amazing. It looks just like lace. Or filigree. Master Leeuwenhoek, are you seeing this?"

"No, Pierre, remember—" replies Leeuwenhoek, patiently.

"Right, right," mutters the boy, "one at a time. But it's stupid, isn't it? We should throw it up on some kind of screen, you know, with mirrors? Then we could both see it." He keeps the eyepiece up to his eye.

"Exactly!" says Leeuwenhoek, "I have thought of that, too. Like a *camera obscura*? But it is impossible to get enough light. It's always the light. It's infuriating. I can't figure out how it would work."

"Well, don't ask me," says Pierre. "You're the one for that kind of thing."

Vermeer walks in. "The maidservant said you were here—" he begins. He sees Pierre by the window, his white hair aglow, holding the tiny silver machine to his eye. "Jesus Christ, will you look at that?" he says, forgetting whatever he was about to say. He is silent for a while, performing calculations in his mind. "The light—"

Shut up, Johannes, thinks Leeuwenhoek sourly. There might be enough for you, but never enough for me. Vermeer stands there thoughtfully, looking at Pierre.

After a moment, he turns to Leeuwenhoek and says, "Who is this boy? Or is he an angel, contemplating the state of man? Where do you find these extraordinary specimens? You already have a holy fool looking after your geese!"

"They just find me, Johannes. Who knows why?"

"Possibly because, unlike most men, you are not a judgmental hypocrite. But the boy, who is he?"

"Pierre DeWitt, son of Matthias, from the guild. He's my draughtsman." Pierre, unwilling to look away from the microscope, waves vaguely in their direction, hearing his name.

"Look at his dedication! Squinting on and on in all that light. He looks like a diamond broker. Too fair, though, too fair. Who has ever seen a Jew that blonde?"

"What do you want, Johannes?"

"Merely to ask you, again, to step over to the house, and have a drink, and bask in your own ingenuity as you admire the camera. And of course, now, to ask to borrow your apprentice to sit for me. Or rather, stand, just like that. Here would be best, of course, though the set-up would be a nightmare. Fortunately, my windows are also north-facing."

"Johannes! You cannot have him! It would take forever! You are far too slow! Dear God, man, he is my amanuensis! How would my work proceed without him? You are determined to make everybody as broke as you!"

"I was not aware that you made any money from your philosophical inquiries, Antoni."

"Well, I don't—yet! Except for selling a few lenses. But the time may come...at any rate, Pierre does the drawings for the letters I am sending to the Royal Society. Anatomical drawings, I guess you would call them."

"The Royal Society of London? With Hooke and those men? Are you really? Well done! You really are taking my advice!"

Leeuwenhoek prays for patience. Before he has a chance to reply, Vermeer goes on: "and have you been pursuing the tapestries? Now that you have found a cartoonist?"

"No, no, not as of yet," says Leeuwenhoek, hurriedly. "We have been very busy setting up this correspondence and so on." In reality, he has been biding his time, not blurting out his half-baked plans to Pierre or getting him embroiled in enterprises that would take considerable investment, and that could, he believes, lead to genuine profits. He glares at Vermeer, who, amazingly, says no more.

Instead he returns to his wonderful new idea. He goes and stands next to Pierre, who ignores him. "Yes, he is just a bit taller than my eldest son. I can probably block the whole painting in if I stand him on a box. Then I would need him for a much shorter time, just for the head and hands. I will need to borrow that silver instrument—or, I don't know, do you have one like it? You see how I am trying not to inconvenience you?"

"Johannes, almost every time I see you I want to kill you."

"Yes, but you never do. It is your unusual decency. So could you perhaps send him over for a few sunny afternoons about two months from now?"

"Sunny afternoons are when I need him here, Johannes. Exactly then."

"But—"

"I will go," says Pierre, suddenly, from the window. He has put down the scope and is looking straight at them. "But only if you give him the painting."

"What?" says Vermeer.

"Hah!" says Leeuwenhoek.

"You are Johannes Vermeer, are you not?" says Pierre. "And you already owe him money. I am not sure what for—"

"A *camera obscura*," interjects Leeuwenhoek.

"Ah," says Pierre, "and it will recompense him for my lost labor, as well."

"Antoni, your apprentices are unruly," says Vermeer, stalling.

"I have no apprentices, except as a draper. Pierre is a free agent, paid by piecework. His time is his own. I cannot constrain him to do anything," replies Leeuwenhoek, smugly.

"Well, it's a ghastly system, little better than slavery anyway. I have had several, and they were all cretins. Couldn't paint worth a damn and wouldn't listen. Barbaric practice," says Vermeer.

"And of course, it is an honor to be painted by you, Master Vermeer," says Pierre.

Vermeer looks at him. Pierre smiles placatingly.

"And what if I don't want your damn fool painting, Johannes?" says Leeuwenhoek.

He stares at the artist, straight-faced. There is no way on God's green earth that Johannes will ever pay him cash money. This could be an excellent opportunity.

"Well, fine! Fine! Then he must sit fourteen days— fourteen sunny days, of my choosing! And you must keep the painting in the great room! You have a piece of shit there now, anyway, so I am doing you a favor!"

"You are, Johannes. You are. Thank you," says Leeuwenhoek. Pierre nods fervently in the background. The two men shake hands, and the painter bows himself out.

After Vermeer's footsteps have receded down the hall, Leeuwenhoek bursts out laughing. Wiping tears from his eyes, he says "You are a canny little bugger, Pierre."

"So that was Vermeer? My father thinks he's an idiot. Paints like a fish in water, though. A pure natural."

"He is."

"So what's this about tapestries?" asks Pierre.

Cartoons

Leeuwenhoek knows he is not going to be able to keep dissimulating. Also, Pierre has just revealed the makings of a good business partner, despite his young age. The fact that he is not affiliated with the guild—which had been one reason keeping him quiet, truth be told—could actually prove an advantage. Come to think of it, his status as a transplanted Fleming might also be of use; weaving had been the backbone of Ghent. The local trade in Delft still consists mostly of artisans whose families had fled eighty years ago. They all know each other.

"Ah. Well, it had occurred to me some time ago that drawings of certain animalcules would make beautiful patterns for fabric. Either woven or printed. At the time I was thinking of some specimens of honeydew from the goose pond, which are, frankly, exquisite. You know regular patterns are best."

Pierre is silent, looking awestruck. "My God," he says finally. "The lace wing from the cochineal—Master Leeuwenhoek, you could make a fortune!"

"Vermeer thought it ridiculous when I mentioned it to him."

"Vermeer!" says Pierre, derisively. "Can I see the honeydew?"

"Unfortunately, the specimens dried, but I can show you the drawings."

"Excellent! Now?" asks Pierre. He is wildly excited. No other work will be got out of him for the rest of the afternoon. Leeuwenhoek goes to the cupboard in which he keeps his notes. They are in no particular order, so it takes him some time to locate the honeydew pages. Pierre sighs audibly behind him. Finally he gets his hands on them and turns them over to the lad. It strikes him that for a grown man he is rather at the mercy of youth.

Pierre looks at the drawings for some time, closing one eye and then the other, moving around the table on which he has placed them. They are, of course, godawful, compared to what he can produce.

"You know my cousin Martin works for DeVeyne?" says Pierre, still circling the table, both eyes open now.

"Really? I had no idea," replies Leeuwenhoek. De-Veyne owns the most significant fabric works in town. Leeuwenhoek knows him, of course; he buys fabric from him. Not tapestry, though; that's a bit rich for his blood. Printed fabrics, mostly. This Martin must be an artisan, like the rest of the DeWitts. So there is no reason for Leeuwenhoek to know him; he is a retailer.

. "Yes, he's a cartoonist. Sometimes. That's only occasional work, frankly. Unless you're some fashionable artist from Amsterdam, and DeVeyne would never get those jobs. The industry's not big enough here."

"Your cousin is a cartoonist for the weavers, Pierre?"

Pierre eyes him. "Yes, and he sees colors, too. For the very little work he can get out of the weavers, he gets guild rates. But he's a drunk. Spends most of the time working for the factory at caffa wages."

"Pierre," says Leeuwenhoek, seriously, "I would never hire your cousin over you. Colors be damned. It is your gift I need to do my work. My most important work. Nor do I need a guildsman to design; I already have good relations with several factories, and we could pretend the designs were mine. You and I—and your father—could work out a contract they need never know about. If we made money, some would be yours."

Pierre gets up and walks away to the open window. He keeps his back to Leeuwenhoek, looking out into the street, toward the canal, for a minute or two. Then he turns, and approaches Leeuwenhoek, and shakes his hand earnestly. In terms of seniority, this cannot be correct, but perhaps what they are negotiating is unprecedented. "My father," he says slowly, "is not a fool. He knows my talent as a draughtsman. He also knows that in the trade, I am a cripple. We have never mentioned it outside our family to anybody but you. And he is richer than you think, and angry. His family never wanted to leave the south. I have never even been to Ghent; I have no idea what he talks about. But if you are serious about this, I think you should talk to him. He could be an investor."

"Could you make a weaving cartoon, or a block pattern?"

"The patterns are easy. Regularity is the thing; it just takes some fancy folding to check it. And you have to mind the edges for the repeats."

"Yes," says Leeuwenhoek.

"Cartoons, you need that big scale, so you use a grid. I have never done it, but it can't be that hard. The complexity of the patterns depends on the capacity of the looms. A few drinks and Martin would tell me all about it."

"Fine."

"You will have to make the decisions about colors."

"I look forward to it. It will be a relief to sell something in the shop that isn't black. Though black is nice and expensive."

"You know God prefers black. This is the Republic."

"Yes, though not for interiors. Those might be mistaken for Persia. The shiny and fancy stuff I sell for drapery would boggle the mind."

"Everyone is Catholic inside," says Pierre.

"Are we discussing religion, Pierre?"

"My mother told me never to discuss religion," says Pierre virtuously.

"Wise woman. Let us keep our minds on domestic furnishings. Do you think you could make a pattern based on the honeydew? We will need a sample."

"Yes. I will get a start on it. I will use the drawings, but it would be nice to see the originals. Could you get more?"

"It might be too late in the season. Tends to be spring. But it lingers in places that are rich in animal droppings. I will ask the goose girl if there is any left in the pond."

"Yes, maybe she will have heard them singing, or something. She's a funny one," replies Pierre.

Leeuwenhoek gives him a long look. "So you have been talking to her?"

"Yes, just now. She claimed to see a mark on the back of my jacket because some geese were standing behind me, and they told her somehow. I was facing her. I have no idea how she did it. It was quite a trick."

Leeuwenhoek considers this. "Yes, it is. That is not one she has told me about. I will have to discuss it with her."

"You believe her, then?"

"Yes."

"That she hears animalcules?"

"Yes."

"That is crazy."

"Yes. She does not inhabit the world of reason. Often I feel she has wandered here out of a children's tale. It's like having an oracle in the courtyard."

"She is a freak. You could exhibit her at fairs."

"What with producing tapestries full of creatures invisible to the naked eye, I have enough alternate sources of income at my disposal. Also, I find her strangely comforting. She accepts whatever I say about the animalcules as perfectly natural. Still, you must never mention her— visions, or whatever they are—outside this house, Pierre. Promise me. It could be very dangerous to her, and even to me."

"Of course not. I am accustomed to keeping secrets about what people see," says Pierre, on his dignity.

"Quite so."

"If I am to work on the honeydew now, we should use it for the next letter to the Society. That is more efficient."

"I agree. I will start trying to make sense of my notes. You know, the goose girl said to me about the honeydew that it had some other way of being alive, neither animal nor vegetable. I think she may be right."

"A new genre of life, eh? Like with paintings? For a while everybody wants flowers, and then, hup, suddenly it's fruit, or maybe it's cows, don't you know, then hey, it's kitchens with shiny pans, and then it's saints…"

"Yes. Much like that."

"Who would have thought that living things would be subject to fashions, too?"

"Categories. God must have some system of headings in his book of life. He's been reading it for a long time. Every now and again he turns a page."

"I thought we were not discussing religion?"

"No, you are right. It is unprofitable. I will ask the girl about the honeydew when she comes back this evening."

"But she hasn't left. She is out there now, geese and all. Says it's going to rain."

"Good God, really? But it's been so silent. Not a squawk."

"They are tired, and resting their sore feet," says Pierre, knowledgeably. "Did you know she wants to see the animalcules, too? I said I would ask you if I could show her some drawings."

"You two seem to have talked a lot," says Leeuwenhoek, with some surprise.

"Apparently, I am a white goose," says Pierre, shrugging eloquently. He looks very like Reinier, doing this.

"Hmm," says Leeuwenhoek. "Well, fly away then, white goose. Take these," —he gestures to the drawings on the table— "and leave me to my notes."

Pierre honks with convincing accuracy and flaps his arms. Taking the drawings, he disappears out the door.

THE WHITE GOOSE

When Pierre gets home, his father meets him at the door. "Pierre, you knocked over that jar of gypsum, didn't you? And then cleaned it up and put it in a new jar? Hoped I wouldn't notice? And now I've gone and wrecked a panel with it! It's streaky! I can't sell it to Bloemfontein, and now his order will be late! You know how bad for business that is!"

His father is a calm, almost emotionless man, except where money is concerned. If a penny too much is paid for butter, or cloth, or candles, he beats his wife mercilessly. Bruised, she has occasionally to stay away from divine service, which distresses her because she is very devout. She attends the not-so-secret masses that the Jesuits hold across town in the *Papenhoek*; usually Pierre goes with her. He is a Catholic, too: born, raised and confirmed in the old religion. Matthias is a Protestant. It is better for business. Religion is not his concern. His wife and son are free to worship as they please, so long as it does not prejudice his trade. With Pierre he is equally harsh about anything he perceives to be wasteful: using too much paper in copying, not eating up every scrap of food at meals. Pierre had endured a dreadful, and seemingly endless, series of beatings for wasting colors early in his apprenticeship, as he tried and failed to reproduce the paintings his father had set him to copy, unable to distinguish the hues.

In the excitement of the proposal about the tapestries, Pierre had managed to forget about the gypsum. Now his customary constricting fear of his father's violence comes flooding back. There is no way that he can avoid a beating now; Matthias sees administering them as a strict part of his duty as the head of the household. Domestic waste of any kind is punishable; as husband and father, he is the punisher. He has never been challenged in this belief; neither Pierre nor his mother would dream of it. Pierre is certain, in his inward, rebellious heart, that if he ever were, he would say that scripture supports him. The doleful, ugly scripture of black-clad merchants. Not the elevated, incense-scented words he hears with his mother. This is why he hates Calvinists.

"I broke the jar, yes," he says. He does not bother apologizing or explaining; these make no difference. Nothing he has said after an admission of guilt has ever made any difference. "But I have also come home with a business proposal from Master Leeuwenhoek. About my designing tapestry cartoons and block prints for him, on contract. He will want to consult you about it."

"We will discuss that later," says his father implacably, gesturing toward the studio. Pierre, with a familiar feeling of mixed anger and dread, leads the way down the short hall. He puts Leeuwenhoek's honeydew drawings carefully on a side table. He places his jacket beside them. Then he crosses the room to the main worktable. There is the small jar of now-useless, dirty gypsum sitting upon it. Matthias has a habit of wordlessly bringing the offending objects—an uneaten crust, an overpriced fish—and placing them before the eyes of his victim. Obviously this is significant to him, part of the lesson. To Pierre, at least, they are never significant other than that they give him a fixed point to stare at. Pierre leans downward slightly and grips the side of the table. Once he used to have to reach up to it. Without speaking, his father strikes him across the back, from shoulders to buttocks, with a flat, stiff ruler, two ells in length, that he uses to measure panels. He hits him exactly thirty times with moderate force, never breaking the skin. This punishment regularly left bruises when he was smaller but rarely does now. Pierre does not cry, or not audibly. Tears moisten his eyes and occasionally leak out. When he was little he would sob and beg and even try to run away. But his father would always bring him back again, position him exactly there, and start over. So he learned quickly not to do that.

Pierre stares at the jar and counts his father's strokes. At thirty he straightens up, walks away, and collects his jacket and the drawings from the table. He walks silently out of the room. His father hangs up the ruler on its nail and returns to the work he was doing before, trying to save the panel for Bloemfontein or whatever it was.

They will discuss the tapestry plans later. Pierre knows that his father is wise enough not to try to do so now, even if there is money to be made. Right now he is not very sanguine about Matthias as an investor in any business of his.

He goes to the kitchen. His mother Mathilde is there, chopping vegetables. The maid is thumping away in the back pantry, setting bread. "Can I work here?" asks Pierre. The kitchen is the only place other than the studio that has a table big enough for drawing on. His sweet and beautiful mother tucks a wisp of honey-colored hair back under her cap, and gestures for him to sit down. She knows why he is here. Before he can place the drawings on the table, she comes around to his end and wipes off the already pristine surface with a rag from her apron pocket.

"There," she says, in her genteel voice. "Now it's ready for your work. You go on." She touches his hand lightly as he puts the honeydew drawings down. Pierre stares down the table's length at the carrots she has been chopping.

Even her carrots are a picture of elegance, lying neatly on the ceramic tiles she has placed there, in perfectly even pieces. They look like a pile of severed fingers, perhaps her own fingers, long and narrow and pale. He knows that the carrots are bright orange, though that is not how he sees them; it is his refining eye that makes the scene macabre. The long kitchen knife, its blade at an angle to him, glints spectacularly in the leaning afternoon light from the window. He imagines plunging it into his father's chest. Being dead, however, would not make him a reliable investor. Pierre's gaze flickers upward to his mother as she moves back toward the vegetables. He smiles briefly.

"Thanks," he says. Mathilde looks at him evenly. She begins to chop potatoes. They are already scrubbed; she does not peel them. That is wasteful. Her knife clicks rhythmically on the tile surface. The mismatched wall tiles she has placed there, in a neat line, are all beautiful, and using them in this way is ingenious. Pierre wishes he could attribute this to his mother's innate artistic sensibility and good sense, which are very real, but he knows that otherwise she might damage the table. That would likewise count as a waste of good money. Pierre and his mother live in a world in which the cost of every action is reckoned to the *duit*. They are both highly skilled at such reckoning. Pierre's mother no longer has to cover for him. He has, on rare occasions, been able to cover for her. He wishes he could do more, but their domestic spheres are very different.

"What will you do with those drawings? Make fair copies, as you have done with others for Master Leeuwenhoek?" she asks, with the faintest trace of a sly grin. She would, of course, never mention how bad the drawings are. "More letters?"

"No," says Pierre. "It is different this time." He goes on, his earlier excitement creeping back. "This time Master Leeuwenhoek wants me to turn these drawings—they are of honeydew, that green stuff from ponds—into prints and cartoons that could be used to make fabric. Isn't that a brilliant idea? If he likes them, he will draw up a contract that will pay me some profits as the artist if they go into production. And he can sell them at his shop. Isn't that amazing?"

"When has Master Leeuwenhoek ever not liked the work you have done for him?" asks his mother, proudly. "What an opportunity, Pierre!"

"I have even thought of asking father to invest," he says, determinedly, after a moment. He and his mother look at each other cautiously. "After all, isn't it about time he made some money out of me?"

"You are already making money, Pierre."

"You know how he despises piecework. This would be something different. Artist fees and a cut of profits. Return on investment."

"And what if he loses money, Pierre? What then?" asks Mathilde softly.

"I don't know how many beatings that would be worth, but I am sure I am equal to it, with all my experience," replies Pierre.

"You know it is not funny, Pierre."

He shrugs his sore shoulders. "No, you're right; it's not funny. But if he sees me turn a profit, maybe he will be less angry."

"It isn't anger. It is his sense of justice," Mathilde replies.

"You know I don't agree, mother. No one is beaten, day after day, for justice. He is filled with rage. I don't understand why." Pierre knows that his mother has her own list of his father's miseries, and that she herself, with her single child, is one of them. He is unpersuaded. His father is such a cheapskate that one child is apparently a burden; why would he be happy with more?

"I will talk to him later. Maybe tonight. I thought perhaps I should talk to Martin. He will know all the techniques."

"If he can stay sober long enough to tell you."

"Yes. Still, get a man talking about his work, you know…and it might keep him from getting too curious if I buy him a few drinks."

"Perhaps. I hope he won't get jealous. His life is a disappointment to him."

Pierre shrugs again and turns to his work. He has providently brought several sheets of paper to experiment on from Leeuwenhoek's house, tucked in among the drawings. Leeuwenhoek does not mind; he is generous with supplies. He looks at the elementary drawings from various angles; they are certainly beautiful, and quite regular. There is a persistent teardrop shape occurring at several scales that reminds him of the fashionable Indian patterned cloth called *cachemire*. It is wildly popular; the French have even banned imports of it to encourage their own industry around Marseilles. But everybody makes it now: the Dutch, the English, too. Perhaps this is what turned Leeuwenhoek's mind to fabric when he saw the honeydew; he knows far more about cloth than Pierre does. The honeydew forms, though, are more rounded, chubby, egg-shaped. Interesting squiggly business is going on inside them. In *cachemire* each curly teardrop has a carefully drawn jagged edge, so they look hairy, like burrs. In this pattern all that would be inverted: each form would have a smooth edge but extra patterning inside. So they could sell it as what—fat, bald *cachemire*? Inside-out?

Pierre snorts mentally. These problems will be Leeuwenhoek's. He is the draper. He puts words out of his mind and lets his hand think. This is the only thing that works. In a moment, as he sits there thinking of nothing, his hand begins, with sudden decision, to translate Leeuwenhoek's drawings into a new design. He makes all the elements bigger. He spaces them out elegantly, at two scales. He regularizes the innards of each honeydew form, using repeating shapes. He keeps all elements a regular distance from the edge. There. He closes his eyes for a long minute, then opens them quickly and looks squarely down at the sheet. He closes his eyes again. He repeats this procedure three times, never looking at the picture for more than a second. His father taught him this technique for evaluating compositions. If, after a few trials, he feels calm and satisfied, then the picture he is carrying in his mind is working; it is well balanced. If, on the other hand, he feels itchy or jumpy or undecided—one sign of this is that his eyeballs will continue to move around while his eyes are closed—it is not. The composition is lopsided, too many elements crowded over here, too much blankness here. Or relative sizes or distances are wrong. Or something. It is a yes or no thing. Sometimes he can tell what the problem is, feeling it as a kind of stickiness or sludginess in places, or hot and cold spots on the canvas of his mind, behind his closed eyes. More often he just knows it is wrong. Instinctive corrections might be able to fix it, but mostly it means it is a dead loss and he has to start over.

It is the same for Matthias. He and his father have discussed this process many times, going over and over the exercise with their own works and with practically every painting they see. The very few investment paintings Matthias has ever bought have been rigorously subjected to this test. The problem is, in doing his own work, Matthias is reluctant to start over. He hates to waste material. He hates to waste time. Yet he also knows, because this infallible sense tells him, that to continue with a useless composition is likewise a waste of time and material. So he gets into a furious bind. This is why, Pierre realizes as he sits at the kitchen table with his eyes closed, performing the test for the fourth time, his father has never made it as a painter.

He is afraid.

This is such a revelation that Pierre's eyes pop open. Unfortunately his mind is so full of words that he cannot see the drawing properly any more. But, as his whole body remained calm the first three times, he can claim the design as a success. Now he can work on re-scaling it to see what density is best.

Emerging from these thoughts, he realizes that his mother is done chopping the vegetables. It is quiet. Mathilde wipes her hands on her apron and comes around the table. She looks down at the design. "Pretty," she says, laying a hand on his shoulder, "they look like goose eggs. Tapered, you know?"

Pierre smiles. "Yes," he says, "it's been quite the day for geese."

THE MECHELEN

The following evening, to his own astonishment, Pierre is sitting in the swanky public bar of the Mechelen, looking out into the square. He has never been in here by himself before, or indeed, at night. Afternoons he has been in various times, dropping off prepared panels or meeting clients with his father. But now he is sitting at a small table in an alcove, a quieter part of the room usually used to transact business, waiting for his cousin Martin. A porcelain jug of wine sits on the table before him, and in his pocket is at least enough money to buy another.

His father gave him the money. This is unprecedented. He cannot remember ever having left the house with a single *duit* in his pocket before, unless under strict instructions to purchase some specific item for the studio, from a specific person, at specific price. That his father would hand over ready cash sufficient to buy two jugs of wine, or perhaps more, without quibble, is remarkable. That he would specifically enjoin Pierre to invite his cousin to the Mechelen, where genever is at a premium and French wine exorbitant, nearly defies belief. Mind you, Pierre thinks, as he sips his wine in tiny increments so as to leave more for Martin, Matthias does bring all his own clients here. The inn's elegance accords with his sense of propriety. It is a business associated with the arts. And it is named after a refined southern city. Money spent here is well spent.

All of this implies that Matthias trusts his son to spend money well. Pierre sits there trying not to let this fact go to his head. Surely there are other, less miserly, signs of fatherly approval and affection? In his father, Pierre can think of none. He does not praise. He does not boast. Pierre could become a cardinal and not a vain word would pass his father's lips, drunk or sober. A fine drawing, a job well done; these merit a firm nod or a faint smile. That is all.

He thinks how little the sum in his pocket would mean to Master Leeuwenhoek—the man who had crazily purchased a whole flock of geese just to get a few quills! Who is friends with Vermeer, a profligate whom his father considers little better than a criminal. The mad microscopist, willing to let a half-blind boy be his partner in an art business! He could get the money for two jugs of wine from him any afternoon, just by asking. Hinting, even.

Still, his father had given him the money. He had nodded briskly over the sample drawing and said that he would meet with Master Leeuwenhoek to talk about contractual matters at his convenience, if the business went forward. All of this had transpired in the kitchen yesterday evening, with Mathilde hovering in the background, trying to keep anxiety out of her eyes.

Suddenly his tall cousin Martin is framed in the doorway. He is handsome, Martin, and fair in a less freakish way than Pierre or his father. He is also much bigger than either of them and heavier in build. A peasant, a potato eater, says Matthias dismissively; he does not like Martin's mother's family, wealthy farmers from Den Hoorn, just outside Delft. His brother, in his opinion, had married beneath him—though, to be sure, the girl was rich, which counts for something. Pierre sees an expensively dressed woman near the bar eyeing Martin as he comes in. Her dress is more lustrous than the fine damask on her table. There are pearls on the combs in her hair.

Martin is a boor. Sober, he is not ill-tempered, though not well-spoken. Drunk, he becomes loud and maudlin. Fortunately, for such a big and powerful man, he is not violent. Booze makes him not mean but lachrymose. He spends a lot of his non-working hours in a melancholy stupor. He is still young and strong, so as of yet he bears none of the marks of the drinker. Hence expensive women give him the glad eye, if they see him early enough of an evening. Pierre likes his cousin, even if he is a failure, so he sympathizes with the lady by the bar.

"Martin!" he calls out. His cousin comes over. He seats himself, looks cheerfully at Pierre, and seizes the wine jug.

"All ready, I see?" he says, in a rumbly baritone. He sings when drunk, often quite well. Pierre earnestly hopes that the mood will not strike him this evening. Such a performance would not endear the family to the proprietors, and his father does a lot of business here. Pierre will pay for any indelicacy out of his own hide.

There is no need to pour Martin's wine. He has taken care of that himself. However, removing that bit of polite duty makes Pierre's task all the harder. Hands in his lap, he pictures himself, wistfully, as the host, pouring wine, and saying: *Martin, my dear cousin, of course, as you will have expected, we are here to discuss a professional matter.* Eighteen to Martin's twenty-five, it is altogether more agonizing to begin in cold blood, with nothing in his hands. This is why noblemen carry swords.

"So," says his cousin amiably, scanning the room. "Why are we here? Your son-of-a-bitch father have some work for me?"

"Would you want work from my father?" says Pierre, surprised.

"I didn't say I would, no. Couldn't think why else, though. He thinks the rest of us are scum. Farmers and wage workers. No offence, Pierre. Not your fault your dad's an asshole."

"No," says Pierre, abandoning forthwith all the feeble stratagems he had worked out beforehand, "I want your advice about cartooning for fabrics. I might be able to make a deal with Antoni Van Leeuwenhoek."

"What, the draper in Hippolytusbuurt? Really? He's not a manufacturer, is he?" asks Martin.

"No. It's a side venture. He's found some interesting patterns and wants to develop them for the local market."

"Ah. From India? China?"

"Who knows, Martin? Who cares? Somewhere!" Pierre rushes on, "The point is, he's asked me to fix them up, and he'll pay a percentage if a factory takes them!"

"What factory?"

"I don't know. DeVeyne, maybe. But I think he knows everyone in the area, at least as a retailer. I guess he will show the samples around. Take the best offer, small batch, sell them in his shop, then see what happens from there."

"How did he fix on you?"

"I've been working for him as a draughtsman in another capacity."

"In another capacity, Pierre? What capacity?"

"Doing anatomical drawings, I guess you could say. Of creatures he sees through his microscopes—"

"His what?"

"It's a kind of eyeglass, like a jeweler's loupe, only much stronger. It can magnify things over a hundred times, so a single hair looks like a tree trunk. It's incredible. There's a whole world of creatures living around us, everywhere, far too small to see."

"Insects, you mean? Bugs?"

"Much smaller than that. Tinier than the tiniest grain of sand. Invisible. Alive."

"You mean, we eat them and breathe them—they're on everything?"

"Yes."

"That's disgusting, Pierre. Are you sure it's true?"

"I've seen them. Lots of them. In water, and milk, and from hairs and feathers and dirt."

Martin, quaffing his wine, looks revolted. "In clean water?"

"Yes. From the well. There are more in the canals, or in ponds, though."

"Jesus Christ, that is disgusting. So they must be inside us? That's unnatural, Pierre."

"Well, I expect they've always been there. It's a part of nature, just we haven't seen it before."

"Are they in wine?" asks Martin, looking moodily at his glass.

"I don't know. We haven't tried looking at wine," admits Pierre.

"If you look, don't tell me. I may never drink water again. Or milk."

"When's the last time you drank water?" asks Pierre.

"True, there are better things to drink," says Martin. "Thank God." He looks with some horror at the abundant vase of flowers on a nearby sideboard.

"Master Leeuwenhoek says it helps if you boil the water," says Pierre apologetically. "Ah, now, cartooning—"

"Cartooning, yes," says Martin, dragging his gaze from the flowers, "any fool can do it. What do you want to know? Does he want woven cloth, tapestry or whatnot, or printed?"

"Both."

"Only a few tapestry looms around here," Martin warns. "As I know too well. I have a gift for that scale. I suppose, if I lived in Amsterdam, I'd make good money."

He is silent a moment. "Well, fuck, eh? Right, so for tapestry you need to know the frame dimensions of the loom; you need to know the thread counts, especially warp; you should know how many colors you're dealing with, whether just two or more—though I don't think anybody here is set up for more than two—and you need to know about the final fabric. I mean, is it silk or wool, on linen warp, or what? This will affect how many threads it takes to draw a line, y'know? With silks you can make tighter patterns, but obviously it is more expensive."

"But basically you just do a big pattern on a grid, and they pin it to the warp and use it for a guideline?"

"Yep, that's it," agrees Martin, finishing the jug. "On the back. That part's easy. The workers use a mirror on the floor to check it as it goes. At least, on a horizontal loom like DeVeyne's. Fucking tricky, but not your problem, if you're the artist. We need more wine. I'll order it, shall I?" Without waiting for a reply, he strides off to the bar. The woman in the lustrous dress shifts restively, glinting in the lamplight, drawing Martin's eye as he stands there. Pierre hears a low rumble of flirtatious conversation. He hopes his cousin will not get distracted.

Moments later, Martin is back, a new jug in hand. "You can pay later," he says, sitting back down. He says nothing, but edges his chair out of the alcove. His view of the pearl-combed lady is still obstructed, but now she, at least, can see him.

Pierre watches this. "Lord and Savior, Martin, do you want to trade places? Ah, for God's sake, look, I can sit there," he says, moving to get up.

"No," says his cousin, authoritatively, pouring wine for both of them, "it's fine as it is."

Pierre eyes him askance for a moment, then continues, "so, does anybody else here have tapestry looms, besides DeVeyne?"

"No. At least, not that I know of. And his aren't always in production, either. Printed fabric's the thing now. Cheaper to make, and faster, too. You know all those fancy Indian patterns the East India Company's always importing? They cost a bomb to weave here, and they're still not as good, so why bother? Dyes are so much better now, and plain cloth is cheap, so if you make a good pattern out of them, just print it. People buy it up like crazy."

They sip their wine. Or, Pierre sips his. Somehow half the jug is gone already.

"Do you know what he wants the fabric for? For table cloths, or curtains, or bed hangings, or dress fabric, or what?"

"I don't know."

"Well, this will affect the scale of the pattern, y'know. So watch out for it."

"Yes." Pierre tries to think of the most efficient question to ask before his cousin gets too drunk. "So, what's the worst mistake you can make, would you say? In making a pattern for printing?"

Martin is starting to look a bit owly. The second jug is almost empty. He ponders this question for a minute. "Well, there's some technical stuff. You want everything a thumb's breadth from the edge, even. The absolute best patterns will have several ways to break, as well—so, that means, y'know, you cut a form in half, it could join on seamlessly to another part of the pattern, another edge— best way to check this is by folding, see if you can get them to line up, see? Wish I had a bit of cloth to show you…"

Pierre is glad he doesn't. Things would get laborious. "Anything else?"

"For my money," says Martin, pouring the last of the wine into his glass with careful concentration, "you don't want a pattern that gets too busy. You want them to breathe, y'know? I hate people who scale patterns down too small. Might as well be dots, what's the point in that? You spend all this fucking time drawing a wheat grain or a bird's head, lovely lines to them, and some idiot prints it so small it looks like an ink blot, completely stupid, hardly worth wiping your ass with it—"

Pierre is immediately worried that the pattern he has spent the last day working on is too fussy, only suitable for ass-wiping.

"Well, a genever then, and we'll call it an evening, eh?" says his cousin, already rising. Pierre, lost in thought about pattern density, waves at him vaguely as he heads back to the bar. Rumbling and light tinkling laughter ensue. Pierre turns to see Martin talking animatedly to the lady in the dress, which now seems to be glowing, nacreous in the dim light like mother-of-pearl. Pierre rarely drinks wine. Martin, on the other hand, obviously has no problem keeping her in focus.

He reappears by their table, two small glasses in hand. "Great dress, eh?" he says, sitting once more. "Maybe she bought it from Leeuwenhoek. Silk taffeta." He downs his genever, and eyes Pierre's. Pierre hates genever. He waves his cousin toward it. It is instantly gone. "Look," says Martin, expansively, "if you want me to look at your pattern, or you want any more advice, just call on me, alright? Now give me the money, and I'll go pay."

Pierre hands him the money and yields up the authority of paying. His father would not approve. But his father is not here, and Martin needs to impress the lady. His cousin heads off toward the bar yet again; Pierre falls back into musing, should he space out the goose-eggs—

the animalcules from the honeydew—a bit more? Scale them up again? He doesn't want the complexity of their forms to be lost. What if—?

A slight clink at the bar. Pierre looks over to see Martin and the lady, who is now standing, raising two glasses of genever. He realizes that whatever change he might be due, it is going down fast. He is at his cousin's side like lightning. Martin, having understood the speed at which he was moving, surreptitiously hands him the remaining small coins so that she does not see. Pierre understands that it is time for him to abscond. All singing, all seduction will then have nothing to do with him, or his father's reputation at the Mechelen. And the lady, it is obvious, will be able to foot even Martin's bill.

He wrings his flushed cousin's hand in genuine gratitude. "Thank you," he says, "and if I have any trouble with it, I will call on you." He nods politely to the lady. She returns his nod, rather conspiratorially, he thinks.

"No trouble, no trouble," says Martin, vaguely but impressively, releasing his hand, "Happy to help." He turns back to the lady. Pierre escapes and makes his way home.

All night, alone in his small, upright bed, Pierre is troubled and elated by dreams in which he is making tiny garments for the animalcules: minuscule waistcoats and dresses and shawls, jackets with many arms, or none, cut from the finest fabrics, all of which are themselves printed with animalcules. In his dreams, he rejoices that his patterns are perfectly to scale.

THE LADY IN THE DRESS

Three days have passed and Martin has hardly got out of bed, and not because he is hung over. Aliette, the lady from the Mechelen, has not let him. He is extremely clean, extremely tired, extremely well fed, aggressively clean-shaven, and confused. He has missed at least one day's work, maybe two; he is not sure what day it is. No one at the factory will be surprised. This has happened to him before, though always because of drink. Not because of shockingly determined, sexually voracious, witty, skilled, wealthy, and as it turns out, hardheadedly entrepreneurial women.

Aliette De Hooch is the rich widow of dream and nightmare. At the moment Martin is not sure to which camp he belongs. Certainly the prolonged, elaborate sex he has been enjoying is like a lustful dream. Though perhaps not his own lustful dream, as many techniques, and even tools, had been unknown to him, and do we dream things of which we know nothing? At the same time, aspects of it all have been humiliating, starting with the fact that it was never clear to him who was fucking whom. This has always been perfectly obvious to him before. He was also, more or less, forcibly, bathed and shaved after their first encounter. Servants have walked in on them twice while they are completely naked, which is a pretty damn surprising state to be in to begin with, to deliver messages or drinks or meals. Aliette has not cared, and neither have they. He, on the first occasion, was ready to wrap himself up in the bed curtains. Moreover, servants keep arriving, regular as clockwork, bearing trays of oysters and red wine and meat and fruit; they are feeding him up like a hound at stud. What will they do when he is no longer able to keep it up? Dump him in the street?

No, they will not, because Aliette has made him a business proposition. She has, in fact, offered him a whole alternate career. He can hardly say he's succeeding at his present one. Aliette is a procurer. This beautiful house, which she inherited at the death of her husband, a serge merchant, is also her place of business. Several—though not all—of the unflappable servants, women and men, work for her, entertaining clients with sex and comfort and conversation and music. Martin has never really thought of the last three as being important in whorehouses, but Aliette assures him that they are. Nor has he thought of men working in them. The idea of a male prostitute is ridiculous. But Aliette claims that although they are rare—indeed, because they are rare—they make excellent money. It is, however, more typical of the few men she employs that they do not work under her roof, but in the private houses of the women who summon them. Or the men: the best paid assignments of all, says Aliette, but work not undertaken by everybody. Good God, he remembers thinking, how much money would it take for me to do that?

He feels the bed slowly spinning as he lies there, as if he's had a whole bottle of genever. The inside of his head is whirling, like one of the tiny spiraling dust storms you can see on roads in summer. He has no idea what to do. He hates choices, and life is always so full of them. Aliette has risen to attend to some task or other. While she was next to him, everything had seemed crystal clear; this was a great opportunity. That clarity departed with her. He lies there feeling generally at risk. Some of it, he realizes, is because he is still naked. People are rarely naked. Most places are too fucking cold. Aliette's room is as hot as a stew pot, with its chimney and ceramic stove.

Martin gets out of bed. He finds the clothes he's been wearing, which are certainly not those he came in with, on the floor, and puts them on. He immediately feels less frail. The more clothes, the better. We are born naked – and buried naked. Does it count as naked if you're in a winding sheet? He thinks of himself, yesterday or the day before, yelling with shock and about to grab the bed curtains. He sits down at a small round table of elegant marquetry, turns his back on the luxurious bed, and wills one of the clockwork servants to show up with wine. Nothing happens. The world does not conform to our will, even in a whorehouse.

Of course, this is why there are whorehouses. The unending intractability of the world. Buggering thing. It doesn't give a shit about us. At least in a brothel you have a little control for a while. Sex is good, and money is good. You trade one for the other, that makes sense, whichever way you look at it.

Aliette comes in. Martin looks up at her from his seat at the table. "I will do it," he says.

PATTERNS

Leeuwenhoek has made sense of his notes on the honeydew. To them he has added a number of other observations, so he has another long letter ready to go. He tries not to dwell on his now all-consuming desire to impress these wrongheaded Englishmen. He tries to think of his efforts to convince them—all the money he is spending on Pierre, all the time he has invested when he ought to have been concentrating on business—not as groveling but as rational argument. For the advancement of philosophy. Pierre, unusually, has not been to the house for two days. But then, he has two sets of illustrations to do instead of just one. Leeuwenhoek has no doubt that he went straight on, after the philosophical drawings, to sketching out some fabric cartoons; a brick wall couldn't have stopped him.

It continues hot and unusually dry, so some afternoons the geese are home, huddling in the shady courtyard, rather than out in the field. The goose girl has been taking them to graze at night, sometimes staying until morning, despite Leeuwenhoek's protestations. She says there is some honeydew left in the pond. He has given her a jar and expects it back today. It is curious and faintly unsettling how he has come to depend on her. At any rate, he will soon have some live specimens to show to Pierre. The yard is empty and quiet this morning. She and the geese must have departed before dawn; the geese like to drink the dew on the grass stems, and it burns off fast in this weather. They will likely be back before noon.

So now, like a general, he waits for the reports of his lieutenants. This role is boring. He prefers to do things himself. The shop is not yet open. He could do more work in the study but is not in the mood; he is too eager for the honeydew to concentrate on anything else. He drifts backward through the house, away from the street, toward the kitchens, with the thought of getting something to eat. Passing through the great room, he sees Marieke playing with the dollhouse as she waits for breakfast. She rises early. Clattering comes from the kitchen; Barbara and the maid are in there. He will be underfoot. He sits down and watches Marieke in her silent concentration. She is setting the table in the tiny kitchen, carefully setting out plates and cups. "One for me and one for mama," she says to him, glancing over. "Would you like me to set a place for you, too?"

"Yes, please," he replies.

She brings a third walnut chair up to the table and sets out another tin plate and ceramic mug. Gleaming brass pans hang on the wall of the dollhouse kitchen over the little iron stove. "Aren't you going to cook?" asks Leeuwenhoek.

Marieke looks at him in surprise. "But mama's cooking! Can't you hear her?" she says.

"Yes, but she's cooking away there, in the big kitchen," he says, amused.

"No, she's right here. There's only one kitchen in this house," replies Marieke, pointing into the perfect little room.

"This one and the other one, they are the same then?" asks Leeuwenhoek.

"Of course. I am helping mama set the table." Marieke smooths down the silk tablecloth with its scalloped edge and makes minute adjustments to the table setting until she is satisfied.

"But then, when you are eating the food that mama has made, where will you be?"

"I will be right here. That's always my place," says Marieke, pointing to one chair. "And mama will be here, and you at the back, here."

"And at the same time, we'll all be in the big kitchen, back there?" He gestures to the rear of the house.

"Yes," she says. "In the kitchen. That's what being in the kitchen means. The room with the cookstove and the pans and all that. For cooking and eating. The kitchen. What does it matter if it's big or small?"

Leeuwenhoek considers. His seven-year-old daughter is perfectly calm, and perfectly convinced, and perfectly correct. But this isn't how he looks at it at all. Perhaps, he reflects, some of the goose girl's oddity is simply that she is a child and never pretends to be anything else. "Does mama know you are helping?" he asks finally.

Marieke looks at him pityingly. "Of course she does. I help her set the table every morning, and I never get in the way. She always thanks me. You know mama is very polite."

"She certainly is." He is not sure what else to say. He has stumbled into the secret proceedings of femininity. Many of these revolve around the dollhouse. He used to think of it as a toy and once made the mistake of saying so to Barbara. She had flared up at once: "It's no more a toy than your microscopes are, Antoni! It's a tool! For teaching girls how to run a household! Don't pretend to understand it!" Chastened at the memory, he asks his daughter humbly: "Do you suppose mama is done now? I am getting hungry."

"No, not quite yet. In another five minutes."

"How can you tell?"

"From the sound, papa. How else? Well, except maybe by the smell," Marieke replies.

He nods and settles in his chair. He is quite prepared to believe Marieke. He himself can't tell that breakfast is exactly five minutes away, whether by smell, sound, or any other means. How can she? A combination of sense acuity, childhood greed, and experience of the morning schedule, he conjectures. He sits quietly, watching the pendulum clock. Marieke rests on the stool that is placed by the dollhouse to make the upper rooms more accessible. She does nothing more to the small kitchen. After a moment, as if to explain her idleness, she says "there is no point cleaning up until after breakfast, you know."

"Quite so," he says.

Exactly four minutes later, Barbara appears at the door, beckoning them in to breakfast. She does not look surprised to see him there, though he does not always eat with them in the morning, and when he enters the kitchen, he sees three places set. He realizes that she must have heard them talking, but it does appear that she and Marieke have performed a magic trick. She gazes at him gravely, yet with a twinkle in her eye—how is it, exactly, that he can perceive such a minute change in her expression?—as he sits himself down in the chair that Marieke had previously indicated. Though he is tempted to sit somewhere else just to see what she would do ("Papa! That is not where you sit!"), he does not dare to. If a thing is perfect, you do not wreck it.

After eating, he leaves Marieke and her mother to the mysterious dual task of clearing up, and goes to open the shop. The morning is already bright and hot. He opens the shutters and the door, sweeps the entrance desultorily, smoothes out some fabrics on the shelves. He does not really expect business this early. He pulls a stack of notes out of a side drawer in the heavy wooden display table and retires to an upright chair in the corner, wincing at the poor drawings on top of the pile. They are in black ink, showing the beautiful and regular interior structures of a linden leaf. The pattern, if properly executed, he reflects, could compete with those botanical *toiles* that the French are starting to print now. He hears Vermeer guffaw in his head. Shut up, Johannes, he thinks: it *is* a botanical.

His assistant Joost, the apprentice he employs as a draper, arrives after about half an hour. The lad knows what he is doing, so Leeuwenhoek leaves him to it. There are no big orders in right now, and the accounts are up to date. Joost is younger, handsomer, and more charming than he is; women buy more cloth from him, anyway.

Heading toward the study, he hears cackling and honking through a window overlooking the courtyard: the geese are back. It will be too hot for them in pasture today. Poking his head through the window, he calls to the goose girl: "Do you have the honeydew?"

"Yes!" she calls back, picking up the glass jar from the cobbles and holding it up.

"Excellent!" he cries, and rushes out to get it.

She hands it over dispassionately, but just as he is disappearing inside with it, he hears her quiet, flat voice behind him asking, "Can I see it, too? Through the special eye?"

Leeuwenhoek is overcome by a surge of guilt. The girl has been living under his roof for months; how is it that she has never looked through a microscope? Because she has never asked? Or because he cannot hear the animalcules, so he jealously prevents her from seeing them? What is he, a dog in a manger?

"Yes, of course!" he replies quickly, turning back to her. "Do you want to come now?"

"Yes."

"Will the geese be all right?" This is a foolish question. They are in a gated courtyard.

"Yes."

"Of course they will. There's the gate, after all," Leeuwenhoek says.

"They don't need a gate. They stay where I am."

Leeuwenhoek is rather proud of his gate. "Well, at least it means other people can't steal them."

"If anyone tried, they would fight and be very loud," she says, shrugging.

"Perhaps just for the look of the thing, so that nobody wonders about your unusual powers as a goose herd?" he suggests.

She gazes at him expressionlessly. He abandons the topic of the gate. He beckons her inside the house. Going through the doorway into the darkened interior, he feels as if he is entering a burrow: a fox's den or a badger's sett. It is the goose girl's animal effect. She follows after him silently.

They enter the study. The goose girl stops and cocks her head. "Ah," she says, "the blood is here. And other things, though they are quieter."

"Can you hear the honeydew?" asks Leeuwenhoek. He is glad that no one else hears him asking such ridiculous questions.

"I think so. I could hear something as I was carrying it along the road. Or feel it. Whatever it is in that jar, it is quieter than blood. More peaceful. It doesn't buzz. I can just feel that it is alive."

"More like a vegetable, you mean? Like grass? Can you hear grass?"

"I think I can hear grass when everything else is very still. It is part of the general hum of things. But there's a lot of it. It's hard to tell."

"Is the honeydew more like that, or more like the blood?"

The goose girl considers. "More like grass than blood," she says finally.

Leeuwenhoek has been piping a little honeydew water into a capillary as they speak. He corks it and hands it to her. "Just take that to the window while I find a scope," he says. She moves toward the big front windows. He searches along the shelves for a viewer that he can clamp on, one which has a good lens with high magnification. He finds one, takes it to her, and shows her how to tighten the clamp onto the delicate glass. "Hold it up so the light comes through it, and look through the center of that little eye, the lens," he says. She does so. "You may need to move around to find the best light," he goes on. "What do you see?"

"I see a web of light," she says, "I see green glass balls floating in a huge empty space. It looks big enough I could walk into it. Could I walk into it?" She takes the glass away from her eye and looks at the tiny object in her hand, just as Pierre had done the first time. "How is it so big? How can it all fit in there? Is that their world?" She trails off, lifting the viewer back to her eye. After a while, she asks "Can they see us?"

"No," says Leeuwenhoek, thoughtfully. "They don't see the way we do. They have no eyes, or nerves, or brains. Nothing to see with."

"And we would be too big. They would need special eyes to make big things small. It would be the other way around for them," she says, still peering into the vial.

Leeuwenhoek pictures natural philosophers among the animalcules—a rare breed—assiduously making telescopes to view the human world. Macroscopes? Brilliant, infinitely small devices to reduce us to their size. Duly noting down our vast, planetary features, discussing them in meetings of their learned societies...

"Yes, I suppose they would. Like telescopes to look at the stars. Have you heard of those?"

"No."

"They do what you describe, in a way: you look through a tube, with lenses at both ends, and you can see something as far away as the moon, or a distant star that looks like a tiny spark, as if it were right in front of you. Huge. It's amazing. They look like you could touch them."

"Do you have one?"

"Yes, I have several. I have even made a few. But I find animalcules more interesting."

"Is the moon alive, like the little animals? Are stars alive?"

"No, I don't think so. Celestial bodies—things in the sky—are very large, and very far away, though, so we are not certain. Creatures may be found living on them, the way they live here on our world. Animalcules, for example."

"How would we ever find out, I wonder? They must be too far away to hear," says the girl vaguely, still poring over the honeydew. "So there are worlds in the sky? There are many worlds, aren't there? Most people think there is just one."

"They are wrong."

"Yes," she replies. She hands Leeuwenhoek the capillary and the scope. "Honeydew is beautiful. I am glad I saw it. It is too quiet to hear well. You are lucky that you can see it, and all the other little animals. You will learn a lot. For that, seeing is better than hearing."

"What is hearing good for, then?" he asks.

"Love."

Leeuwenhoek is struck by a small, circuitous sorrow. Love? He loves the animalcules. He is just embarrassed to say so. It is not philosophical.

"Love, in what way?" he asks her.

"Love? I don't know," she says, turning back to him briefly as she moves toward the door. "Love tells you things are there. You can't love something that isn't there, can you?" She nods, and heads silently back through the house to her geese.

Leeuwenhoek, raising the vial to his eye, looks forlornly at the honeydew. There they are, the bright green globules, tiny stars hanging in their own firmament. Here he is, standing in a shaft of dusty sunlight in his study in Hippolytusbuurt, a colossus. A silence as great as those between constellations hangs between them.

Fortunately, Pierre comes in within minutes to rescue him from gloom. As he had expected, the lad is clutching a folder of drawings and gleaming with suppressed excitement; all the light in the room seems to bounce off him as he rushes in from the darkened hallway. "I met the girl, coming out," he says. "Did you show her the microscopes?"

Leeuwenhoek nods. "And she brought some honeydew. I have it ready," he says.

Pierre puts the folder down immediately and comes to the window. "May I see?" he asks eagerly. He takes the vial and its viewer from Leeuwenhoek's hand and maneuvers to get the best light. "Ah," he says wistfully, after a moment. "God does it so much better than I. Really, it's embarrassing."

"Let us not be distracted by metaphysics, Pierre. Show me your drawings!"

Pierre puts the specimen carefully down on a shelf and returns to the work table. He opens the folder with a flourish and spreads a series of drawings out over the surface. Leeuwenhoek recognizes his own paper. Pierre's father is a cheapskate. "Here," says Pierre, gesturing to one side, "are the philosophical drawings for the letter, based on yours. Now that I see the live specimens, I think they could be improved. So perhaps I will do them again before we send them to England?"

"If you really think you can improve on them. They look excellent to me," says Leeuwenhoek, examining them.

"And then these, obviously," says Pierre, pointing to the others, "are very different. They are my attempts at a block pattern, at several scales. I think it could be scaled right up to the size needed for a tapestry cartoon, though I didn't have enough paper for that…"

Leeuwenhoek picks up a sheet of Pierre's elegant handiwork. It still resembles the honeydew, to his philosophical eye, but is more stylized. He tries to look at it with the eye of a draper.

"I thought it looked a bit like *cachemire*," says Pierre. "My mother said it looked like goose eggs."

"I have several *cachemires* in the shop. Let us go and look at them," Leeuwenhoek replies. Pierre nods and gathers up the papers. They proceed through the midsection of the house to the opposite end, where the shop is located, entering through the house door at the rear— the commercial door is open to the street, a too-bright gap next to the equally blinding window. Joost has the door wide open for air, and to encourage traffic, but has providently pulled the display table back from the window so the fabrics do not fade in the sun.

They have moved perhaps fifty feet and are still under the same roof, but they might as well be on a different planet. Joost looks up from the sample book he is perusing. A look of consternation passes over his face, and Leeuwenhoek can see a list of tasks passing through his mind—is there something he has forgotten to do? This is the look of apprentices everywhere. "It is fine, Joost," says Leeuwenhoek, coming forward. "Do you know my draughtsman, Pierre DeWitt? I don't think you've met."

Joost nods. Pierre nods and inclines his shoulders into a short bow. He is definitely a Catholic. "Are you the son of Matthias DeWitt?" asks Joost.

"Yes," replies Pierre.

"Ah, then my brother knows your cousin Martin. He also works for DeVeyne," says Joost.

Pierre nods.

"DeVeyne just fired him," continues Joost.

"Your brother?"

"No, your cousin. He hasn't been to the factory for three days."

"I wasn't aware," says Pierre. Lord and Savior, he thinks. How rich was that woman? Is Martin still off somewhere with her, half-drowned?

"News gets around in a place like DeVeyne's," says Joost. Pierre shrugs in agreement.

"Joost, can you find those *cachemires* we got in a little while ago? I'd like to get a look at them against this new design," says Leeuwenhoek. Joost heads to a shelf and begins to scan through bolts of printed muslin. After a moment he pulls two adjacent ones off the shelf.

"Here," he grunts as he heaves them onto the measuring table. He places them side by side and unrolls an ell of each, as if displaying them to a customer. "Two different grades, you see?"

Leeuwenhoek and Pierre move up to the table. Pierre puts his drawing down next to the two fabrics. Both samples of *cachemire* feature the complex little pear-shaped form with its jagged edge, each at a different scale. Leeuwenhoek says to Pierre, "so, which do you prefer, blue-and-red or purple-and-green?" He taps each one lightly with a finger.

"I prefer this one, on the left," replies Pierre coolly. "I like the larger print. Though it doesn't seem as well executed," he says, peering down at it closely.

"Cheaper. Bit of bleed," agrees Joost. "French. You can't get much quality from there in these prints now. Only some cheaper stuff floating around from a while ago. This pattern is probably a couple of years old."

"Likely," says Leeuwenhoek as Pierre glances at him for confirmation. "And the other is probably Dutch. More recent. Cleaner print. These patterns have been getting tighter, too, wouldn't you say, Joost, over the last few years?"

"Would you like me to look it up?" asks Joost.

"Yes. That would be helpful," says Leeuwenhoek. Joost checks the number on the bolt and heads toward a row of ledgers on a far shelf.

"Thanks," says Pierre in an undertone to Leeuwenhoek, "about the colors."

"Leave the colors to me, like I said," replies Leeuwenhoek, smiling. "They'd just be getting in the way for now. We need to think about the design."

Pierre looks at him gratefully and then turns his gaze back to the table. "I prefer the bolder look, the larger pattern, you see? That one is closer in scale to mine—though mine is even a bit bigger—what do you think? Too loud?"

"Good for curtains, carpets, table covers. Shawls, even. For dresses, no. But we mostly sell solid colors for dresses.

Stuffs with sheen, taffetas and so on, or subtler weaves like damask."

"Waistcoats? Handkerchiefs? What else do people make out of patterned cloth?" asks Pierre.

"Petticoats, linings, underthings of various kinds."

"Why, as people can't see them?"

"I have no idea. But people must get some satisfaction from it. And the toilette of rich women takes so long, and requires so much help, that at least lady's maids see them, for hours at a time."

"And husbands. Or lovers," adds Pierre.

"Though perhaps they are not looking primarily at the fabric," returns Leeuwenhoek.

Pierre thinks of Martin assessing the dress of the lady at the Mechelen. He is pretty sure his cousin could have put a price on everything she wore down to her shift, perhaps better than she could.

"Are you thinking of proceeding with the print first?" asks Pierre, "rather than full-woven tapestry?"

"It might make more sense. Less costly and more competitive. Easier to find a manufacturer. DeVeyne is the only local who has any tapestry looms at all. So we float the idea with a print, and if that sells, invest some of the profits into a more ambitious tapestry design: honeydew, or anything else that comes along."

"I can see the wisdom of that," says Pierre.

Joost returns with a ledger. "Yes, it is Dutch, that one. From Huisman in Amsterdam. Printed this year." He looks at Pierre's drawing on the table. "That isn't *cachemire*, is it?" he says. "But it's nice. Did you do it?" he looks at Pierre. "Where does it come from?"

Pierre looks at Leeuwenhoek uncertainly. Leeuwenhoek nods his permission. "Ah," says Pierre, "that is a bit surprising. It is honeydew, that stuff that grows in water, as seen through the master's microscope."

"Honeydew, that stinky stuff from ponds? Jesus. Why not just dye the whole sheet bright green and be done with it? How can that be honeydew?" He jabs his thumb at the pattern on the table.

"I assure you, Joost, it is honeydew. Each one of those forms is a tiny speck, so small you can't see it with your eye alone, but the microscope reveals them. They float around in rafts or colonies, just like that," says Leeuwenhoek, firmly.

"God. I was thinking it came from China, and you can scoop it out of the canal," replies Joost. "Wouldn't it be better just to say that? Who wants cloth covered in pond scum?"

Pierre represses a snort of laughter, causing a violent fit of coughing. Joost eyes him with a mixture of suspicion and fellow feeling, unsure how his master is going to react. Leeuwenhoek pounds the red-faced Pierre on the back a couple of times. He leaves off after a moment as Pierre, eyes streaming, recovers and waves him away. "You are not alone in thinking so, Joost," Leeuwenhoek says, "Vermeer told me something similar. Perhaps we won't mention it. But I had hoped that people might be interested in the beauty of natural philosophy."

"I wouldn't count on it," replies Joost. "Not if you want to make money."

"But, as a draper, what do you really think of the pattern?" asks Pierre, still wheezing.

"Oh, I like it. It's pretty. Like eggs or water droplets. It would look good in that purple-and-green. Or maybe just green, but a bit lighter. The effect would be quite different then. More French. Very good for curtains. Or upholstery."

Leeuwenhoek thinks back to his earlier reflections on the linden leaf. "Like those botanical *toiles*, you mean? With plant patterns and garden scenes and so on?"

"Yeah, those," says Joost. "Real money-spinners."

"Then we could just say it was a water plant. Put a fancy name on—" begins Leeuwenhoek.

"Water Garden," says Pierre abruptly.

"Yeah," says Joost, "perfect. Water Garden."

"Otherwise known as Pond Scum, though only to connoisseurs," says Pierre. All three of them laugh.

LIME

The geese do not like the heat. They insist on staying in the cool courtyard as much as possible. The problem with this is that their shit builds up abominably. Antoni has told her that the neighbors cannot be given any reason to complain, since he is not supposed to have fowls in the yard at all. So now she has to clean it constantly. She has never had to do this before; usually they are on the move, or in the fields. Goose shit is smelly, and sticky, and it gets everywhere. It's easiest to clean up when dried, but she can't let it wait around that long. So what should she do? Barbara is getting impatient with the mess. She has been haranguing Antoni about stench and vapors and disease, worrying about the child. She is very protective of the child, like a cow with a calf. Something must be done.

The girl spends a lot of time sweeping and has ruined the courtyard broom. She swills foul areas down with buckets of water, but it doesn't really drain, just dries again in the sun, and is almost as bad as before. So, now she is in the market, buying a new broom. Barbara told her where to go and gave her some money. She is heading toward a stall across the square, squinting in the bright sun. Her eyes are watering.

A voice speaks at her elbow. Peering up through the glare, she sees a bright blur. But the voice is familiar. It is that painter. Johannes. "What?" he says. "Usually it's only creditors who cry at the sight of me!"

"What is a creditor?" she asks, looking down at his feet. They are surprisingly small.

"Oh, people I owe money to. Never mind. What are you doing here? Where are your geese?"

"They are in the courtyard. They hate the heat. I need a new broom because they shit everywhere."

"Yes, it must be disgusting in this weather. Have you tried lime?"

"What is lime? What do you do with it?"

"It is white, powdery stuff, finer than sand. You can dig it out of the ground in some places. Mix it with water, and you can paint your walls with it: whitewash, they call it. Mix it with some other stuff, and you can make panels or canvases white with it. Painters know all about lime. But if you sprinkle it over the shit, it should help it to dry up and take the smell away."

"Where can I get some?"

"In the meat market, I imagine. I bet they use it there to clean up blood and so on. Come with me. I'm going that way anyway."

The goose girl follows the footsteps of the neat, small boots. It is still too light to look up. She has money. This will be more useful than a new broom. "What did you do with my hairs?" she asks him as they go along.

"Ah. Made paintbrushes with them, attached to the ends of goose feathers. Or, Antoni did. They are marvelous! You have very talented hairs!"

"Do I? Maybe the geese have talented feathers."

"I don't know. Both, perhaps. I have good luck with them, anyway. Do you know that apprentice of Antoni's, the pale boy, Pierre? I am doing a painting of him with one of those brushes right now. It is going superbly."

"Pierre, the white goose? Why are you painting him?"

They pass under the shadow of an awning. She sees two shrewd brown eyes looking down at her under the shade of a broad-brimmed hat. "The white goose?" he says, looking delighted. "Yes! Him! He is standing at the window in your master's study, looking through a silver microscope. The sun is breaking over his head like a wave on the beach."

"I have never seen the sea," she says.

"No? What have you seen, then?"

"Roads. Woods. Towns. Canals. Fields. Houses. Barns. Tall houses with huge spinning wings, except they do not fly—"

"Mills. They grind flour with big stones. Or pump water."

"They groan and scream in wind. We were near one once in a storm. Its neck stretched up, and it howled and beat and beat its wings. The geese were filled with fear and sorrow. They stood up high and stretched their necks and flapped and flapped, trying to show it how to take off. They still remember it, when the wind rises: the broken bird, in its vastness and thunder."

"My God," says the painter. "How do you know they remember?"

"They tell me. I can hear it in their minds, a huge whooshing noise. Their feathers bristle. They get very excited."

"You are a very strange child," says the man, Johannes. "Some kind of prodigy."

She ignores this. "In your painting, what little animals is Pierre looking at?"

"Little animals? Oh—through the microscope! Those creatures! Pierre? I have no idea."

"How can you have no idea, when you are doing the painting?"

"Really, I have no idea! Why should I?"

"You are looking at Pierre, and he is looking at the little animals. If your painting does not include them, it isn't showing everything that is there. What is the use of that?"

He stops and stares down at her. "What?" he says, "you cannot seriously expect me to be responsible for painting creatures not visible to the naked eye—if they are even there at all!"

"Of course they are there."

"A painter paints what he sees!"

"Antoni can see them. I have seen them, and Pierre."

"Well let them paint them, then!"

"Pierre draws them all the time."

"There you go. It's fine. Art can account for them. Just not mine."

"If Pierre was looking through a microscope, he was looking at little animals. You should have asked him what kind. Now they are missing. The painting is not true."

"Oh my God!" says Johannes, taking off his hat and crushing it to his breast, beginning to walk on. "Did Antoni put you up to this? It's insane! You're insane!"

"Isn't your painting one of Pierre seeing through the microscope?"

"Yes!"

"Then why doesn't it show what he is seeing?"

"Well, how could it? Pierre stands there, and we look at him. We are the same scale—the same size—as him. So what we see is him. The little animals are too small. He needs a microscope to see them himself! How could we see them, without a microscope ourselves?"

"So it only shows Pierre from the outside, your painting?"

"What?"

"It doesn't show what's in his eye, or in his mind? The little animals—he loves them, he sees them, that's why he's there with the special glass, looking. They are the most important thing. What's the point if we can't see them, too? I can see Pierre any time."

"Oh my God," says the painter, again, crushing his hat. "You must be joking. I'm sure Pierre is a very nice boy, but he'll be dead in fifty years. Or less. Gone. This painting, if I finish it, will still be here. Pierre will be there, inside it, his hair blazing, his eye glued to that little machine, looking, looking… What people will see, then, when we ourselves are dead—yes, even you!—is Pierre, in the light, with his passion. Understand me. People will see Pierre, in his effort at seeing. What else is there? I don't give a shit about your little animals!"

"I suppose that is something."

"Oh my God," mutters the small man, putting on his crushed hat. They continue across the market.

"Of course, there will be little animals there, anyway. On the painting. They are on everything. On the hairs. On the goose feather. Everywhere. Maybe not the ones Pierre is looking at through the glass. But some. Maybe you don't need to paint them."

"Well, thank all the saints for that! I have enough to be getting on with."

"Though it would be more fair if you did. Why not do a painting of Pierre, and the little animals, too? Paint them as small as they are, and keep a microscope near it? Then people could look through it and see what Pierre is seeing, just like him…see the inside…"

"But how could I paint so small? Who ever could?"

"I don't know. Maybe you would need to use a microscope to do it."

"But the tools! The brushes! They would need to be so fine you could hardly see them—not even your hairs are fine enough for that!"

"I guess not. Maybe you could do them a bit bigger. After all, Pierre is really much bigger than he would be in one of your paintings. Sizes are different in paintings."

"Yes."

"Why?"

"If I were to do a painting of Pierre as big as he really is, who has a wall big enough to put it on? Might as well just invite him over and be done with it. That's not the point. Paintings like mine show scenes of the world that we know, but small, so you can carry them around in your hands. Concentrated. Like genever. It takes half a field of grain to make a bottle of genever, and you can carry that around in your hands, too."

"Geese would rather just have the grain. They'd stay to eat it, and carry nothing."

"Liquor. Paintings. People make those. We're desperate to store everything. To keep hold of pleasure. Geese are not."

"If you did a painting of the geese, in the courtyard, say, would it just be from the outside, too?"

"Obviously that would not satisfy you? How else should it be? I should turn them inside out and paint their guts, too?"

"No. You said painters paint what they see. Geese also see. If we look at them, they look at us. That is what happens in the world. Why isn't the painting like that, too?"

"Ah, I am getting it now. You want the goose's perspective—what things look like if you are the goose in the painting. Not just what a person sees looking at the goose. Both. That would be a complete picture to you?"

"Yes."

"How do I know what the world looks like to a goose? Now, I know what you're going to say—" he holds up a warning finger, glancing at her— "you're going to say that you can, and I might even believe you. But I can't. So I can't paint it. Unless I make it up, and I hate pretending. It's why I don't paint angels. Did a few on commission years ago, and they were godawful. So who will paint your goose paintings? Can you? Can they?"

"No."

"I don't deny it's a lovely idea. Wonderful, in fact. I may never be able to get it out of my head. The seer and the seen, you might say, in conversation. A painting of the whole act of seeing. Miraculous. —I wonder, could it be done with inset panels? But no— No. I am not your man. I find painting hard enough as it is, even if it's just—what did you say?—from the outside…"

The child trots silently beside him for a moment. "I guess hearing is just better than seeing for that," she says in her flat voice.

"For what?"

"For getting to the inside. So you know how things are. How they feel. What it is like to be them."

"You mean, if people tell you in words and you hear it? Then you know how they feel?"

"In words, yes. People do that. But not geese, or little animals. They just make sounds. They can be big or small. But the sounds tell you how they are alive. How they live. The sounds, the voices, that is them. Themselves. Pictures are never like that. They just stop on the outside."

"Jesus," says Johannes. "That is practically a mortal insult. So what have I been doing all these years?"

The girl says nothing. His speech trails off. They are at the meat market. Smells, fresh and rancid, are rising around them. Fodder and blood, shit and offal. There is bleating from pens along one side. A man with blood on his arms up to the elbow is chopping lamb on the counter of the central booth. The painter leads her toward him.

"This girl," he says to the butcher, "needs some lime to dry up goose shit in a yard. Do you sell it?"

"Well, I can sell her a little," says the man slowly, "from my own supply. But not much. How much do you need?"

"I don't know," says the goose girl. "There are eleven geese, and it's not a big courtyard. A house courtyard."

"They been there some time?"

"Yes, over the hot spell. Mostly they are pastured."

"Four-five cups should do it. Every two or three days. You know what to do?"

She shakes her head.

"You sprinkle it, thin like, over the wet areas. Leave it an hour, maybe two. Then sweep it up. Helps dry it out, keeps the smell down. Wash your hands after. Lime burns your eyes."

She nods. She holds out the money Barbara gave her to buy the broom. The butcher looks at it in surprise. He glances at the painter, who smiles back at him cheerfully and also looks at the money. The man places the coins carefully on an unbloodied area of the counter and moves a few steps away to the rear of the booth, dries his hands, and opens a barrel off to one side. He scoops several heavy scoops of what looks like flour out of the barrel into a rough fodder sack, ties the neck, and brings it back to the counter. "Enough for three sweepings, I'm guessing," he says, weighing the sack in his hands. He takes one coin from the three lying on the counter and nudges the other two back to her. Johannes looks on, unperturbed.

"Much obliged, now she knows where to come," says the painter, politely, as she takes up the sack and turns away. The butcher nods judiciously and returns to his chopping.

"Well, he probably would have ripped you off worse if I hadn't been there," says Johannes, "but I can't be sure. I couldn't tell you what raw lime costs. I wouldn't pay more than that in future, anyway."

"All right," she says. "I hope it works. I don't want Antoni to get in trouble."

"Antoni, eh?" he says, his brows rising toward the brim of his hat, "well, no more do I. Best to keep the neighbors happy. And the geese. Phew. It stinks. Let's move along." The goose girl nods.

"And it's loud," she says.

"The flies, you mean? The animals squealing?"

"All those, yes. And the little animals, buzzing, buzzing, underneath it all. There are many here. Very many."

"You mean those microscopical creatures that Antoni sees? Those again? You hear them buzzing? Is this what you meant before? I hear nothing. Are you sure?" He glares down at the girl. "Does Antoni know this?"

"Yes."

"So you are standing here in this market and hearing the voices of *invisibilia* all around us, while I, the blind painter, stand here like an idiot, seeing none of them, missing half the world?"

"Yes."

"I might as well just set myself on fire," says the painter. "You are infuriating, and I am sure you are mad. Still, Antoni is on your side. The creatures he has seen through his microscopes, I know they are real. I have even seen them." He tugs on the brim of his tortured hat. "I will just have to accept that painting is a smaller enterprise than I thought. And I must say I don't like it at all."

The goose girl stands before him, clutching her sack of lime.

"For God's sake, don't mention this to anybody else," says the painter abruptly. "It's too odd. Most people don't want their world to expand this fast. It makes us feel irrel-evant. So keep your mouth shut."

"That is what Antoni says, also."

"Good. I hope the lime makes some improvement. My best to your master, and to Barbara," says the small man. He makes a short bow and leaves with a brief, quiz-zical smile.

The goose girl returns home. She will have to use the old broom.

THE CLIENT

Martin stands just inside the door of a handsome great room outfitted in mahogany panels. Candlelight gleams out into a polished hallway. He is about to entertain his first client. He has just arrived and has not yet taken off his hat. He is to wait in this room for the lady.

She is a musician. A fine spinet stands in one corner. Music, which he cannot read, is displayed on a bracket in front of it. He has been told that he may be expected to sing. If the lady wants him to sing French songs to her accompaniment, she is about to be sadly disappointed. He will have to try and make up for it in other areas. About those, at least, he is reasonably confident. Aliette is a firm tutor.

He is exquisitely dressed. His hat alone, with its white cockade, cost more than any suit—breeches, vest, coat, shirt, and all—he has ever worn before. His linen is stark white, spotless. His boots are made of glove leather. He wears a half cape lined with sable. Every inch of his skin is clean, his hair is washed; even his teeth have been scrubbed and his breath scented with mint. He feels himself practically glowing as he stands there.

He looks good in this room. He lives up to it. He is just as beautiful as the heavy silver flagon on the table, the delicate green wine glasses, the perfect chilled and misted grapes in the porcelain bowl. He had not fully appreciated his own beauty before. He hadn't been able to put a price on it. Women's beauty is much easier to assess. It's clear what it's good for. What good is handsomeness to most men, in most trades? It might impress your tailor. Let you stand up faster at village dances. Earn you a little extra respect in your business dealings: a fine figure of a man. But really, only women like it, and who cares what women think?

Martin is used to being noticed by women, in the same way that he notices attractive women himself. So what? How many women can you fuck in a day? Assuming that, by a series of miracles, such a thing is on offer, that the woman in question is not too polite, modest, married, maidenly, devout, snobbish, filthy, or entirely surrounded by her male kin? Ninety-nine times out of a hundred, female attention is no use to him. Most women are too busy, too cautious, and too supervised even to flirt. And as for actual business, he conducts it with very few of them, even in the garment trade.

Aliette has opened his eyes to the fact that the attention of women can be money in the bank. And probably not just his clients or patronesses. Many women. Rich women. Married women. Ones who would never pay outright for his services, but who will introduce him to women who will. Who will take him into the charmed circle of their lives, and introduce him to their husbands and sons and nephews, and all the patronage that they command, just for being handsome and attentive. For being a beautiful man.

He hears rustling in the hall, near silent footsteps approaching the door. The lady is wearing soft shoes, leather or silk slippers, not wooden pattens that click on the floor. Evidently she is not concerned with preserving her footwear. Or getting cold feet; not in this weather. He stands like a sentinel just inside the door frame, allowing passage for her wide skirts, waiting to doff his hat.

Sarah Tolmie

A glistening, whispering presence, all silver reflections, glides up to the door. At the threshold, the lady stops, inclines her golden head and performs a brief curtsy. Martin removes his hat and bows. He feels like a nobleman in a pantomime. What does she feel like? It is odd and exciting, meeting a stranger, one you might end up fucking in a very short time, skipping all the usual preliminaries. Such is the power of money.

"Mevrouw," he says, rising from his bow. He does not use the name of her late husband.

"Martin," she replies. Aliette has told him to expect her to use his Christian name. He is a servant and an intimate. Already.

She swishes by in a crackle of taffeta, heading to the spinet. "Please come in," she says, glancing over her shoulder at him, "and pour wine if you would like some. Can you sing?" She has a long patrician face, close-set blue eyes, and an overbite that gives her words a slight shushing sound. Her dress would buy a farm. The hair that has artfully escaped from her elaborate pinned-up braids frames her face in soft curls. She looks to be in her middle thirties, a matronly age, though her skin is pale, perfect, and unlined. She has no children.

Martin moves to the table, pours two half-glasses of wine, and brings one of them to her as she settles at the spinet. She inclines her head graciously. "I can sing, yes," he says, "I have a fine repertoire of vulgar songs. I am afraid I may know none of yours." He gestures to the music before her.

"No matter," she says. "Perhaps you can turn the pages of this music? I can tell you when." She sips her wine and puts it down on top of the instrument. Martin nods and sips his wine and also puts it down. Aliette has warned him not to get drunk. He waits at her side and a little behind her, within reach of the music book. She squints at the page briefly, flexes her fingers, and begins to play a fast, pretty, and complicated tune that he does not know. Her fingers hit the keys with considerable force. Her hands weave a series of repeating patterns across the board. He is reminded of himself at the loom. The instrument probably has strings inside it. He would like to get a look at the interior. Are they plucked somehow, or struck with hammers? Weaving. He can't get away from it.

"Now," she says.

Now? thinks Martin, contemplating her moving hands. Now what? Then he remembers what he's doing and turns the page. He hopes he wasn't too slow.

She does not look up or pause. He sees her eyes flickering across the page. He has no idea what the notation means, except that it is obviously a pattern that tells her what keys to press. Like a loom pattern: when to hit the treadles to raise and lower the threads. The bit she is playing now reminds him of a dance tune. She is weaving it out into the air. Her chest rises and falls as her breathing quickens. She has freckles on her *décolletage*. He counts fifteen pearls at the front of her necklace; the rest are hidden under her hair.

"Now," she says. He turns the page. She races for the finish. A slight flush is rising in her cheeks, and her bosom is blotchy under her pearls. She is working hard. She is probably also nervous. Why is she doing this? To impress him? To calm herself? Or does she need someone to listen to her playing? Someone other than the housemaids, or the cook?

"Hah!" she says, blowing out her breath as she completes a final trill and comes to an end. Martin claps, not too loudly. She smiles and pushes back her dampening hair, looking demure, triumphal, and sheepish all at once.

She picks up her wine and takes a hearty swig. Martin picks up his and does likewise. They look at each other over the rims of their glasses. The half moons of her fingernails are pink with exertion. "So," she says, after a minute or two, "let's see, do you know 'The Wind That Shakes the Barley'?"

"What?" says Martin, surprised and a bit embarrassed. "That old thing? Mevrouw! Here?" It's a popular song, of course. He's sung it many times. It doesn't sound rude on the surface but really it's quite dirty. Her eyes twinkle.

"Yes. Here."

"But surely you can't play that on the spinet?"

"You'd be surprised at the things I can play," she replies. "On the spinet."

Martin looks at her, aghast. There's nothing for it. He will have to sing. He moves to the side of the instrument. He takes another sip of wine. He keeps hold of the glass. Usually he sings with a glass in his hand. The lady watches him closely and sits with her hands poised. "Go on," she says.

He takes a deep breath and begins "The Wind That Shakes the Barley." His deep voice seems incredibly loud in the small, echoing room. Usually he sings in pubs, at parties, outdoors, over noise. He tries not to shout. After one verse, the lady joins in. She plays simply and sparingly, nothing so complex as before. She does not sing. She listens, and adds a few notes here and there. The spinet is louder than a lute, which is the only instrument he has ever sung to before. Tactfully, she keeps it in the background. He is impressed. He is so busy keeping track of things that he does not worry about all the bawdy jokes he is making as he sings the words. He sings right through to the end, and then, not knowing what else to do, raises his glass to her.

She nods in acknowledgment, picking up her own glass. "You sing very well," she says. "I thought that song would suit you because of your speaking voice. But you are trying to be quiet. There is no need. You are a big man; you have a big voice. Just sing. And breathe from your belly." She stands up, comes over, and prods him gently with two fingers, just below the navel. "From there." She is back sitting down at the instrument again, shaking her lace sleeves back, before his mind has fully grasped that she has touched him. This is really not what he expected whoring would be like, at all.

"So, let's do it again," she says, looking at him expectantly. "Though you might want to pour more wine?"

He does so, carefully not overfilling the glasses. He brings hers over and places it on top of the spinet. He keeps hold of his, not sure what else to do with it. He draws breath to sing.

"No," she says peremptorily. "From the belly. Remember? Down there." She points to his abdomen. "Your chest should hardly rise at all. But your breeches should feel tight. Ready? Again."

Martin takes another breath, trying to force the air down into his belly and keep his chest still. It feels odd. The waist band of his breeches tightens. He had anticipated feeling tightness in the breeches over the course of the evening, but certainly not for this reason. The thought is so comical that he lets out a short bark of laughter, which he immediately disguises as a series of coughs, using up the rest of the enormous breath he has drawn. The lady looks at him with concern. "I know this can be hard," she says.

He gathers his wits, breathes from his belly again, and sings. She lets two verses elapse before she joins in at the keyboard. He sings right through the song, trying not to hold back. This time, he is much more aware of all the *doubles entendres.*

"Again," she says, as soon as he gets to the end. "Stand up straight. Don't thrust out your chin. You will get a better tone."

He sings the song again. He tries to stand up tall, tuck in his chin, breathe from his belly, and remember the words, which seem to get more obscene each time he repeats them. He actually blushes at the chorus. His belly is getting sore. Much more of this and he may keel over. Is she going to keep him singing all night?

This time when he finishes he drinks off his wine in two gulps, holding the glass up with trembling fingers. She takes pity on him. "Breathing like that is hard until you get used to it," she says, "I'm sure that's enough for tonight." She comes over to him once more and pokes him unceremoniously just below the third button of his waistcoat. He can feel his muscles protesting. "Just practice. Practice filling this up with air." Then she reaches up and strokes the hollow of his throat very gently, just below the Adam's apple. Her fingers are hot. "And here, keep it loose. No stretching, no pressure. You will sing so much better."

Martin catches her hand as she rests it lightly there, and kisses her fingertips. She has touched him twice now. She can't be expected to do everything herself. "I am sure I will," he says, kissing the back of her hand, then her wrist. The pulse there is jumping, fleet as her fingers on the keyboard. She watches him steadily, as if assessing his technique. Slowly she reaches up her other hand and strokes the side of his face and his hair. He does the same to her, and bends down, grazing the edge of her face between chin and ear with nibbling lips. He does not kiss her on the mouth. He does not boorishly grab her. He is supposed to be a professional. Ten thousand instructions from Aliette flood his mind. He pushes them away. Right now, in this room, with this woman, he figures that what he will do is what she just showed him. He will follow.

He will be the accompanist.

BLOCKING

Pierre did his part in making the design. Now Leeuwenhoek must do his own part. He would prefer to get
the job done locally to save time and shipping costs. So
he is talking to DeVeyne. His is the largest fabric operation in Delft.

He waits in the factory office, surrounded by account
books and sample books. He has been here many times
before, but as a buyer. It feels quite different, being here
in order to sell something. He has to admit it makes him
nervous. DeVeyne is out on the factory floor, examining a
machine. This is fine with him. How do salesmen do this?
He is a retailer himself, but people come to him. You go
to a draper's shop if you want to buy cloth or at least price
it. That is simple. It's not like he's out hawking brocade
on the street.

DeVeyne comes in, a tall thin man with a long nose.
He is famous as a harsh master, but he still employs more
people than anybody else in the area. And famous as a
hard bargainer, but he still sells more cloth.

"Christophe," says Leeuwenhoek, rising to shake his
hand. He lays the folder of drawings down on the desk
to do so.

"Antoni," says DeVeyne, "what have you got there?"
He looks at the folder. "Sit down."

Leeuwenhoek sits. "A fabric design. I am looking for
someone to print it, in the first instance."

"In the first instance?" says DeVeyne, "and then what? You might want tapestry weave then? Is that why you've come to me?"

"Yes," replies Leeuwenhoek. There is no point in indirection with DeVeyne.

"Let's see it, then. Show me," says DeVeyne. He lifts up the spectacles that are dangling around his neck on a leather cord, perches them on his long nose, and sits down at the desk. Leeuwenhoek pushes the folder toward him. He opens it carefully and spreads several drawings of the pattern at various scales and densities over the surface. He squints at them silently, one after the other.

Leeuwenhoek is encouraged. If the man had not liked them, he would have pushed the folder back at first glance. A man for snap decisions, DeVeyne. "This isn't quite your normal line, is it?" asks DeVeyne. "Where'd you get it?"

"My apprentice and business partner—in this—Pierre DeWitt."

"Where'd he get it?"

"It's a common botanical. We call it Water Garden."

"Chinese? Indian? What?"

"No, it's a local design. We worked it up from nature."

"From nature, eh? What the hell does that mean? I've never seen anything like it before."

"No, you wouldn't have. Do you like it? Would it print well?"

DeVeyne picks up a sheet and holds it at arm's length, peering over his glasses. "Yeah, I like it. Strong. It would compete with those bloody French prints. God, I'm sick of those things."

"Could you do up a couple of color samples?"

"Yeah," says DeVeyne, putting the drawing down and turning to pick out a sample book behind him. "Cotton? Linen? What kind of weave?"

"Better see both. Mid-weight muslin; light linen. Plain weave. Nothing too fancy for now."

DeVeyne pushes the sample book across to him. "What about colors? Take a look here. Green, right, if it's a botanical? What shade? And indigo. You can sell just about anything in indigo, I swear to God. And then there's this rust color, kind of like a red brick, or bright ochre, very fashionable now."

Leeuwenhoek leafs through the book of swatches. Cottons. Linens. Dye formulas in DeVeyne's spidery writing. He hadn't thought of indigo, but it makes sense. There's a craze for it. The rusty color is quite nice. The bold print would look rather demure in it. He had been thinking chiefly of green, of course, like the honeydew itself. But he needs to get away from that whole idea. He is not going to say anything about honeydew at all. Nobody cares what color it is except him. Not even Pierre.

"Indigo, yes. Rust, yes. And green, obviously. Which would you choose? I like this lighter one, like a lime leaf..." says Leeuwenhoek.

DeVeyne comes around and looks over his shoulder. "Yeah, that's good. I think you want to keep it light; that print's loud. It's going to poke your eye out in indigo. But some people like that."

"Right. Go with that one, then."

"So," says DeVeyne, taking off his glasses and looking down at Leeuwenhoek, "I will do your samples. A couple of times each to get a clean print. 10 to 12 ells per; it's not worth doing less than that. I'll do them free, but I get right of first refusal if you want to print in bulk. You know what it'll cost me to set up the machines."

"Done," says Leeuwenhoek. He had already decided to accept any reasonable offer from DeVeyne. The man is canny, and when he decides something he moves fast. You have to know exactly what you want when dealing with him, and no dithering. He stands up. They shake hands again.

"I'll let you know as soon as they're ready," says De-Veyne. "Set-up will take a while." Leeuwenhoek nods and strides out of the office.

Water Garden is on its way. Soon the ladies of Delft will be carrying handkerchiefs covered with microscopic creatures. He thinks suddenly, Just like the goose girl. Probably the ladies will not hear voices emanating from them, however. Not even if they spotted them with their mothers' blood. The very idea is macabre.

What about a pattern based on blood?

Those handsome discs? In cherry red? In that rust color? He shakes his head. The idea is fantastic. Ridiculous. Human blood?

Then again, he has just sold the hard-headed Christophe DeVeyne on pond scum.

WATER GARDEN

Finally the heat breaks. There is a terrific thunderstorm, and the air changes. The girl and the geese depart at dawn for the pasture. The courtyard, now whitened with lime, is finally silent.

Everyone is relieved. Especially Barbara, at least once the storm is well over. That she had lain through, rigid and silent in her bed, rising at dawn with her hands cramped from clutching the bedclothes. Now she takes Marieke on walks through the town, along the canals, out to be fitted for new shoes. The little girl is delighted to be outside, freed from three weeks of domestic captivity; her mother had kept her at home, out of the hot sun and away from the reeking water. Even the best efforts of the Water Board, flushing the system, keeping the canal water constantly moving, had not been able to prevent it from stinking. Now it is approaching normal again.

Business, which had been flagging, picks up again. Joost is busier in the store. Leeuwenhoek assigns him a few extra hours, as he himself is so busy with Pierre. They have embarked on a series of observations of summer plants: grasses, weeds, and flowers. They have looked at samples of the goose shit ("Might as well get some good out of all this crap," said Pierre). And Leeuwenhoek has taken a long series of samples out of the canals, on different days, to see what changes occur at the microscopical level during this unaccustomed heat. The samples become more and more active as the heat mounts; the density and variety of animalcules climbs drastically. He even sees some honeydew-like particles, though sheets or ropes of green stuff are not visible in the water. This is really information that he ought to share with the Water Board, but he is not sure how to explain it to them. The whole nation is built on water, he thinks, surely it would be best to know what is in it? But he doubts that the impatient engineers and pompous guildsmen of the Board would listen. Perhaps if he lived in Amsterdam, where Hudde, the philosopher, is mayor...

Busy as he is, he feels in his heart that he is waiting. Waiting for the fabric samples, or for the next letter from the Royal Society? If he is being honest with himself, he knows it is the latter. After the *débacle* of their first one, why should he even bother? Why should he allow himself and his work to be insulted? And Pierre's? Yet he finds a constant narrative running in his head as he works, explaining, defending, justifying. Somehow he has got to get those Englishmen to believe him. Why is he so much more concerned with their good opinion than with the Water Board? It makes no sense. Except that to interest the merchants of the Board in animalcules, he would have to talk to them in terms of profit and loss or civic safety. It is difficult to explain animalcules in this way. He has ascertained their presence, but not their function. He cannot make their practical implications clear to the Board because he is not yet sure of them himself. Of course he would like to be. Yet practicality is not his sole concern. There is a part of him that desires the study of animalcules to be disinterested. An end unto itself, with its own intellectual nobility, like the more rarefied parts of theology. What did Reinier say about the Society? The new clerisy? An international body of learned men, pursuing topics that most people do not even know to exist? In Latin, moreover? As a member of a reformed church, there is much about this of which he ought to be suspicious.

And of course to expect the English to be disinterested is ridiculous. The English are obsessed with money. In trade, they are rank profiteers. Pirates. To imagine the members of the Society as exempt from such crassness—as selfless, dedicated amateurs—is folly. Most people participate fully in their national vices. Probably his desire to please the Royal Society is just a new form of snobbery: the wish to belong to an elite international brotherhood. And yet, and yet—these are the only men in the world with whom he can discuss the amazing anatomy of wheel bugs! Other than, perhaps, the goose girl. But no one is going to give him a certificate for that.

The color samples, predictably enough, arrive first. Writing to a Delft haberdasher is hardly the Royal Society's main priority. DeVeyne, on the other hand, is pursuing a business opportunity. Joost taps on the study door at midday. He pokes his head in and says "Master, some cloth has come from DeVeyne. Looks like samples. You said I should tell you."

Pierre, who is usually impossible to distract when he has a scope to his eye, looks up at once. Leeuwenhoek puts down the fragment of leaf he is preparing. He is curious, too. "Thank you, Joost. We will come at once," he replies. Joost disappears.

Pierre puts the scope on a shelf, and the two hurry through the house to the shop. Joost is there, unrolling the samples. He spreads them on the big table, cottons in a row, linens in a row, the ends of the short bolts drooping off opposite ends. He lines the three colors up. Joost has an orderly mind. "Hey, these are great!" he says. "Isn't that the pattern you made?"

"Water Garden," says Pierre. He comes up to the table hesitantly. Leeuwenhoek has never seen him look so self-conscious before.

Before Joost can say anything else, Leeuwenhoek says heartily, "So, Pierre, which do you prefer? Red, indigo, or green?" He gestures casually to each. He turns to his apprentice: "And you, Joost? What about you?"

"Ah—" say Pierre and Joost, at exactly the same time. Joost subsides respectfully. He really is a good sort of lad, thinks Leeuwenhoek. "I like the darkest one, the one with the most contrast, I have to say—so, indigo," says Pierre. "I realize it's loud. But I like the pattern. I happen to know the designer."

Joost laughs. "I like the indigo," says Joost. "I love indigo, like everybody. I don't mind a dark line; it makes the forms nice and clear. But I also like the green. It has that elegance. I can see it in the Mechelen, say, for curtains…"

"But not the rust?" says Leeuwenhoek.

"No," says Joost. "I like the color but it doesn't seem right for that pattern."

"I agree with you," says Leeuwenhoek thoughtfully. "So, one bold and one subtle? I think I can persuade De-Veyne to that."

"Yes," says Pierre.

"You putting up the money yourself, master?" asks Joost.

"Some," replies Leeuwenhoek. "And I think De-Veyne will want to invest, if only costs, or he wouldn't have agreed. He already has, in effect, by producing the samples."

"And my father," says Pierre, definitely.

Sarah Tolmie

"You looking for any other investors?" says Joost. "I could see my uncle being interested, but of course I can't speak for him."

"If you think he might be interested, I can't see the harm in talking to him," says Leeuwenhoek. Pierre nods. Always share the risk, his father says. Probably another reason Matthias isn't a serious artist. You can't share the risk of painting.

"I propose one cotton and one linen. The question is, which should be which?" says Leeuwenhoek. "My thought is soft green linen, indigo cotton. What do you think?"

"I think so, too," says Joost. "Softer print for draperies, and bolder for scarves and shawls and linings and whatnot."

"As I am not a draper, I defer to your expertise," says Pierre. "Seems sensible to me."

"Joost, you can take the samples to your uncle, as long as you are careful with them. And don't let anybody else see them, within reason," Leeuwenhoek continues, "while I talk production terms with DeVeyne. Pierre, I guess I had better talk to Matthias?"

"Yes," says Pierre, "I will let him know this evening. And—" he hesitates— "you'll want to watch DeVeyne."

Leeuwenhoek raises his eyebrows at the much younger man. Joost looks profoundly glad that he did not make this remark himself, but immediately agrees. "He's hell to work for, my brother says."

"It's more that stuff he produces he assumes he owns." Pierre goes on, doggedly. "Martin has designed tapestries for him. He's been paid a pittance and can't use the designs again, according to DeVeyne. I don't know that Martin or the family has ever offered to invest, though. That may make a difference."

"I will keep that in mind," says Leeuwenhoek.

"Should I take the samples tonight?" asks Joost.

"Yes," says Leeuwenhoek, "faster is better. Pierre, tell Matthias I will drop by tonight or tomorrow night, if that is convenient. Actually, no, tomorrow—so I can bring the samples with me."

"Yes, he may have trouble believing you if you don't have those," says Pierre dryly. A snort from Joost. Dear God, thinks Leeuwenhoek, am I really going into business with apprentices? He soothes himself with the thought of their solid, respectable families.

"One moment," says Leeuwenhoek, and vanishes through the house door. Pierre and Joost listen to his rapid footsteps fading into the house, then returning. He bursts through the door once more, carrying a bottle of genever and three tiny glasses. He fills all three and hands them round.

"To the Water Garden!" he says.

"Water Garden!" say Pierre and Joost, raising their glasses. "The Water Garden!"

TRUST NO MAN'S WORD

MnH Antoni Van Leeuwenhoek,
Hippolytusbuurt, Delft in Holland

MnH Van Leeuwenhoek,
The Royal Society is in receipt of your letter dated 18
April, describing and illustrating in detail the plant-like
formation apparently to be found in stagnant water, the
which you term honeydew, and containing as well a variety
of other microscopical observations, viz. of insect wing cas-
es in cochineal, solid particles in soot, the eye of a pismire,
and further *animalcula* of diverse kind that you claim, just
as in your first letter dated 3 December, to have discovered
in pond water. Certain of your microscopical observations
fall into line with ones that have been made by our members—those of cochineal, and of the insect eye, for example, both of which seem to us exceedingly well observed
and illustrated—while others we have remained unable
to reproduce or confirm. The variety of translucent and
motile bodies that you claim to have discovered in water
is particularly astonishing to us, and if true, must indeed
represent a major microscopical discovery. How you can
have achieved these results using only a simple single-lens
microscope defies our understanding.
    In my previous correspondence with you, which I am
sure you cannot but remember with displeasure, I con-
veyed the initial view of the Society that your results were
fantastical. In light, however, of the provable quality of
many of the observations contained in your second letter,

this position no longer seems tenable. Moreover, in the interim, we have received a letter from MnH Dr Reinier De Graaf, anatomist and graduate of Angers, attesting to the indubitable quality of your lenses, which he claims are the best he has ever seen or used. He goes so far as to say that he considers them the best in Europe.

In light of the foregoing information, we propose the following course of action, if it is acceptable to you. At our earliest convenience, we will dispatch a learned observer, either a member of the Society or a responsible delegate, to you in Delft, so that he may look at the samples you have prepared, through your optical devices, with his own eyes. If, indeed, your microscopes have reached such impressive powers of magnification and resolution, he will doubtless be interested to obtain some, should you be willing to part with any or to impart instructions as to their fabrication. If he is able to verify your observations of the *animalcula* in water, in particular, he will then be able to congratulate you on a very significant discovery, one of enough consequence to admit you to the Society as one of our (decidedly rare) foreign members. As arranging such a visit will involve considerable efforts, the which, of course, cannot be undertaken without your consent, we would appreciate your reply to our proposal as soon as may be. We hope that you will accept this hand of friendship, knowing that it is extended not in the spirit of inquisition but of free inquiry, and that the further association with the Society it might afford will prove valuable to you in your work.

Respectfully, sir, I remain,

Henry Oldenburg.
Secretary, The Royal Society of London

"What in hell is that stamped at the bottom?" says Pierre, holding the elaborate English letter in one hand and the short and inept Dutch *précis* in the other. "Trust no man's word? Lord and Savior! That's disgusting. It's unchristian. What? It's an insult!"

"It's the motto," says Reinier De Graaf languidly from his place on the window sill. "Coat of arms with it and all. It's the *royal* Society, don't you know? They slap that *royal* on everything in England now. Mind you, those republicans who were previously running the island weren't that big on philosophy, whereas I've heard the king actually attends their demonstrations." Leeuwenhoek chuckles, but Pierre looks scandalized. "Don't worry about it. It means: trust no man's opinion. Use your own eyes. It's the motto of empirical inquiry. Though it could just as well be a religious one: trust no man but only God."

"Which are we after?"

"Both," says Leeuwenhoek firmly. "God made animalcules; we confirm them with our own eyes, to his glory. As far as I am concerned, there's an end to it."

De Graaf looks at him with approval. "You will end up a diplomat."

"It's amazing luck that you turned up on the very day this arrived," says Leeuwenhoek. "We've been waiting for months."

"It's divine providence."

"I notice they had no trouble trusting your word, Dr De Graaf," says Pierre, still staring at the letter.

"The English can't open their mouths without lying. They say two things at once as naturally as breathing. Once you realize this, they become much easier to deal with," replies De Graaf. Pierre does not look mollified. He regards the letter with loathing.

"I can't believe they don't trust you! Sending out this observer like an inquisitor from the Vatican! Who do they think they are?"

"They are the men who sponsored Hooke's *Micrographia*, which everyone in Europe has read, Pierre. The guild masters of a fast-growing new trade, along with the French Academy," says De Graaf. "We have to accept it."

"Well, then, we should have one here, in the Republic! We should be reporting to them! Not these foreigners!"

"Have you discussed this with the mayor? The regents? They are very busy men. Too busy for natural philosophy," replies De Graaf.

"But—"

"You might talk to Huygens, of course. He is a learned man. Or Swammerdam, though he is completely crazy. Draws even better than you, though, Pierre," continues De Graaf. "Frankly, I think you're well out of it. Let the Englishmen come, be duly impressed, sign Antoni up, and go away. You'll have someone to talk to, but they'll be too far away to control you. Even if you were in Amsterdam, you'd have Hudde looking over your shoulder; he's a nice fellow and a fine mathematician, but he is the mayor. Here you are on your own. It's ideal, don't you think, Antoni?"

"So you think I should say yes and let them come, Reinier?"

"Yes. You have complete confidence in your results. Anyone can see them who is not blind."

"All right. I will write back directly. I just hate to seem slavish." A white flame of hope and relief is secretly burning in his heart.

"They are offering to send someone across the North Sea to see your observations, Antoni. Can you even get your neighbors to look at them?"

Leeuwenhoek shrugs from his place at the study workbench, trying to appear unperturbed. Pierre sets his mouth in a thin line and returns to impaling a fragment of butterfly wing on the mount of a scope in front of him.

"So, how was Paris?" asks Leeuwenhoek, pulling a sheet of paper toward him. He picks up a quill—one of Caligula's—and checks to see if it needs sharpening. It does not. He opens the ink pot.

"Hot. Catholic. Full of opinionated Frenchmen," says De Graaf. "But I got lot of work done. We know far more about the breeding of animals than people, you know. It is ridiculous. Rams, rabbits—or in Paris, pigeons—go at it in front of our eyes all the time, yet one cross-section of a man's cockstand brings the whole faculty of medicine into uproar."

"And yet you persevere, Reinier."

"I do. I can't help it."

"I know what you mean," says Leeuwenhoek, scratching away at his reply to the Society. "I won't include any observations this time, just say yes to the request."

"You can send their observer back with a flea in his ear and enough observations to sink the ship in the crossing."

"Hmmph," says Pierre, finally succeeding in skewering the tiny fragment of butterfly wing on the mount and moving to the light of the window. Once he lifts the scope to his eye, his jaw relaxes and he becomes rapt and silent. The work claims him, and he is untroubled by the pretensions of faraway Englishmen.

Later that evening, after the supper hour, Leeuwenhoek takes the fabric samples over to the house of Matthias DeWitt. Joost had left them, carefully wrapped in burlap, for him to collect in the shop. Joost's uncle, a fancy ironmonger by trade, with a good eye for line and an investor's instinct, has expressed a cautious interest in the deal, depending on the terms that can be worked out with DeVeyne. Leeuwenhoek feels therefore that he has a propitious venture to offer to DeWitt, especially given the interest he will naturally have in promoting the work of his son. Transferring the bundle of fabric under his arm, he raps on the front door. The dwelling is considerably more modest than the house in which he lives now, in Hippolytusbuurt, or the family house in which he had been born, at Lion's Corner, but everything about it is as neat as a pin. The door is newly painted a handsome dove gray, and a small window box is full of flowers laid out with mathematical precision. Leeuwenhoek reflects with some wistfulness on similar window boxes at his own home long since devoured by geese.

A truly beautiful woman opens the door. "Mevrouw DeWitt," he says, blinking as if at a bright light, and bowing slightly and awkwardly, "I am here to talk to your husband about some business."

"Mijnheer Van Leeuwenhoek! Please come in," she says. "You must know how delighted we are about all the help you have been to Pierre. He never ceases talking about it." Her voice is as refined as her face. He had not expected Pierre's mother to be a creature of such exquisite elegance and feels obscurely that Pierre ought to have warned him. Looking at her, like a painting in rose and gold and cream, he feels, for the first time, sorry for the boy that he only sees in black and white.

Dazed, he is ushered into a pristine great room. Its proportions are not large, and it shows signs of being little used. A large linen closet stands to one side, topped by a classical bust in plaster. Four very fine small paintings adorn one wall, and a modest collection of silver and porcelain lines the mantel of the unlit fireplace. Nothing is lavish, and everything is well chosen. The elder DeWitt and Pierre are seated at a small mahogany table nearest the wall upon which the paintings are displayed. A fine ceramic jug of wine is on the table, along with a small bowl of handsome walnuts, their stippled shells chiaroscuro by candlelight. A third chair is drawn out and waiting. The woman curtsies at the door and withdraws, closing it behind her.

DeWitt and Pierre rise, and then sit down as Leeuwenhoek seats himself in the waiting chair, depositing his bundle of cloth on the floor behind him. "Welcome, Antoni," says DeWitt, "Wine?"

"Thank you, Matthias, yes," says Leeuwenhoek. The man pours out three small glasses. "To an interesting new enterprise and the draughtsmanship of Pierre!" says Leeuwenhoek, raising his glass. Pierre looks gratified, his father austere. All three sip their wine. Leeuwenhoek glances at the walnuts and the silver nutcracker beside the bowl and decides it would be too much trouble. Besides, a single fragment of shell on the floor would disturb the propriety of the room to an extent for which he cannot be answerable.

"I have of course seen Pierre's original drawings of the design, which I judged to be excellent," says DeWitt, sipping his wine. His lips are so pale that the wine stains them almost immediately in a disconcerting manner. "I assume that you have brought the cloth samples with you? What did DeVeyne think of them?"

"I have them right here," replies Leeuwenhoek. "I believe that DeVeyne was impressed with them right away, or he would not have agreed to print them. But I haven't yet talked to him about terms."

"Pierre tells me that Frans Hoek may likewise be interested to invest?"

"So I have been told informally by his nephew Joost, who works for me."

"He is astute, Frans. He has invested in several East India voyages to great success over the years," says Matthias. "I take his interest as a good sign. While I am not a rich man, I am a prudent one, and have some savings I could contribute to this venture. But only provided that DeVeyne shows full confidence and contributes costs or cash; that seems to me definitive of final profitability. How much will you print first off?"

Leeuwenhoek finishes his wine, as does Pierre. DeWitt swigs the last of his quickly and clears the table of the half-full jug, the glasses and walnuts. "Here. Put them up here."

Leeuwenhoek reaches behind him, picks up the parcel, and unrolls the two small bolts from their burlap coverings. He lays them out on the table. Pierre, who has been utterly silent so far, coughs tensely. His father glances at him. "Apologies," mutters Pierre immediately.

DeWitt stands up to view the cloth. He picks up each bolt, examines the forms minutely, holds the cloth up to let the light shine through it, fingers the weave. Pierre, still seated, is as pale as bleached paper. He watches his father wordlessly. "Did you tell DeVeyne that this design was the result of your microscopical investigations?" DeWitt asks, still peering at it.

"No. We merely said it was a botanical. Pierre has named it Water Garden, which we thought excellent."

"Yes, a tactful choice, Pierre," says DeWitt. "Most people would simply be confused by these animalcules or whatever they are."

Pierre nods in his chair without a trace of a smile. He is clearly terrified of his father. Leeuwenhoek had not been aware that the colorless DeWitt was a domestic tyrant. He thinks of the silence and alacrity of his wife in closing the door. Yet more evidence that she is a Catholic. A good Protestant woman would not put up with it; as *Camerabewaarder*, he's seen plenty of them challenge their abusive husbands in court. But then, the consistory has been behind them every time: they have no say in what happens to a Catholic woman, nor would they be inclined to care. The reformed church disapproves of mixed marriages. No one will help Mevrouw DeWitt. Her religion will not let her divorce. It is a shock to realize how other people live. He had not known that Pierre's father was a brute or his mother a captive as beautiful as a fairy princess, and he sees the lad nearly every day. And every day he goes home from the brave new world of natural philosophy and lives in the stark confines of a children's tale.

"I am going to ask DeVeyne initially for a six months' supply for my shop—which should be about 400 ells, 200 per pattern. Not a large job for DeVeyne, but worth doing. If it sells well there, I would be willing to consider allowing other Dutch retailers to carry it, after a time," says Leeuwenhoek. "I don't want to undercut my own business."

"I cannot see DeVeyne accepting a deal exclusive to one retailer, or not for long, if the pattern were selling," says DeWitt. "He would invoke some guild rule or other."

"But then again, so could I, as a draper. Or investor."

"True, but he is rich and fights like hell at law. I don't say this in the spirit of judgment, merely as a practical measure. Contractually, everything would have to be watertight."

"Yes. Should I proceed to hammer out a contract with DeVeyne, and name you as an interested party? Do you have a percentage or a lump sum in mind that you intend to invest?"

"Not knowing the exact figures, I would say I can put in up to one quarter of initial costs, given the solidity of my fellow investors. As to what profit I expect to realize from that, I will have to leave that up to your negotiations with DeVeyne and your own pricing as retailer, mindful of the fact that I am doing this for money, not vanity."

"Yes. And Pierre, there are a number of options about your reimbursement. You could take a one-time cash payment for the design. I understand that is what your cousin has done for DeVeyne in the past? This does not seem advantageous unless you have immediate needs for the money. The other would be to take a smaller cash payment and invest the rest of the fee in costs, making you eligible to receive profits. That is the middle road. Or, you could commute the whole fee into investment, the riskiest option."

Before his father can say anything, Pierre, amazingly enough, asks directly, "But what would be the amount of the fee? That is the question. How much investment will it buy, as a percentage, do you think?"

"I have thought about it. I was going to offer 30 guilders. By my current rough estimate, that should be between 15 and 20% of initial costs."

"Then I would prefer to do that," says Pierre, without hesitation, not looking at Matthias. He does not dare. Yet at the same time, he is determined to proceed independently. Leeuwenhoek has to admire his nerve. Matthias regards his son impassively.

"Matthias?" asks Leeuwenhoek, "Are you agreed? You will have to sign for him, as he is a minor."

"Thirty guilders is a respectable amount. Enough for three paintings of investment quality," says DeWitt, "so a fair fee for a commercial property. You agree, Pierre? And you are certain about investing it all? You must decide now."

"Yes."

"Then I will sign for him. It is his decision."

"Excellent," says Leeuwenhoek, relieved that there is not going to be a parental explosion. "I will set up a meeting with DeVeyne and report back with a preliminary contract. Much obliged, and good luck to us all!" He rises and begins to wrap up the samples in their burlap again. DeWitt waits for him, then walks him through the hall and out of the house, shaking his hand. Pierre remains behind, his white hair glimmering in the candlelight against the sober darkness of the walls.

⟫

After seeing the microscopist to the door, his father walks back into the room. Pierre remains seated and returns his glance, carefully neutral. "We could end up being the primary investors in this, between us," Matthias says, after a minute, "so it had better work out. Keep the animalcule foolishness out of it. No one will understand it. This is business."

"Yes," says Pierre. Then he is silent. He holds his silence like a white veil.

He has won.

⟫

Finally, there is the matter of DeVeyne. He is no pushover. Negotiating a contract with him would try the patience of a saint. Leeuwenhoek has done it before, but never one of such complexity involving so many parties. The cloth will be woven in Tilburg from materials imported by the East India Company; DeVeyne has managed to argue his way into the same deals that the locals there are offering to the big factories in Amsterdam. This is a coup: costs are lower. It will be dew-bleached and baled and sent to his factory, where the linen will be printed with the soft green design and the cotton with indigo. Two hundred ells of each fabric will be delivered to the shop in Hippolytusbuurt in six weeks' time. Leeuwenhoek will sell it at retail, and the profits will be divided amongst the investors: roughly 20% each, though there will still be fierce haggling over the details. The sticking point, as DeWitt had predicted, is DeVeyne: he will not concede that the finished cloth is to be sold only at Leeuwenhoek's shop. "Look, man," he says, time and again, "I'm a wholesaler. And so are you, now. If it takes off, you have to let the fashion run its course and sell as much as you can, wherever you can. That's the way things go with a craze: the stuff has to be visible. You can't let concern for your one little shop slow it up. I can give you six months' exclusive, but after that I want to be able to sell it to the Great Khan himself."

Finally Leeuwenhoek concedes. He's still making profits when it's sold elsewhere, isn't he? And isn't the point of all this to get the animalcules out into the public eye? In their tasteful disguise as Water Garden? How is it that he has ended up with another secret? Unlike the technique of making his best lenses, this secret he would be only too glad to share, but everyone keeps telling him not to. It seems Vermeer was right: natural philosophy and industry are uncomfortable bedfellows.

BOOM

"**Barbara** is with child," the goose girl tells Leeuwenhoek as he stands by the well, three months later, in autumn. "Did you know?" She and the geese have just returned from pasture; it is early evening, with a chill in the air.

"What? Did she tell you?" asks Leeuwenhoek, amazed.

"No. I can hear it inside her. It is very small."

"Have you told her? Talked to her about it?"

"No."

"Are you sure? You are not just hearing animalcules inside her?" He cannot believe he is asking this question. "We must all bear them around with us, all the time," he goes on, feeling at sea.

"My mother had a child inside her when she died. I had been hearing it for a long time. I expect that is why I heard this one. It even lived on for a short while after her death. But it was trapped there and died, too, quite soon," says the girl.

"Dear God," says Leeuwenhoek. The child's gift is appalling. And now he and Barbara will be dragged through the mill again. He is not sure if either of them can stand losing another child. "Do not tell her. Let her find out, if she doesn't know already."

"No, I won't," she agrees. She goes back to watering the geese. Their sinuous necks ripple like white ribbons in the dusky light. They chatter and rustle as if talking among themselves.

He stands there gazing at them sightlessly. Is it right that he knows this before Barbara? Or that the goose girl knows it at all? Never before has her power seemed so invasive. He is filled with a brief, creeping dread.

"Is it a girl or a boy?" he asks. "Is it healthy?"

"I do not know," she says, putting down the bucket. "It is very early. Though I am not sure if I could tell, anyway."

"Then what is the use of you? Why did you tell me?" he asks bitterly.

She faces him. "I don't know. People are not very useful. Not like geese."

He snorts incredulously. "Geese?" Never has the girl seemed more alien.

"Geese, yes. You can eat them, and you can write with their feathers, and they guard you, and they show you which plants are poisonous…"

"And people build houses, and courtyards, and wells! And share them with other people!"

"Yes, but this house and this well, they are not you. You own them. Did you even build them? I thought they were old? I live in the house; it keeps me warm. I drink from the well; it gives me water. Not you. Everything the geese do, they do themselves. All the time. They are useful, just themselves, without anything."

Leeuwenhoek, uncomfortable and on edge, is filled with rage. He wants to throttle the strange child. She does not understand people at all. How they extend themselves into objects around them. His house, his well: they are part of him, in a way. To insult them is to insult him. To use them is to owe him. She cannot see that. She is blind to the way people live, to what passes through their minds. To the connections they make to things. It is maddening. It is like a punishment.

"Why would you tell me this?" he asks again.

"You said you like to know things," she replies.

He is brought up short. He did say that. It is not right to blame her. Tact, privacy, these are things that mean nothing to her. Her mind is otherwise filled up. His anger wanders off course as he explores this new thought. Most people's passions flow out of them, settling on everything around them: people, objects, ideas. She, on the other hand, is constantly receiving signs, voices, forms, from everything around her. Perhaps it is impossible to do both. A river that flows one way in most people flows the opposite way in her.

That is why, he thinks, she always seems like a lone island, or a standing stone far upstream. She is at the other end of a compass needle: we are north, and she's south. He is astounded at his own insight. He glances at the girl: it is as if she is suddenly standing in a patch of illumination cast by an invisible lantern. She goes about her goosely business, unconcerned.

"You're right," he says to her, "It is just better to know things." He draws a deep breath, fills his two jars from the well bucket, bids her good night, and goes back inside.

As he passes through the kitchen, Barbara is standing there, in a sober dark blue dress. She looks beautiful and serene. He stoops and kisses her forehead briefly. In so doing, he manages to spill water on her from one of his jars. She jumps back quickly, mopping herself with her shawl.

"Cold, Antoni, cold! Augh! It's freezing! What the hell is that?" She pats at her soaking breast with the shawl that she has whipped off her shoulders.

"Sorry! Sorry! Well water, for an experiment! Sorry!" yelps Leeuwenhoek.

"I hate natural philosophy!"

"Sorry! Barbara, I'm so sorry! What an idiot I am, clumsy oaf!" He moves to help her, still holding a jar in each hand.

"Put them down, you silly ass! Before you spill even more! On the table!"

Leeuwenhoek puts his jars down. Barbara looks ruefully at her dress and moves closer to the fire. She gathers up the shawl and holds it out as well. He goes to her and kisses the top of her head apologetically. She waves the shawl at him. It is indigo Water Garden.

"What if it runs?"

"What? Never! Only quality products at Leeuwenhoek's!" He puts his arms around her. She is certainly damp. "Besides, it is Water Garden, so I had to water it…"

"Feeble, Antoni," says Barbara. "And what will you do if I catch my death?" But she is already smiling, and nestles her head on his shoulder. The two stand quietly together for a moment. Then she flaps her shawl briskly. "Go on," she says, "back to those little animals of yours. Go! Take the jars."

Barbara is hardly alone in wearing a shawl of Water Garden. Now that the weather has turned, it seems that every woman in Delft has one. Leeuwenhoek sees the pattern everywhere. He is beginning to find it unnerving. The indigo is almost all sold already; more has been ordered from DeVeyne. The green-printed linen is not moving quite as quickly—the rush for autumn and winter clothing is always the fastest part of the market—but it is still outselling all his other drapery fabric. Pierre walks around looking a foot taller.

They have their next print almost ready to go: Lacewing. The translucent insect wing from the cochineal.

Another elegant pattern from Pierre, another pretty, deceiving name. After much debate, Pierre has persuaded Leeuwenhoek (and Joost) to print it in black and white. There is no doubt that it looks superb, refined as an ink drawing even when machine printed. Pierre has not said so, but Leeuwenhoek knows that he considers it a vindication of his way of seeing the world. He himself had favored printing it in cochineal. He allowed Pierre to override his private joke, however. Besides, cochineal is expensive.

This time they have decided to print the same design on two fabrics: the filmiest, thinnest muslin and fine silk. It is their belief that women will use it in lieu of lace in collars and slashes, and that it will make a striking lining for capes and jackets. People enjoy luxury in winter. This is something new. All the same investors are involved; the contracts signed; the East India silk and cotton are due at the factory within days.

DeVeyne is champing at the bit to get Water Garden out into the wider market. He is pressing Leeuwenhoek hard to forego his monopoly. He has sent samples out to drapers in Amsterdam, Deventer, and Den Haag and promised them stock immediately, though Leeuwenhoek's exclusive deal has another three months to run. Without consulting anyone, he has gone ahead and sent stocks of both fabrics to London, Paris and Marseilles, paying the costs and import taxes without demur. What he really needs, DeVeyne keeps insisting, is to get the pattern picked up by fashionable drapers in Amsterdam. This will immediately create demand in London and almost certainly Paris. "Believe me, these piddling sales in Delft and the villages are nothing to what we could get out of this. Forget them. I smell a run. We've got to get our product out there before people start knocking it off."

Leeuwenhoek is tempted just to let DeVeyne have his way, but Pierre is firm. His authority has suddenly blossomed. "Don't do it, master. Antoni. You have a monopoly in the Seven Provinces, at least. Use it while you can. People are coming from further afield to get it all the time. Rarity is driving the price up. You're making great return for all of us. Use every minute you can while you control the trickle; then open the floodgates wide. And you mustn't let DeVeyne win. You won't be able to work with him if he thinks you are weak. He will exploit you. You must force him to honor his contract exactly."

"You are becoming a cutthroat, Pierre!"

"Tell him you will withhold all further designs."

"He already has Lacewing at the factory."

"But he does not know how many others we have. He will not risk it. We could go elsewhere."

"We have no others, Pierre."

"We have a million animalcules, your lenses, and me."

"I see. Put it that way, and we could print enough cloth to cover the whole earth. The fleet could use it for sailcloth," laughs Leeuwenhoek. "But Pierre, listen to me, we cannot get distracted. We are natural philosophers first. Promise me."

"That is the wonderful thing about investments," replies Pierre. "Your money works, and you stay at home looking through microscopes at saltpeter and blowflies."

"Pierre!"

"I promise. I will not let this get in the way of the real work."

"Fine, then I will take your advice."

"Do you have any idea what we might use for the next design? Then we really will be one step ahead of DeVeyne."

Sarah Tolmie

"Well," admits Leeuwenhoek slowly, "I had thought of blood. It is very handsome through the scope. Regular, rounded forms like loaves of country bread."

"Excellent!" says Pierre, "We can call it Staff of Life. If anyone asks us about it, we can say innocently: don't you think it looks like bread?"

"Do you have any poets in your family, Pierre?"

"No. Only liars. And salesmen."

"Come to the study, then. I can show you the blood."

"Marvelous. Pond scum. Parts of bugs. And now blood. We're going to be rich."

"Vermeer will be shocked."

"The man's a fool," says Pierre. "If I could paint like that, I'd be the richest man in Europe."

THE USE OF PEOPLE

Lacewing sells even faster than Water Garden. By the time Leeuwenhoek's monopoly on the latter is up, they have sold three printings of Lacewing in silk and two in cotton. Joost can hardly keep it in the store. The mayor's wife wears her sleeves slashed with it at the Stadthuis Christmas festivities. The pantlers' guild buys 200 ells of it to line their new vestments. At the Mechelen, not to be outdone, they retire their layered taffeta draperies and outfit the taproom windows in filmiest Lacewing muslin to make the most of the low winter light. Fashion trumps even frugality, as now they are surely buying more peat without the protection of their heavy curtains.

Water Garden goes on sale at an expensive haberdashery on the Ververgracht the day the exclusivity contract lapses. Within weeks it is selling like wildfire in Amsterdam; the drapers start selling it in London. Then Marseilles. In many shops in the Republic that are supplied by DeVeyne, Water Garden is outselling *cachemire* and French *tuile* by two to one. It is a verifiable craze. It is a heady time for the investors. They are making excellent money, but spending it, too, on the rising costs of production and shipping. DeVeyne is used to this, but the rest of them are not; some weeks the outgoing expenses for Water Garden are actually greater than Leeuwenhoek's shop in Hippolytusbuurt brings in. This makes him anxious every time; he wonders if he is really cut out for this league of commerce. Whenever he sees Matthias DeWitt, he can tell the man is also feeling the strain. Only Pierre is calm.

DeVeyne is counting the hours until he can get Lacewing out of Leeuwenhoek's exclusive hold and out to Amsterdam and the wider world. He is pressuring them to get another pattern out as soon as possible. But they are having some trouble with the Staff of Life design. Everyone is satisfied with the strongly three-dimensional discus shapes Pierre has designed; the pattern is bold and modern. What they cannot decide upon is the scale. Pierre thinks it is too fussy at high density, too much like dots; Leeuwenhoek and Joost fear that the shapes are too stark when they are scaled up. As to color, they like it both in dark red and in black. Both give an almost *bas relief* effect against a plain white background, very striking.

"Yet I wonder," says Pierre, "if this might be the time for two colors. Red on black, or black on red? Or a tapestry fabric that could use both colors?"

"More expensive, even it was just dyed cloth with a print on it, though. And much more expensive for a full tapestry weave. Is it worth it?" asks Leeuwenhoek.

"I don't know. Color ought to be your province, I realize. But it seemed worth considering. This form is simpler than the honeydew form; it might look quite sophisticated, say, as a deep red fabric with the forms woven in black. Shiny fabric, matte form. Or as a cut velvet, black with a red form."

"I don't know. Black and red? Don't you think it would look too clerical? I don't know, too Spanish?"

"Like I said before, everyone is Catholic on the inside. Of their houses, I mean. I could imagine either one for tablecloths, wall hangings, cushions, bed covers, that sort of thing. There's no end to it. If my mother were a rich woman, she would positively drown in luxurious fabrics for the house. I have known her to go into a trance at the sight of them."

"A woman of queenly taste as well as queenly appearance," says Leeuwenhoek.

"Yes. Though the taste, at least, is common."

"You could be right, Pierre. Could you do up some color samples somehow? We need to work this out before we go to DeVeyne."

"All right. Just to get the idea. I know my father's colors well. I had to work with them for years. The red tones will be notional—I can only judge their degree of light and dark. It will take a little longer than my usual drawings."

"Fine."

Pierre goes home to work. Leeuwenhoek thinks of Mevrouw DeWitt, that beautiful and sweet-voiced woman, pining after silks and velvets that her husband is too cheap to buy for her. He thinks of Barbara's dollhouse, newly outfitted with indigo curtains and a bedroom wall upholstered in silk Lacewing. It is really too bad. Such a simple thing.

~

Barbara is showing now, some six months' gone. She is subdued and nervous. Leeuwenhoek cannot blame her. Labor is a terrible ordeal at the best of times; now she fears both the birth and what may happen after. Reinier has talked to her about eating healthful food and taking frequent but not exerting walks; he has advised her about the necessity of rest, and of keeping up her spirits. He has been permitted to examine her, once, in her shift. There is little else he can do, and it is still unclear whether she will allow him to attend her during the birth. The midwife is strongly disapproving of men in the birthing chamber, and of physicians in general.

"There's a baby in there," De Graaf says to Leeuwenhoek, after his brief examination. "It's kicking. That much I can tell you. Of course, so could anyone. It's no wonder midwives think we are useless. Suspicious lot, they are. It's like dealing with the *Wacht*. They spend half their time reporting to the regents: who is having sex outside marriage, what kids are born out of wedlock, and who is the father of this child, please sign here, and so on. They're practically agents of the court. I have been reported twice merely for conducting examinations. What, Dr De Graaf, you are discovered with a married woman in her shift! In intimate contact with her! *Ontucht!* You will both be banished for fifty years! It must be adultery! The fact is, Antoni, I need to examine Barbara much more intimately, and most women just won't stand for it, not to mention the state of our laws. How are we to advance in this area at all? I may be of a bit more use in examining the infant. The others, I know, died of respiratory failure…"

Leeuwenhoek winces. Reinier looks at him helplessly. He claps him on the back lightly and strides out.

The goose girl is more forthcoming about the baby, but it is hard to make sense of what she says. Leeuwenhoek feels strange asking her, but he can't help it. If there is an oracle at hand, people will consult it. "Yes, it's definitely alive," she says. "No, I don't know if it's a boy or a girl. I guess I can't tell. I think you would have to see it. It is much bigger now. I can hear its heart beating. But it feels…cold. Yes, cold."

On another occasion, she tells him: "it is salty."

He says nothing of these consultations to Reinier. Or Barbara.

Pierre comes back with a black-on-red and a red-on-black design, and it is clear that his instinct was right: they are terrific. Much more interesting than the pattern on a light ground. Moreover, he has scaled the pattern down to the mid-range, which suits all of them. Now that Leeuwenhoek sees them, even as colored sketches, he can imagine the textiles precisely: a shining deep crimson satin with the design picked out in black threads, and a heavy black silk velvet with dark red cutouts. He can feel the nap of the velvet and the slickness of the satin scored by the raised threads as clearly as if they were already in his hands. Pierre watches him mull all this over, and nods to himself. "This is going to cost a bomb," says Leeuwenhoek. Pierre nods again. "I don't know if DeVeyne even does velvets. And we'll have to do the tapestry in silk, I think. These will be deluxe fabrics. Very expensive."

"We might need a lawyer to keep DeVeyne in line," says Pierre, "what with the heavy costs. Also, I am not certain my father will be prepared take them on. He is cautious. I, on the other hand, will invest as much as possible."

"We could easily find other investors now," says Leeuwenhoek. "I have already been approached by several people, asking about it."

"So have I," says Pierre. "Among them my cousin Martin."

"But the last I heard he had been fired! How does he have the money?"

"He has moved into another, much more lucrative, profession," replies Pierre, without elaborating. "Also, he knows a lot more than I do about tapestry fabrics."

"Talk to him, in that case, by all means. I am sure we can find someone else one way or another. Meanwhile,

I will discuss this with DeVeyne. I am sure this will be a longer process altogether."

Yet the very next day Leeuwenhoek is talking to De-Veyne. The dour manufacturer is transfixed as soon as he sees the sketches. Leeuwenhoek can see him doing furious calculations in his head. "Ambitious, aren't you?" he says, biting his thumbnail and taking a sample book down, and then another and another. He flips through them, muttering to himself, without speaking to his visitor, for almost ten whole minutes. Leeuwenhoek waits patiently; he knows better than to interrupt. Finally De-Veyne turns to him, and says, "I'll be honest with you, this job will stretch me. Stretch my resources. Now, maybe they ought to be stretched. So let me think about that. The satin tapestry, that I can do. Two colors, no problem. I'll have to refurbish that loom; it hasn't run for a while. But the velvet's another story. I don't have a double loom to do it on, and it's hard to compete with Bruges, not to mention Italy. Even Utrecht, now. Velvet looms cost a lot, and you need skilled laborers for cutting pile. So I'd have to buy a loom and hire extra men, or contract it out, and as a rule I hate contracting, except for simple thread, of course, and flat weaves for printing like they do out there in Tilburg. And then, you know, if you want two colors in a velvet, you have to flock it: or were you thinking *devoré?* Anyway, whichever one, down to a red satin warp for the forms, is that the idea? It'll be a nightmare. My God. A nightmare. But then—if we've already got a red silk satin going for the other one, well, at least we've bought the thread, and—" He stops and bites his thumb again.

"Christophe, you wouldn't seriously buy a double loom for this, would you?" asks Leeuwenhoek in amazement. "Maybe we should just start with the tapestry?"

"The tapestry, you're on. I'll start re-tooling tomorrow. But I will need a much fuller design than this; I had better talk to Pierre. The velvet, well, I confess, I have been thinking along these lines already. Zuidermann there, in Utrecht, he's been making this crushed velvet, see, for a while now. People get pissed off, buying from Bruges, and half the time you can't, anyway. He's making a killing. Everybody wants velvet. Especially black. It's a staple. So this job could be the thing pushes me over the edge, makes me reach a decision. And double-quick, before you take it elsewhere—to Zuidermann, for example, that asshole, can't stand the man. So, give me a day or two to think about it. Big commitment. But the payoff could be huge. The thing is: everybody's cut velvets look the same, the same forms, the same shapes, all leaves and trefoils and greyhounds and whatnot, stuck in the Middle Ages. Yours is different. Just like the other patterns were different. That Pierre, he's amazing, that kid. And you, wherever you're finding this stuff. Never seen anything like them, never."

Leeuwenhoek does a mock bow in his chair. "But how much would a double loom cost?"

"Oh, say, two thousand guilder."

"Christophe! You could buy my house for that!"

"It's a capital investment. My investment. Don't worry about it. It's not a cost I'll pass on. It would be part of the factory. Might need to factor in increased labor costs, though, for everyone. Anyway, let me think about it." Leeuwenhoek nods and leaves him to it.

DeVeyne, as usual, thinks fast, even when sums of this size are at stake. He decides to buy a double loom for velveting. The rest of the investors are staggered. There are a series of anxious meetings between Hoek, DeWitt and Leeuwenhoek; it is clear that DeWitt is seriously concerned. "If DeVeyne runs his business into the ground, I don't want to be on the hook for it. And what happens to our enterprise then?"

"Matthias, there are other fabric manufacturers, if it comes to that," Leeuwenhoek says reassuringly. "Though I trust DeVeyne's judgment. He is an extraordinarily successful businessman. And if you feel uncomfortable with the financial commitment that this particular pattern might compel, you do not need to join. You will remain an important investor in producing the others."

"True," says DeWitt. Pierre, at his side, remains silent. Leeuwenhoek can almost hear the clock ticking in Pierre's head, counting down to his majority. He hopes that his father cannot hear it.

Within days comes the news that a fashionable hotel near the Louvre has done up its drawing room in green linen Water Garden. Sales in Paris pick up dramatically: some are bulk orders for the great houses of the nobility. It is a triumph. "Better dump as much there as we can, right now," says DeVeyne, practically, stepping up production, "once the crown realizes it's foreign, they'll ban it." He hires extra workers, keeps the mill running almost round the clock. "And we'll need some cash to bribe import officials. Better see how much we can raise."

Pierre talks to Martin and shows him the designs for tapestry and velvet. Martin has some excellent suggestions about the thread counts in the formal design for the tapestry. They have a long talk about loom dimensions. He puts a surprising amount of money in immediately. He is obviously delighted to be dealing with DeVeyne in this capacity, as an investor. "Show him he can't treat me like a caffa any more, eh, cousin? So the old fox has gone out and bought a velveting loom? Well, well. Out to smash that poor fellow in Utrecht, is he? Zuidermann can kiss his ass goodbye."

Martin is astonishingly well dressed. He looks quite the gentleman. His manners are much improved. Pierre cannot figure it out. "So you work for that fancy woman now, the one from the Mechelen? What exactly do you do?"

"Aliette De Hooch. Yes. She's a madam."

"A what?"

"She runs a whorehouse."

"Oh my God, Martin! So you're a—"

"Yes."

"Lord and Savior! I didn't think men did that. You mean to say women actually pay you for—"

"Services. A variety of services. Singing, sometimes. I play chess with one. The world is full of lonely women. Lonely people, hiding in their houses."

"God above! Well, from the looks of things, you're doing quite well. Is this all your own money you're putting in?"

"No. A lot of it is Aliette's. She needs respectable enterprises. And so do I. Now I can say I am a fabric merchant as I float around these expensive houses."

"How does she keep the civic guard off her back?"

"She pays them. A lot. Discreetly. Contributes to charitable causes. Knows the regents, does jobs for them. Gets some of her girls from the orphanage. As housemaids, officially. Though some of the girls are foreign; two are French. One Bohemian."

"And this business is in Delft?"

"Yes. Not too far from Leeuwenhoek's, actually. In Prinsenstraat."

"Lord and Savior," says Pierre faintly. "I wonder what I should tell him. Leeuwenhoek, I mean."

"Don't tell him anything. Just give him the money and use my name."

"You're sure you can keep up these payments? I will look like an idiot if you default."

"Yes."

"All right then." The cousins shake on it. Now it does not matter if Matthias contributes or not. Staff of Life has enough investors.

DeVeyne is busy and dangerously short tempered. He is having a loom shipped from Italy. He will have to hire southerners, from Bruges, perhaps, or Antwerp, to run it. The contract negotiations are particularly sharp and explosive because of his state of mind. The sums involved are exceedingly high. Matthias DeWitt opts out. For a while it appears the whole project might founder. But by dint of arduous meetings, day after day, they finally arrive at a deal.

Leeuwenhoek is exhausted. He hasn't been in his study for weeks. Not to do observations, that is. Only accounts. It is driving him mad. He wishes he had never thought of the whole fabric business. And he is worried about Barbara, who seems more and more wretched and distraught.

Then he receives a letter from the Royal Society, explaining that their delegate, a Mr. Hugh McFarlane, a wool merchant and amateur microscopist, accompanied by an English priest who is traveling to the Republic on the business of the faith, will be arriving in three weeks' time. This English priest, the Reverend William Davenant, is acquainted with the rector of the English church in Delft, the Reverend David Forsythe, and suggests that he also attend, if only to assist with translation. Leeuwenhoek, who knows the rector and his Dutch, thinks that the man's usefulness is likely to be limited. And he himself is so tired that his own ability to conduct a philo-sophical conversation in Dutch, let alone English, is not something he would put money on. He feels resentful, even though his determination to impress them remains as high as ever. This inspection could hardly have come at a worse time. Plus, the presence of the priests is rath-er worrying. What exactly is their role? He recalls Pierre muttering about the Vatican. The letter assures him that they are all "reasonable men."

Reasonable men. Perhaps they'll be a relief after all these merchants and midwives.

INCONVENIENT TRUTHS

"Antoni," says Barbara, suddenly appearing in his study, which she almost never does. "What does that girl know about my baby, and how does she know it?" Her voice is at once anxious and peremptory. Leeuwenhoek puts down the sample he is preparing with a silent sigh. It is the first time he has had an opportunity to work in weeks. But this crisis has always been inevitable.

"My love, I don't know exactly what she knows and certainly not how she knows it. She has some kind of gift. All I know is that she was aware of your pregnancy very early, and that she can somehow hear or sense the baby's presence inside you."

"Is it well?" says his wife, instantly.

"I don't know, Barbara. What has she said? What has happened?" asks Leeuwenhoek uneasily.

"Did you know about this before?"

"Yes," he admits.

"Why did you not tell me, Antoni? Antoni?"

He hesitates a moment. "I did not want to worry you. I didn't know whether to believe her myself. Geese, animalcules, that is one thing. A child of ours seemed quite another."

Barbara clutches the edge of the work table with white fingers. Her voice is tight. "You should have told me. I am the one bearing this child, Antoni. She came in for bread just now, to the kitchen, and remarked that the baby was sleeping. At first I thought she meant Marieke. But Marieke was playing in the next room; I could hear her. The girl meant the baby inside me. And it was sleeping, too. Now that it is this big, I can tell. Now, explain that, Antoni!"

"I can't. I don't know anyone who can."

"We should take her to the church and have the pastor examine her. Perhaps it is a miracle, or a devilish power."

"Please, Barbara, I beg you not to do that! There is no telling what might come of it. We might be blamed for harboring her! The Stadthuis will require endless examinations, should she need to be admitted to the madhouse! And the Englishmen from the Society come in just a few days! Please, not just now!"

"But—"

"Do you feel that she means you harm? That her knowledge could hurt you—or the child?"

"No! But I want to know what she knows! I must know, Antoni, if…just in case. I must know!" says Barbara, trembling. "You must bring her in here, right now, so we can talk to her!"

Leeuwenhoek acquiesces instantly. Barbara is in a pitiable state. It is his fault. He ought to have told her. It is that damnable girl. Why does he keep her around? Other people are beginning to believe him. Reinier. Cornelis s'Gravesend. Perhaps now the Royal Society. The child is uncanny and unreasonable, like a remnant of a previous age of the world. But he, he is the future! And now he has gone and upset his beloved wife in her fragile condition with his irrational allegiance. What could be more selfish?

He rushes out to find the goose girl. Fortunately, she has not yet left for the pasture. He finds her in the courtyard, sweeping. "Thank God! You are still here!" The girl looks up in surprise at his agitation.

"You must come with me! Barbara has discovered that you can hear the child inside her, and insists on knowing everything." The goose girl leans the broom against the wall and comes with him. She seems reluctant. They pace across the courtyard and through the kitchens and the narrow hallway. "Barbara is upset," he warns the girl. "She is worried about the baby. Others have died, before. Try not to scare her."

The goose girl looks at him expressionlessly. They reach the study door. Leeuwenhoek opens it and they go in. Barbara is waiting, standing at the head of the work table, pale and anxious. He goes to stand beside her, taking her arm. The girl enters a few feet into the room and takes up a position at the opposite end of the table. She stands there, straight-backed. Leeuwenhoek is reminded of a prisoner at examination.

"You! Do you hear this child inside me?" Barbara asks the girl, without preamble, staring at her.

"Yes," says the girl.

"What can you tell me about it? Is it sick or well? A boy? A girl?"

"It is there," says the child. "That is all I can tell you. Its heart beats; it grows; it wakes and sleeps. Sometimes it is warmer, sometimes colder. Sometimes hungry. I don't know if it is a boy or a girl. Just that it lives."

"Not much use," says Barbara.

"No," the girl agrees.

"But it lives and thrives—it grows normally?"

"As far as I can tell."

"When did you first hear it?"

"When it was about the size of a pea."

"And now—how big is it?"

"The size of two apples. Big ones."

Barbara puts her hands over her belly, disengaging her arm from her husband's. "When will it be born?"

"I don't know. I might be able to tell, when it starts. If things change. The saltness. The sourness. The tightness. How things feel, or taste. How they are. Does it take long, being born?"

"A fair time," replies Barbara. Her voice is steadier. "Can you hear other women's babies?"

"Yes," says the girl. "And calves inside cows, and kittens in cats."

"God!" says Barbara. "How embarrassing."

"Most animals, really," finishes the girl.

"It is like Reinier says," ventures Leeuwenhoek. "Animal processes, you see?"

Barbara looks at him sharply. He says nothing more. She looks back at the girl. "I do not understand how you can do this," she says, "but Antoni says you can see many things others cannot."

"It isn't seeing," says the girl.

"No matter," says Barbara. "So long as you tell no one else what you know of my child. These are private matters. And if you learn anything else, you must tell me at once. Only me."

"Yes," says the girl. A guardedness disappears from her posture, one that Leeuwenhoek notices only as it passes off. Clearly the girl knows this is a reprieve. She looks steadily at Barbara. "I will take the geese to pasture now. That was very good bread." Without saying anything more, she turns and departs.

Barbara lets out a long breath and leans on the table. "I had to know, Antoni. Even from her. What a fool…consulting her like a prophet. I should be ashamed of myself."

"No, Barbara," says Leeuwenhoek firmly, "you shouldn't." He hugs his wife lightly, so as not to squash her belly.

"I'm starving from all this inquisition," she says, and heads for the door. "And then I suppose Anneliese and I had better start baking for these important Englishmen." She sails out in a rustle of linen. Leeuwenhoek picks up his abandoned specimen thoughtfully.

⟡

"Johannes, I need a favor," he finds himself saying, two days later. Vermeer is in his study, urging him to allow Pierre to sit for him on the next bright day.

"What?" says the painter.

"I need you to look after the goose girl for a few days, while the party from the Royal Society is here."

"What, surely she speaks no English? What can she say to them?"

"They are bringing priests."

"Ah, and you need to get rid of your heretic for a few days?" Vermeer looks shrewd. "Well, I will take her if Pierre comes as well. That is fair. What the hell do they need priests for?"

"One is a translator—Forsythe, from the chapel. The other is merely acting as a witness for their delegate."

"So they say. They may even believe it. But if anything gets the wind up them, for any reason, everybody will listen to them, not to this so-called Royal Society. Who even knows what that is? But everyone understands the authority of priests, even across borders. I will take the girl. She is too odd for scrutiny. She could get you all in trouble."

"Thank you, Johannes," says Leeuwenhoek, relieved. "I hope they won't be too much of a burden. They will mostly be at pasture during the day. I will provide grain.

The child is quiet and can sleep anywhere. What will your wife say?"

"She is pregnant, as usual, and as sick as a dog. She will say nothing. She may not even notice. Just tell your goose girl to come to my house when she returns from pasture. The yard has a gate. It will be fine. But Pierre must come to sit, also! How long are they here, this official party?"

"I should think about three days."

"Excellent. That should be almost enough time to finish the head and hands."

⤙

Now De Graaf is in his study, also talking about the Englishmen. No one seems to talk about anything else. Leeuwenhoek is beginning to dream about them, horrible dreams in which all his specimens suddenly vanish or he makes elementary errors in arithmetic.

"It is a pity about the meeting at Leiden, but I cannot afford to miss it," says De Graaf. "I think I should be back in time for their visit, though. I will hurry back. So I hope I may yet meet them. After all, my reputation is at stake!" He drums his long fingers on the work table and looks around at the tidily labeled jars lining the walls. He is suddenly admonishing and businesslike: "And whatever business you have to transact about cloth with DeVeyne and all those fellows, tell Pierre to take care of it. Keep them out of your house. Do not show them the fabrics! You do not want these fancy philosophers thinking that you practice microscopy for money. You must appear disinterested."

"When did you become so concerned about English opinion, Reinier?"

"Antoni, I hear that one of the investors in your fabric business is a whore. Such are the rumors. Even I am capable of prudence if that is the case. Keep the English away from it. Priests will fear for your soul, and philosophers are snobs. Most of them are gentlemen. They will despise you if they think you have commercial intentions. Especially if your machines are better than theirs, which they are, or they would not be coming. Do not shame them; give them no opportunity to shame you."

"Or you, my guarantor?"

"Or me," agrees De Graaf, nodding firmly.

Under the Microscope

The Englishmen arrive. It is a Wednesday afternoon, a nasty, chilly day with bursts of freezing sleet. The party have come by barge from Amsterdam, where they landed. They are tired and chilled; the priest, in particular, had a bad sea-crossing and has retired to bed. He is staying with the rector at his home. McFarlane is staying at the Mechelen. Leeuwenhoek receives this information in a brief note that a boy delivers from the hotel. They will call upon him in Hippolytusbuurt tomorrow morning if it is convenient, to view his microscopical specimens.

Nothing about this is particularly convenient, but he can hardly put them off now. He sends the boy back with a reply of yes. He tells Pierre, who is in the study drawing, not to come in tomorrow or the following two days. Pierre is obviously disappointed.

"But shouldn't I be there in my capacity as your amanuensis? I could help explain the drawings…"

"No, Pierre, I need you to keep the investors away from the house. I cannot be seen to be mixing natural philosophy up with moneymaking enterprises. Reinier was adamant on this point. I have told DeVeyne and Hoek to call on you at your house or at Vermeer's. You are expected there tomorrow at noon to sit for that damned painting of his. The goose girl will also be staying with him."

"All equally embarrassing, are we? Might ruin your prospects?" asks Pierre with venom. Leeuwenhoek looks at him in astonishment. Pierre colors under his gaze but continues to look grim. "I've put a lot of work into those drawings!"

"I know, Pierre! I know! But I need you to take charge of the cloth business!"

"What business? Nothing is happening."

"But something could come up! And I must be left undisturbed. It's only for three days."

"Three days when members of the Royal Society are here. And I've never even met an Englishman before."

"Pierre, you despise Englishmen! You didn't want them to come. Do you even speak any English?"

"I've changed my mind. When will I have the honor again?"

"Pierre, we will meet other representatives—many!— if we end up working with the Society."

"And if we don't?"

Leeuwenhoek is getting angry. He is sorry for the boy's disappointment. Pierre's work, as much as his, has brought the English delegation here. But nothing must get in the way of this opportunity. Nothing! Plus, he has promised Vermeer. And De Graaf.

"Pierre! Please! I had to let you sit for Vermeer so he would take the goose girl off my hands."

"Damn that crazy girl. What's the use of her? Compared to me?" says Pierre. He looks shocked at his own bitterness. "I am sorry, Master Leeuwenhoek," he says stiffly. "That was unpardonable."

"That girl! That poor girl! Thank God this is not France, where she would be burned at the stake! Do you want to see her locked up at the madhouse? Because of some foolish thing she says with a house full of witnesses? Priests and foreigners?"

"No, no, of course not!" Pierre makes a small, flailing gesture of denial. He continues, more calmly, "Of course,

I will go to Vermeer's tomorrow, and look after any fabric business, and sit for the painting. I understand." He turns back to his drawings, taking a long breath.

Leeuwenhoek stands there feeling guilty and then goes to seek out the goose girl. She, at least, will not care about the Royal Society.

The girl and the geese are still in the courtyard. The weather is threatening so they have not departed for the field. Leeuwenhoek goes out to her. "Are you pasturing them today?" he asks.

"Yes," she says, "we are just going to leave. It won't rain for a while, so we should go now."

"When it's time to come home, go to Vermeer's house—Johannes' house—in Oude Langendijke. You remember him, the painter? His house has a dark blue door, and there's a yard at the back. You go there tonight, and tomorrow night, and the night after, instead of coming here. Three nights. There will be grain and shelter for them, and somewhere for you to sleep. I know it's strange, but we both think it's for the best."

"Why? Why not here?"

"You remember we talked about those learned men from England, across the sea, and how they might name the animalcules? Well, some have come here to see them, through my microscopes, all the way from London. It is great honor. I cannot afford to have any distractions while these important men are here. Not you. Not the geese. Not even Pierre. It should just be me, and them, looking at them together, and talking."

"At the little animals from the blood?"

"I think so. And some from water. They are very interested in those and have not seen them before. I don't think they truly believe that they exist—that they are really there."

"That is stupid," says the girl. "Of course they are there."

"Well, you must give me time to convince them. These men will only believe things that they see with their own eyes."

"That's stupid, too," she says. "What if they were blind? The little animals would still be there. What does it have to do with them?"

What indeed, he thinks. He says to the girl: "Vermeer and his family will take good care of you, and you can come back as soon as they are gone."

"All right," she agrees. "The geese hate strangers, anyway."

"Isn't Johannes a stranger?"

"No." She shrugs, " I know him." She steps away from him, and the geese move after her soundlessly, waiting for her to open the gate. "We will go to pasture now and then to Johannes," she says. She wraps her heavy woolen shawl over her head and around her small form, tucking the ends under her arms. She pulls knitted mitts from her belt and puts them on as she walks. The geese follow her, dignified, in single file, their backsides twitching back and forth.

Leeuwenhoek is struck by a sudden, senseless fear that he will not see them again. They are leaving his world, as he has faithlessly sent them away. "Goodbye!" he calls after them, panicked. None of them turn, or stop. They proceed quietly away from him down the narrow lane, turn left, and are soon lost to sight.

Coming back in, he passes Pierre in the hall, heading home, and avoids his eye. The lad is subdued, but he says politely, "I'll give your best to Vermeer." Then, sounding more like himself, he adds "I won't ask him to invest, though."

"He might try," replies Leeuwenhoek. "Don't let him."

"No fear," says Pierre, wrapping a scarf about his neck and slipping out the door.

Leeuwenhoek feels abandoned. The goose girl, gone. Pierre, gone. These two children, not even his own, who have changed everything for him. One mad and one half-blind. It is a strange world. And now these important English philosophers will come, reasonable men in possession of all their senses, and he will strive to impress them, and he will probably succeed in doing so because he, too, is a reasonable man in possession of all his senses, and then they will leave, and all the while the goose girl and Pierre, the crazy child and the cripple, will be just a few streets away at the house of Vermeer, both of them capable of perceiving animalcules more clearly than any of them.

～

Next morning, early, there is a polite knock on the door. Barbara answers it, wearing her best dress and her Water Garden shawl, and admits three men: a tall, thin man with fiery red hair, who must be MacFarlane, David Forsythe, the rector, and a pale, fair man with dark circles under his eyes, the priest, William Davenant. The priest does not look well. He is practically swaying on his feet. Barbara looks at him with concern and offers him some coffee. Her English is still quite good though she only practices occasionally. Davenant looks surprised and relieved, both at the excellence of her English and at the prospect of feminine care. The rector lives alone in a tiny flat.

Barbara goes to the kitchen to prepare coffee, while everyone else performs introductions. Leeuwenhoek is glad, after all, that Forsythe is there. His accent is bad, but he knows perfectly well what is going on and is helpful. Leeuwenhoek has always liked him, and he is, at least, a known quantity. MacFarlane, of course, is a Scot. He lives in Edinburgh, where there is a famous school of medicine, and keeps his own microscopes at home, which he uses primarily for botany. A lot of his friends are doctors, which is how he knows the Society. He is in the Low Countries acting in the interest of a great landowner in southern Scotland, who sells huge crops of wool to mills in Amsterdam, Antwerp, and Bruges. As everything to do with the wool trade is taxed at London, he had been in the city on that business when he heard that the Society wanted an emissary to Delft. "Hooke showed me those drawings of the *animalcula* in the water. I have never seen the like of them. So I came," he says, nodding vigorously. The miserable, shivering priest, Davenant, has crossed the water to supervise the printing of some pamphlets in Amsterdam and then is going on to attend a Protestant conclave in Geneva. Unless he drops dead of the ague first, Leeuwenhoek thinks, looking at him.

They take sugared coffee, hot wine punch with fruit, and pastries in the great room. The room looks lovely, thanks to the efforts of Barbara (who had worked all afternoon preparing it the previous day) and Marieke (who arranged the flowers). Marieke, who in her own mind had done the bulk of the work, serves cream for the coffee with a proprietorial air. She looks quite darling in her miniature, perfect dress and apron, with her crisp white cap and thick, braided hair tidily pinned. Silver glints on the table. Cinnamon and clove scent the air. There is a small, hot fire. Davenant looks around gratefully and tries not to collapse too obviously into the large chair nearest the hearth. MacFarlane holds a mug of punch in his chapped red hands and looks around at the beautifully furnished dollhouse, the layers of tablecloths on the table, the shining dress of Barbara as she passes by. "There's enough good cloth in this room to outfit Whitehall," he says approvingly. "It's easy to see you are a draper by trade." Forsythe does not need to repeat this in Dutch. He is hovering near the fire with a cup of coffee in his hands, wearing the inquisitive, birdlike aspect of a translator, head cocked slightly to one side.

"Now that is a remarkable contrivance," says the priest, gesturing toward the dollhouse. "Splendid craftsmanship. To whom does it belong?" He addresses Marieke in passable Dutch: "Is it yours, young lady?"

"Oh no!" says Marieke. "It's mother's. But she lets me look after it. I set the table and do the dusting, every day." Davenant nods solemnly. Marieke nods solemnly back. She is pleased to be part of the adult conversation.

When everyone has finished, they depart for the study. Barbara says tactfully, looking at the weary priest, "I will put out some fresh food and coffee in one hour's time. It will be there all through the morning, until dinner time."

"Thank you, Mevrouw," says Davenant, bowing and trying not to stagger.

With four men in it, the study feels crowded. The priest sits on the window sill. The rest stand. Leeuwenhoek opens the shutters for light. Fortunately it is not too overcast. He has laid out a number of vials and viewers on the work table. These, he knows, because he has already checked, contain wheel bugs and straight wormlike forms and translucent round bodies from pond water. One contains honeydew. The lenses in the viewers are excellent quality ground glass. He has also laid out several microscopes for them to examine. These they will use to look at solid samples.

All of the lenses on display are good, up to 200x magnification, but none are his best. Those remain hidden under the lathe, where they will stay. Not even Pierre knows where he keeps them.

MacFarlane looks delighted. He rubs his hands together. "Let's see, then! Let's see! Do you mind?" He points to a vial on the table, its viewer attached neatly to its side.

"Take it," replies Leeuwenhoek, in English. He is proud of himself.

The red-headed man picks up the vial and goes to the window. Needing no instructions, he looks through the viewer and maneuvers around to get the best light. He is silent, doing this. "Ah," he says suddenly, "there it is. Rafts of stuff, joined all tidily. Look at that clarity. Best lens I've ever seen. So much light coming through. This is what you call *honeydew*, is it? From the letter?"

"Yes," says Leeuwenhoek. At least he understands the question.

"Well, that's certainly there, all right. We can consider that confirmed," says MacFarlane, not taking his eye from the viewer. Forsythe, smiling, translates this: it is important. "What do you think it is, this stuff? Is it a tiny plant?" asks MacFarlane. He is a botanist, after all.

"I don't think so," replies Leeuwenhoek. He figures he might as well be honest. "It doesn't seem to have all the parts of plants that I have seen. Wouldn't you agree? But it needs light to grow, I think, and blooms out in spring and summer, so it is plant-like."

Forsythe does his best with this. "I see," says MacFarlane thoughtfully. He beckons Davenant over. "You'd better have a look, too, Father. You've come all this way." It is evident that MacFarlane is not too worried about the priest's opinion. He is the kind of man who is used to judging things for himself.

Davenant takes the viewer and looks through it. After a moment, he gives a little jump of startlement. "Good God!" he says, "will you look at that? Like floating emeralds! Clear as day! Good God! This is just floating around in ponds, you say?"

"Yes," affirms Leeuwenhoek.

"So we can confirm that the Church of England sees it, too, then, can we?" says MacFarlane with a hint of malice. "Maybe we can include it in the Book of Common Prayer?"

The rector does not translate. Davenant looks at the Scot wearily and says, "Yes. I can confirm it."

Leeuwenhoek wisely says nothing.

"Can I see?" says Forsythe, after a moment.

"Of course," says Leeuwenhoek. Davenant hands him the vial. Forsythe looks through the viewer, fiddles about with angles, and says, "Merciful heavens!" He gazes dumbfounded at the vial for a little while. "It's a whole new world!" he says. The two priests look at each other meditatively. Thoughts pass through their minds that they do not share with the others. Forsythe passes back the vial.

"Do you have some of those lively little beasties from pond water?" asks MacFarlane. "I am dying to get a look at those." The "oo" in "look" has a nice Dutch sound to it that reminds Leeuwenhoek of his old master, Davidson, years ago.

"Yes, right here." Leeuwenhoek hands the man another vial.

After a moment an explosive "Christ!" comes from the window. "Incredible! Amazing! There they are, wriggling around, look at that, moving under their own power, holy God... It's a whole village!" He hands the vial to the waiting Davenant.

The priest looks into the vial silently. He passes it to his comrade, the rector. Forsythe looks as well, silently. Leeuwenhoek feels a rising anxiety. Forsythe passes the vial and its viewer back to the hovering MacFarlane, who is immediately absorbed again. He pays no attention to the two clerics.

Forsythe says quietly, "We can certainly both confirm that there is life in that vial. Some kind of life. It is like a miracle. I cannot quite take it in."

"Nor me," says Davenant, sitting back down on the sill, looking haggard. "Dear God. Are such creatures everywhere? We have been sharing the world with them all this time? Why are they not mentioned in Genesis? Or are they, and we've failed to see it? As we've failed to see them? Are we meant to see them? Or is this part of the privacy of creation, that we have just invaded? Oh my God."

Leeuwenhoek does not get every word of this, but the gist is clear. He understands the man's distress. He has had similar thoughts himself. On the other hand, he is not a priest. It is not his duty to make determinations about blasphemy. Mind you, is it the duty of an English priest to make such determinations in Holland? No. Is it the job of any man to suppress the light of divine reason? No. Is it, in fact, even possible for a man to injure the grace of God? No. Any mistake we make, he can rectify. So we should be fearless. The most disastrous inquiry of all time, in Eden, led to the Passion of Christ. People were left more godly than before. All this races through Leeuwenhoek's mind as he watches the English priest struggling.

"Tea," says Davenant. He makes an unsteady gesture and walks to the door and away down the hall. Leeuwenhoek earnestly hopes that Barbara has set out tea as well as coffee. He wonders if he should go after the man. But

Forsythe lets him go, unworriedly. And Barbara is there, and her English is far better than his, anyway. He had better stick with MacFarlane, the official envoy.

"Wonderful!" says MacFarlane, from the window. "Aren't you the lucky man, to have discovered all this? It's like finding another continent! I congratulate you!" Forsythe says a few words for clarification. "Now, what else have you got for me?"

Leeuwenhoek shows him the variety of scopes on the table. The man picks them up carefully, one by one, examines their simple mechanisms: the pin mount, the screw for focus. "I have to say, I've seen finer metalwork; some of these are a bit crude. But you can't argue with their effectiveness. We can't all be beauties. Still, we get the job done, eh? I've never seen lenses like yours. Make mine look like children's toys. Can you show me how to mount a specimen?" Forsythe translates all this.

Leeuwenhoek shows the man how to stick a fragment of willow leaf onto the mounting pin. He goes happily to the window. Leeuwenhoek puts a small slice of oak on the pin of another scope. Then an insect wing. Finally, a tiny chip of dried blood. McFarlane goes through these, one after the other, with many oaths and exclamations. He is agog. Leeuwenhoek understands that his reputation with the Royal Society is now secure. A happiness, though one not unmixed with anxiety, floods through him. It will not be entirely unmixed until he receives some sort of document with a gold seal.

Now comes the part Leeuwenhoek has been dreading. Putting down the last scope with a sigh of satisfaction, MacFarlane says expansively, "can you tell me a bit about how you make these? If you don't mind? Why are your lenses so much better than others'?"

There is no way Leeuwenhoek can explain all this in English, so it is slow going as he takes MacFarlane through the process of scoring, cutting, and grinding the lenses out of the panes of optical glass he buys from Amsterdam. He demonstrates the use of the lathe. He does some hand buffing. He explains that he uses various grades of glass, sometimes even cheap glass beads, grinding them down but keeping the convexity on one side. The trick, he explains, is to make them as much as possible like a human eye. Not flat, but round. And small. As small as possible. This minimizes distortion. This is why he never uses two lenses and doesn't believe in barrel mountings: too much distortion. It's just not worth it.

All this takes over an hour, and the rector is beginning to look harried. There has been no sign of Davenant, either. They decide to take a break, and rest and wash before dinner. As they are walking back along the hall to the great room, MacFarlane asks if he has any scopes for sale. Leeuwenhoek says that he does: they agree to look over them in the afternoon. McFarlane says he wants one for his own collection but that he had better buy one or two for the Society, as well. Leeuwenhoek thinks of Hooke, that eminent philosopher, using one of his microscopes, and swells with irrepressible pride.

In the great room they find Davenant, Barbara, and Marieke drinking India tea and playing with the dollhouse. Marieke is moving the various items around, in consultation with the other two. An odd but comfortable mixture of English and Dutch conversation can be heard as they enter the room. Barbara is seated on the stool in front of the house, her teacup on the floor beside her. She looks happier and more animated than Leeuwenhoek has seen her for months. The priest looks peaky and feverish, his eyes and cheeks bright, but he is highly engaged in talk with both Barbara and the little girl. He seems to have gotten over his shock.

"Papa, we have been playing you in the study," says Marieke proudly as he comes in.

"Ah, have you?" says Leeuwenhoek. "What does that involve?" The priest eyes him sheepishly, but he is too ill to be much embarrassed. He looks ready to keel over. Barbara has provided him with a blanket that he has laid over his lap. He is still shivering.

"Well, I don't know what you do in there, so I just make it up," replies Marieke.

"I do that myself," admits Leeuwenhoek.

"Mostly it's moving bottles and jars around. And some cleaning."

"I do those, too," he agrees. "But which room is it?"

"Oh, it's this one," says Marieke. "Didn't you know?" She points to the storage room and pantry that connects to the kitchen of the dollhouse by a small spiral staircase. It is indeed full of tiny bottles and jars, some of which he made himself. He sees a tiny golden thing on the table of the room.

"What is that?" he says. "On the table?" The object is minuscule. Looking at it closely, he sees that it is a miniature pair of *pince-nez*. It must have come from some doll long since broken.

"It's a microscope, of course," says Marieke. MacFarlane lets out a hoot of laughter from the doorway.

"Of course it is, wee girlie!" he says. Turning to Leeuwenhoek, he says, "Ach, man, you must have known that!"

"Indeed. We all practice natural philosophy in this family," says Leeuwenhoek, in perfect English. The sentence comes out of his mouth as smoothly as if pulled by a string. He and Barbara look at each other in momentary disbelief, almost horror. Then they burst out laughing. Marieke also laughs uproariously, without knowing or caring why.

"What? You speak English?" says MacFarlane, looking at him comically askance.

"No!" says Leeuwenhoek.

"It was a miracle," says the rector, lightly. Everyone chuckles.

"Big day for miracles," says Davenant, falling out of his chair in a dead faint.

Marieke utters a little scream. Leeuwenhoek and Forsythe dash forward as Barbara is struggling up from her low stool. They pick the priest up from the floor and lean him back in his chair. Fortunately, he had crashed over directly onto the heavy blanket and thus had not hit his head on the floor.

"Best get him to a bed," gasps Barbara, leaning on the dollhouse for support. She gets lightheaded when she stands up too fast. There is a box bed in the second kitchen. The maid sleeps there. Leeuwenhoek and Forsythe lug the unconscious man there. They prop him on extra pillows to help his respiration. Everyone knows it is unsafe to lie flat. Davenant's eyes flicker open, and he mumbles something. He is hot to the touch. "Give him some water. Small sips," says Barbara, coming in, clutching her side. "Antoni, I think you should get Reinier."

"Yes," says Leeuwenhoek. He turns to MacFarlane, who is standing there, pale with shock. "My friend Reinier De Graaf is a doctor. He should be home at this hour. I am going to get him," he explains. Somehow, magically, he again says this in English. No one notices. He grabs his coat from a peg in the rear kitchen and clatters out the back door.

The rest are left standing about in the kitchen. Its surfaces are crowded with food for dinner, ready to be brought through to the great room. The maid is clinking and thumping through the wall in the rear kitchen, making pastry. Barbara passes through to speak to her, and she emerges momentarily, wiping her hands on her apron, to take Marieke upstairs. Barbara dips a cloth in a bucket of cold well water and mops the priest's brow and cheeks.

"He had a bad journey," says MacFarlane hoarsely. "Sea-sick all the way. Awful. But it didn't go away when we landed. Seemed to get worse. Now it looks like a fever. Poor fellow. Who is this doctor?"

"Reinier De Graaf," says Barbara, still mopping. "He trained in France, at Angers. And at Leiden. He is very skilled. An old friend of Antoni."

"Lucky he is in town. A physician is best if you can get one," says MacFarlane. "Though any port in a storm, of course. Apothecaries and whatnot."

"Mevrouw Leeuwenhoek," says the rector, "Would it be helpful if we were to take this food through to the other room, if this is to be a sickroom, at least for a little while? We can get around to eating it sometime, I hope, and meanwhile the area will be free for De Graaf when he arrives? You and the maid are both occupied."

MacFarlane nods in agreement as he stands next to him. Barbara blushes at the thought of guests doing such work in her house, but agrees. She stays sitting with the drowsing, muttering priest. The two men carry dish after dish out onto the table in the great room, using cloths to protect their hands. Then they come back and stand awkwardly around the bedside. After a moment, Barbara rises, goes through to the rear kitchen, and gets the chilled silver jug of wine waiting there. "Perhaps we could all use a glass of wine after this excitement?" she suggests. She paces heavily through to the dining table and pours two glasses. She brings them to the men and then returns to fill a smaller one for herself. All three of them settle within sight of Davenant, on the edge of the bed or on kitchen benches. They are uneasy leaving him alone until the doctor arrives. Barbara thinks wistfully of the delicious meal getting cold on the great room table. She is always starving these days.

Barbara and the two men sip their wine. The whole situation is uncomfortable. She tries to think of the last time she has been alone in a room with two men she hardly knows. Three, counting the poor priest. Foreigners, even. At least the rector speaks Dutch, after a fashion. Finally Forsythe speaks, in English, swirling the wine in his glass. "It is so very hard to make small talk in a language not your own, isn't it?"

"Small talk," replies Barbara in the same language, smiling. "Why is it called that? Not large talk, I suppose. In Dutch, too, we have small talk, you know, *praatje*—a little chat? But what is the large talk?"

"It's what your daughter thought we were doing when we were shut away in the study," says MacFarlane.

"Yes! Just so! But did you think it was large, at that time?" she asks. The priest mumbles beside her and she strokes his clammy hand absently.

"No," says Forsythe, "I rarely think of my speech as large. Except maybe when preaching. In olden days, you know, in English, *large language* was rude, insulting. So you could challenge me to a duel, you know? French, of course. Now we might say 'talking big' and mean bragging or boasting, I suppose. Thinking ourselves important."

"Ach, but I am important," says MacFarlane with mock gravity, "If not large." He gestures to his belly. He is a tall man, but very thin. "It's only priests who say they aren't."

"And why is that?" asks Forsythe.

"Presumably God's important enough for the lot of you. The rest of us have to get on as we can. You work for the Lord Almighty. I work for Lord Firth of Dunvernie."

"Well then, Mijnheer MacFarlane," says Barbara to the Scotsman, who looks bemused at the title, "what speeches of yours have been large?"

He looks thoughtful. "I may say, I am a dab hand at swearing. Cursing, that is. Speaking insult. It's an art where I come from. I could curse you out such that your hair would turn white overnight, Mevrouw."

Forsythe laughs. McFarlane looks affronted. "There's never been an Englishman who could swear like a Scot!"

"Well I know it," says Forsythe. "I once had a sister-in-law...well, best leave that alone. I believe you."

The back door rattles, and Leeuwenhoek comes charging into the room, followed by De Graaf, who is carrying a heavy black bag. Both men are breathless. "Here is the doctor!" says Leeuwenhoek.

De Graaf looks around at them all. "Go and eat that dinner I smell," he says. "Leave him to me. Barbara needs to keep up her strength." They all file out. Leeuwenhoek is last to leave. He and his friend glance at each other as the doctor opens his bag. "Did you really need to kill the priest?" says De Graaf, "There is such a thing as taking natural philosophy too far."

De Graaf's lips twitch as he turns to his patient. Leeuwenhoek turns on his heel and goes in to dinner with the remaining delegates of the Royal Society.

Falada

"There are horses in the market," says the goose girl to Vermeer as she leads the geese into his courtyard. He is outside smoking one of his rare pipes of tobacco. His wife will not permit him to smoke indoors. Tobacco is expensive. He only smokes when he hits a rough spot in a painting, or anticipates one. He knows that Pierre will be coming tomorrow, and he will have to start grafting the apprentice's head on to the body of his son Jan, who modeled the figure. He is not happy about it. There are a thousand ways for the process to go wrong.

"Horses?" he says to the girl, as the geese stream by, "that's unusual. It's not time for the horse fair. How many?"

"I don't know. More than ten. A flock."

"A herd. Maybe they are there for slaughter. People eat horse meat. Not nearly as good as beef, in my opinion. It's often fed to dogs. And horsehide is strong and is used for many things. I suppose if I go over tomorrow I could get some horsehair for coarse brushes..."

"I spoke to one. He said his name was Falada."

With any of his own children, he would assume that this was make-believe. The child wants the horse to be named Falada, so the horse tells her. With the goose girl, he is not sure. "How did he tell you?" he asks.

"I heard it in his mind. Horses are like dogs, you know. They remember the sound of some words, like names. Not like geese."

"Don't your geese have names?"

"Yes, but that's just for me. I thought them up on the road. And I like to talk to them. They don't use them, or remember them."

"What did Falada say?"

"He was tired and had pain in him somewhere, I think in his legs. But he was happy to be out in the fresh air. He had been in a dark place. He didn't mind the cold."

"Those do sound like things a horse would say. What kind of horse was he?"

"A big gray one, with dapples and hairy feet."

"There's a kind like that that comes from France, around La Perche. They are beautiful, huge animals. Perhaps he has come a long way, on a great adventure. Or his ancestors did. Those horses used to be used for war. Knights rode them. But now they are mostly used on farms."

"Knights like Lancelot?"

How does this illiterate girl know about Lancelot? "Yes, like Lancelot. Did Antoni tell you about him?"

"Yes. He said he wasn't real."

"What?" says Vermeer, scandalized. "Of course he is real! He's just dead! So what? Hundreds of books talk about him!"

"Maybe they lie. He lived long ago. How do we know what happened then?"

"Because the books tell us! That's the whole point of books! And paintings! To tell us what happens! If you can't believe them, what's the point of anything?"

"I don't know. Do things need a point?"

"For me they do," says Vermeer, drawing heavily on his pipe and then coughing. Smoking is a bizarre thing to do. It always makes him uncomfortable, and he finds this distracting, which is the point, when he is troubled.

"What is burning in there?" asks the girl. "Grass?"

"The dried leaves of a plant called tobacco. It grows in the Americas, and in the West Indies. Far away, in hot places. This is from the West Indies."

"It smells nice. The geese like it. Like fires in autumn."

This remark focuses his attention on the geese for the first time. "You haven't shut the gate. Will they stay, without it?" he asks.

"Oh yes. They stay where I am. I don't know how to latch that kind of gate."

Vermeer shows her. "Would they stay even if you left? Can you command them, like dogs?"

"If I told them, they would stay for a while. A long while. Especially if there was something here with my smell on it. Clothes or something. Or if I peed on the ground."

"If you pee on the ground, all my children will want to do it, too, so don't do it where any of them can see, I beg you," says Vermeer.

"No. I won't."

"Come in and have a bit of supper. I have a little grain in the kitchen that you can scatter for them, too. You can wash inside."

"Oh, I don't need to wash."

"You do, or I will never hear the end of it," says the painter. "It is hard enough getting the children to wash already. Hand washing it is, with the rest of them!" He thinks for a minute. "Just like Lancelot. All the knights and ladies used to wash in silver basins, with fine linen, before feasts. It's in all the stories."

"Why?"

"It was a ritual."

"What's a ritual?"

"Something people do to make themselves feel safe." He knocks out his pipe. "Now come in, you exhausting child!"

The goose girl follows the artist into his house. She is not happy. She does not like children; they are unpredictable. But she is very hungry. There is little in the fields at this time of year, for her. The geese are fine.

She washes her hands and face in a long wooden basin, almost like a trough, in the rear kitchen, along with three other children. They are younger than she is, or at least smaller. They are shy at that age, at least at first, so she ignores them. She may be able to eat and get away before they work up their courage to do anything.

Entering the first kitchen, she finds a huge crowd sitting around a table. A blur of adult faces—including one old woman who looks hard and mean—and some more children, a bit older, more like adults. They will be controlled by the presence of their parents, so she doesn't have to worry about them. Still, this is far too many people. She hopes the food is good. She must get back to the geese as soon as possible. She can water them and give them grain. It would be so much simpler if she could just eat grain, too. But she has tried. It does not work. She can hardly chew it, and she just poops it out; it does not seem to stay inside her. For food, that cannot be right.

The food is good. There is bread, for one thing. She loves bread. There is a stew of meat, and bowls of various roots. Then some more bread with sweet stuff. She keeps her head down, eats quickly, and speaks as little as possible. So do most of the other children. Vermeer speaks to a woman with a baby inside her, who must be his wife. The baby is about the size of a pear, and it is sleeping. Soon it will wake up because of all this food. The old woman also talks a lot. She corrects the children, and complains that the bread is burnt. She wears rich clothes and looks discontented. The goose girl does not trust her. She is the kind of person who will always be as cruel as she can get away with. Fortunately, the old lady also considers herself too important to talk to a goose girl, though she glances at her from time to time with loathing.

As soon as the girl is done eating, she rises silently. "I must go back to the geese now. They need water and grain. I saw the grain by the door. I will take my plate back to the basin." She edges past two other children, holding her dirty plate up over their heads, and heads for the rear of the house. They look at her in amazement. One of the older children laughs. The painter shrugs. Then she is through the door and away.

That night, she sleeps on a pile of blankets by the stove in the rear kitchen, close to the door of the yard. She can hear the geese fluttering and hooting as they settle to sleep, huddled close in the cold. She has many times slept with them like that. It is the only way that makes sense in this weather. The ones on the outside of the huddle keep watch, sleeping with one eye open. She has always wished she could do that, too.

In the morning, she takes them to the pasture. Vermeer's wife gives her some bread. It is not as good as Barbara's. She smells fear and blood as she goes by the market, and the geese are uneasy. They hurry through. In the field, the day passes slowly. It is cold, so the geese do not want to stay out too long. As soon as the light begins to fail, they clamor and fuss to go home. The girl wishes she could lead them back to Antoni's house as usual. But she has said that she will go back to Vermeer's tonight. It never occurs to her to do other than she has said.

They troop back into town. On the outskirts of the market, the geese are once again uneasy. The horses are gone. The smell of blood is stronger, now mixed with lime. They are about halfway through the square when she sees a solitary figure standing by a cart. It is Johannes.

She recognizes his hat. As she comes up to him, she sees that he is holding what looks like half a horse's tail, a big handful of long, coarse hairs. Still and mournful, he is gazing down at something lying in the back of the cart. Coming abreast of it, she sees that it is full of dim, lumpy shapes: the heads of horses, piled up. At the nearest edge lies the head of Falada, light gray and bloody. The one dark eye showing is misted over. The head lies on its side, one flat cheek down, one up, its tongue protruding over the edge of the cart. From the tongue slow drops of blood, thick and black, drop to the ground like quiet words.

"Is it Falada?" asks Johannes.

"Yes," she says. She is sad, and angry. Horses die. All creatures die. Some are eaten, some not. Such things do not normally upset her. It is just that she had met Falada so very recently, just the day before. His funny, horsey mind had been happy and snorty and full of glee to be out in the air, away from darkness. So she is sad for him. It is at the little animals that she is angry. She can hear them everywhere, covering the heads of all the dead horses, buzzing and spreading and growing in the skull of Falada. In his blood, in his spit, in his hair. Feeding on his death. It is unfair. She is rarely angry with them, but she is now. They are cruel. They care nothing for Falada. Nothing for her.

Vermeer watches the goose girl clench her fists. Tears slide soundlessly down her cheeks as she looks at the horse's head. He pats her small shoulder hesitantly. Under his palm her slight frame is quivering with powerful emotion; he can feel it coursing through her like a mill-race, dark and turbulent, with bright flashes. Its direction is not single; it is like touching a school of fish or a swarm of bees. He feels on the edge of some enormity, an abyss or a whirlpool. He takes his hand away.

"Horrible creatures!" she says, "triumphing over him like that! I hate them!"

"What creatures?" he asks, confused.

"The little animals! Vile things! Death-feeders! Everywhere!"

"They are on him, those ones you can see through the microscope? Is that what you mean?"

"Yes! And so it sounds like Falada is speaking, poor Falada, but he is not! It is them! They lie! Liars! Liars!" she says. She begins to sob.

Vermeer has no idea what to do. He is afraid to touch her again. She is full of some huge revelatory power that makes his spirit quail. So he stands feebly beside her as she cries and cries, muttering soothing words that make no sense even to himself. Behind him, the geese scream and squawk and flap their wings, standing up high. It is like being caught in a storm.

After a few moments the girl calms. Then the geese. Vermeer feels his heart racing. "We must go home," he manages to say.

"Yes," says the girl impassively, wiping her red eyes. She begins to walk across the square again; the geese fall into line. The painter trails after them, like a goose himself. He has about as much idea as they do about whatever has just happened. His thoughts feel jumbled in his head. At least, he thinks shakily, he and Antoni were right to keep the girl away from the English priests. Who knows what they would make of such a display?

PIERRE AT THE WINDOW

Reflections from the silver microscope are dazzling Pierre's eyes and giving him a headache. He has been standing here by the window for over two hours, staring at the empty mounting pin of the scope through the glass. He has been cursing himself continuously for not having the presence of mind to bring a specimen with him. A nice little fragment of that butterfly wing, say, would liven things up considerably. He is getting a crick in the neck. He never gets sore from actually working. He can spend hours squinting through tiny scopes with no problem at all.

He is wearing an elaborate sort of velvet tunic that he suspects is red. It is absolutely not the kind of thing he would ever wear, and it does not fit him. It is also dusty, and it is making him sneeze intermittently. Whenever he does this Vermeer roars at him. He has a loud voice for such a small man. At least he is wearing his own breeches. The tunic is quite long and he is standing behind a desk, upon which are artfully displayed a number of specimen jars, some empty, some full of colored liquids. From where he stands he can see that each jar stands in its own circle of chalk, traced precisely around its base. If he picked one up—which would undoubtedly lead to another roar—he knows that he would see numbers, on the desk and on the base of each corresponding jar. He can also see, from behind the desk, where all the jars have been carefully, almost invisibly marked to indicate their levels. These are not things that can be left to chance.

A significant amount of the painting is already done. Vermeer's son Jan, whom he has seen around the house with red eyes and a sniffling nose, no doubt from this vile tunic, has been standing in for him for weeks now. The lad is a bit shorter than he is and has had to stand on a pile of books, which are now stacked in a corner. He is fairly sure that one of them is a Bible, though its spine has been turned inward toward the wall. The rest of the composition has been thoroughly painted in, save for the last layer of highlighting that must necessarily wait for all the final reflections from the scope, his hair, the window-pane, and so on. Whatever drawing and underpainting Vermeer has done that involved the *camera obscura* is now hidden—obscured. Pierre is annoyed. This is the stage he would most have liked to see. The rest is pretty boring, and he has seen it many times before.

The man has had the grace, at least, to show the camera to him, as it is, after all, the whole reason Pierre is sitting for him. It is a beautiful instrument. As Vermeer had been demonstrating it, a gray horse had stopped outside the window. The man had looked down at its perfect, flattened image on the drawing surface as if he had never seen a horse before. He had looked positively stricken, his hands clenched on the table edge. After a moment, noticing Pierre looking at him curiously, he let go his hands and turned away, but not before giving the image of the horse a long, steady, measuring glance of at least ten seconds. Pierre knows that glance. If a horse shows up in one of the man's paintings soon, he will not be surprised.

Another explosive sneeze. Seconds later, it is overcast as a bank of cloud moves in. "Goddamn it!" says Vermeer, "you've sneezed out the sun, you cretin! Jesus! Well, better give it up for today. I think I've got somewhere."

"Thank God," says Pierre, putting down the scope and massaging his neck. He takes off the tunic immediately. He is just putting it carefully over the back of a chair when he looks out the window and sees Frans Hoek hurrying down the street toward the house.

Moments later there is a knock on the door. Mevrouw Vermeer answers it and then ushers the big, bluff man into the room. Hoek looks a lot like his nephew Joost except that his coloring is dark: tanned skin, even in winter, dark eyes, and hair. He has enormous, powerful, muscled hands from ironworking. "Johannes!" he says, shaking the painter's hand. "And Pierre! Antoni told me I would find you here. An interesting opportunity has just come my way. I came to tell you about it."

Vermeer looks at the cheerful merchant sourly. "Frans," he says, "take Pierre down to the great room. Kick the children out if you must. I must clean up here. And the fact is, when I am painting, I hate everybody. It saves time and helps me concentrate." He turns to the task of cleaning his brushes.

"Right," says Hoek unflappably, seizing Pierre by the shoulder and steering him out of the room, pausing only to let him pick up his jacket. They march down the hall to the great room. It is crowded with children, women, workbaskets. Some of the children are immediately sent away.

The two of them sit at a small table in the corner. There is a squawk as Frans sits down. A cat is in the chair. He grabs it in both hands and dumps it unceremoniously on the floor, where it flounces away indignantly. "Busy in here," remarks Hoek. "Now, this is what I've come to tell you. I want you pass it on to the other investors. I've just had a large order of fancy grillwork—balcony railings— to be sent to Prague. They're to be sent on from there because some big family is building a huge castle in Poland.

Why they aren't ordering locally I have no idea; some trade dispute or other, I suppose. Anyway, it's to be there by spring, when they break ground and start building. There's a huge team assembled. I think we should send along some fabric samples on the barge, eh? They have a whole castle to decorate. They'll need miles of cloth. If they like even one, we'd make a killing. And you know how Frenchie they are in Poland; the fact that it's selling well in Paris will impress them. Don't you think?"

"I agree," Pierre replies. "How much would we send? Some of everything? I wonder if we could have Staff of Life ready by then—sounds like they could afford it?"

"Exactly what I thought. Not everybody can. We'd best get on to DeVeyne and see how he's getting on with that velvet."

"Right," says Pierre. "I will tell Antoni. When do you ship?"

"As soon as I know the firm date, I will drop by Antoni's house. Why aren't we meeting there, anyway?"

"Oh, he's entertaining some guests from England. Natural philosophers interested in his microscopes." A stab of annoyance passes through his mind.

"Natural philosophers? Not your everyday draper, is he, Antoni?" says Frans, shaking his head.

"No."

Hoek, who never stays in one place for long, rises and shakes Pierre's hand. He nods politely to the women, avoids treading on the small children, and makes his exit. He nearly collides in the doorway with Jan, bearing a tray of pastries. Jan's eyes are much less red, Pierre observes. The boy, who is about fifteen, slight and blonde like his mother, puts the tray of sweets down on the table, where it is directly set upon by the children. He grabs one and hands it to Pierre before they are all gone. "Here," he says, in a low voice so his mother and the maid cannot hear him. "Thanks for wearing that fucking tunic." Pierre raises his pastry in a salute.

"Now hold on, hold on," he hears Mevrouw Vermeer saying the background. "Slow down. We must save some for the others. Jan, can you call them, please?"

"Yes, mama," says the boy dutifully. He goes out to the hall and shouts upstairs. Shuffling feet are heard, and three more children come trooping down. Chattering happily, they squeeze between Pierre and Jan and rush through the door toward the tray. "Little fuckers," says Jan, squashed against the wall of the narrow passage. He looks exhausted. Pierre, finishing his pastry, reflects that being the only son of his mother is not so bad. On the other hand, more of them might spread the beatings around.

He goes to find Vermeer. He will have to excuse himself to go and find the other investors. Antoni was right: something important has come up in the cloth business. He will have to take care of it. It takes a little of the sting out of missing the Royal Society visit. Just a little.

CONGRATULATIONS

"Congratulations, Mijnheer Van Leeuwenhoek!" says MacFarlane, wringing his hand heartily as he stands in the great room. He has congratulated Leeuwenhoek several times before, in passing, but this is evidently the final flourish. "As the Royal Society of London's official delegate, I hereby confirm your findings of *animalcula* from pond water, the impressive quality of your microscopes, and the trustworthiness of your philosophical investigations. I extend the Society's invitation to send whatever further observations you like, at any time, and a formal invitation of membership will be sent in due course."

Leeuwenhoek bows. MacFarlane bows. He feels like they are about to launch into a country dance. He hates this solemn rigmarole, and yet there seems to be no realm of human endeavor free of it. The goings-on in the guild of St Nicholas are sometimes enough to drive him to distraction. He always wishes he could send Barbara in his stead. She has a gift for such things. And it is by no means true that all women do. He has seen many of them, poor souls, crammed into the ridiculous layers of their finery—half the contents of a drapers' shop at once, it looks like—red-faced, anxious, their hair straggling, walking like ducks. They talk too much; they talk too little. They do no better than men do. But Barbara, a draper's wife, daughter of a brewer, can act like a duchess when the occasion requires. She does not fuss. She does not stumble. She is somehow queenly and yet puts everybody at his ease. Her clothes are stylish; any room

she decorates looks superb. She handles all the arrange-
ments for important occasions in his irritating job at the
Stadthuis. These are very real gifts. He himself has none
of them.

"Thank you," says Leeuwenhoek, "thank you very
much." He has sold the man three microscopes and two
unmounted lenses. He has convinced him of his claims.
He has shown him practically every specimen he has in
the study. Now he is desperate to be rid of him.

MacFarlane is clad for traveling. Cape, muffler, boots.
His hat is in his hand. Leeuwenhoek, hoping his patience
will not snap, bows him out the door. It is a delicate operation, like backing a horse into traces. He has almost
done it. McFarlane covers his red hair with his tricorne as
he passes the threshold. "Goodbye," he says, and strides
off toward the inn to meet his party traveling back to Amsterdam. Leeuwenhoek slumps against the doorframe.

❧

"Congratulations, Mevrouw Leeuwenhoek," says De
Graaf, seated on the edge of the box bed in the kitch-
en. "Your guest has influenza. So you have done well to
keep Marieke away. Unfortunately, you have not kept
away yourself. This is unpropitious for a woman in your
condition. If you feel any signs of fever coming on, please
inform me immediately. Meanwhile, I will do my best to
get him out of your house forthwith."

Davenant, the priest, is awake. He is pale and thin, and
he looks ghastly. He knows he has been well cared for, and
hearing the doctor speak, he looks extremely contrite.
"Mevrouw!" he says, "I am so sorry to have put you and
your household to this trouble, perhaps even into danger!
I should never have come. I should have declined, and
stayed at Forsythe's. Forgive me!" He presses his forehead

against her hand as she sits at the bedside. He looks absolutely wretched.

"Hush now, hush, do not worry about it," she says, as she would say to Marieke. The man is sick. He has been nothing but sweet-tempered and kind. She and Marieke have just had one of the best afternoons in recent memory in his company. Still, she has to fight down a rising panic. She has felt so precarious while carrying this child. Everyone knows that influenza kills children. She feels faint.

De Graaf looks at her with concern. He says soothingly, "Forsythe is at home preparing his apartment. We have hired a nurse and fixed the broken stove. I will look after him there, and he will be entirely comfortable. It is even a bit closer to my apothecary. I will bring news and come to check up on all of you. We have hired a wagon that should be here within the hour."

"Thank you, Reinier," whispers Barbara, waiting for her knees to stop trembling. She is late setting the bread this morning. She must get on with it. The maid is looking after Marieke upstairs. She is well away, as De Graaf said. Well away. Safe.

❧

"Congratulations, Aliette," says Martin, as he walks into the bedroom, carrying a long legal document. She is sitting up in bed in a Chinese silk nightgown with a desk over her lap, doing accounts. "Here is the contract from DeVeyne. We are now part owners of that fabric enterprise, for the tapestry and velvet. As proper as you please."

Aliette gives him a long look. She has just given him a lot of money. He has signed the contract in his name. She has learned from experience that it is sometimes best to keep her name out of things officially, even when investing her own money. Women in Holland, especially widows like she is, are allowed to enter into contracts and to operate financially on their own. Not like in England or France. Her constraints are matters of etiquette, not of law—though as any woman will tell you, the one is as binding as the other.

Her operation is illegal only insofar as it facilitates fornication. *Vleslijke conversatie*, such a pleasant, civil phrase for fucking. It makes the Dutch sound so very tolerant. Unfortunately, fleshly conversations are illegal between unmarried parties throughout the whole Republic. Ridiculous, of course. Such stupid laws are widely, though carefully, flouted. However, they are prosecuted enough to keep magistrates busy everywhere, and they make many bailiffs rich. Many people, mostly women, endure miserable exile.

"Thank you, Martin," she replies. "Coffee?"

He sits on the bed beside her and helps himself to a cup from a silver urn. She and Martin are beginning to understand each other. At first he had been so overwhelmed by her confidence, beauty, wealth, rank, voluptuousness—by everything—that he had been nothing but flattered, thinking himself wholly in her debt. He was flattered to be allowed into her bed, flattered by her attention, flattered by her quick offer of employment. Now he is beginning to see how useful he can be to her. Even perhaps, how necessary.

That is fine. It is good for people to feel necessary, especially when they actually are. Martin had been feeling superfluous; that was why he was unhappy. He is a much happier man now. Aliette prefers to proceed by keeping people happy. People are less cruel, less unpredictable and more honorable when happy. Her husband had been a regent; she comes from a family of regents. She understands how to keep them happy. She pays taxes on her legitimate investments, and the tactful equivalent of taxes on her other business: donations to civic and guild causes, gifts to the bailiff and the *rekkers*. Free services. Occasionally she has allowed an adulterer to be exposed on her premises, though she protects her workers to the best of her ability. She has a midwife in her pay and has been known to take unruly girls from the orphanage.

Delft is not Amsterdam. People come from all over the world to go whoring there; everyone knows it; every now and again city officials are elected who need to make a show about it. Now is one such time. Hundreds of women have been prosecuted and shamed and banished in the last five years. It is grotesque, but it is good for Aliette's business in Delft. The Council of Forty understand this quite well. They are happy to deal with a woman of their own class and not the poor whore-mistresses of Amsterdam and Rotterdam, wives of common sailors, who run tiny businesses out of tenements. Aliette's establishment is run out of a serge merchant's mansion, with mahogany paneling and Chinese porcelain. Her catering costs compete with those of the Mechelen. She spends a lot of money in town and invests heavily in local enterprises, such as this one of Leeuwenhoek's. There is a lot of money for the city in textile taxes and retail tariffs.

The *Herren der Wecht* are all merchants, too; they are happy that Aliette's elegant business keeps common whores off their streets, preserves Delft's reputation as a town with good morals. They are happy that the young foreign traders, single men or men far from their wives, perform their fleshly conversations with paid women rather than their own daughters. Or wives. Or servants.

Everyone knows whose agent the yokel Martin Dekker actually is. In many respects, he is at greater risk than she is. Though she will not push that idea too far: he is still a man.

"You should have seen DeVeyne," says Martin with satisfaction. "He was beside himself. He wanted the money, but not from me. Finally I convinced him I was representing myself as well as another investor, who was as solid as the East India Company. He really needs the cash. He's bought a fancy new loom, and he's being gouged by these fellows from Lucca he's hired to train up workers to use it. He's in a panic."

"But the investment is safe?"

"DeVeyne's a prick. I don't mind seeing him sweat a little. But in my opinion he'll do as well with this as he always does—very well. There's a reason he's the biggest operator in the area."

"Excellent, Martin. Thank you," says Aliette. Martin kisses her hand and eyes her speculatively as she sits there in her loose gown. Then he finishes his coffee and departs. She is not to be distracted when she is doing accounts.

THE ENGLISH PRIEST

There is no doubt the man is very ill, thinks De Graaf, as he cleans off his smallest fleam. He has had to bleed the poor fellow. This in itself is an admission of defeat. It is a simpleton's technique, worthy of barber surgeons. Still, loss of blood volume is a surefire way of reducing body temperature, though it weakens the patient. Soaking the feet in cold water, cold compresses on the forehead, neck, and wrists; these have not sufficed to keep the fever in check. Usually he would let it run its course, but the man seems too weak to bear it; several times his eyes have rolled up and he has gone into convulsions. De Graaf is glad he was able to get the man out of Barbara's kitchen before these began to happen. They are ugly to see. She is already distraught.

Forsythe has done his best to make his dour little apartment at the rear of the English church a better place for a convalescent. A small ceramic stove breathes out proper heat. He has bought, or otherwise procured—perhaps from parishioners—more blankets. He no longer tries to feed the poor man whatever lamentable cooking he was able to do with his three dented pans on the surface of the poorly drawing stove (unused to it in its proper state, he had scorched the first meal he cooked on it after the repair beyond recognition). Instead, the nurse he has hired to assist De Graaf brings decent, nourishing food and a copious supply of meat broth twice a day. They are able to get the latter into the starving priest, spoonful by spoonful, hour after hour. He will probably live. But he will be as weak as a new duckling for weeks. Traveling will be out of the question. Forsythe seems resigned to having Davenant as his companion until spring.

No, not resigned, thinks De Graaf: eager. He does not doubt the rector's Christian charity, but looking at the way he lives, he must be a lonely man. He himself has lived in dire little rooms like this, in Paris and Angers. It is hard to be a foreigner. Endlessly anxious. Nothing is easy. And his French is fluent, unlike Forsythe's Dutch. Why has he put himself through all this? Religious fervor? Obedience? Desire for adventure? Misfortune at home? Or to help the English cause, whatever he thinks it is?

For that matter, why had he himself done it? To study medicine. To live in France, that great nation. To get away from his overbearing father. To think more broadly. Perverse that to think great thoughts one must live in small rooms. A tidy thought, worthy of an epigram. Though he is no writer of epigrams. Dissection notes are more his style. He is a new man. Not like Huygens, with that father of his, all classical quotations.

Davenant coughs from the opposite corner of the room. His cough, at least, is improving. Here medicine is actually of some use. De Graaf has compounded expectorants that have cleared his lungs a little. He has spent hours pounding him on the back. People can drown in their own phlegm. It is one of the body's many stupidities. One of his professors from Angers has had recourse to holding patients upside down, especially children, and using a siphon to clear the throat and nostrils. It sometimes works when nothing else will. But why the body should produce the vile stuff, let alone in such quantities, is a mystery. It must have some purpose. Yet it is obviously a purpose that can easily turn back on itself and produce disaster. The flesh is just as immoderate as the will. He has never been convinced that the substance rattling around in the chest of William Davenant is the phlegm spoken of by Aristotle. Leeuwenhoek's two infant sons did not die because their constitutions were too cold and moist. There is some other reason altogether. It is frightening and exhilarating to live in a time in which people are beginning to realize that all the old authorities are wrong.

"Have you seen these animalcules that Leeuwenhoek has discovered with his microscopes?" whispers the weak voice of the priest from his corner, unexpectedly. He is just barely audible.

"Many of them, yes."

The priest coughs and gasps. "As a doctor, what do you think their role is in human life?"

"It is not yet clear. But I think it will prove to be tremendously important. There is obviously a whole world of life at the microscopic scale, probably as various as life at our scale, the scale of men and animals."

"I have been thinking about it until I am exhausted," says Davenant.

"You are exhausted because you have influenza," replies De Graaf, dryly.

"But doesn't it alarm you?"

"No, not particularly."

"I feel as if I have been charged with some great responsibility, but I have no idea what it is."

"Have you talked about this with Forsythe?"

"A little. When I can talk. He seems less disturbed."

"You are likely to be overwrought in your condition. What can you be expected to do about the existence of animalcules? Stamp them out? Suppress all knowledge of them? What happens to freedom of conscience then?"

"No, no, nothing like that! It's just that I can't believe they've been here all the time and we haven't known. Or could they be something new? How can we know? I think about Adam naming the animals, you know, or the lists of creatures going into the ark—where are they? Do we reckon them among the creeping things? Or as fishes, if they are in water? There are thousands and thousands of these creatures, you say? How can the ancients not have known of them? Pliny? Galen? Do you know of any mention of them?"

"No. I have thought about it, and I don't think I have. People have described very tiny insects—water fleas and the like—and Greek philosophers used to talk about atoms. But those were tiny particles, I think, not necessarily alive. What Antoni sees, some of those are clearly alive."

"It is incredible to me that I can know Augustine's thoughts in Africa in the fifth century *anno domini* and not know this. There are probably hundreds here right now, listening to our conversation!"

"Hearing it, perhaps. Or feeling the sound vibrations. But listening to it? No. I have never seen evidences of reason in animalcules, or any organs of perception that we recognize. No more than in plants. There are millions of unknown plants in the new world, Father. Is it your duty to catalogue them—or to convert them? Like St Francis preaching to the birds?"

"What about governing them? Don't they need government?"

"They have taken care of themselves all these years. Surely they can go on a bit longer. Perhaps indefinitely. But as to killing some, and breeding others, and figuring out what they all do, and how they can be used, you can rest assured, Father, that people will take care of it eventually. We are born interferers."

"What Leeuwenhoek is doing, will it contribute to the glory of God?"

"Yes. Why should it not?"

"But to think that they are in our water, in our air, crawling all over us, the divine image! It is obscene!"

"Davenant, how complete is your idea of the divine image? You, a fallible man? Who is to say that this inhabitation has not always been part of the divine image? You realize that Christ himself lived among animalcules, and was likely covered in them, like us?"

"Christ was immaculate!"

"He was without sin. But perhaps not without animalcules, if they are part of the human condition. Part of the dirty, fallen, unpredictable world that he chose to live in."

"That is horrifying. Christ was fully himself. As we are fully ourselves. What does it mean to have these creatures living on us, and in us, and through us? Are they part of us? Have we become corporations?"

"What, like the East India Company? Or the nations of Europe? Each one of us our own body politic? You know, those corporations work quite well, much of the time…"

"De Graaf! You are joking! One person, one soul, one salvation!"

"Do you imagine the soul to be susceptible to infestation, Father? Why animalcules any more than fleas?"

"No, you are right, doctor. Quite right. Still, this whole conversation has been very disquieting," says the priest, wiping sweat from his brow.

"Father Davenant, you are still running a high fever. It is a wonder you are able to talk at all. Try to rest now," replies De Graaf. The man shifts restlessly, twitching his heavy covers, but says no more. In a moment he is once more in an exhausted sleep.

Homecoming

The goose girl is back. Leeuwenhoek is very glad to see her. His heart lifts as he hears the slap-slap-slap of goose feet on the cobbles and sees her small, stately form, wrapped in shawls, coming along the alley.

Vermeer is with them. He must have joined their procession as they came by his house, as surely he was not in the frosty fields with them all day. He, too, is bundled in layers against the creeping cold. "Antoni!" he hails him, clapping his gloved hands together. The goose girl says nothing. The geese cackle, cheered to be back in the familiar courtyard. "I have a tale to tell you!"

"Come in!" says Leeuwenhoek, to them both. The girl shakes her head. She heads for the well to water her charges. She will likely feed them and settle them before she appears in the kitchen. Vermeer accompanies Leeuwenhoek inside and starts to shrug out of his winter clothes in front of the hearth. "It's about your goose girl," says Vermeer, unwinding his scarf, loop after loop. "And about me, too, I suppose. But mostly her."

He tells Leeuwenhoek the story of Falada, with many stops and hesitations. Leeuwenhoek agrees that it is odd, but obviously does not consider it as remarkable as Vermeer does. He is used to the girl's strangeness. "I can see I have done a poor job," says the artist, "of convincing you how utterly freakish was her power, and her passion, as she stood there. It made my hair stand on end."

"I believe you, Johannes," replies Leeuwenhoek.

"Those foreign priests would have burned her at the stake, I guarantee you. Didn't you say one was from Scotland? They're crazy for witch-hunting!"

"The Scot was not religious. He was a wool merchant."

Vermeer goes on, "Anyway, perhaps this may convince you. You know I never paint animals. It's sentimental, not in my line at all. You've heard me scoff at barnyard painters a thousand times, I'm sure. Yet since I saw you last, I have almost finished a painting of that blasted horse. In two days. Me! I can't do the final touches because the paint's not dry. It's unheard of!"

"Why paint the horse?" asks Leeuwenhoek, puzzled.

"I have no idea! I was just compelled to do so. I never even saw this horse, Falada, alive. Only his head in a cart. So I had to make it up from one I saw in the street. You know I have a horror of working that way. But I did it. It's bizarre. It came together almost instantly. That child was so sad, and so angry…she made the horse's thoughts so clear to me, so vivid, as if I were he, trotting through the market… I felt I had to make a memorial… or something…"

"But what will you do with it? Sell it? Give it to her?"

Vermeer has not heard him. He is gazing into the fire thoughtfully. "You know, she said something before. Now that I think of it. Back in the summer. She talked about making paintings from the inside. She was talking about the geese—of course—and she said, what about a painting that showed them from the inside, what they see, what they feel? Not just from the outside, as we see them. My God. And now I've gone and done it with the horse! That's amazing." He pauses, and then goes on in wonder, "Jesus Christ, Antoni, do you suppose that's why I didn't need to see him? I already knew, I had felt it—from the inside? So I painted that? Usually I have to look at everything for hours and hours. From the outside. God! You should have heard her. She was so dismissive. Of every painting I've ever done. It was humiliating. But just for that one moment when I touched her arm, the world was inside out."

"This sounds rather mystical for you, Johannes," says Leeuwenhoek.

Vermeer glances at him shrewdly. "No, my friend, I have not lost my mind and begun to see visions. Or hear them, or whatever she does. I just got a blast of her insight at second hand. But it's a great little painting of that horse. Remarkably full of life. You'll see what I mean. I've never done anything like it before. It's all down to her, somehow. I suppose I should be angry. I had it all worked out before. I really thought I was capturing everything. Telling the whole truth."

"And what of the painting of Pierre?" asks Leeuwenhoek.

"Oh, it's going well. Only a few more sittings, and it'll be done. I just need one good bright day for the highlighting. Bad at this time of year, but maybe I'll get lucky. If you see it getting bright at about eleven o'clock in the morning any time soon, better send him straight over."

"But—"

"Think of your investment!"

"Very well, Johannes."

The door to the courtyard opens and closes quietly, and the goose girl appears by the hearth. She unwraps the shawl from about her head, another from about her body, takes off a wool jacket and heavy gloves. Already small, she is now smaller. In the year that he has known her, Leeuwenhoek reflects, she does not seem to have grown at all. Soon Marieke will be as big as she is. Without speaking, she takes off her kerchief and begins to unbind her hair. The two men watch in uncomfortable fascination as she untwists the coronet of braids, unties ribbons from the ends, and undoes the heavy plaits, each as thick as her arm. As it comes free, her hair gains in length, tumbling and swirling and parting in curtains as she unbraids the ends closer to her scalp. Finally she stands in front of the fire, her hair touching the ground all around her. She gathers it up, handful after handful, smoothes it down her back and turns her back to the fire. "Your wife made me wash it yesterday," she says to Vermeer, looking at him, "so it is still wet."

"It takes so long to dry?" says Vermeer. "Really, your hair is extraordinary. You realize how much money you could make if you cut it and sold it?"

"For paintbrushes?"

"No, for wigs and false braids. Rich women buy hair all the time to supplement their own. Yours would be worth more than all your geese together. Much more."

"Really?" says the girl. "I had no idea. It could be traded for money?"

"Johannes, why would she need to sell her hair? Why put these ideas into her head?" asks Leeuwenhoek in some exasperation.

"I don't need to now. But I might sometime. We always need money on the road," says the goose girl, matter-of-factly. "So it is good to know."

Leeuwenhoek experiences a chill despite the warmth of the fire. "But isn't this your home now?" he asks her. "Why would you be on the road?"

"The flock is my home," she replies.

"Aren't you happy here?"

"Yes."

"Are you planning to leave?"

"No. I never plan. I just let things happen."

"Antoni, you might as well ask the wind to stop blowing. She is here now. That's the main thing," says Vermeer. "Right?"

"Yes," says the girl. She shakes out her hair, spreading it with her fingers. "Is there any bread?"

Leeuwenhoek gets her a plate of bread, butter, and cheese and puts it on the floor beside her. She grabs a slice and chews it with satisfaction, still spreading and fanning out her hair. It steams slightly, flowing around her. Her very dark blue eyes gleam in the firelight. Her pale fingers cut through the masses of gold, again and again, shifting, shifting. It is like having a gnome or a wood spirit standing there on the hearth tiles, thinks Leeuwenhoek. Eerie. Or perhaps a wet dog, he thinks, watching her eat her bread and enjoy the fire with an utter lack of self-consciousness.

"Welcome back," he says at length. The girl regards him, finishing her bread.

"Where are the men who were here? Have they gone?" she asks.

"Yes. Or, one has. He has gone back to London, via Amsterdam. The other one, a priest, took sick and is staying with his friend here in Delft until he is better."

"And did the priests name the little animals, like you said?"

"No. But they did confirm that they were there. Perhaps they will name them later."

"I think you should name them. It is nice to have something to think with, in the words that people use. That is why I named the geese."

"But why not yourself?" Leeuwenhoek has always wondered this. "If you forgot your name from before?"

"Why? I am already here. I don't have to think of myself. I am myself. What for?"

Sarah Tolmie

"But then other people could call you something. They could think of you more easily."

"I don't want other people thinking about me."

"No?"

"I want them to leave me alone."

Leeuwenhoek and Vermeer look at each other. The goose girl begins to braid up her hair again. "Every time I talk to her I think I am drunk," says Vermeer.

ESTERHAZY

It is spring again. *Pinksteren* is the most propitious time of the year for baptisms. And this year, they have a baby to baptize: Philips Cornelijs, their third son. He is a month old, and, so far, thriving. The birth had been hard, and Barbara is only just recovered. De Graaf had not been present. He and Leeuwenhoek had been overruled. She has, however, taken his advice and is nursing the baby herself, although they could easily afford the services of a wet-nurse. Several of the more ostentatious members of the family think this is scandalous. Barbara does not care. Her only concern is for the health of the baby. He bawls his head off lustily as the water droplets from the fount in the Nieuwe Kerk hit his damp forehead. Leeuwenhoek, standing beside his beaming wife, looks down at the infant in his trailing gown and thinks that if he were wearing that much lace and linen and ribbon and a silk cap and all the other folderol to which the poor child has been subjected, he would be screaming himself. He inwardly apologizes to Philips; this is one instance in which it is not an advantage to be the son of a haberdasher.

Leeuwenhoek is now a fully fledged member of the Royal Society. An impressive parchment scroll with a wax seal, bearing his name, arrived not long after McFarlane's departure. *Trust No Man's Word.* Except now they do. Two of his letters have been published in their *Philosophical Transactions* (translated, of course). He is elated. Several more extracts, including some of Pierre's illustrations, are due to be printed in the next one. Pierre, too, is thrilled.

He seems to have forgiven his master for his temporary exclusion. For one thing, it turns out that Hoek's announcement about the opportunity in Prague had kept him quite busy with the investors throughout McFarlane's visit.

Staff of Life has finally reached the market and is selling exceptionally well for such an expensive fabric. They have hopes that it will catch on in Paris, where the stock has only just arrived. DeVeyne has also arranged to send some to Madrid, in the wake of the newer and more cordial relations the Stadthouder has established with Spain. "The stuff looks Catholic as hell, anyway," says DeVeyne, signing off on the shipment, "I reckon it'll do well there. Not that I ever want to do business with one again." He has been frantic for the past three months trying to cope with the elaborate techniques required for *devoré* velvet and dealing with a bitter series of labor disputes with his expert weavers from Lucca. Now that he has production established, he has sent them all packing and is having an easier time of it with the Dutch and Flemish artisans that they have trained for him. "Fuck it," he tells the other investors. "If we have any trouble, I'll just steal the help from that fool Zuidermann in Utrecht."

The superb painting of Pierre at the window with the silver microscope is hanging in state in the great room, displacing the flower painting that had hung there since Leeuwenhoek's marriage to Barbara ("Now you can burn it," said Vermeer, as he took it down). Every guest who enters the house is transfixed by it, though most don't know what Pierre is doing and have to have it explained to them. Marieke has devised a perfect little speech about it that she can produce on cue. Vermeer finds this especially charming and has her repeat it whenever he comes by. "I guess you could call it *The Microscopist* and put a sign underneath," he says to Leeuwenhoek. "Though I'm not sure that would help."

Pierre is quite in awe of the painting. "It makes even having to wear that stupid tunic worth it," he says privately to Leeuwenhoek. "It is red, isn't it? And the liquids in the jars—what colors are they?"

"Deep blue and emerald green."

"Lord and Savior—lapis, eh? He does splash out, doesn't he? No wonder he's broke."

The geese are happy at all the green grass and have grown even bigger. The feathers that the girl harvests from them are like swan pinions, with shafts harder than deer antler. They last so long that Leeuwenhoek has given several extras to Vermeer. The goose girl leads her inscrutable life, pasturing the birds every day and often spending nights out with them in the good weather. She spends as little time in the house as possible, though she does not seem discontented. Leeuwenhoek no longer sees her talking to her handkerchief. When he asks her about it, she says, "The little animals are much quieter now. And I know it's not my mother. So it is less important. And I am still angry at them about Falada."

"Do you miss your mother?" he asks.

"I don't know," she says. "I hardly remember her. Can you miss someone you don't remember?"

❧

Hoek's barge full of wrought iron has long since sailed, bearing its unasked-for cloth samples. Word comes back that the castle in Poland is well underway. Then, one day in late June, he receives an astonishing letter from the agent of the family of Esterhazy in Prague: the count is very taken with the Staff of Life fabrics, both the tapestry and the velvet, and wishes to place orders to outfit the drawing room and the ballroom of the castle in Poland, as well as the second drawing room of the family house in Eisenstadt. The order is absolutely enormous—pretty well the entire output of the factory for the next two years—and the noble family of Esterhazy is willing to pay a considerable premium for exclusive use of the fabric in the Austrian Empire. While they do not wish to put their crest upon it, they prefer that it not be sold on imperial soil, and certainly not to commoners, in order to maintain the dignity of the house.

Hoek arrives, breathless, hatless, and with unbuttoned coat, at Leeuwenhoek's door at ten o'clock in the morning with this letter in his hand. Pierre has just arrived. They pass the letter around. All three stare at each other, dumbfounded. "DeVeyne will have a bird," breathes Pierre. He is silent a moment. "And so will my father. This is one boat he has missed." He closes his eyes as if in prayer.

"I had better come with you to DeVeyne's, Frans," says Leeuwenhoek, after another moment of stunned silence. "Pierre, can you let Martin know? I imagine we will have to have a meeting."

"Yes," says Pierre, looking chalky. He puts down his pen and walks out the door. Everything seems faintly unreal. The water lapping in the canal is far too loud. If the numbers mentioned in the letter prove true, he is about to be rich. Richer than his father has ever been. He is not sure if his dazed feeling is pride, or fear. There is no telling how Matthias will take this news. So far he has been pleased to see Pierre make some money; pleased to make money himself. Pierre now stands to make a lot of money. The question is, will Matthias see his own failure to invest as a loss? And will he blame Pierre for it?

He knocks on the door of the elegant house in Prinsenstraat that he now knows to be Aliette's. A pretty maid in a fine uniform lets him in. He wonders if she is just a maid, or also a whore. He inquires after his cousin. He is not certain if Martin lives here, but he is often to be found here. "A moment, Mijnheer," says the maid and disappears into the depths of the house. Pierre sits on a sumptuous divan in an open foyer and pictures the room re-done in red and black tapestry. Maybe some cushions in velvet. He is just finishing this off in his mind's eye when he hears rustling behind a hallway door: it opens and closes and Aliette comes up the passage. She is alone.

Pierre leaps to his feet. He has not met her since that night at the Mechelen. He has no idea how to address her, or even exactly what her status *vis à vis* his cousin is now. At a loss, he simply bows as she approaches him. She inclines her head and says graciously, "Pierre DeWitt? Please sit down. Martin is away from the house on business at the moment, but as I am his partner in the fabric enterprise, you may speak to me. I assume that this is what you have come about?" She sits next to him on the divan. Her shot silk dress is lustrous, and she smells of roses.

"On business?" says Pierre, flustered, "You mean, he's—" He flushes to the roots of his hair. He jams his mouth shut tight. Aliette regards him imperturbably until he calms down. "Yes," he says eventually. "It is about the fabric business. The investors have just heard from Frans Hoek that a family called Esterhazy has offered to buy the next two years' supply of Staff of Life—the tapestry and the velvet—at a premium price. They have two estates that they wish to outfit using them."

"Ah, the count Mikkael Esterhazy? Which houses?" asks Aliette.

"You know him?" asks Pierre, trying to keep his voice even.

"No, not personally. I am, of course, familiar with the name, and we have some business connections in common, though at a remove."

"The houses—there is a castle in Poland, and the family house in a place called Eisenstadt."

"Excellent! The family house! Well, if the Esterhazy are decorating with it, I had better buy some—from myself—to use here, don't you think? Nothing too extreme, just a touch here and there."

"I was thinking that myself, earlier," admits Pierre.

"Were you now?" says Aliette, playfully. "As designer or investor?"

"Both."

"Or even client?" continues Aliette, glancing sidelong at him. Pierre blushes furiously again. His hands clutch his knees.

"Mijnheer DeWitt," says Aliette, patting his arm, very briefly, very lightly. "This is wonderful news! Congratulations! I suppose the investors are meeting? I will tell Martin immediately. Please leave a message here for him when it is arranged."

"Will you be attending yourself, Mevrouw De Hooch?" asks Pierre, formally.

"No," replies Aliette. "I will send Martin to speak for me, and for his own interests. Women are rarely welcome at such meetings. We are considered distracting." Her eyes are hard.

"Very well, Mevrouw," says Pierre, rising. "Please greet my cousin for me and thank him for the advice he has given me along the way. I am glad of the opportunity to speak with you. Good day." He bows again.

"Good day, Mijnheer DeWitt," replies Aliette. The maid appears magically to usher him from the room.

Mijnheer DeWitt, he thinks, trotting happily down the front stairs of the grand house. I am Mijnheer DeWitt. Sobering, he thinks, Well, to everyone but my father.

THE SIN OF DESPAIR

William Davenant is having a rough spring. He has nearly died of influenza. He has missed the meeting of great Protestant minds that happened three months ago in Geneva, for which he pawned everything he owned and forwent a preferment in the deanery of St Paul's, an offer that will never be made again. Worse, having received the pamphlets that he, and a small number of Anglican radicals, had printed in Amsterdam, that oasis of English reformers and hotheads, he despises them. He perceives, now that he has crossed the narrow sea and seen Europe in its wealth and scale, that their liturgical concerns are petty, their vision of a Protestant Europe spavined; everything they could ever say has already been said by Calvin, the terrifying logician, or Luther, the institutional bulldog. It is empty air, the tiniest of pennants snapping in the wind.

What consolations does he have? His Dutch has improved. Dutch is just English spoken by drunk people. Unlike French, it makes sense. He has the friendship of David Forsythe, a good man, a funny man, a calming preacher to the anxious English congregation of Delft. A man who saved his life, and paid for it, for months with little hope of recompense, as claims for what goes on beyond the channel can languish in church and court for years. Who also took care of the fees of that disconcerting, brilliant, freethinking doctor, Reinier De Graaf, which were probably not inconsiderable. Who gave up his bed and sleeps on a pallet on the floor. Who provides English conversation, confession, communion. He thanks the Lord above for David Forsythe. It was a long winter.

Forsythe also saw Leeuwenhoek's animalcules. Davenant thinks in his heart that he might have gone mad these last months, cocooned in blankets and meat broth, had he not had the rector, a sensible English Christian, with whom to discuss the animalcules. They have been over every inch of ground upon which they might be discussed, from the Old Testament to the New, the Fathers, the Apocrypha. He no longer really regrets missing the great conclave in Geneva, their talks were so fruitful. Some were downright heretical. Truly, what is more worthwhile than discussion between two rational men?

Now he is able to get up and walk. He has explored Delft, roaming around slowly, pausing for breath, enjoying the sunshine. The little city is beautiful; there is no doubt. It is clean and orderly; the architecture is lovely; everything looks magical reflected in the ever-present water. It is also very green: willows lean over the canals; there are small lawns and green verges, gardens of tulips, flowerpots, and tubs of herbs. He is surprised at the quality of care that the town offers to its citizens: there is a hospital, a home for old men and one for old women, an orphanage, a madhouse, in addition to a jail. The Dutch do not want the poor and suffering cluttering up their narrow streets. The people seem prosperous. Even the lowest classes are decently dressed. The inns and public houses are full. They seem be open constantly and offer huge quantities of food. Stores sell every conceivable thing. People are apparently spending money like water.

Davenant grew up in London, in a ward near St Paul's. Before this, he had hardly even left the city. If you live in England, there is very little reason to leave London, especially if you are a churchman. Oxford, and even

Cambridge, are all very well, but he is not of the class that attends. He has been ordained, but has no degree. This is typical. Since the reform, the value of a theological degree has been hard to assess in every venue except the highest royal service. During the blasphemous commonwealth, of course, such royal service had largely been in France, far out of his purview. Religion on English soil had made no sense and was mostly war. The king is barely returned, the church barely restored. There are plenty of other ways up in the Church of England now.

He grew up amidst crowding, filth, and squalor, with a palpable gap between rich and poor. The streets around Paul's are filled with cripples and beggars. They are regularly swept aside to make way for city merchants, provincial magnates, members of the royal family, and all their various retinues to attend divine service. The level of ostentation he is used to seeing on those occasions is not in evidence here. Wealth is a bit more spread out, or displayed in other ways, ones to which he does not have access, as a foreigner.

He has kept clear of the area around the fish market where Leeuwenhoek's house is located. For a long time, he knew he was not ready to go back. Now he is. It is his last duty before he goes home.

On a morning in the last week of June, he knocks on the door of the house in Hippolytusbuurt. Mevrouw Leeuwenhoek opens it. In one arm is a spectacular bundle of cloth that he assumes is a baby. "Congratulations, Mevrouw!" he says, peering into its tiny face. It is sleeping, so still it looks like a wax doll. "Is Marieke happy with her new brother—or sister?"

"Brother," says Barbara, smiling, "Philips, the name of Antoni's father."

"Is your husband at home? I have come to say farewell to him, and indeed to all of you, as I am soon to depart for England. I could not leave without saying a final thank-you to your family, for helping me when I was so ill."

"You look much better now, Father, thank heaven," says Barbara, beckoning him into the hall. The infant lets out a small, treble snore. The two adults look at one another comically.

"I love babies," says Davenant. "They show us so much about the helplessness and comedy of human life. I was the eldest of a large family, with many children much younger than me. I helped look after them, all those that lived, anyway. They are so very fragile. That is the only terrible thing about them, though perhaps an instructive one for a priest…"

"What? Not the noise? Not the smell?" says Barbara, leading him toward the great room.

"Life is full of noise and smell," replies Davenant, sitting down on the nearest chair. To his surprise, Barbara deposits the baby in his lap. He cradles it with practiced hands. Barbara looks at him critically. Seeming satisfied, she walks to the door.

"Antoni is in the study. I will fetch him. Call me if he wakes up."

"I have no doubt he will call you himself," says the priest mildly. He sits contemplating the infant. He can see its minuscule face and feel its warm weight, about the same as a cat. Otherwise, it is a cipher. Even its hands are covered with swathes of lace. It is silent except for the occasional tiny, rattling snore. Perhaps its lungs are congested. He wonders if De Graaf has seen it. Him. Philips Van Leeuwenhoek. A lot of name for such a tiny being. Babies are curious things. It has always struck him as odd that we use adult names for them, adult pronouns: he, she. They really have nothing to do with those categories.

He remembers, with a sudden chill, performing his first baptism—of sorts, unofficially, a desperate final blessing—on his infant brother as he lay dying in his arms. He himself had been about eleven. The boy—what had his name been? Mark?—had been a few days old. His mother was still abed. He was sitting in the kitchen with the baby, who was very small and weak, born early, when the tiny form had begun to stiffen and convulse, twitching and gasping. Not knowing what else to do, possessed by a sudden, horrible fear that the tiny soul should be eternally lost, he had stuck his fingers into a water jug on the table, made the sign of the cross on its forehead, and whispered, in English, "You are a Christian. I save you." Then the child had stopped breathing, and he had run to tell his mother. Not long after that, he had decided to become a priest. He had been tortured for years, never knowing if he had managed to save his tiny brother. He was determined that it should never happen again: he was going to have it, that sacramental power. To be sure.

Later he had learned that this was retrograde theology. Calvin had already declared that people are born elect, or not. It has nothing to do with the power of priests. Nothing to do with baptism or any other old rituals. We are in God's hands, and his alone. These facts had provided some comfort to him, when he finally learned them. Indeed, he has always felt that the Church of England is insufficiently Calvinist. The church he had been raised and trained in had retained much more faith in those old rituals, including baptism, than the Swiss theologian's radical mind would ever have tolerated. Enough that he has never been able to free himself entirely of the fear that that little boy had been damned due to human error. His error. He had not been a priest at the right time. Really, either an ordained priest must be available every single second, or every living person must have the power to be one at need. Otherwise life is simply intolerable.

He remembers himself at the age of twelve: skinny, half-starved, terrible at Latin, stumbling through cathedral school. He was going to be a priest. He was going to have the power to fix things. He was going to be able to walk through life with the power to save people in emergencies: himself, or anyone else. Ready for anything. Better than any doctor. A man who could save people from the true terror of death, which was everlasting damnation.

Philips snores on. Davenant hears distant footsteps in other parts of the house. Philips, this tiny Dutch baby, has been born into a God-fearing family. There is nothing to do but assume that he is already saved, along with his father and mother—and everyone they know, everyone in this town, everyone in this Protestant republic that they are still managing to run. The numbers cannot possibly be that good—the elect are shockingly few in number, according to Calvin—but there is no other way to live. To assume that one is damned is to live in despair. Despair is the sin against the Holy Spirit. So there is no escape that way. He has heard people talk about Protestant fatalism. Nothing could be more wrong. To live as a Calvinist is to struggle to accept, constantly, daily, hourly, that every person in Christendom, indeed, in the whole world, is as helpless and witless as this baby in his lap, when compared to the power of God. If you think this is easy, you have never tried it. It has nothing to do with resignation.

There are footfalls in the hallway, and Leeuwenhoek enters the room, followed by his wife. "Father Davenant! Excellent to see you up and about. You are a credit to Reinier. We have had regular reports about you from

Reverend Forsythe. I hope you received the wine, the ham and the cheese? We waited to send them until the doctor said it was safe for you."

"I did, thank you."

"When do you depart? Are you going straight back to London?"

"Yes. I have missed my opportunity in Geneva."

"A great pity."

"Yes, it was. But strangely, a winter of sickness and contemplation has been good for me. For my faith, at least. It has been tested."

"Sickness is one of the great tests of our faith, our pastor is always saying."

"And so, I may say, is natural philosophy," says Davenant. "I have been meditating all this time upon your animalcules."

"Ah," says Leeuwenhoek, "you know they are not *my* animalcules. They are no invention of mine. They are part of God's creation."

"I believe you, Mijnheer," says Davenant seriously, "but you would not believe the fight I have had with myself to say that. Or perhaps you would—"

Leeuwenhoek nods at him solemnly.

"I have finally come to the conclusion that it is no business of mine. Why that should have been so hard, I cannot say. I mean—we are as small and insignificant as animalcules ourselves, in the eyes of God, are we not? At the very least, that is something we can learn from them, the vast differences in the scale of creation."

"I have always thought so," says Leeuwenhoek, looking relieved.

"And God made them for his own inscrutable purposes. Perhaps they know what they are, as we have some inklings of his purposes for us. Or perhaps they don't.

More and more I wonder if it is right to assume that we know his purposes at all. *Sola fide.*"

The baby wakes up with a surprisingly loud roar. Everyone jumps. Philips' arms flail without direction, shaking his lace sleeves. Davenant hands him to his mother. "You see he disapproves of Latin. Already a right-thinking child." His parents chuckle and look at him fondly. Held upright, he quiets down quickly. He looks at the English priest out of his dark eyes, with tear-fringed lashes. What he sees, not one of them has any idea.

THE ALLEY

Davenant has made his farewells. He is just heading away from the fish market, back toward Forsythe's, when he sees a very small girl in a white kerchief emerge from the alley behind Leeuwenhoek's house. This is unexpected; he had not thought they had any other children. She appears young to be a servant. To his surprise, a line of huge white geese is following her. He has not seen fowls in the town before, except on market days. The girl turns out of the alley and marches straight toward him, her geese waddling obediently behind.

As the child and her strangely silent geese come abreast of him, she looks up at him and stops. "Are you one of the priests from England who came to see the little animals?" she asks, in a clear, flat voice.

He is amazed. "Yes," he replies.

"Did you name them?"

"No," he says.

"But you saw them?"

"Yes, I did."

"So now you know what Antoni says is true?" asks the child fiercely.

"Yes. It is true."

"Good," she says, and begins to make off toward the fish market. The geese, who had paused politely behind her, begin to move again.

Perplexed, he calls after her, "Wait! Have you seen them, the animalcules?"

"Yes," she says, stopping. "I was glad to see them. Antoni showed me. But I already knew they were there."

"You did? How?"

"I heard them. I hear them, everywhere."

"What?" says Davenant. "What do you mean?"

"I hear them, speaking, or singing, or buzzing. All the time. From all over."

"Speaking?" whispers Davenant, and then louder, "but surely not in words?"

"No," says the girl, "just so you know they are alive. Like animals. Little animals."

His mind reels. He puts his hand on the rough brick wall for support. "Do you live at Leeuwenhoek's house?" he asks, "Who are you?"

"I keep the geese," says the girl.

"And you can hear his animalcules, you say? The ones he can see through the microscope?"

"They are not his. They belong to themselves. They have always been there. Like people, or geese."

"Oh my God," says the priest, "and you hear them?" He pauses to collect himself. "Are you Leeuwenhoek's daughter?"

"No."

"But you belong to his household?"

"I belong to myself. Though Antoni keeps us just now."

"Does your master know that you can do this? Did you tell him about the animalcules in the first place?"

"He knows I can, yes. But he had already seen them before I came. Many kinds. I just told him about the ones in blood."

"In blood?" says Davenant, "in people's blood? Even when it is inside them? You can hear that?"

"Yes," says the child, impassively. "Inside, or outside. I first heard them on a handkerchief with blood on it. My mother's blood."

Her mother's blood? Why would she have her mother's blood? From some unthinkable demonic ritual? Has this child killed her own mother? Davenant considers the girl. A horror rises inside him. Should he flee from this monstrous child—from this whole insufferable, alien town? Or should he just strangle the little imp? Is she the one responsible for this confusion, this carpeting of the world with tiny, invisible voices? Is she lying? Is she in league with the microscopist to deceive him, for some incomprehensible reason?

Could the child be possessed? He has always acknowledged the devil, in principle, though Satan has never impressed him. What is he, after all? A failed angel. Why should people let themselves be led around by the nose by a mere angel, no more than God's vicar in hell? No. It is undignified. Had angels been perfect, there would have been no need for man. They were not; men were not. Both fell. God is the one to worry about, the supreme power.

Should he denounce her? What would that entail, exactly? He is in a foreign country. He barely speaks the language. This is the kind of thing that one imagines as so easy for the papist priests, or vengeful laypeople, in Foxe's *Book of Martyrs*. But what, precisely, did those people do, to have their countrymen tried and executed? Talk to a bishop, inform to a beadle? Perhaps he could do it at home, where he understands the hierarchy. How could he do it here?

Why would he do it, here?

What would happen to this girl? If he reported her remarks to the local consistory, for instance? Would they even believe him, a foreigner? And why would he shame his hosts, the Leeuwenhoeks, who had treated him so well? In what imbroglio would he involve Forsythe, that excellent clergyman?

The child would likely be confined to the madhouse. He has seen it. It is a source of civic pride. It is clean and orderly. Its inmates are well fed. It is like a school, but with no curriculum. He remembers school. There is no point to such suffering but the curriculum. And his companions had been sane. What might the insane do to each other? Does he want that for this girl? Does he?

Davenant struggles to get a grip on himself. He feels as though his fever has returned. Ten minutes ago he had been sitting in Leeuwenhoek's great room, explaining calmly that he had made his peace with the animalcules, this new form of life, the ark of creation expanded. This peace has gone up in a puff of smoke. It had been as brittle and dry as a resinous branch. He clutches the wall behind him. He tries to think clearly. God is the creator of everything, and therefore, of the animalcules. He has seen them with his own eyes. They exist. What this girl can hear, or not hear, is irrelevant. Living at Leeuwenhoek's house, she could have got this idea in her mind and embellished it in her own way. Or, if she does really hear them—and he can think of no way to prove or disprove it—then she is simply attesting to a part of God's creation. Why should this be harmful? What, he does not trust the creator? That would be true madness.

The girl stands, arms at her sides, gazing at him unreadably, as the infant Philips had done upon waking. Who knows what goes on in the mind of another? God will take care of this girl, as he does everything. *Sola fide.* Her relationship to divinity is foreknown and foregone. *Sola fide.* He is not responsible. He cannot save her or damn her. Not this child. Not this time.

He lets go the wall. A glow of relief spreads through him. Tears rise in his eyes. Perhaps God has placed this girl here, now, as a sign that the knowledge of animalcules is admissible to men. Even a child can know them.

"I see," says Davenant, finally, graciously, to the girl. She nods once, firmly, and marches past, the flock following. He moves aside to let them by. The last goose, as it passes him, lets out a derisive honk.

THE RECTOR

The Reverend David Forsythe is sad to see his guest leave, even though he has been a considerable burden. It was nice to hear an English voice during those bleak months of the year. He always finds he makes it well enough through Michaelmas—there is something about the power of Advent, and the bustle of harvest—but after Christmas he can find his solitary life hard to bear. He has his parishioners, of course. Indeed, they are a needy lot. They live in touchy circumstances. England and Holland are frequently at war in the changing play of European politics. Yet no-one, Dutch or English, is willing to forego the profit that can be made through trade, even in time of war. The merchants stay. On both sides of the channel, colonies of foreign traders live, protected by law. Occasionally they are rounded up and incarcerated. Some are killed by mobs. Always, they pay exorbitant taxes. Yet they stay. The money is too good. Also, they are co-religionists. Their languages are similar. They have a lot in common.

Forsythe has lived in Delft for seven years. He ministers to a changing roster of between twenty and thirty English families, and more single men, from the city and surrounding area. He helps newcomers to settle; he finds servants and tutors for their children; he acts constantly as witness and unofficial notary; and he looks after their spiritual welfare. He leads a busy life. People confide in him. They expect a lot from him. Yet he is still lonely. He brought his library of eight books with him, and he can get English books in Amsterdam, but only for purchase.

He doesn't have much money—and less now that he has been looking after Davenant. In Oxford there had been a lending library, a most remarkable thing: scholars and some wealthy citizens had pooled some of their books and set up a fund to buy new ones that could be used by all the members in common. He would not be surprised to find that such organizations exist in Holland, though the books would be in Dutch, which he finds difficult to read for pleasure.

He has no wife. He is not attracted to women. He does not like the timbre of their voices. He does not like their shape. He knows this is a defect in him, and once it worried him gravely, though less and less as time goes on. This may be one reason that he lives abroad. Facing the endless challenges of living here keeps him happier with himself. Bravery is constantly required. Not that he is running around with a sword and buckler, delivering the oppressed. He is really quite a shy man; sometimes just buying eggs in the market is quite enough.

He has been dropping by the Leeuwenhoeks' house from time to time all winter and spring, telling them about the progress of Davenant. They have been very kind, and Barbara welcomes the chance to practice her English, which she has used but occasionally since she was a girl. He has met their new baby, of whom she is anxiously proud. He understands she has lost three other children, so he cannot blame her. Barbara insists, in particular, that he is welcome to keep coming, even now that Davenant has left. "I get out very little with Philips, you know, Father," she says, "so it is a relief to me to have company during the day." So he has got into the habit of coming by the house in the mid-morning, once every week or two, usually on a Wednesday, sometimes bringing flowers or a small treat for Marieke. He has few Dutch friends. He is not sure if this is his fault, or theirs. The Dutch, although social, are reticent. Perhaps he is too occupied with the English communion. He is happy to be inside a Delft household, to eat their food and chat with their children and admire the art on their walls. Here common people of the merchant class own fine paintings and display them, trade them, and commission them. At home, it is only princes and great magnates. The scale and magnificence of some of the paintings he has seen here in guildhalls (he has witnessed contracts in many of them) has left him flabbergasted.

On the first Wednesday of August he calls at the house just as a party of men is leaving the great room, investors in Leeuwenhoek's cloth business. He is introduced to them in due form: DeVeyne, the factory owner, a thin, hard man obviously keen to be on his way, who departs directly; Frans Hoek, the ironmonger, whom he knows slightly, having witnessed some contracts for him; Pierre, Leeuwenhoek's assistant, a talented artist whom he has talked to once or twice; the last is Martin Dekker, a cousin of Pierre's, a strikingly handsome man, very tall, finely dressed, carrying an extravagant hat. Hoek, an endlessly busy fellow, also leaves at once. The two cousins seem disposed to stay and drink coffee with the family and their English guest.

Soon Pierre, Leeuwenhoek and his wife, Martin Dekker, Forsythe, Marieke, and the infant are all sitting around the great room, variously occupied with eating, drinking, talking of this and that, and playing with the dollhouse. This is another difference Forsythe has noticed. People of any wealth or standing at home would never entertain with their children, at least not those as young as these. Family visits would be the exception. On the whole, children are relegated to the care of servants.

Sarah Tolmie

Here they are much more omnipresent. Marieke is the kind of little girl his grandmother would describe, unflatteringly, as forward; she is quite comfortable with adult company and talks easily and pertly to visitors. She asks a lot of questions, and her parents do not shush her. They let her speak. Perhaps it would be different if they had more children, reflects Forsythe. Philips is alternately in his mother's arms or in a handsome, beribboned basket near the table. This is normal to them. Whether this is the domesticity typical of Delft families, or if it is just the Leeuwenhoeks' way, he doesn't know. Certainly Pierre and Martin Dekker seem familiar with it. After about twenty minutes, he looks over to find the enormous lanky figure of Dekker sitting on the floor in front of the dollhouse, deep in a discussion with Marieke about the cloth used for decorating it. It transpires that he used to be a weaver. This explains his interest in Leeuwenhoek's fabric business. What he does now that allows him to buy the superb clothes he is wearing is not exactly clear. "Oh, I do a bit of investing, you know," he says casually, "and I work for Aliette De Hooch, here in town."

Pierre chokes on his coffee. "Hot! Very hot!" he says apologetically, making fanning motions in front of his mouth. His cousin chuckles at him from his place on the floor, tossing back his curly blonde head. There is no doubt he is a fine figure of a man. Why are men so much handsomer than women?

Overall, the visit is a pleasure, as usual. He is invited to hold the baby and does so for a moment so as not to offend. But he hands the child back quickly. Infants make him nervous. They are too breakable. He exchanges a few remarks with Leeuwenhoek about microscopy. The man is evidently frustrated; he has not been able to spend as much time as he would like in his study, being too busy with the haberdashery business.

"Poor Antoni," says Dekker, from the floor, helping Marieke to straighten the silk cloth on the kitchen table of the dollhouse, "forced to make money hand over fist."

"Martin, you frivolous dandy, just because you have no other passions—" begins Leeuwenhoek.

"I have passions, no fear," laughs Dekker. Barbara looks over at him warmly. He is the kind of man women admire.

Pierre has another fit of coughing. Perhaps he should not drink coffee. Everyone looks at him curiously. Red-faced, he waves off their glances.

"Dear God, I had better be going, before my wit kills you," says Dekker, scrambling up from the marquetry floor. Marieke looks disappointed. So does Barbara. He suddenly looms over them all, rumbles some good-byes in his deep voice, and strides off toward the front door in his glove-leather boots. Barbara and Marieke gaze after him wistfully. Forsythe admits that he is probably doing the same himself.

≈

Three days later, he is frantically sweeping the aisle of the English chapel. Usually the sexton does this. He will be surprised when he comes in later and finds the aisle swept, the pews dusted, and all the silver polished. Forsythe is desperate to keep himself busy.

He has just learned that Aliette De Hooch is a procurer. She runs the most expensive whorehouse in Delft: one of the most deluxe in all the Seven Provinces, he has heard from parish gossip. So Martin Dekker is a—what? His head is boiling with the most insidious ideas. All of them are sinful, and several are lascivious in ways he has not hitherto allowed himself to imagine. It is like a dam has broken in his mind. He is appalled, and he is running out of things to clean. Usually he is very moderate doctrinally, but at the moment he wonders if extreme Catholic mortification of the flesh might not be a good idea after all.

It is inappropriate for any good Christian man to work for a whoremonger. In any capacity. But what capacity? In any capacity whatsoever. Managing her investments. Running her errands. Anything. Anything. Should he beat the dust out of the tapestry that hangs in the vestry? Could it be time to scrub the chapel steps?

Prostitution is a blight. It is an assault on the sacrament of marriage. It is an encourager of adultery, a spreader of disease. It fills the world with bastards and discourages the begetting of lawful children. It propagates unnatural practices. To make money selling the human passions is a crime, worse than usury. This vile woman, what has she got Martin Dekker, once a virtuous craftsman, into? Foul corrupter!

He is perfectly aware that there are male whores. *Mignons.* Some of them even dress as women. You can find them working certain streets in London—Lad's Lane, for instance—and in Oxford, in Jericho. It is a dangerous job, and they have to keep clear of the beadles, but everybody knows about it. Most of them are, or were, soldiers. The army is the home of sodomy. Likely it is the same here. More sailors, perhaps. But brothels? Men working in brothels? Does that happen, too? Can that be the work that Dekker does for this Aliette De Hooch?

He will beat out the tapestry. It is a godawful thing, heavy wool with embroidery and appliqué, with dwarfish images of the English saints Edmund, Edward, and Alban on a murky background. It looks a hundred years out of date and had been brought here from England by some misguided predecessor. The fabrics decorating Leeuwenhoek's dollhouse are probably worth more. It is a lamentable object. Fortunately it is in the vestry, so only he has to look at it. It would be embarrassing if Dutch citizens saw it.

Once in the vestry, he realizes that it weighs a ton only as it comes crashing down on top of him in a floury cloud of dust. More dangerous is the heavy oak cross pole, longer and heavier than a lance, and the long and freely swinging chains that had affixed it to the wall. The pole deals him a heavy blow on the temple, and one chain, whipping through the air in a lash of iron, connects with the side of his face, striping it from ear to jaw, bloodying his mouth and knocking out one of his molars.

He passes out and awakes, probably just a few minutes later, seeing only pitch black. Opening his eyes, he is filled with horror, wondering if he has been struck blind. Feeling with his hands, he finds that he is just buried in the filthy dark tent of the tapestry. He wrenches his way clear. Standing up, he is weak and nauseated. Blood is dripping from his face onto his shirt. He is confused, and it is hard to make decisions. The church is empty. Parishioners will not be coming until the evening service. He needs help, and for that he needs a place with many people, where someone might recognize him and send for a doctor or a surgeon. He staggers out the door, pausing for a moment to hold onto the frame. He will go to the Mechelen. It is nearby, and many traders gather there, including Englishmen. There will be water and spirits at the bar to clean his wound. He sets off, weaving erratically. There is a roaring sound in his right ear. It sounds like waves and gives him the impression he is walking thigh-deep in water. The air seems somehow resistant.

Holding the walls most of the way around the square, he makes it to the inn. He pauses to clutch the doorframe and then enters the taproom. A few paces in, he collapses onto the floor, cracking his knees painfully. Startled faces turn toward him, this bloodied apparition, gray with dust. A man in a white apron helps him up and half-carries him to a chair by the bar. Forsythe does not know the man. He must be the barkeep. Slumped in his seat, the battered priest looks around but sees no familiar faces. The man in the apron comes swimming back toward him from behind the bar, carrying a cloth and a tub of water. He says something helpful but Forsythe cannot really take it in; the man begins to wash the blood from his face and mouth. He gives Forsythe the cold cloth to hold against his cut and swollen cheek and returns with a glass of genever. Looking carefully straight into the wounded man's eyes, he mimes drinking and hands it over. Forsythe drinks it. The liquor burns horribly in the cut on his lip and in the bloody gap where his upper front molar had been. The pain is quite amazing. He gasps, and the room comes into clearer focus.

"Who are you?" asks the man. "Have you been attacked?"

"No," mumbles Forsythe through his agonizingly sore mouth, "not attacked. Accident. I am—"

"Reverend Forsythe? Is that the Reverend David Forsythe?" says a deep voice unexpectedly from behind the barkeep. "Good God, what has happened to you? Do you need a doctor?" In an absolutely perverse stroke of fortune, there is Martin Dekker. He comes forward and sweeps off his hat. "Would you have any ice in the back, Smits, d'you think?" he says to the barman. "I know it seems a waste at this time of year, but it would be just the thing for the father's busted face here—this is the priest from the English church, Reverend Forsythe, I met him not long ago at Leeuwenhoek's—" The man bustles off into a back room. "Should I get De Graaf?" he asks Forsythe. "Jesus! You English priests! What happened?"

"A tapestry fell on me," mutters Forsythe, feeling ridiculous.

"A tapestry did that? Are you kidding?"

"With a heavy pole and chain."

"Jesus. I've known men seriously hurt by looms, but none by the finished product. That's an achievement, Forsythe, it really is. It smashed your head? Can you walk? Can you see and hear? Did you throw up? Pass out?" He is businesslike, like a foreman on a factory floor, assessing the damage.

"I walked here from church. I think I passed out for a while."

"Better get De Graaf then. I'll be back with him. At this rate he might as well just move to England. Clap that ice on. Drink some genever," says Dekker, taking charge. "Smits, I'll take care of the tab when I get back," he says over his shoulder as the barkeep comes out with a chunk of ice wrapped in a towel.

"Jesus," says Forsythe, who never swears, taking the ice and holding it to his temple.

De Graaf, when he arrives, pronounces him out of danger. "I don't think you have cracked your skull," he says, passing his hands carefully over Forsythe's scalp. "The swelling is superficial. The cut may scar. You'll look like an English pirate. Follow my finger." He moves it around in front of Forsythe's eyes. The priest manages to track it with his aching eyeballs. "If you start vomiting or your vision changes, send someone for me. Give me that." He takes a half full glass of genever from the priest's hand. "Close your eyes." De Graaf throws the spirit with surprising vigor into Forsythe's face, all over the right side. The alcohol burns in the cuts. Forsythe splutters. He feels a cloth wiping his eyes. "Just let that dry. Wash it later. Your shirt is a mess already," says the doctor. He looks amused. "I've never done that before. My first bar fight, Father. You are a bad influence." He packs up his bag. He is off out the taproom door before Forsythe can ask him about the bill.

Another glass of genever appears before him. Forsythe sips it absently. He prefers gin, but he can hardly argue. He hears a low voice rumbling off in a corner. Dekker is standing there, talking to a matronly woman in a glistening dress and a soberly attired man in his fifties with iron-gray hair. They are negotiating something; he hears dates and numbers, queries and replies. "Fine, fine, excellent," says Dekker at length. He and the man shake hands. The woman looks on levelly. The tall man turns around and sees Forsythe staring at him with bleary concentration. He comes over.

"You look a bit better, Forsythe." The man pronounces it with a *t, foresight.* There are *th*'s in Dutch; he can never figure out why they pronounce some, and not others. In Europe everywhere *th* is a bad deal; it's an English thing. Nobody gets it right. He does not feel filled up with foresight at the moment. Foresight. Jesus. "De Graaf says you will not die. It would be too much to be killed by a tapestry," he says. "Let us drink to your survival! And the fact that I have just sold some extraordinarily expensive curtains!" He beckons the barkeep. "Smits, two genevers!"

Forsythe looks on with horror as Dekker slides coins over the bar: quite a few coins. More than two glasses of genever should cost, certainly. He realizes that Dekker has just paid for all the spirits used in his revival, and probably the ice, too. With his vile whoremongering money! The rector feels queasy. He has been implicated in a dreadful, sinful trade. This is the worst thing that's happened to him all day. He fears that he may burst into tears.

"Do you preach tonight, Father?" asks Dekker. "Your congregation will wonder what happened. And where is that tapestry now? Are you going to need help moving it?"

"Blasted thing," says Forsythe shakily, staring at his morally compromised genever, "it's on the floor in the vestry. I should just set it on fire."

"Is it English?" asks Dekker shrewdly. "Then you might as well. They smell awful burning, though, especially if they're wool. Come on. I will walk back with you. You still don't look too steady. I can help you lug it out the door, at least."

This is the last thing that Forsythe wants to happen. The day has been such a catastrophe, though, that it seems inevitable. He quaffs his genever. Standing up, the floor rises up to greet him in a nasty way, and he is reminded of his horrific channel crossing. Dekker catches his arm just as he is about to pitch over. It is a pity. He seems a genuinely nice fellow and is so very handsome. But he's either a whore or a pander. He's not sure which is worse. The tall Dutchman pilots him carefully out the door. It is clear to both of them now that Forsythe will never make it without his assistance. They limp across the square, the priest leaning heavily. "Not to worry, Forsythe," says the man jovially. "Everybody's well used to seeing me stagger out of there. Not so much lately, though. They'll just think I've relapsed."

"What?" says Forsythe miserably, stumbling along.

"Used to be a famous drunk," says Dekker, righting him. "Had a tab a mile long at every place in town. I've paid them all off now. That's why Smits is nice to me, y'see? It's been a bit better since I'm—"

"A whore? A pimp? Which is it?" says Forsythe. He cannot believe he has just said this to the man in cold blood. By rights Dekker should knock him down, which will certainly not be hard.

"Reverend! Who have you been talking to? What, those parishioners of yours? When the English stick their pricks into everything that moves, right across the world? Some of Aliette's best clients! Come on now, Forsythe. Don't be an idiot. What's it to you? Unless you want to hire me?"

So many utterly contradictory ideas burst into his mind that he feels like an exploding gunpowder magazine. The second Delft Thunderclap, right inside his head. He stops moving. Dekker looks at him closely, still holding his elbow so he doesn't collapse.

"Ah," he says. There is a momentary pause as Forsythe teeters on his legs. "Look, Father, we've got to get you home. You're drunk, and you've had a bang on the head. This is no time to discuss such things. You likely won't even remember any of this tomorrow."

I will, thinks Forsythe despairingly, as he struggles to remember how to walk. If there were a fire handy, he would throw himself into it. Go up like a Guy in a blaze of guilt.

"Forget the damn tapestry," says Dekker. "You need to get yourself to bed. You couldn't help with it just now; you'd do yourself an injury. I can come back tomorrow to help you shift it. If we're still speaking. I'll get you round the back to your rooms." They are almost there. Dekker half-carries him the rest of the way. Fortunately, the door is unlocked. Who would rob a poor, foreign clergyman? Steal his catechism and penitential and six English romances? The books are the only things of value, and he's hardly the Duc de Berry. Thank God his little apartment is on the ground floor. He really doesn't think he could bear it if Dekker had to carry him up the stairs.

"Thank you," gasps Forsythe, holding onto the frame of the open door. "I should be all right now."

"I doubt it," replies Dekker, looking at him dubiously.

The rector closes the door, carefully, finally, without slamming. He latches it. He stares at it with bloodshot eyes, thinking: I doubt it, too.

SPERMATOZOA

"**Look,**" says De Graaf with some asperity. "I just need you to check it for me. You are the better microscopist. I won't mention your name in the book if it makes you squeamish. But how can I possibly write a treatise on the organs of generation without a proper investigation of the male element?"

"But how are we going to get it, Reinier? That is the question."

"Antoni, after all the children you have fathered, you must have some idea."

"I mean, with propriety, Reinier!"

Pierre, who is investigating some pepper water by the window, says hesitantly, "I think I might know somebody."

"Great heaven, really, Pierre? Who would be willing to do that? I can't even imagine asking," says Leeuwenhoek.

"Martin," says Pierre. "I bet." He looks at the older man seriously. "Are you entirely aware of his...other... profession?"

"News has reached me, yes," says Leeuwenhoek dryly. "You really know how to choose an investor, Pierre. Just don't tell Barbara. She would be horrified."

"What on earth are you talking about?" asks De Graaf, looking from one to the other.

"Martin Dekker," replies Leeuwenhoek, "who works for Aliette De Hooch. Pierre's cousin."

"Jesus Christ, does he?" says De Graaf, suddenly grinning. "Well then, he's our man! He's accustomed to dropping off his seed all over the place. Likely even sends it through the mail! It shouldn't prove any problem at all! Easy!"

"But what do I say?" asks Pierre, "Hello my dear cousin, as the most shameless man I know, would you consider—?"

"You brought this up, Pierre. How do I know?" says Leeuwenhoek. "Just ask him directly. Tell him we'll pay the going rate."

"We can't afford the going rate chez Aliette," replies Pierre.

The microscopist and the doctor raise their eyebrows inquiringly at him.

"It's ten guilders! Is it worth that to you?" says Pierre. The eyebrows climb higher.

"According to Martin!" says Pierre hotly.

"Maybe there's a family discount?" says De Graaf.

"Agh, that's disgusting!" says Pierre, looking mortified.

"I mean," corrects De Graaf hastily, "perhaps you could come to an individual arrangement, for the sake of natural philosophy?"

"Well, I'll try," says Pierre.

"Tell him it has to be fresh," warns De Graaf.

"Lord and Savior! You mean he has to—"

"Commit an act of onanism, yes," confirms De Graaf. "Philosophically."

"And then what? I rush it across town, and then we examine it?"

"Exactly. Bring a vial."

"Jesus," says Pierre. He turns back to the pepper water, trying not to blush.

❦

It works like a charm. Martin laughs uproariously. "Pierre, that's the most fucking ridiculous thing I have ever heard in my life. Well, that'll really put Aliette's place on the map, eh? Do you mean to say that this Royal Society that you're always going on about is going to be looking at my spunk like it's some precious relic?"

"Well, we probably won't send it to England—"

"Yes, what would you put on the export license, really?" interrupts his cousin.

"We'd examine it here. And if it proves interesting for some reason, I guess I'll draw it, and we'll send that. Plus Antoni's description."

"That's probably incest."

"Lord and Savior, Martin, are you going to do this or not?"

"Fine, fine!' says Martin, "but you owe me. I wouldn't do this for just anybody."

"Come on Martin, you already do," says Pierre.

~~~

There it is. Two ounces of milky fluid in a capped vial on Leeuwenhoek's work table. Pierre had handed it sternly and silently over to him a minute before, as if daring him to say anything. Uncapped, it releases a faint scent of flour-and-water paste. With unusual sobriety, Leeuwenhoek sets about preparing a sample. He gets a tiny dab on the mount of his best scope. This is precarious but direct. If it doesn't work, he will dilute it with water in a capillary and try that way. He carries it to the window and squints through the lens, fiddling with the focus pin. A moment elapses, and he lets out a gasp.

"Don't!" says Pierre, "you'll disturb the sample!"

"We had better get Reinier," says Leeuwenhoek. "Maybe he will know what this means."

"What what means? Let me see! Then I'll go and get him, if you want." Pierre hovers near Leeuwenhoek's elbow until he hands over the scope. "Savior!" he mutters after a minute. "He's afflicted with fish! Little fish, swimming everywhere! Can this be natural? Or could he have some disease?"

"I have no idea. I suppose we would have to compare it to another sample," says Leeuwenhoek. "One thing at a time! Go and get Reinier!"

De Graaf comes barreling in, hot on the heels of Pierre, within a half hour. "Pierre says the stuff is wildly active! Is this true, Antoni?"

"See for yourself," replies Leeuwenhoek, extending the scope. "I've never seen anything like it. Like eels, or polliwogs."

De Graaf immediately puts it to his eye. After a moment, he too gives a gasp, a long indrawn breath. This is immediately followed by a sigh of satisfaction. "Amazing, Antoni, amazing. Your lenses triumph again. I can't say I expected anything as dramatic as this, but I expected something. Some active principle. This is perfect! They are capable of self-motion! You see, I believe there are sections within the female body, fairly long ones, anatomically speaking, that these—creatures? animalcules?— must traverse. I could not understand how. Now I see it!"

"So you think this is normal, then?" says Pierre. "It's not that he's got the clap or something?"

"I would guess not. I think this is the mechanism of life itself. The male, animating force made visible. It's miraculous!"

"I don't know," says Pierre, "I feel as if animalcules are invading my privacy. I mean, we know they are everywhere—but even here?"

"Our bodies make them, these little eels, for some specific purpose," says Leeuwenhoek. "We must consider them part of ourselves, not foreign bodies."

"Yes, Antoni," says De Graaf, "exactly! These tiny things, they are somehow signatures of ourselves. We should not fear them. Soon enough we will figure out exactly what it is they do for us."

"Hmmph," says Pierre. "I have always heard this stuff spoken of as seed. These are not like seeds at all. They are creatures, not little grains."

"Now we know that is a misnomer. *Semen*, that's the Latin word for seed; obviously the Romans didn't know, either. You realize we are probably the first three men in the world to see them?" says De Graaf, pacing. He looks transfigured.

"I guess I had better do a full description for the Society," says Leeuwenhoek, again peering into the lens at the tiny, flailing bodies with their whiplike tails.

"They'll probably make you a knight," says De Graaf. "Better send it in Latin, though."

"Well, I imagine accepting an English knighthood would be treason, so let's hope not," says Leeuwenhoek.

"Give it here," says Pierre, shortly. "How do you expect me to draw them if you won't let me see them?"

"And after all, they are your relatives," says De Graaf.

Sweet and Salt

Philips is not thriving. He is not growing very fast, and he coughs a lot. He has lived longer than their other two sons, and the one little daughter who died before Marieke. This is small comfort. De Graaf says to keep him out in the air as much as possible and not to smother him with bedclothes during the night. The midwife, who thinks that babies need to be protected from drafts and kept nearly at roasting point at all times, does not approve. On this occasion, Barbara sides with De Graaf; the little fellow has less struggle to breathe if he is more lightly clad and in cooler air. He greatly enjoys being carried around in the autumn wind and gets wildly excited by the moving boughs and fluttering flags and blowing leaves and all the other sights of fall. Walking on the edge of town one afternoon, they see a windmill in the distance, its great sails turning and turning, and Philips goes into transports of joy, his little arms and legs stiffening into rods. Barbara is afraid that he is suffering from apoplexy, but his face is wreathed in smiles, and he laughs and laughs.

"His lungs are not strong," says De Graaf, looking concerned. "That is all I can say. Nurse him as much as you can."

Barbara is walking Philips around the courtyard briefly on a windy afternoon, giving him an airing. The girl returns with the geese. They squawk and chatter proprietorially, settling in. The baby watches them with bright interest. After a while, the girl comes over. She looks at Philips for a long time. Barbara is surprised, as she has

Sarah Tolmie

shown no interest in him heretofore. After the interrogation Barbara had put her through during the pregnancy, she can hardly blame the child for caution.

"Can I hold the baby?" asks the girl, unexpectedly.

Barbara is reluctant. The girl is not clean. She has been with these geese in pasture all day. On the other hand, she would not have to touch the baby's skin; he is entirely swaddled in cloth, only his face showing. It is so rare that the girl shows human sentiment that she does not want to discourage her. Battling with herself for a moment, she hesitates, then hands the infant to the goose girl.

The girl looks down at Philips dispassionately. She is calm and holds him firmly. Barbara has no fear that she will drop him. To her utter shock, the girl raises the baby up toward her face, still cradling his head carefully, and licks his right cheek. Philips considers this hilarious; his lips smack and his little arms wave. Barbara nearly screams. What is the mad girl doing?

"Salt," says the girl. She holds the infant back out to his mother, still supporting him precisely. Barbara snatches him back.

"What?" she says stupidly, peering at Philips' round cheek, checking that he has not been bitten.

"Salt. He tastes of salt," says the girl, "You try."

"What? Why?" says Barbara, "What are you talking about? Why should that matter?"

"Try," says the girl.

"Why?" asks Barbara, in increasing desperation, "Why?"

"He tastes of salt. More than you. More than me. More than Antoni."

"If you had licked me, or Antoni, I am sure I would have noticed! How would you know?" says Barbara.

"From the smell. Lick him," says the girl.

Barbara holds the small package that is Philips up to her face and licks his left cheek. The baby thinks this is a wonderful new game. He tastes of salt. Barbara lifts up his bonnet, checks his layers of swaddling. He is not hot. He is not sweating. He was bathed this morning. He tastes of salt. Like a grown man who has worked all day, in summer. Like the sea on your skin after swimming.

"He does," whispers Barbara, her heart seizing in her chest. "He does. Why? How did you know?"

"I know he is salty," says the goose girl, "but not why."

Barbara begins to cry, silently. She does not want to upset Philips. He is delighted by the game of licking, perfect for babies.

"Will he die?" asks Barbara. This is an appalling, ridiculous question, one that no one should ever have to ask of anyone, or to have answered. She is tired of asking it. She had asked it about her other two sons.

"I do not know," says the goose girl, simply, "but no one else is as salty as that."

Barbara cries quietly, wiping her eyes on the baby's trailing robes. The girl's expressionlessness is horrible. She thinks vindictively of chasing her out of the gate, slaughtering the geese and eating them...who would blame her? Let the orphanage take her—let her be made a slave or a whore! Let the madhouse take her, crazy girl! Salt! What does that have to do with anything? Why should that condemn her child to death?

Why has Antoni insisted that they keep this unnatural girl and her filthy geese, when they need none of them? Only the fact that she is holding Philips prevents her from seizing and slapping the girl and pummeling her with her fists. She who has never hit anyone. She takes a deep, dragging breath.

Salt. Maybe her womb has been sowed with it. Poisoned. As a punishment for her terrible doubts after the disaster. Week after week she had gone to church with her aunt, her hand still on fire, and been unable to pray, unable to hear the words of the pastor, her heart and mind filled with a boiling fury. God was a cruel parent. He had allowed this awful thing to happen to good, plain people; the citizens of Delft had been crushed under the wreckage of their town. They could not possibly have deserved it. She could not have deserved it. No manner of accounting could render it just. A year or more had passed before she had been able to rid herself of these hateful and rebellious thoughts. She was just coming out of them, and then Klaartje had been born, red and ruined all down one side, living only for minutes before dying in her arms. Months more of rage had followed. Finally she had passed into an exhausted stupor and then a kind of peace.

She clutches her tiny, living son to her chest. She had brought him into the world in all that pain and terror, and now she is going to lose him, just like the others. This perfect little spark that is Philips will be blown out, leaving her with nothing. A furious desolation wells up inside her. It has been waiting there for ten whole years, right from the day of the Thunderclap. Her aching bitterness, preserved in salt. This hateful girl child has seen it and named it. It is more than she can bear. Shifting Philips to one hip, she takes a step toward the girl. She will throttle her, choke her, smash her on the stones.

The goose girl stands, staring at her steadfastly. She shows not a trace of fear. All around Barbara, the geese close in, absolutely silent, their necks taut, expectant. She sees their glittering black eyes like shiny pebbles. They do not honk. They do not rush or gabble. They wait with a kind of excruciating politeness.

Barbara lowers her raised hand. She steps back. The fury drains out of her. The taut watchfulness drains out of the geese. All the while the girl has not moved. How had she known that Barbara's nerve would fail? How had the geese known?

Suddenly, as if nothing had happened, the girl says, "Maybe Antoni will know about the salt. Maybe he can find out. He likes to find out things."

Barbara lets out a short, despairing laugh, almost a bark. The baby on her hip starts, wails and then coughs. She dandles him up and down. He calms at once, wheezing gently. "I will be sure to tell him," she says to the girl. Then she resumes her pacing. The geese ignore her, or make way for her, as they usually do, unruffled.

Leeuwenhoek finds that he is going around with his teeth clenched, as if expecting a blow. He wakes up mornings with a sore jaw. Barbara is suffering because the baby is suffering. She is brave and says nothing, but she goes to church more and more. She has prayed with the pastor. Leeuwenhoek knows she is fighting despair. She is looking haggard, with dark circles under her eyes. She is having trouble eating, and her ankles swell. She is almost never off her feet, constantly walking the baby. He has remonstrated with her, trying to get her to take care of herself. She does not listen. She even snaps at Marieke.

"Let me take him for a while," he says to her, on a chilly early fall day, stopping her in her endless pacing of the courtyard. "You go in for a few minutes. Sit by the fire. Have some of that excellent soup," he continues, holding out his arms for Philips.

"I can't, I can't," she replies, hoarsely, "I have so little time to do this, Antoni! You know it! I have to be with him now, in this little time we have!"

"But Barbara, please, you must think of yourself as well!" says Leeuwenhoek, persisting in trying to take the baby from her, "You are exhausted. You must be strong yourself, in order to care for him! It's only sense, my love—"

"I can't, I can't!" repeats his wife feverishly, holding Philips to her breast. Leeuwenhoek sees his son's wondering, blinking eyes looking over her shoulder. Barbara begins to walk again, holding him upright so he can breathe easily. He stops trying to get hold of the baby and walks along beside them.

"Then I will come along, too," he says. He puts his arm around Barbara's shoulders, trying not to interfere with Philips, surreptitiously trying to take some weight off her swollen feet. Her shoulders feel thin through her heavy dress and shawl.

"Thank you, Antoni," whispers Barbara. Their tiny son is drifting to sleep, peaceful in the rocking motion of her arms. Leeuwenhoek walks along with them quietly, so as not to wake him, gazing at both of them, sadly, tenderly. They walk for a long time. Up and down, up and down, up and down.

❧

Leeuwenhoek buries himself in work. He fills pages with notes on every kind of observation. Pierre is busy keeping up with him. Letter after letter goes off to the Royal Society. His correspondence increases; now he is exchanging letters with Constantine Huygens, a very important man, and Swammerdam, and Claes Oldenburg, and even with a few members of the French Academy. Reinier goes back to Paris; he writes to him, too.

Vermeer's eleventh child, a son, Ignatius, had been born around the same time as Philips. He is fine, small but tough like all the others. Vermeer is looking the worse for wear, however. His mother-in-law, who owns their house, is a harridan. She is also exhaustingly devout and uses her religion to punish the rest of the family. Finances are straitened. Vermeer is not a prolific painter and he has strange views about clients. "I hate selling art to people I hate," he says to Leeuwenhoek. "These fine paintings in the houses of assholes. It's really unbearable."

"Johannes, you must get over this or all your children will starve."

"Do you want a few? You can afford them. They're a very nice lot, really. A playmate for Philips, perhaps? Ignatius is about the right age."

The grisly idea of exchanging the sickly Philips for the robust Ignatius steals through Leeuwenhoek's mind, like something from a fairy tale. He is revolted with himself. He says nothing and waits for the evil notion to pass off. The painter looks at him with a certain grim acuity, perhaps guessing what is passing through his mind.

Even Pierre seems under a cloud. His jokes have tapered off. He is unusually silent and works with ferocious concentration. Leeuwenhoek suspects that all is not well at home. Matthias DeWitt did not invest in Staff of Life, which is now almost unbelievably profitable. Every time Leeuwenhoek thinks of the noble family of Esterhazy with blood globules displayed in state all over their drawing rooms, he wants to laugh. It had been DeWitt's own timidity that kept him out of the deal. However, a miser's view of money is not one governed by reason; he may blame it on Pierre. His assistant has not confided in him, though, so there is little he can do.

On a drizzly day in late October, he goes out to the well. The goose girl is there with her charges. They are sheltering under the eaves, muttering grouchily. The girl puts down the foot of Scratch, which she had been examining, and comes over to him. It is unusual for her to initiate a conversation.

"Did the painter show you the painting he did of Falada?" she begins.

"Yes," he replies. This was months ago, so he wonders why she should bring it up now. "It was marvelous."

"He painted it with my hairs, you know."

"Yes, I suppose he might have," replies Leeuwenhoek.

"Do you think my hairs knew about Falada?"

"Knew what?"

"Knew what it was like to be him, the way I do, from talking to him. Would the hairs know that, too, because they are part of me?"

"No," says Leeuwenhoek. "I can't imagine that they would. I don't think hairs know anything. You need a brain and a heart for that. They are inert—not alive, I mean."

"I wonder how he did it then, Johannes. How did he know what Falada was like?"

"Did he not see him?"

"Only dead. Just his head."

"Then he must have used his imagination. That's the part of the mind that makes pictures. He made it up. Some artists do that. Plus, he could have looked at other horses."

"No, it was exactly like Falada."

"There are many dapple gray horses."

"No, the painting shows Falada from the inside. What he feels like. That's why it looks so much like him, from the outside."

"I confess I don't remember the painting all that well. And I never saw the horse myself."

"I wonder if he heard it from me, from inside me, like I heard it from Falada."

"Well," says Leeuwenhoek, reluctantly, "maybe. But I've never met anyone else who can do that. I think it's your own, special, gift. Though I think, as I've said before, it would be best not to talk about it."

"I told that priest."

"What priest?" he says sharply.

"That English one who visited, who got sick. We talked once, when he was here."

Leeuwenhoek thinks of all the trouble he and Vermeer went to in order to keep her out of the way. He sighs inwardly. Secrets will out.

"What did he say?"

"He was afraid, for a little while. Then he was fine. Happy, I think."

"That is strange. What on earth made you tell him?"

"I don't know. I was angry at him for doubting you."

"So was Pierre."

"Pierre is your white goose. He protects you."

Leeuwenhoek pictures Pierre, honking and hissing at fleeing members of the Royal Society; forcing DeVeyne to honor his contracts, beak upraised. The girl is quiet for a moment.

"Did Barbara tell you that I licked your little baby?"

"Yes, she did. She thought you had gone mad, at first. But she said you found him salty. Is that true?"

"Yes. Do you know why?"

"No."

"Is there a way to find out?"

"Not that I know of." He shrugs, defeated.

"Barbara is sweet. Her skin, her sweat. I can smell that, too. Do you know why that is?"

"No," says Leeuwenhoek. "No, I don't." He sits down on the coping of the well. "Really? Sweet? You are certain, I suppose?"

"Yes," says the goose girl, "but you can lick her and make sure."

"No, I can't do that. Not now. She is far too worried about the baby."

"Is it bad, the sweetness?"

"Probably," says Leeuwenhoek. "If nobody else has it. She is a sweet woman, Barbara. Naturally sweet. God forbid it should kill her. I will ask Reinier." His shoulders slump. He puts his head in his hands.

"Maybe I should not have said anything," says the girl. Unusually, she comes to sit beside him on the coping. She does not touch him. She smells strongly of geese.

"It is better to know as much as we can," he says heavily, after a time.

"I remember you said that before. Even if it does not help. That's why I told you."

"Thank you," says Leeuwenhoek, though he does not feel thankful. The girl nods. She sits stolidly beside him, as one goose will sit by another if it is sick or miserable or in pain.

They sit unspeaking, side by side, on the edge of the well. The light rain soaks their clothes, making them heavier and heavier. It beads and slides easily off the feathers of the geese huddled around them. Finally the girl looks up and says, "Antoni. We should go in."

Eggshells

Pierre and his father have reached a standoff. Exactly as Pierre had feared, Matthias has not taken his son's extraordinary success with Staff of Life well. At the same time, he cannot fail to be impressed by the amount of money it is bringing into the household. Thus he is in a bind, the same kind of bind he is in about his own paintings. This indecision is slowly filling him up with a murderous rage. He does not show it overtly. He maintains his calm, implacable manner. But Pierre can sense it. His fear is less for himself now than for his mother.

Matthias has not laid a finger on Pierre since the success of his first designs. Evidently he does not see investing in someone's business as compatible with beating him. The ruler has remained on its nail in the study. However, Mathilde remains in her usual Purgatory, receiving beatings for every shortfall in the kitchen budget, every burnt loaf of bread or sleeve cut too wide. These beatings have not become obviously more savage or more frequent, but they are all the more noticeable now that he is not receiving any himself: the silences, the absences, the muffled cries in distant parts of the house. His mother's bruises. It makes even less sense than it did before because, as a family, they now have so much more money.

Time and time again he is on the brink of intervening, but Mathilde begs him not to. She says it would only make things worse. He pleads with her to tell Father Grotius, maybe he can do something. Why would your father listen to him? she replies. He is not a Catholic.

Exactly one half share of the weekly budget now comes out of Pierre's purse. "Now that you're suddenly the golden goose," his father says. So now, seemingly, he is partly responsible every time his mother runs over budget and gets her face slapped or her back striped. His solution is to give her money, a little at a time, just leaving it in the kitchen unobtrusively at odd hours, when Matthias is out of the house. She does not seem to use this money, or at least, not to spare herself. Perhaps she is saving it for something. Either that, or Matthias is, in fact, losing control and punishes her regardless of her frugality. Pierre doesn't know. He and his mother do not discuss it.

He can easily afford to leave his father's house if he wants to. It would be unusual to do this before he gets married, but not impossible. It might be considered a shameful family breach, though, one that could impact his father's business. What would happen to Mathilde then? Pierre doesn't feel that he is doing her a lot of good as it is, but that would definitely be worse. She would be entirely at his father's mercy, and all alone. Hanneke, her kitchen maid, does her best to shield her mistress, but she has little power. She is dependent on Matthias for all her earnings. Such is the tyranny of money, in the world of Matthias DeWitt.

The goose who lays the golden eggs, thinks Pierre derisively, trudging across the fish market to Leeuwenhoek's house. That's why we're all walking on golden eggshells.

Arriving at Hippolytusbuurt, which he usually finds an oasis of calm, he finds disarray. Philips has had a respiratory attack. His lungs had been so full of phlegm when he woke up that he had been unable to cough it all up. Remembering the instructions that De Graaf had left him when he departed for Paris, Leeuwenhoek had managed to save him by holding him upside down by the heels and drawing off the worst of it with his largest pipette, time and time again. The child is much better, breathing well, now sleeping in exhaustion.

Leeuwenhoek is a shattered wreck. All he says about the morning's events is: "I'm going to need a larger pipette." Barbara has retired to bed with nervous prostration. Pierre excuses himself and is about to depart for home again, but Leeuwenhoek, looking up, says "Stay, Pierre. Let us work a while."

However, his master is unable to settle to any work. This is so unlike him that Pierre is quite concerned. He bustles around, making a show of things, which Leeuwenhoek seems to find comforting. He tidies up, though the place is already tidy. He checks on various experiments that need no oversight. Leeuwenhoek sits at the study table, leaning on his elbows, looking gray. At length he looks up and says, "Thank you, Pierre, for doing all this. Do you know, the goose girl says you're my white goose? My guardian."

Pierre feels himself stifling a sob. He knows that the phrase is mere accident. It's just that, at home, he is failing so horribly to protect the one person he loves most in the world. Keeping his back to Leeuwenhoek, he wipes off a shelf, lifting and replacing a collection of scopes and vessels, one by one. Once he is sure that his voice will be steady, he says the first thing that comes into his head: "Do you ever find her a bit frightening, that girl?"

The microscopist reflects. "I have," he replies. "But then I tell myself: she's just a child. And she attests to things that we know, by our own observations, are truly there."

"And maybe to some we haven't seen. What was that motto—trust no man's word?"

"But then, she's not a man."

"Do you trust her word?"

"Yes. I'm not sure why. Do you?"

Pierre considers. "I guess so. At least, I think she doesn't lie."

"Animals don't lie."

"You think she's an animal? A goose, maybe?" says Pierre, only half-joking.

"No," replies Leeuwenhoek thoughtfully, "not if you mean like in an old tale: transformed by a witch's spell. She's not a princess; she's a peasant. I suppose she's a savage. Like a red Indian. Though talking with her often makes me feel that I'm an animal myself, only wearing clothes and walking on my hind legs. But she does it better. More completely."

"But man is the noblest being in creation!"

"I never doubt it except when I'm with her."

"I expect that's a sin."

"Likely. But then, so is pride. She always knocks mine right out of me, if I'm feeling too clever."

"But you are clever! The cleverest man I know!"

"Really, would you say so? That's very kind of you, you know. We live in an age of clever men. I am touched, Pierre. Thank you," replies Leeuwenhoek.

"You're welcome," replies Pierre stiffly. "It's no more than the truth. Antoni." He gets on with the dusting.

MARTIN

Forsythe has managed to get rid of the tapestry. He wishes he could burn it. He blames it for all his problems. He and the sexton managed to roll it up and carry it out the door; they left it on the midden next to the churchyard, where it was doubtless scavenged by somebody within hours. As cannon wadding or rags or carpet, it may do somebody some good, thinks the rector, massaging his aching jaw. His face is scarred and remains a little swollen on one side. For weeks he had looked a fright as his bruises healed. His parishioners think he still looks peaky and keep bringing him condolences and soup. He puts up with one for the sake of the other.

He does not deserve condolences. If his congregation knew what was going through his head, they would report him to the regents. He would be sent back to England in shame. He would be defrocked. There are severe punishments for sodomy here in the Republic, like there are everywhere, though they keep them very quiet. He has heard that such men receive private trial and are quickly garroted. Holland does not want to be thought of like Italy, or England. He might not be subject to these laws as a clergyman and a foreigner, but he does not want to find out. And it would be the most sophistic quibbling to point out that he has not committed any palpable acts. Sodomy is a state of mind. It is linked to treason in every state in Europe: treason against the state of things.

Realizing that Martin Dekker is available for hire has made his own desire known to him concisely and clearly.

He had been right to rail against prostitution, in his own mind and from the pulpit: putting a price tag on a set of human actions makes them thinkable, and therefore covetable. It mixes lust up with greed, as he has heard himself say in countless sermons against the sins of the tavern: concupiscence is that generalized state of desire, excessive, grasping desire for everything. Its objects are mutable: food, drink, money, fame, song, and dance. Men.

People have paid to have *vleslijke conversatie* with Martin Dekker. Women. Possibly men. "What's it to you?" he had said, "unless you want to hire me?" He had been defiant. He had been joking. Had he been joking? Forsythe's mind runs on this question endlessly. He wishes it had never, never been asked. He despises Dekker for asking it. He despises himself for entertaining it.

Two weeks ago the thought of hiring a male whore would have been impossible. Now it is possible. Here it is: the slow creep of sin. The force that unknits moral order, stitch by tiny stitch.

Fucking another man is a sin. Paying for it is likewise a sin. If you're going to do one, why not do the other? This is where the logic leads you, the logic of despair. It's just so much easier this way, all in the one package; no dangerous seduction, less risk of exposure. Whore and client are already sharing a secret, what's one more? It's as easy as throwing yourself out of a boat.

Forsythe's mouth is sore—he keeps rinsing his torn gum with salt and water, as De Graaf had advised, and it still hurts like hell every time—and he is pale and restless and sleepless, but he is preaching better than ever before in his life. His sermons have never been more than passable. Suddenly they have the profundity of St Paul: *sin, taking occasion by the commandment, wrought in me every kind of concupiscence. For without the law, sin was dead.* So there's something to be said for temptation, he thinks bitterly, writing out sermon heads in his lonely rooms.

He wishes Davenant were still here. At least he could confess to him. The seal of the confession would offer him some protection, no matter how much the man despised him afterward. Mind you, Davenant had confessed to bizarrely heretical notions himself as he worked through his agony at the discovery of the animalcules. He had departed for England full of strange theories. God knows what theological *cul de sac* he will have gotten himself into by now. Perhaps he will found his own church or become an evangelical. The thought of Davenant, in his Englishness, in his struggle amid irreconcilables, is strangely comforting.

He is afraid to go back to Leeuwenhoek's lest he meet Martin. What would he do, denounce him in front of Barbara, their good hostess? In front of little Marieke? How much does Leeuwenhoek know? That he would take the man's money and permit him into his house with his wife and child bespeaks either ignorance or a degree of laxity he would not have expected even of the Dutch, who are notoriously permissive. This would be positively *louche*. He cannot believe it of Antoni Van Leeuwenhoek, the respectable merchant. But then, what would he believe of himself, the respectable clergyman?

But it is not at the house of the microscopist that he again meets Martin Dekker. It is at church. At the English church, during a sacrament. The Dekkers are a wealthy farming family from outside Delft. Martin's youngest sister has married an Englishman, Matthew Carver, a felt merchant from Harwich.

Here they are, the family, at the fount, baptizing their first boy into the Church of England. Here is Martin Dekker, solemn and proud, dressed in black velvet that would buy a plow and team, standing next to his aged mother with her pursed mouth, prissy-looking old cunt. Does she know where he got the money for it? Nauseating crone in her sober silks; her son is a whore. He should throw her out of the church bodily. What has he told her? That he's a diamond merchant? Here he is, Dekker, the picture of elegance, offering to act as the infant's godfather, profaning the sacristy by his very presence. Peasants, the lot of them. Farmers make too much money in Holland.

Forsythe is only too glad of the overpowering grace of God, for he makes a hash of the service. Had it been up to him, poor little Stephen Carver would still be a heathen. He shrugs off the jubilant clan as fast as he can with forced congratulations. He feels positively soiled. He is rushing up the aisle, two steps away from the vestry, lifting the dalmatic over his head, when he is hailed by Dekker, the new godfather.

"Reverend Forsythe!" he says, laying a hand lightly but insistently on the sleeve of his robe so that he has to turn around. "How are you? I have been meaning to call on you. You look much better. Did you manage to shift that tapestry?"

Forsythe turns to confront Martin Dekker, so tall, so handsome, looking so very decent and concerned, head to toe in black like something out of a guildhall portrait, the model citizen. "I got rid of it, thank you," he replies tightly.

"Did you have to send for De Graaf again? Or were you all right? You looked terrible."

"I was fine. Lucky. I remain much obliged to both of you," says Forsythe.

"To the tune of eight guilders you are, Reverend, indeed!" says Dekker. "And so, I insist on taking you out for a drink. You look angry. Best to give an angry man a drink and see what he's angry about. And we can celebrate my godfatherhood."

"While I congratulate you on becoming a godfather, Dekker, I—"

"Have no intention of boozing with you because you're a vile, whoring sinner?" says Dekker, at once jovial and wounded. "I believe that you have some recollection of our last, interrupted conversation, father, and that we would do best to finish it." His whole demeanor is such a heady mixture of contrition and challenge that Forsythe, as man and clergyman, cannot say no. He merely nods. He continues into the vestry and beckons Dekker after him. Having already begun to take off the dalmatic, he pulls it off over his head and lays it carefully on top of the vestment chest, acutely conscious of disrobing in front of him. He refuses to countenance the ironic lift of blonde eyebrows that he believes he might have seen and marches on toward the rear door of the chapel. Dekker follows.

"Let us go back to the Mechelen," says Dekker, once they are outside. "We might as well return to the scene of the crime."

"Very well," says Forsythe shortly. They cross the square. As they sit down in a corner of the taproom and order two genevers, he asks the tall Dutchman: "Are you really prepared to discuss this in a public place?"

"I have entertained clients in this public place," replies Dekker, smiling. "It isn't all fucking, you know." The priest is silent, his mouth a thin line. "How did you find out about Aliette, anyway?"

"From my parish."

"So you asked about me?"

"Yes."

"Why?"

"I couldn't figure out what you did for a living. How you could afford your expensive clothes."

Dekker strokes the lace that emerges from the sleeve of his jacket, pulling it down over his hand. He has fine, strong, long-fingered hands, clean and agile-looking. "I see. But why would you care?"

"I don't know. Curiosity, I guess."

"How do you come to know the Leeuwenhoeks?" asks Dekker.

"I was a member of a party sent out from England by the Royal Society to examine his animalcules. Just a translator, really."

"Were you now?" says Dekker. "The famous Royal Society?" He appears quietly delighted, as if at a private joke. "I have had professional contact with them myself."

"What? What do you mean?" asks Forsythe. He has an instant, terrible suspicion of Davenant. He tries to quell it, disgusted with himself.

"It is a long tale and a rather improper one," replies Dekker, now grinning at the horrified priest. "Suffice it to say that my services have been of use to them."

"Oh my God, your services—?"

"Yes," says Dekker, nodding. "Now, Reverend Forsythe, it seems to me that you disapprove most highly of me, and of my work. Is that correct?"

One stiff nod.

"Have you given any thought to why that might be?"

"Your profession is a sin, and a crime."

"A sin it may be, Forsythe, but it is not, precisely, a crime in our Republic. Selling our bodies is not against the law; fornication outside marriage is, though. It's adultery that gets the magistrates most exercised, in fact. And that can happen without us."

"Quibbling," says the rector.

"Are you going to denounce me? Preach against Aliette and her house from your English pulpit?"

"No. Or at least, not by name."

"Well, that is some consideration, at least," says Dekker.

"Do you feel no pain at what you do?" bursts out Forsythe. "Adultery? Bastardy? Sodomy?"

"I can give lonely people pleasure. I don't feel it as pain. And it is excellent business, a fair trade. People get what they pay for."

"But what about your soul?"

"What about it? It is inside me. I don't fuck people with my soul, do I? It takes care of itself. It's already saved or damned, isn't it? Predestined?"

Forsythe snorts. Dekker gives him a long, speculative look. "I think, Father, that you want to fuck me," he says quietly, with astonishing bluntness. Forsythe stares at him, aghast. A very dangerous thing to say in a public place. He moves to get up. "Now as it happens," continues Dekker, "I do not perform with men. I have never fucked one before. We have another fellow who does that. I suppose I could introduce you to him—"

"What? No! Jesus Christ!" splutters Forsythe. He feels faint. He folds his hands carefully on the table.

"No, I didn't think so," says Dekker. "It's me, isn't it? We desire one person, and not another. Who knows why? Understand me, Forsythe: I am not accusing you. You can be a sodomite or not, for all I care. I'm not about to report you. I just don't want you to be angry at me because you feel guilty at your own desire. That could be dangerous for me. Likely for you, too. One thing I have learned in this business is that there are few things stronger than desire, and it can go many ways. It is very unpredictable."

"So you are trying to blackmail me? By suggesting these calumnies?"

"No. But you can look at it that way if you wish. If it makes you feel better. As long as it keeps both you and me safe. Think what you will. It's really just that I prefer to drink with people who don't act too high and mighty." Dekker pulls down his other lace sleeve so that the two are even. He sips his genever, watching Forsythe. "Come on now, Father, say something."

"So very businesslike, Dekker. This is all just business to you, is it?" replies the rector after a moment.

"Yes. Mostly."

"So you really would let me hire you, for the right price?"

"Well," says Dekker, raising his blonde brows. "It would have to be a seriously good price, Father. More than you would be willing to pay, I think. As I said, my taste does not run to men."

"But then you would?"

"Yes. Why not? If it were worth that much to somebody."

"Money is evil."

"Men are evil, Forsythe."

"And you would seriously introduce me to your friend, the catamite?"

"I would."

"And you would not care if I fucked him in the sight of God? Or any other man, money or no, for that matter?"

"No. That is none of my business."

"You are utterly corrupt, Martin Dekker," says Forsythe, "I don't know what else to say."

"Then have a drink, Father," says the tall man, smiling once more, "and say nothing."

Never Paint Animals

Suddenly, Vermeer is dying. He gets a fever that will not abate. He does not have the strength to fend it off. Everybody knows he has been exhausted for a long time. De Graaf is still in Paris, or Leeuwenhoek would send him to his friend, at his own expense. As it is, the painter is stuck with apothecaries and an old barber-surgeon who has known the family for a long time. His pious wife and even more pious mother-in-law insure that he is given the last rites every time he flags, though he keeps rallying.

"I'm well sick of it, to be honest," he tells Leeuwenhoek during one of these periods of lucidity. "If I see that damn priest one more time, I will scream. I'm sure I've been saved by now. He can just piss off." He gasps for breath for a moment. "Now listen to me, and for God's sake don't interrupt me with condolences. It's a never-ending parade of consolation around here, and it's driving me mad. I need that girl. Your goose girl. Bring her to me."

"What?" says Leeuwenhoek. "Johannes, what can she possibly do?"

"I want to give her something. Get on with it, Antoni! Please! I'm a dying man!" Vermeer is so insistent, and he looks so awful, pale and sweating, that Leeuwenhoek finds himself bolting out the door. It is still early; he hopes she will still be at home.

She is. The geese are drinking and pecking desultorily at scattered grain in the yard. The girl is sitting on the upturned bucket, silent as a statue. Leeuwenhoek dashes through the gate, skidding on a goose dropping, flailing his arms for balance. Hilarious as this no doubt appears—the geese jump and cackle—he has never felt less comical. "Thank God, you are still here!" he says to her. "Will you come with me to Vermeer's? He is very sick, and he wants to see you."

She stands up immediately and follows him. The geese all come up to the gate as she clicks it shut and stand in a solemn line before it like sentries, their grain forgotten. Leeuwenhoek sees their eyes shining like a row of black beetles between the wooden slats as he and the girl disappear up the laneway.

They walk fast. The goose girl asks no questions. Within minutes they are back at Vermeer's. Knocking, they are admitted by a defeated-looking Jan. The wails of children rise from behind him, in further rooms of the house, and he turns away directly, leaving them to find their own way to the sickroom. The painter is lying there, small and upright in a box bed. He opens his dark eyes in his pinched white face, and Leeuwenhoek is reminded of a goose. Seeing them, Vermeer motions the girl forward. Quietly she moves toward the bed.

"You are sick, Johannes the painter," she says, stopping before him, "and there are little animals all around you. Everywhere here. On your bed, and in the air, and inside you. I hear them singing."

"Oh, not them again!" says the artist, smiling faintly under his sheen of sweat.

"They will kill you. They are a bad kind. Strong," says the girl, hoarsely. "I am sorry." Leeuwenhoek has never heard her utter these words before.

"Never mind that," whispers Vermeer impatiently. "Take these. They are for you." From beside him on the bed, partly under cover, he pulls out two tiny paintings.

The girl takes them. One of them Leeuwenhoek knows: the horse, Falada. The heavy, powerful gray trots diagonally through the picture, over cobbles, heading away. The painting is barely two hands wide, and you can feel the weight of him. His huge haunches and right flank dominate the foreground. You can just see a slice of his right eye in his receding head as he escapes at a dramatic angle. He is bridle-less, halter-less, pounding through the cold. Leeuwenhoek realizes it is the first painting of a horse he has seen without a man in it.

"Falada!" says the girl, stroking one side of the tiny unframed panel. She is speaking to the horse.

The other painting is new. In the goose girl's grubby hand Leeuwenhoek sees his own courtyard, the brick wall, the gate. The geese. All the geese, even Caligula in his red boots. The white birds are milling, moving, facing this way and that. Only Caligula looks out, straight out, his button eyes just visible, challenging, on either side of his upraised beak. He could be speaking. "Redboots!" says the girl, directly to the painting. "I thought I would never see you again!"

Vermeer looks on with quiet satisfaction. "He looks at us; we look at him. Just like you said, remember?" he says to her. "So tell me, just this once—is everything there?"

"Everything is there," she says.

The artist lets out his breath. "There, then, now I can die happy," he says to her. "Do you believe me?"

"No one dies happy," says the girl, "but it is a great painting. It has an inside and an outside. Everything."

Vermeer nods. The goose girl looks at him. "Did you paint it with my hairs?" she asks. He nods again. "Thank you," she says. Leeuwenhoek is thunderstruck.

The painter turns to him. "I used brick dust in that wall. Feel it. Gritty. Pity I just thought of it now, eh? Well, let her keep them. She may need them. And that old bitch Maria won't get them. Plus, you know I never paint animals."

"Sentimental," says Leeuwenhoek.

"Sentimental," agrees Vermeer.

INHERITANCE

The funeral of the domestic painter Johannes Vermeer, of Delft, is no great affair. He is buried in an obscure corner of the Oude Kerk, along with the children who had predeceased him, surrounded by paupers and nobodies. The family cannot afford an elaborate monument. Why should a man who left eleven surviving children and a host of brilliant paintings need a carved lump of stone, after all, says his pious mother-in-law, Maria Thins. Then again, she is too cheap to buy one—though she had paid for the plot.

Unsurprisingly, his legal affairs are a nightmare. Leeuwenhoek knows this because he has been named executor. Looking at the tangle of it all, he expects to be engaged with it for the next two years at least. But it is the last thing he can do for his recalcitrant friend. Nineteen paintings are left without liens on them for his wife to inherit. A number are owed as collateral on defaulted loans. The guild of St Luke, of which he had been several times President, owns a couple; he might be able to get them back for Catharina to sell or borrow against, but not without spending more money. He lets them go. There is also a considerable amount of work by other artists, stock from Vermeer's other trade as an art dealer. He had inherited his father's taste for this business, and unfortunately also his colossally bad timing: paintings are hard to sell in time of war, and the whole Republic has been rocked by wars for the last ten years. Some of these paintings Vermeer had bought and was retailing; some were

Sarah Tolmie

on consignment; almost all the deals had been made verbally and had no contracts. Now everybody is contesting them. Artists are a grasping lot.

The main problem, thinks Leeuwenhoek to himself, as he makes out endless itemized lists of things to be sold from the cluttered house, is the women. Vermeer's life had been run by women: his wife and his mother-in-law. This is all very well in life, but it's bad in death because they have comparatively little power in the law. All their expertise is wasted. The man had clearly spent the last fifteen years casually signing this document and that document as Catharina or Maria brought them to him; they did it all. Now they can't. He has to, and he doesn't know their system, such as it was. This is all very, very stupid, Johannes, he lectures his old friend in his head. Fuck off, he hears Vermeer's ironic voice reply: let the women do it. They are better at it than me. I'm just a painter.

The goose girl keeps the two little paintings by her pallet in the pantry. It appears that they have become her conversational companions now. Barbara and the maid report that she can be heard talking to them at night or in the early morning. She still carries her handkerchief, but can now only rarely be seen to spread it out ritually on her knee and consult it like a map or a sybil. "It's dead now," she says to Leeuwenhoek when he asks her about it, one day in the courtyard. "The little animals are dead, or sleeping. I can't hear them anymore." She continues in her unemotional way, "I cried about it. I cried and cried. But now I have Falada. And Redboots."

"Do you miss Johannes?" asks Leeuwenhoek. He misses his old friend terribly. There is a part of him—the part that Vermeer himself had been so good at bamboozling—that actually relishes the infuriating struggle of the painter's account books. Vermeer is managing to annoy even in death. When that is over there will be nothing left of him. Except the art. And that, he had always insisted, has nothing to do with him at all. "Painting isn't about personalities, Antoni. It's mechanical. A machine could do it. It's about accounting for what's there." The man himself had been much more affectionate than this severity would suggest. He and the goose girl had made a curious bond.

The girl cocks her head reflectively. "Yes. Do you?"

"Yes. A lot. He was my friend. He was funny and talented and brave. He went his own way."

"Like us," replies the girl, "me and the geese. We go our own way."

"You do," says Leeuwenhoek. "But I wonder if it's the same way."

"I don't know," says the girl. "Johannes saw things, though, that other people don't see. He saw the insides, finally. I was glad for him, because he told me that paintings were about making things last for a long time. Like genever, he said. But nothing stays the same if you only see it from the outside; it's always changing. It's not itself. Stupid. But he saw Falada, and Redboots, in the end. They are there, in the paintings, forever."

"Like genever, did you say?"

"He said it takes half a field of grain to make a bottle of genever and that his paintings were like that. I thought it was too bad because genever is disgusting. But I love Falada and Redboots anyway." She pauses a moment. "I guess they are like Lancelot now."

"Are they?" asks Leeuwenhoek, "How?" He imagines Lancelot, the heroic white goose of the Table Round. A horse is more plausible.

"Well, they're dead. But they're also alive, just in a painting instead of a story."

"But what if you had never known Falada and Red-boots? I remember we talked about this before. You said it would be impossible to tell if stories—or paintings—from the past were true, if you hadn't been there yourself to see it. What if I showed the paintings to someone else, who had never known them? Would they be alive to them?"

"I don't know. I never know what other people think. But for me, they are alive. I can feel what it is like to be them. That is what matters. They are real. They have voices, like the little animals do."

Leeuwenhoek hears Vermeer's voice in his head: *It's about accounting for what's there.* Somehow he doubts that this is exactly what he meant, but perhaps it is related. He goes off on a tangent of reminiscence, "Then I guess Johannes has proved his point that art can preserve nature just as well as natural philosophy can. We were always arguing about that."

"Why?"

"Well, philosophical specimens can be dried or treated with chemicals, or put in sealed bottles. In botany, say, or medicine. Then they can last for many years. Hundreds, I imagine. And there they are, still perfect. Or perfect enough to investigate. That is good enough for me. It wasn't good enough for Johannes. He was filled with scorn. Dead bugs in bottles, Antoni, he said, will never be worth a painting. A painting doesn't need to be *investigated.* It is already there. He laughed at me."

"Do you still have the blood from the handkerchief?" asks the girl, unexpectedly.

"Yes, in water. In the study. Do you want to see it? You never did, did you, under the microscope?"

"No, only the honeydew."

"Let's go and look at it, then," says Leeuwenhoek, glad to get away from the interminable lists of Vermeer's possessions for a while. "I haven't seen it myself for ages. It won't take long. You can take the geese out afterward." They go into the house, leaving the geese milling about the yard. They always look aimless when the girl is not with them.

In the study, he throws open the windows. He putters around, looking for the specimen. He thought it was in one place, but Pierre has tidied it away into another. It takes him a moment to locate it. He brings it gingerly down from the shelf. It is a bit like handling a dangerous sleeping animal. He realizes he ought to have warned Pierre about it, or put a label on it, or something. If his assistant had dropped it, would he now be dying of the plague? What if he dropped it into the well? Or into the canal? Would these animalcules pass through air, or water? Would the goose girl, out in the fields, see the towering, misty figure of Plague gliding toward the town? Leeuwenhoek's mind has been running entirely too much upon death. He tries to curb his wild speculations.

The girl stands peacefully in the sun from the window, waiting. Her hair glints under her cap. Her hands are still. Her gaze is directed down at a slight leftward angle. She could be a painting, as beautiful as the one of Pierre with the silver microscope, standing in that very window: one that Vermeer will never do. Leeuwenhoek recalls that he was going to ask Vermeer to paint a portrait of Philips. He had anticipated a big argument about it, knowing that his friend would object that he was not really a portrait painter. He had never been able to have that last debate, as Vermeer had fallen sick so suddenly. So the portrait of Philips will have to be done by some other, lesser artist. Probably one who paints deathbed pictures. There are a couple of them in town, even one who specializes in children. Barbara is going to need something.

Tears suddenly wet Leeuwenhoek's cheeks. He had not wept at the funeral. It is not appropriate for men to cry at funerals. Even Vermeer would have disapproved of such carry-on. Leeuwenhoek wishes that he could scream and wail and gnash his teeth like a savage or a hurt animal. The goose girl would tolerate it. She would continue to stand at the window, unperturbed, unjudging, in her accidental homage to Johannes. But Leeuwenhoek could not tolerate it in himself. He struggles to focus, returning to the task at hand.

He brings her the tiny capillary with its scope attached. As he is placing it into her small hands (which are filthy, as usual; he will have to wash the glass), she says: "Yes! I can still hear them, the ones from the handkerchief! And some others, too." She looks delighted. She peers through the viewer. "I see some things. I wonder which ones they are?"

"I will look, after," says Leeuwenhoek. "At least the ones that are common in water, I know." He lets her look for a long time. The size of her hands, he reflects, makes her a likely worker with philosophical instruments. Also, her stillness. Eventually, she hands him the tiny phial. He examines the sample. Softly rounded blood globules; water animalcules. Exactly what he saw before. "You are sure you are hearing the plague ones?" he asks. "Because I think we are still not seeing them." He describes the visible animalcules to her, as best he can. She looks through the viewer again to confirm.

"Yes, it is them I hear. The same kind as before. The ones that are gone from the kerchief now," she says.

"Damn! Too small!" replies Leeuwenhoek.

"You are angry that I can hear them, and you still can't see them?" asks the girl.

He winces slightly. "A little, yes," he admits. "But maybe I will someday. My lenses are getting better."

"Maybe it is just more important to me." Leeuwenhoek is taken aback. This is not a philosophical idea. Yet he may still agree with it. He is just beginning to wrestle with it in his mind when the girl says, "I am sorry." Now he is truly surprised. He has only heard her say this once before, to Johannes on his deathbed. It makes him uneasy. Still, he reckons, such are the small triumphs of civilization. Geese do not feel sorry.

"Sometimes a setback just makes us more determined," he replies. "I am just about to make a few more lenses," he goes on, the plan forming in his mind even as he speaks. "So maybe we will see them yet!" He has not worked with the glassblowing tools for some time. The state of concentrated attention that they demand will be good for his scattered state of mind. "If they turn out well, I will give you one," he finds himself saying. This is also unexpected. But why not? A bit of brass, a glass bead? Vermeer has given her two little masterpieces. It's the least he can do for her, his strange companion on the voyage to the world of the animalcules. For a year and a half she has acted almost as his translator, as if she were a native of the place. The girl can carry her scope out to the fields and try to see all the little creatures she is always hearing around her. It is an incredible prospect. Heaven knows what she might discover. She will outstrip him instantly.

"That will be very interesting," she says, "but I think I had better take the flock out now."

"Yes, of course," says Leeuwenhoek, and lets her go.

Sarah Tolmie

≫

    As the goose girl leads her charges out to the pasture, the Reverend David Forsythe sits on a bench in the vestry, reading and re-reading a letter from England. His uncle and his entire family—his wife, and Forsythe's two cousins—have just died in a house fire in Bampton. Forsythe, named in his will as the next heir, has just inherited their property, aside from the movables lost in the fire, which had destroyed a whole block of the village. He was close to his cousins and had grown up in the village. It is horrible to make money from such a catastrophe. But he has. He's just made a lot of money.

THE GIFT

Radix malorum est cupiditas. Greed is the root of all evil. He'd said something similar to Martin Dekker only two weeks ago. It's not that he now disbelieves it, just that he is in the equivocal position of inhabiting the statement more fully: he has more to be greedy about. Forsythe thinks about this as he writes out a letter to his family that will greatly increase his sister's dowry. It is appropriate that family money should be used for family purposes.

Should he go home? He is now a man of means. Of relatively modest means, but enough to support the life of a gentleman—outside London, at least. Like many younger sons, he had gone into the church. He had been happy to do so. It is a more interesting life than running an estate, with all its petty concerns. Spiritual sheep are more rewarding than literal ones, as he knows only too well from his father's flocks. He had been prepared to be a clergyman for life, going wherever God and his career called him, but then his elder brother had died of a wasting sickness two years ago, leaving no children. He really ought to have returned to England then, but his parents had not felt particularly urgent about his return. Things were well in hand on their farms. His father had finally succeeded in enclosing enough land to run the sheep properly. A son in orders in a foreign (but Protestant) land was a credit to them. He and his father had never gotten on especially well under the same roof. The man is a philistine; there is nothing Forsythe, with his precious degree in theology, can do about it. He had been glad to stay in Holland, being his own man.

Due to the wonders of international banking, he can draw on his new funds almost immediately. He could re-furnish his dreadful rooms, or even move into a spacious flat. Perhaps he should replace the tapestry in the vestry. It is, after all, his fault that the previous one is gone.

He could call on Martin Dekker. See if he really is as good as his word, or if it was all bluff. Be the sodomite Dekker had accused him of being, and make Dekker into the whore. Hah! Tit for tat. The only thing stopping his precipitate fall into this temptation is his own paralyzing terror. Not terror for the state of his soul, but the fear of figuring out what to say. Of having to make an offer and then stare him down. He cannot imagine it. The fleshly conversation ensuing he can imagine just fine. The process of getting to it seems altogether more perilous.

He is already damned. That is perfectly clear. He would not be filled with these wrongful desires otherwise. So really, there is hardly any point in worrying about it. Insofar as it is possible to make peace with one's own damnation, he has done so. Doctrinally, he is assured that his own pollution will not make any difference to his parishioners. His job is to exhort them to find the best in themselves, to live up to the burden of being chosen. Not to enforce it. Not to enact it sacramentally. He could do it from jail. This is the point of being a Protestant.

If only he had someone to talk to. On the other hand, when contemplating something illegal and dangerous, the less said, the better. What to do? What to do? Why is everything important so bloody terrifying? The fact is, the only person in all the Seven Provinces he can talk to is Martin Dekker, and this is exactly the problem.

So he will talk to Martin Dekker. He finishes his letter.
He will leave it in the vestry for the sexton, who will get
it on a boat. Should he add a postscript—if you haven't
heard from me for a while, it's because I've been arrest-
ed as a sodomite, please send help and money? In Latin,
perhaps? But then his father couldn't read it. And if he
could, he would disown him. He drops his pen and leaves
the letter on the vestment chest. Feeling like a knight on
a suicidal quest, he goes in search of Martin Dekker. Dirty
schoolboy jokes crowd his head. The brave Sir Fucksalot
couches his lance—

He has no idea where the whorehouse of Aliette De
Hooch is, so he goes to the Mechelen. There he inquires
after Dekker. Smits, the barkeep, congratulates him politely on his recovery. Forsythe thanks him and thinks privately that it would have been better had he simply died, no
matter how humiliating it might have been to be smoth-
ered by a tapestry. He might have imagined, with his dying
breath, that it had been the sacred arm of the church,
smashing his head in so as to save him from himself.

As it is, he heads to Prinsenstraat. De Hooch's establishment is in the most imposing house on the street. Her
husband made a fortune as a serge merchant, and she has
been able to keep it up in style. He knocks immediately
in order to prevent himself from running away. A finely
dressed house maid opens the door. "Good afternoon,"
he says to her, "I am looking for Mijnheer Dekker and
was told that he might be here." He is for some reason
exquisitely conscious of his appalling accent as he says
this. Even if he were to bolt right this second, the maid
would certainly tell Dekker that some Englishman had
been asking after him.

The maid invites him inside to sit in a handsome foyer
decorated boldly in black and red, and goes off to see if

Dekker is in. Forsythe sits there, every now and again wiping his palms on the knees of his breeches. After a matter of minutes, he hears the long stride of boots in the hall. A door opens and closes, and Martin Dekker is standing before him. "Forsythe!" he says, "Good God! How did you manage to find me here? You realize you have now been seen entering a brothel?" His eyes twinkle. Forsythe wants to throttle him.

"I went to the Mechelen. And as half my parish is here all the time, according to you, I don't suppose it really matters," he replies, rising to shake his hand.

"You look positively desperate, Forsythe. Come in here and sit down. I'll get you a glass of wine," says Dekker, opening the door to a small, fine parlor. They both enter, and he closes the door behind them. Now they are in a mahogany box about twelve feet square. It really might as well be his coffin, thinks Forsythe. Dekker pours wine into two beautiful green glass goblets. He sits down at the small table and looks attentive. Forsythe sits down opposite him. He looks at the tall man with his mane of curling hair and his pristine linen shirt and his perfectly pared nails. He may be utterly surrounded by elegance, but he is the son of a farmer. He is a cheese-eating Dutchman. He is the most beautiful thing Forsythe has ever seen.

"I've just come into some money," he says abruptly.

"And—" says Dekker, expansively. He is determined to make Forsythe say it.

"And so I can afford to hire you."

"And you want to?"

"Yes."

"That'll cost you twenty guilders, Forsythe. You could replace your tapestry for that. And then some."

"I see you have thought about this."

"I made some very rapid calculations when I saw you sitting in Aliette's foyer."

"You weren't kidding when you said the price would be steep. I could book passage back to England for that."

"That might be your better option."

"No."

"I could set you up with Immanuel for twelve. He's a Spaniard, though. Would you fuck a Catholic?"

"Are you trying to back out, Dekker? I thought you were a good businessman?"

"I am," replies Dekker, with a glint in his eye, "an excellent businessman. Seriously, Forsythe, do you want do this? Have you done it before? Seems to me you're at a bit of a crossroads. A dangerous one."

"I have to know, Dekker."

"Would it help if I apologized for calling you a sodomite?"

"No."

"Is this desire or revenge?"

Forsythe pauses a moment. "Desire," he says, looking down at the shining tabletop. "And maybe a bit of revenge. I don't really know."

"And it is truly worth that money to you?"

"Yes."

"All right then," says Dekker, "just a moment. I must tell Aliette." He finishes his wine. He looks at the rector's untouched glass. "And you should drink up, Father, while I go talk to her."

Forsythe picks up his glass and looks into it despairingly. "Fine. But please, don't call me Father. Or Reverend. Just Forsythe." The excellent French wine smells nauseating.

"Right," says Dekker, briskly. He strides from the room. When he returns ten minutes later Forsythe still hasn't touched his wine. He is pale and utterly wretched. "You know, Forsythe," he says gently, as if speaking to an invalid, "that stuff might actually help you."

"Can't," says Forsythe. It's all he trusts himself to say. He feels like he may vomit.

"We'd better get you out of here before you puke on the floor," says Dekker, assessing him. "Not that it would be the first time. People in whorehouses are usually drunk or scared stiff. We'd better get you moving."

"Where to?" says Forsythe. "I thought it would be here."

"Definitely not," says Dekker. "I never work here. And certainly not for this."

Jesus, thinks Forsythe, with terrible clarity: the madam doesn't want to be liable. We are about to commit a crime. He wants to run home and close the door and never come out again.

"It'll have to be your place," continues Dekker. "Though I'm sure it can't compete in terms of décor. Just please tell me it's not freezing."

"I fixed the stove when I was looking after Davenant," replies Forsythe.

"Thank God, that's something," says Dekker. "Let's go." He looks at the other man, still sitting there. "Really, drink the wine. Just knock it back." Forsythe chugs it down in a couple of gulps. He wishes he could hold his nose as he had always done as a child when forced to eat spring asparagus. He stands up and follows Dekker out of the room.

They walk along Prinsenstraat and across the square in front of the Mechelen. "Well," says Dekker, looking at him, "someday I may walk through this square with you and you will not look like you are about to die. Remember, this was your idea."

"Shut up, Dekker."

"You'd better just call me Martin. Considering."

"Shut up, Martin."

"Dear me," he replies. "Other clients ask me to sing." He grins suddenly. His long arms swing at his sides as he saunters along. He looks completely relaxed. "I think it's going to be a most unusual afternoon."

They arrive at the rear of the chapel, at the door of Forsythe's dismal flat. They go in. Having filled the stove before he went out, it is warm. That's about all that can be said for it. Dekker looks around. "What a shithole," he says. "You're hardly a prince of the church, are you?"

Forsythe looks at him warningly.

"Then again, it's not the only shithole I'm going to be seeing, is it?" he says.

"Martin!" says Forsythe, appalled.

"Christ, Forsythe, we're all men here. Come on. I'm not your grandmother," says Dekker, challengingly. It is possible he is not quite so relaxed as he looks. Forsythe suddenly feels a bit better.

"She wouldn't have come up to your navel," he replies. "Absolutely no fear of mistake."

"That's better, Forsythe," says the tall man. "Now I reckon we both need a drink, don't you? What have you got?"

"Gin." He has one precious bottle of London gin that he has saved for emergencies. This is an emergency. It may even be the Apocalypse. He removes the stoneware jar from the wardrobe. He goes to his little kitchen area to find glasses. He does find two, but they do not match.

Martin follows him over. He takes a glass. He looks around. "Grease," he says. "We're going to need grease. You must have some." The sheer practicality of this is too much for Forsythe, and he nearly spills his gin. "Keep hold of it, Forsythe, for God's sake," he says, poking through various small covered pots and lidded vessels. "Because, I assure you, if there's no grease, we're going to need more gin." He finds a small crock of goose fat. "Aha, saved!" he says jubilantly. He turns around to Forsythe, who is blushing hotly and clutching his glass of gin. He raises his own. "Let us drink," he says, "to your inheritance!"

They drink. They drink more than half the gin, in fact. Things are seeming a bit less dire. "Now listen, Forsythe," says Martin, after a time. "We have to stop or we won't know what the fuck we're doing. It's not that I'm so fucking desperate to know, but much more of this, and I can't guarantee you're going to get what you've paid for. And that is seriously bad for business."

"Why don't you take off your clothes?" Forsythe suggests.

"Clothes?" says Martin. "Right." With complete matter-of-factness he stands up and takes them all off. He is standing absolutely naked in the middle of Forsythe's room. There is a naked man in his room. Martin Dekker stands in his room with no clothes on. It is impossible. Forsythe has not seen a naked human being since he was eleven years old, swimming in the river with his cousins. He remembers once seeing a painting of Adam naked. That would be the only time he has seen an unclothed, adult male body. But there is a pile of clothes: that fine linen shirt, some black breeches, a jacket and vest. Those superb glove-leather boots lie there, keeled over on to their sides. There is Martin, without them.

He does not seem in the least embarrassed. "It's a bit surprising, eh?" he says, quite companionably. "I remember I nearly screamed and wrapped myself in the curtains the first time," he says reminiscently. Forsythe actually laughs. He gets up from the floor, which is where he has been sitting for some time, and comes over to the other man. Martin is a lot taller than he is; he only comes up to his Adam's apple. He is powerfully muscular in the arms and chest, more obviously on the right side. The hair on his body is a shade or two darker than that on his head, but still fair. On his right arm, wrapping right around the shoulder where it joins the body, there is a raised, ridged scar.

"Jesus," says Forsythe, touching the terrible scar. "Far worse than mine."

"Got myself caught in a loom," says Martin. "Nearly tore my arm off. One more reason to leave DeVeyne's. It happens sometimes when you cast the weft over. I was probably drunk. I can't exactly remember. At least I can move it now." He circles his arm in the air. A clovey, gingery scent breathes from him as he moves. "Not quite as good as before, but not bad. Now that I'm not weaving, the two sides are evening out, you see? You always know a weaver, built up like that on the right side."

"Or a knight," says Forsythe.

"Really?" says Martin.

"From jousting. Or fighting with a lance," says Forsythe, stroking his arm.

"Here we fight on the ground, with pikes. Or at sea. Not on horses."

"My family probably fought on horseback once, ages ago, I suppose. I just read a lot of romances," says Forsythe.

"Your turn," says Martin, tugging gently on the collar of his shirt.

❧

Several hours later, when they are wholly out of grease and almost out of gin, Martin rouses from a stupor on Forsythe's small upright bed and says, "Well, that wasn't really too bad at all. I mean, not quite as good as the

Royal Society, but—" Squashed next to him, Forsythe lets out a regrettably high pitched giggle.

"What was that, you fucking English Ganymede?" Martin says, elbowing him in the ribs, "You bloody giggling girl?"

"Shut up, you vile whore," replies Forsythe deliciously, "or I shall go straight back to England, and no one will ever pay you this much money again."

"I wouldn't be too sure," says Martin. "Besides, you fuck a single Dutchman and suddenly that's it for Holland, is it? What? I can personally introduce you to—"

"Put a bung in it, Dekker," says Forsythe, "and go back to sleep. You're drunk."

"Well, that makes a change," says Martin, and passes out again. Forsythe crawls over him, over to the desk. He sits there, wrapped in a blanket, and composes a letter to a friend in the deanery of St. Paul's. A letter on behalf of William Davenant. The man is poor and will undoubtedly turn out a radical. It has become clear to him that the Church of England needs more radicals. Men like Davenant, who will suffer and struggle and kick and then grudgingly admit more forms of life into the scheme of creation. There is no other way to do so. It will never be an act of seamless grace. And why should a good man's life be ruined by one ill-timed bout of influenza? Forsythe may now be in a position to help Davenant out with his lost preferment. If not, he's just realized that as the new lord of the manor at Bampton, he has the village church in his gift. He'll be needing a vicar.

As to what has just transpired between himself and Martin Dekker, what is he to think, now that the unthinkable has happened? Impossible to say—and no one to say it to. This is a truth that will take a long time to settle over him. History is full of sodomites, as everyone knows who has read the Roman poets. But that was a different world. Perhaps he will spend the rest of his life afraid. Right now, however, right now he is not afraid, after having spent most of the day in terror. He is sore in the fundament, and everything smells of goose grease. He is still drunk from the gin. But his leading emotion is not fear. He is not sure what it is. It may, perhaps, be peace. One part of it that he can clearly recognize, though, is gratitude. To the tough, the crass, the canny, the just and generous man who is Martin Dekker. The whore. Who has just sold him a whole new world for twenty guilders.

TWO EYES

Really, it is superfluous to offer the goose girl a microscope. She doesn't need it. She is content in her auditory world. She is at home there. He would never be, thinks Leeuwenhoek, as he gets out his lamp and blowpipe. He would find her life a continual, frustrating game of blindman's buff, knowing that the creatures were there but unable to see them—and so, to draw them, to diagram them, to compare them, to figure out how they work. He is not primarily concerned with communicating with them. Nor do they seem to say much. Plus, he can look at a host of other things through the scopes—tree bark, crystals, insects, anything—and examine the structures from which they are composed. He can read the secret book of matter. For all this, he needs to *see*. He would never be content just to hear.

He has closed the shutters and locked the door. He knows this urge for secrecy is unreasonable, even a little bit mad. Other people have made blown lenses in similar ways. Hooke even describes one process in detail in *Micrographia*, which is read all over Europe. It's just that his lenses are so much better. It's a combination of luck, manual dexterity, and trial and error. His materials are not exalted, and he learned the technique from an Italian bead-maker in the Delft market square during the horse fair. Still, the results he occasionally gets from the lenses he makes this way are so astounding that sometimes he can't help but wonder if they come from the hand of God. His own hands work the glass, and his own breath infuses it through the blowpipe; his mind counts out the seconds between each slow drip as he burns off the ends. Yet he has from time to time imagined an angelic presence at his elbow, a fiery and subtle spirit shaping the swelling parison with ethereal hands, telling him exactly when to cut to leave the perfect scar that will be the lens. Certainly these little glass lentils, polished and sandwiched between plates of brass, capable of extending man's vision by two hundred, three hundred, five hundred times, are miraculous, each one a demi-pearl of wisdom offering insight into another dimension.

These rarified thoughts intermingle themselves with the prosaic business of assembling the small lamp, waiting for it to heat, and sorting through the hollow clear glass rods that he carefully unwraps from a series of plush velvet coverings. These are the tubes used by bead-makers, though his are better quality than some. He uses them to make capillaries for liquid specimens, too, when he doesn't use the cheap East India Company beads, especially if he's in a hurry. There's nothing special about them, really, yet choosing one for this process is a curiously mystical business. His hands can hover over them for up to ten minutes. He will pick them up and put them down, feel along their lengths. They all look the same to the naked eye. Yet he will have good luck with some and not with others. Each piece of glass has its own temperament.

He picks the glass rod third from the right to begin with, finally. The lamp is hot. He wants to get two done today. So he will blow four. That is cutting it fine in terms of his usual success ratio, which is just under 50/50 for a usable lens. He holds the tube in the middle—about as thick around as a child's finger—with small brass clamps. It will get hot. He holds one end to the flame, heats it, and draws it out to about a quarter of its original circumference, then seals the end, carefully and slowly. Then he draws out the other end. This end he leaves open. While everything is still malleable, he affixes his tiny blowpipe with its very small aperture—a bead-making pipe—and starts to blow out the glass. He passes it over the flame occasionally, but he doesn't want the bulb that is slowly growing at the end like an onion to get too thin.

Judging the thickness of the walls of this bulb is the trickiest part of the operation. It forms at the end of the wide part of the tube, just before the narrower, drawn-out section, so that the further, skinny end sticks out like a nose. He is suddenly, comically reminded of the long, thin nose of DeVeyne, but he does not dare laugh with the blowpipe to his mouth.

He gets the bulb to what feels like the correct curvature (too big and the lens will be too flat, too small and it will be too curved) and stops. Then he burns off as much of the protruding nose as he can, right down to the bulb, leaving a small scar or knot. This will be the lens. Once it has cooled, he will cut or burn off as much of the surrounding glass as he can, and clean up the edge. The surface he will not touch at all. Unlike the agonizingly slow process of grinding and then polishing an optical lens, this is a one-shot deal. It will work, or not. After this, it is just skill in setting it between the plates and determining the ideal size of the apertures on each side. There is some math involved in this, and a lot of practical experiment.

Right now, he has no idea whether it has worked at all. He leaves the odd-looking shape on the table to cool on a tile, and begins the process again with a new tube. And another, and another. He nearly loses control of the third one and is pretty sure it will end up too thin. These lenses just break. He lets the bulbs cool. He lets the lamp cool. There is a lot of waiting around in glassblowing. When they are set, he taps the bulbs quickly and firmly to break them—a bit like cracking an eggshell—and keeps only the pieces surrounding the little scars of the lenses. They always remind him of nipples at this stage. Very small ones. From gnomes, perhaps. Or babies.

He puts away the lamp and supplies, and cleans up the broken glass. Taking a swift glance around to make sure everything looks normal, he opens the shutters. He unlocks the door. Now he can sit innocently at his worktable, next to the lathe, with polishing tools to tidy the edges of his four new lenses. He sits and does this. They do not have to be perfect at this stage. He is eager to see their capabilities. He carries the first one to the window, picking up a fine metal screw on the way. Holding it right up to his eye, which is exceedingly difficult because it is so very small, he peers through it at various angles, holding up the fine screw and trying to see the tip. This is his initial, cumbersome and infuriating method of determining the basic quality of a lens. Sometimes he drops the minuscule objects and they roll away, never to be found again.

No one else could do it. He could never explain all the variables, and it depends in large part on his magnificent natural eyesight. After many minutes, and many adjustments of hand, screw, and eye, Leeuwenhoek gives a staccato gasp. The screw tip before him has suddenly turned into Mont Blanc, hanging in front of his eyes. It is covered in gouges and striations like it's been through an earthquake. The turnings on the top of the shaft make huge, dark crevasses, each one lined with fierce, jagged edges. It is like looking at the surface of the moon.

The power of this tiny lens is incredible. It is a porthole to a new world. He has seen this screw many times before—he always uses it to test—but never like this.

Never anything like this. This could be up to twice the magnification he's ever achieved before—it might be 500x—with almost no distortion. He cannot believe it.

Can he have caught up with the goose girl? Could he ever catch up?

He tries the others. The second one is nearly as magnificent as the first. This is astounding. The third one is too thin. He grinds it casually under his heel. The fourth one is very good; on any other day he would be most impressed with it. It is as good as some of his best lenses tucked away under the lathe. Now it seems about as useful as a brass mirror. He sits and contemplates these miraculous new tools, holding them in the palm of his hand. Two new eyes.

Compared to his own eyes, they are ridiculously tiny, like the eyes of a fly. He himself, he considers, could now be compared to a fly: one creature with many eyes. A kind of interchangeable cluster of eyes. He has recently written off to the Society with his observations of flies, stating his opinion that their multifaceted eyes are actually many single ones, compounded. His are wonderfully separable.

It will take a while to set these tiny lenses into plates and to optimize their focus with the size and alignment of the two apertures: eye- side, specimen-side. Still, not long. He works fast. Soon he will have a new scope, and the goose girl will have one. He is going to give her the other superb one. It feels like the right thing to do. He could give her the fourth one—he himself works with ones no better than this all the time—and she would still have one of the best instruments in Europe, out in her goose field. But, obscurely, he feels he can't. He set out to make a pair. By skill, by accident, by the grace of God, he has done so. They ought to go to the people for whom they were destined: one for him, one for her. Anything else would be greed.

She will be out there, leading her animal life in pastures and on roads, pulling it out of her apron pocket to look at grass stems and goose droppings and who knows what. Talking about it to the geese and to Falada. And he will be here, in his study, Mijnheer Antoni Van Leeuwenhoek of Delft in Holland, doing much the same and talking about it with the Royal Society of London. He experiences a brief pang of sorrow. She has no amanuensis. She does not read or write. The knowledge she gains will be as ephemeral as wind in the grass.

He puts the new lenses into a small felt-lined box and puts it in the niche under the lathe. He leaves them there, in the muffled quiet, staring into darkness.

KNOCK-OFFS

"Well, it's started," says DeVeyne at the next investors' meeting. Everyone is sitting in Leeuwenhoek's great room, going through the accounts. "I saw three of them yesterday. And four more when I was in Amsterdam last week. Sloppy, though. It seems to be Lacewing they're going for. I guess it's the most unusual—or better for clothing, anyway. Saw them all outside, cut into women's collars. I wonder who's making them?"

"Someone in Amsterdam, probably. Or London," says Martin Dekker. "Not much we can do about it, especially if it's London."

"Nah, you're right," says DeVeyne, wrinkling his long nose and then adjusting his spectacles. "We should just be flattered. That's a battle you can't win. Once the knock-offs are out there, there's no stopping them. I imagine half France is flooded with fake Water Garden by now. Bastards."

"At least Staff of Life is so expensive it's a bit harder to copy," says Pierre. "*Devoré* and all that."

"Mark my words, you'll be seeing cheap cotton prints of it soon enough," replies DeVeyne. "It'll look like shit, but people will buy it anyway. And any Italian could do the real thing standing on his head. I'm sure those ass-holes from Lucca took it with them when they left."

"At least we know the Esterhazy are keeping tabs on it up at the godforsaken end of the Rhine there," says Martin, "for the good name of the family."

"Who really gives a shit what goes on in that empire?" says DeVeyne, "Might as well be Mongols."

"Rich Mongols, and the prince likes them," says Hoek mildly.

"Twat," says DeVeyne, "He can't even hold up his own wig. We've been knee-deep in blood and shit for ten years because of that bunch of Orange clowns."

"Never discuss politics at a business meeting," says Leeuwenhoek, rapping on the table with his knuckles. "Is there anything else?"

"Yes," says DeVeyne, looking at Pierre. "When are you going to have something new for me?"

"Soon," says Pierre. "We have several designs in the works."

"Good," says DeVeyne. "Got to keep getting new stuff out there, now that the copies are coming out. That's the way to make it work for us: Delft, home of the new stuff! Hawked on every street corner, so good people are faking it! Crazy demand! Buy the new along with the old! Decorate your whole house in it! In blue, in green! Delft, Delft, Delft!"

"I understand," says Pierre, nodding. "You'll have it! Soon."

"All right, then," says DeVeyne. "Everything else is fine. Factory's going like blazes, and supply is still coming in well from Tilburg. And things are so shitty down south around Bruges that my Flemings are all staying on to work the velvet, thank God. Show me what you've got as soon as you can." He rises, as does Hoek. After a flurry of handshakes, they both leave.

"Do you really have anything?" Leeuwenhoek asks Pierre, smiling.

"No," says Pierre, "but I have about ten thousand drawings and could knock one off by tomorrow if need be. Do you have any ideas?"

"It's obvious," says Martin, pouring them all wine from a decanter neglected during the meeting. "Use my—"

"No!" say Leeuwenhoek and Pierre together.

"Gorgeous, it was," continues Martin, looking at them innocently over the rim of his goblet. "So lively. Virility itself."

"Absolutely not," says Leeuwenhoek. Pierre twitches with disgust.

"Well, maybe I'll pitch it to DeVeyne on my own…" says Martin. "Back it with Aliette's money…"

"Not with my drawings, you won't," says Pierre.

"I can draw, too, little cousin. Who was it advised you about cartooning in the first place? I could do great things with those fine, curling tails," counters Martin, chuckling. "But no, this is supposed be my straight job, isn't it? Pity. It seems like a lost opportunity… So, what'll it be, frog guts or something?"

"Did you know you can watch gunpowder explode through a microscope?" says Leeuwenhoek, idly. "In tiny amounts? It's quite dramatic."

"Fantastic," says Pierre, "We'll call it Thunderclap."

"Which has a nice Delft ring to it that will please De-Veyne," says Martin, coolly, "while it wins all the prizes for good taste."

Leeuwenhoek has a horrible moment imagining how he would ever explain this name to Barbara. He may have to put his foot down. She cannot take much more strain. Philips is failing day by day. The end of it is clear to all of them now. He curses natural philosophy for its uselessness.

"True," says Pierre. "But you just never know what people will buy, do you?"

KINDLING

Matthias DeWitt is chopping wood. The kindling that they are forced to buy at extortionate prices from the woodcutter is always inadequate. The pieces are far too big. It is as if the man doesn't understand the difference between a piece of kindling and a log. *Lomperik*. They have quite different functions. Kindling consists of small, dry pieces to get the fire started, while logs are for maintaining it. Not that he uses logs; the price would be exorbitant. Like everyone else, he burns peat. The stuff this fellow sells as kindling, they are practically logs. It's infuriating. Is there no such thing as a responsible professional left in the world? At this rate there will be no trees left in Holland.

So, as usual, he is chopping the kindling down. He keeps a small axe for this purpose, hanging in its place on the studio wall. It is not very weighty, but it is lethally sharp. It is impossible to work with ill-kept tools. He stands in his customary place in the rear courtyard, with a chopping block, and carefully halves, and then quarters, all the pieces. Every now and again he stops to collect the chips and shavings that fall. He puts them in a basket laid by for this purpose so they do not get too wet or dirty. He will burn them and use the ash for black pigment; he wants it pure.

He does not rush. There is no point rushing. He is already doing the work of the just. He has his own methodical rhythm for this task, as he does for all his tasks. It is mid-morning, and he is about halfway through. The job is progressing. Just for a moment, a brief moment, he has that pleasurable feeling that things are solid, that they make sense. A blessed silence reigns, broken only by the regular thumping of his axe and the crack and splinter of wood. His wife and the maid are in the kitchen in a hum of silent industry, preparing the afternoon meal. Pierre is at work, if only briefly; he has gone to drop off some new drawings. The boy has proved much less of a disappointment than he once feared, despite his shortcomings. Indeed, he must be called a success.

Just as he raises his axe to swing, a tremendous crash comes from the kitchen. Rage flares within him; he hates loud sounds. They are signs of disorder. And some expensive item has been carelessly broken. These thoughts pass through his mind with lightning speed as his axe goes wild on the downstroke and drives into his left thigh, on the inside, just above the knee. He lets out a roar of pain and fury.

In the rear kitchen, Mathilde stands frozen in horror. The best and largest crock pot, filled with stew, is on the floor in pieces. The rag she had used to wrap her hand as she removed it from the stove was too thin; she burned her fingers and could not stop herself from dropping it. The dinner is gone, wasted. The pot is trash. And aside from a bit of bread and preserves, she now has nothing to feed her husband or Pierre. The last of the week's meticulously managed supplies lies steaming on the floor; she doesn't get the weekly pantry money until this afternoon. What is she going to do? She and the maid stare at each other in mute terror.

A roar from outside. Mathilde does not even glance out the window. Instead she runs to the mantel, picks up a small earthenware pot, and rummages inside it. This is her emergency money. Pierre gave it to her. Leaving the stew where it lies, she turns to the maid and says "Come with me." The two women, aprons still on, run through the house and out the front door. "Eggs, cheese, milk, greens—mushrooms—a couple of sausages—thyme," pants Mathilde as she runs. The maid nods breathlessly beside her. "That ought to do. We can do that fast. Here." She thrusts half the hoarded coins into the servant's hands. "You get the cheese and milk; I'll get the rest. Quickly!"

The two women dash through the market in separate directions, heading from stall to stall. No lingering. No small talk. No bargaining. No sedateness. They have come without baskets. People look after them in surprise. Fifteen minutes later, they are running back up the street, clutching turnip greens and cheese and eggs in their aprons, the maid carrying a borrowed milk jug. Milk has spilled over its ill-fitting lid due to the speed of their progress. "No sausages. Ham instead," says Mathilde, as they rush back through the door. "I will cook; you clean up. Throw it all out." The maid nods soundlessly, clutching a stitch in her side.

In under half an hour, there is omelet keeping warm on the back of the stove. The floor is scrubbed, all traces of the accident removed. The table is set. The maid is pretending to clean dishes at the sink. She cannot really wash them because she is afraid to get fresh water from the pump in the courtyard. Mathilde is sitting in a chair, her trembling hands in her lap. The smallest kettle is boiling on the fire. She is wondering how much valerian to add—how bad the beating will be. If she takes too much, she will get woozy. But she can't use genever; Matthias can smell it on her. The kettle begins to sing.

Pierre walks into this domestic scene: the singing kettle, the smell of omelet, a whiff of lye and lemon from the scrubbed floor, Mathilde sitting still, staring into the fire. His mother, pale and drawn, turns to face him, and he knows something has happened. "Where is father?" he asks quietly.

"Out back," she replies. "You can call him for dinner." She rises to make her tea. Pierre nods and walks out to the courtyard.

His father is lying in a pool of blood by his chopping block. There is so much of it that it seems profligate, unlike Matthias. The edges of the spreading pool are beginning to darken. The center of it is still light, obviously bright red. There is blood on the kindling lying around him. There is so much blood that he surely cannot be alive. Pierre walks around the chopping block and sees Matthias there, his white shirt and white hair blotched and sticky, his eyes glazed. Blood is seeping slowly from a huge wound in his thigh. It must have been spurting before; there is spatter on logs lying two feet from him.

"Father," says Pierre, looking down at him. Matthias blinks and focuses his eyes on his son. He cannot raise his head but makes a feeble gesture with his hand, his fingers twitching. "I expect you are going to die now. No one could survive this. I am sorry. No point going for the surgeon. That would be a waste of good money. We'll need it for the funeral."

For once he has spoken the exact truth to his father, in terms that Matthias can understand. His father says nothing. He probably can't. His eyes remain focused on Pierre, but it is impossible to say if they are seeing or not. Pierre waits there. He glances around at the kindling, wondering if it can still be used. Would it smell? The blood has ceased to well out of Matthias's thigh now. His chest is still. Pierre waits a few more minutes just to be sure. Avoiding the pool of blood so he won't get it on the clean floor, he goes back to the kitchen.

His mother, seated at the table with the omelet pan in front of her, looks up at him. "I broke the big pot," she says.

"Father is dead," says Pierre. His mother sits there, utterly silent. "He cut himself chopping. I guess you didn't know."

"No," his mother whispers. Pierre believes her. Even if she had stood over him as he bled to death, he would still believe her. "I broke the pot. I broke the pot and spilled the stew. I had to run to the market. Hanneke and I, as soon as it happened, we both ran…"

Hanneke stops pretending to wash dishes and turns around, her face stricken.

"Hanneke," says Pierre. "Come and sit down. We can't waste this omelet. Think what it cost. Let us eat." The stunned maid leaves the sink and slides into Matthias's place at the table.

Mathilde serves the omelet. It is delicious and still hot.

WINTER

People who live in towns are afraid of winter. They have feasts and festivals and pray to their saints and burn trees and peat and wear the fur of animals. They are not good at living through things just as themselves.

Geese are. That is all they ever do.

It is hard on the roads in winter. But the goose girl has good clothes and blankets and boots. Better than she's ever had. She has money. She has food, and a bag to carry it in. She has Falada and Redboots, and the old handkerchief with the blood of her mother. She has eleven guards, fiercer than most men: inconspicuous, excellent foragers, so she can fit in anywhere, country or town. With them, she can swim and fight and fly.

She remembers seeing Plague walking through the woods, all that time ago, going to Kampen to kill all the people. Now it is not Plague she fears, but Sorrow.

Sorrow will not arrive as a dim and misty figure striding through a clearing. The goose girl has been living in a town for many months; now she thinks like people who live in towns. They think in words. They have reasons. They try and try to see ahead.

Sorrow will come to her friend Antoni. It will come in the death of that baby, who tastes of salt. It will come in the death of Barbara, whose blood is sweet. She had hoped that Antoni might know why. She had thought he might be able to change things because of it. That is the gift of people who live in towns. But even though Antoni sees so much more than most people, he is not going to be able to change things.

When she is on the road with the geese, she does not worry about how things are. Whether they stay the same or whether they change. But she has lived here, in this town, Delft, for too long now. With Antoni. With Johannes. Antoni is her friend. She would like things to remain as they are for him. But they will not. Once things have begun to break, they end up broken. Even a goose knows that. For Antoni, she would like things to be other than they are. That is where Sorrow comes in.

Geese have no sorrows.

⤳

Antoni comes to her in the courtyard. There is a thin skin of ice on the well bucket. Scratch has been complaining all morning because her foot is sore. "Come inside," Antoni says. "I have something for you."

She goes in. He gives her a little instrument of brass, a microscope. He reminds her how to use it. "It is hard, in full light, like in a field. You need a little slice of light. Then you get the best image. You can try shading it with your hand. I often do that."

They practice, standing here, standing there, inside the house. She sees many things through the microscope. She will see many more things on the road. The little animals will call to her and tell her where to look.

"Thank you," she says. Antoni looks surprised.

"You are welcome," he says. That is what people say.

She puts the little instrument in her pocket. "We are going now," she says. "Goodbye." Antoni glances at her quickly.

She wraps her shawls around herself and leads the geese through the gate. In her bag is food from Barbara

Sarah Tolmie

and the two tiny paintings. The handkerchief and the money are in her bodice, right down next to her skin, safe. Antoni stands with a stiff, white face. He raises his hand to them as they go by. The gate clicks shut.

FEATHERS

The girl and the geese have not come home, though it is evening. Rain, perhaps snow, is threatening. She should be here. He thought he had managed to persuade her that she and her charges would be safer at home at night in this weather.

He remembers her saying, as he gave her the tiny scope with its magnificent lens: "People give each other gifts when they go away, don't they?"

"But you're only going to pasture!" he had said. He had given her a lesson in microscopy.

He leaves Barbara preparing supper and sets out on the road to the field. Perhaps he will meet them coming back, the geese marching through the dull light in a glowing line with the girl at their head.

He does not meet them. Out of town, the road is empty. A misty drizzle, almost sleet, begins. He approaches the pasture with an anxious foreboding. His long-sighted eyes see nothing. No geese, waddling and honking at his approach. No girl. Not a soul, not an animal in the pasture, except for the millions upon millions of the littlest animals, who are of no concern to him now.

She is gone. The goose girl, oracle of the animalcules. Heart of the flock. He could go after her, and the geese, which, in the law, he owns. She can't have gotten far at herding pace. But he knows: if she has left, she chose to go, and would only come back under duress. He would have to hold them all captive. He could never do this.

Why would she go? Why now, in winter?

Sarah Tolmie

There is no need for him to set foot on the soggy, half-frozen grass, but he does so. He walks to the pond. It is flat and unreflective, prickled by rain. As he comes up to the bank, he sees a cluster of white objects, close to the ground. He comes closer, and sees that they are feathers. Twelve perfectly white goose feathers, the best long flight feathers, stuck into the earth. They are spread out into a neat semi-circle, all but one, which is thrust into the turf above the U that they make in the grass, right in the middle. The goose girl, with her flock listening attentively. Leeuwenhoek recalls the first day he had ever seen them thus, in his courtyard, just back from the market: the group of them standing like silent choristers. Tears leak from his eyes. He wrecks the knees of his new woolen breeches, kneeling in the mud to collect the feathers. Cold rain slips down his collar.

He stands up again, holding them in his fist like a strange bouquet, staring at the murky water. Animalcules live there, infinitely more of them in a goose pond than there are people in the Republic, or in Europe, perhaps in the whole world. If they are singing tiny wailing songs for the goose girl's departure, he cannot hear them. But he knows that they, unlike him, are not weeping.

EPILOGUE

There he stands, Antoni Van Leeuwenhoek, a respectable man in black in a goose pasture. He will write over four hundred letters to the Royal Society and become one of their most esteemed foreign members. He will become the second most famous citizen in the history of Delft, after his initially neglected, then celebrated, friend Johannes Vermeer. Royalty will visit him to look through his microscopes into the hidden world of the *animalcule*. He will live to ninety-two and be buried in the Oude Kerk. His daughter Marie, his only surviving child, will look after his legacy, long outliving his second wife. She will spend her life tending his house in Hippolytusbuurt, which came to be known as *Het Gouden Hoofd*.

Perhaps the goose girl is a creature like Lancelot. The paintings Vermeer did with her golden hair—of the geese in the yard, of Falada, of Pierre at the window—cannot be found. Today we know Delft as a town for pottery, not for cloth. The animalcule fabrics of Delft, worn by women all over the world, outselling *cachemire* in their time, have long since unraveled.

Meanwhile, Leeuwenhoek stands alone in the field. He is almost done crying. In his hand he holds twelve new quills.

A Note on Historicity

It will be immediately clear to any expert on Leeuwenhoek that many liberties have been taken with the timeline. This is in addition to the fact that he never met a goose girl, whose story is broadly drawn from the brothers Grimm. And his relations with Vermeer remain conjectural, though he was indeed the painter's executor.

Most of Leeuwenhoek's dateable discoveries seem to have occurred during his second marriage, to Cornelia Swalmius, who was a pastor's daughter. Here they have been backdated into his first marriage with Barbara de Meij, mother of his surviving daughter. The Royal Society delegation is likewise fictitious, though his association with that learned body was very significant to his career and posterity.

Many important works have been written about Leeuwenhoek. The ones I relied on were chiefly the dated but excellent *Antony Van Leeuwenhoek and his Little Animals* by Clifford Dobell (1932) and the magisterial multi-volume edition of Leeuwenhoek's letters by Lodewijk Palm. A cheap Ecco reprint of the 18th-century English translation of his selected works by Samuel Hoole is also available. Partway through my research I discovered Laura J. Snyder's *Eye of the Beholder: Johannes Vermeer, Antoni van Leeuwenhoek and the Reinvention of Seeing* (2015), a wonderful book, though one that gives a very different (and probably more accurate) picture of the Vermeer/Leeuwenhoek relationship. Another invaluable resource is the website *Lens on Leeuwenhoek* curated by Douglas Anderson. Likewise important to this book was information about the sex trade contained in Manon van Heijden's *Women and Crime in Early Modern Holland* (2016).

ACKNOWLEDGMENTS

The Canada Council and the Ontario Arts Council both provided grants that allowed me to travel to the Netherlands to conduct research for this book in 2015 and 2017. While there in 2015 I was hosted, as a Special Guest of the Director, by the Descartes Centre for the History and Philosophy of Science and Technology at the University of Utrecht. I owe both Prof. Bert Theunissen and Ariane den Daas a great debt for all their help. While there I also briefly consulted Prof. Lodewijk Palm. Also incredibly helpful was Tiemen Cocquyt at the Boerhaave Museum in Leiden, who laboriously explained the optical principles of single lens microscopes to me and put me on to valuable scholarship, including the controversy about the possible role of glassblowing in Leeuwenhoek's lens manufacture. The library staff at the Textile Museum in Tilburg—a lovely institution—were likewise very helpful. Sheelagh Carpendale advised about glass techniques; several scientist members of SF Canada also clarified things about histology, algae, and pre-Darwinian classificatory systems: Geoff Cole, Barb Galler-Smith, Ann Dulhanty, and Paula Johanson.

About the Author

Sarah Tolmie is the author of *The Stone Boatmen, Two Travelers,* and the short fiction collection *NoFood* (all published by Aqueduct Press). McGill-Queen's University Press published her first poetry collection, *Trio,* in 2015 and her second collection, *The Art of Dying,* in 2018. Her work has been anthologized in *Year's Best Weird Fiction* (Vol. 4) and *Year's Best Canadian Poetry* (2018). She is the recipient of grants from the Ontario Arts Council and the Canada Council for the Arts. She has a BA and MA from the University of Toronto and a PhD in medieval literature from Cambridge, and is on faculty in English at the University of Waterloo, where she teaches British literature and creative writing.